BETHAN ROBERTS

Graceland

VINTAGE

1 3 5 7 9 10 8 6 4 2

Vintage
20 Vauxhall Bridge Road,
London SW1V 2SA

Vintage is part of the Penguin Random House group
of companies whose addresses can be found
at global.penguinrandomhouse.com

Penguin
Random House
UK

First published in Vintage in 2020
First published in hardback by Chatto & Windus in 2019

This novel is a work of fiction. In some cases true life figures appear
but their actions and conversations are entirely fictitious. All other
characters, and all names of places and descriptions of events, are
the product of the author's imagination and any resemblance
to actual persons or places is entirely coincidental.

penguin.co.uk/vintage

A CIP catalogue record for this book is available
from the British Library

ISBN 9781784708641

Printed and bound in Great Britain by Clays Ltd, Elcograf S.p.A.

Penguin Random House is committed to a sustainable future for
our business, our readers and our planet. This book is made
from Forest Stewardship Council® certified paper.

For Mum and Ted, with love

Graceland, 20 December 1957

Elvis has made his wishes clear: every decoration on the white plastic Christmas tree should be red. Reaching almost to the ceiling, the tree's stiff branches burst forward into the dining room like stars. Gladys sits beside it, surrounded by boxes of baubles and tinsel, searching for old things to match the new.

Her son is still in bed, and the house is quiet. She's determined to wait for him to rise before dressing the tree, so they can do it together, but has decided it won't hurt to select a few items before he appears. She's been sitting for almost an hour now, letting the late-morning sun warm the side of her face as she picks through the ornaments. She's put aside a pile of red things Elvis bought last year for the Audubon Drive house – glass stars, glittering snowflakes, miniature Santas, striped stockings and candy canes – and has given herself over to the examination of the angel he made from a clothespin and shiny paper in elementary school. The wings are a little ripped and the face he'd painted has faded to a couple of vague splotches. That angel moved with their family from Tupelo to Memphis, and has been displayed in more homes than she can count, from two-roomed duplexes to rooming houses to public housing to private apartments. Last year Elvis wouldn't let her put it at the top of the tree because, he said, it would ruin the photographs taken of the Presley family Christmas for the newspapers. Gladys straightens the wings with a flattened hand, tidies the four strands of yellow wool that make the angel's hair, and struggles to her aching feet. Then she buries it deep inside the needles at the back of the tree. This year she will refuse to leave it in the box.

The telephone rings. Gladys ignores it, taking her time to rearrange the tree's branches around the angel, thinking perhaps one of the maids will answer. But the phone continues to trill, forcing her to cross the white carpet and pick up the receiver.

'Presley residence.'

'That you, Glad?'

It's Vester, her brother-in-law, calling from the front gate.

'Course it's me.'

'I got a Mr Milton Bowers here. Wants to see Elvis.'

A shot of fear goes through her, weakening her legs, and she has to place a hand on the door frame to steady herself.

'Looks kinda official,' says Vester.

Stretching the phone cord to its full length, Gladys goes to the window and pushes back the brocade drapes, peering down the long drive. The windshield of her visitor's car glints in the distance. It looks to be a black Cadillac, though not as new as her son's.

'Glad? You still there?'

She could send him on his way. Vester could keep those iron gates firmly shut. But she'd just be delaying the inevitable.

'Send him on up,' she says.

With trembling fingers, she attempts to arrange her hair, then positions herself behind the drapes to watch the car's progress. The gates swing open. Elvis had been careful about their design: they had to be tall enough to deter climbers, but see-through enough for the fans to feel close to his home. The car follows the roadway up the slope and through the tall trees. The blue lights lining the drive are turned off now, but on the lawn is a giant illuminated Santa on his sleigh, bearing the message, MERRY CHRISTMAS ALL — ELVIS.

Mr Milton Bowers is sometimes mentioned in the *Memphis Press Scimitar*, and Gladys knows what his arrival means. Almost a year ago, her son completed his pre-induction physical, was classified 1-A, and the press went crazy over the idea of Elvis joining the army. She's been dreading this moment ever since.

The Cadillac stops just short of the steps, and Gladys inches away from the glass. A large man emerges, tucking an envelope into his breast pocket. Then he buttons up his overcoat, replaces his hat, and slams the car door.

Gladys braces herself, expecting one of the family, or a maid, to come running, but nobody appears. Her mother-in-law, Minnie Mae, rarely leaves her basement room, joining the family only for meals. Gladys imagines that her husband, Vernon, is in the small building he calls his office, out by the car porch, counting Elvis's money. If she lets the maid answer the door, as her son has instructed she always should, there's a chance the envelope will go directly to Vernon, or even to Elvis. She must intercept Mr Bowers on the porch.

First wiping her palms on her dress, she steps into the hallway and pulls back the bolts on the heavy door. Opening it, she squints against the glare of the sun on the white columns. Her visitor has yet to make it up here, having paused to admire one of the marble lions to the side of the entrance. He pats the squat creature's curling hair before taking the steps at a sprightly pace.

'Well, good morning to you, sir,' Gladys manages to sing.

'Good morning, ma'am. You must be Mrs Presley.'

'The same.'

He removes his hat and smiles. He has a wide neck that pushes at the boundaries of his collar. His narrow eyes fix her with the kind of confidence she's often seen in the faces of people who work in offices, whose questions are always a test.

'I'm Milton Bowers,' he says. 'Chairman of the draft board.'

Because she strongly suspects he will refuse, Gladys says, 'Well, do please come in, Mr Bowers.'

Even if he agrees, she can put him in the music room and there's a chance nobody will be any the wiser.

3

'I'm sorry, Mrs Presley, I can't do that. I did want, though, to deliver this note to Mr Presley personally ...'

He fishes the envelope from his pocket.

Gladys smiles and stretches out her hand to receive the letter, but he drops it into the upturned bowl of his hat and asks, 'Is Mr Presley home?'

'My husband is busy in his office—'

'I meant your son. This is an important document. I'm sure you understand.'

Mr Bowers cranes his neck to see past her. She spots a little perspiration on his forehead, a gleam in his eye. These high-class Old Memphis folk are all the same. Too proud to admit that they want to catch a glimpse of her son. Gladys steps forward, blocking his view, and lowers her voice.

'Truth is, Elvis is sleeping right now. He's just gotten back from Hollywood and they work him so hard!'

Mr Bowers sniffs and looks around, taking in the height of the portico and the size of the glass lamp suspended above his head. 'Quite the mansion you have here,' he says.

'We've been blessed,' says Gladys.

'What your son has achieved is certainly impressive, particularly coming from his background.' Mr Bowers shows his teeth, which are small and straight. 'I'd like to commend Elvis myself, if you'll let me, ma'am.'

The clouds are gathering now, and the branches of the leafless trees knock together in the wind.

'That's right kind of you, sir,' says Gladys, 'but I won't wake my boy.'

Mr Bowers stares at her for a moment, clearly surprised. Then he shakes his head and chuckles. 'He'll have to rise earlier than this when he's in the US Army! The officers at Fort Hood won't make exceptions.'

'Elvis won't expect no special treatment.' Gladys holds out her hand. 'Don't let me keep you from your business, now.'

He sighs and offers her the letter, but then hesitates, holding it in mid-air as he takes a good look at the diamond cluster of her cocktail ring. 'You'll see he gets it right away?'

'The very moment he wakes.'

Only then does Mr Bowers surrender the envelope. As he descends the steps, Gladys calls, 'Elvis will be real disappointed he missed you.'

Sitting on her pink silk bedspread, she tears open the envelope.

Selective Service System
Order to Report for Induction

President of the United States to,

   Elvis Aron Presley

   Mailing address: Graceland, Highway 51 South, Memphis, Tennessee

   Greeting: You are hereby ordered for induction into the Armed Forces of the United States, and to report at Room 215, 198 South Main Street, Memphis, at 7.45 am on the 20th of January 1958, for forwarding to an armed forces induction station.

It is entirely as she expected, but still a shock. The signature is not Milton Bowers's, but its large black loops speak of the same smooth confidence. She tosses the thin paper onto the pillow, away from her body. For a long time she has feared for her son's life at the grasping hands not just of his fans, but also his enemies, who lurk on church boards and youth committees up and down the country. Now she sees that her worry was over nothing when compared with this. Before they know it, Elvis could be at war. Vernon often speaks of the crazy Russians and their stockpile of bombs big enough to blow them all to kingdom come. And their nephew, Junior, hasn't been right in the head since he returned from Korea.

Her instinct is to run to her son and break the news. It will be better coming from her. But first Gladys must steady herself. She finds the small bottle of vodka hidden in her velvet purse and takes a swig, letting the alcohol sink warmly to her stomach. Talking with Mr Bowers, she could forget the pain always pulsing through her legs these days, and the way her body seems to have become a burden she must carry around. But now the weariness floods back. She takes another drink, knowing she must guard against letting herself drain the entire bottle. Perhaps it would be better, after all, to slip the letter beneath her pillow and lay her head on it. She could swallow one of the pills Elvis gives her to help her sleep.

Then it hits her: if she can get Tom Parker on the phone, she can beg him to stop all this. Ever since speculation about his draft began, Elvis has said his manager will set things straight. Perhaps if she can convince Mr Parker that Elvis will not survive the ordeal – that he's already a nervous wreck, prone to mood swings and insomnia, exhausted by the whirlwind of his rise to stardom – Parker will take action, if only to save his own behind.

Heart rushing, she lifts the receiver next to her bed. A flat drilling sound fills her ear. Gladys has her finger on the dial before she remembers the truth: she doesn't have the number. Only Vernon and Elvis know Parker's direct line, and if she were to ask her husband he would tell her straight that Colonel Tom Parker would not take kindly to being bothered by a fretful mother, especially when his only concern is making a success of their boy. And if she were to point out that Elvis is already a success beyond any of their wildest imaginings, Vernon would merely counter that there's always more to be had, especially when it comes to Elvis.

She snatches up the letter, takes another slug of vodka, and heads for the door.

It's quiet in the hall, and her house shoes hardly make a sound on the dense carpet of the stairs. Outside Elvis's bedroom she hesitates, but decides against knocking. She knows that his girl, Anita, sometimes stays the night, although Elvis would never admit it. But Gladys hasn't time to consider Anita's embarrassment. She must break the news. The girl can blush and scat if she has to.

She opens the door and steps into the darkness. There's the low whirr of the refrigerator and what sounds like the breath of two bodies. The heating is turned off, and the room is chilly. She feels for the switch on the wall and, finding it, floods the place with light.

Elvis is asleep in the massive bed, black covers pulled up to his chin and a silk sleep mask covering his eyes; his body is curled into a tight ball, just as it used to be when they shared a bed. On the floor beside him is his friend Cliff, who is now awake.

'Miss Gladys,' he says, squinting at the light. 'What time is it?'

She has always liked Cliff. He's handsome in a homely way, with soft brown eyes and a gentle voice. Elvis says he's crazy, but unlike the rest of Elvis's male friends, Cliff takes the time to sit with her some afternoons and share a few beers.

'Cliff, I need to speak with my son.'

He throws back his coverlet – he seems to have slept right on the floor.

'Cliff, why don't you use one of the guest bedrooms, dear?'

'Elvis likes to have me in the room, Miss Gladys.'

She nods. He never did like being alone.

As Cliff tugs a pair of pants over his undershorts, Gladys turns to face the door.

'You sure you wanna wake him?' asks Cliff. 'We didn't make it back till real late ...'

'This is important,' says Gladys.

'You know best, ma'am.'

'You're a good boy, Cliff,' she says.

He leaves the room, scratching his behind.

Through all this, Elvis sleeps.

Gladys sits on the bed and watches her son. His breathing is steady and deep. He used to sleep badly and dream so hard that he'd walk from his bed, into the night, but you'd never know that to look at him now. On the nightstand is a half-full glass of water, a Bible, and a bottle of pills.

'Baby,' she whispers.

He doesn't stir.

It has been a while since she has had the power to make any changes in his life, but now she has the letter. And although she hates its every word, Gladys feels an undeniable thrill at being the one to deliver its message.

She touches his shoulder, noticing how taut and smooth it is compared with her own hand, and raises her voice. 'Elvis. It's Mama.'

Still nothing, so she removes his sleep mask, revealing his dark lashes and brows. These always come as something of a surprise to Gladys, who remembers Elvis as a fair-headed boy. She takes his wrist in her hand and squeezes, gradually increasing the pressure. A doctor at St Joseph's once told her this was the best way to wake a patient gently.

'Come on, son.'

He groans.

'Wake up.'

He buries his face in the pillow.

'Son. You gotta wake up.'

Without moving, he slurs, 'Is somebody dead?'

'Elvis!' Gladys takes hold of the bedclothes and whips them from his body, revealing his white undershorts.

'Don't!' he cries, trying to pull the sheets back.

But Gladys won't let go. 'This is important,' she says.

'Damn,' he mutters.

'Don't you curse, now.'

He hauls himself into a sitting position and rests his head on the white leather board, his hair awry, his face puffy, a light crust of saliva at the corners of his lips. The sight of his naked chest and muscled arms makes her pause, and she has to stop herself from telling him that he's a man, now. The fact of it amazes her, every time.

'What's so important?' he asks.

'It's just – a letter.'

Handing it over, she holds his gaze, and knows he understands exactly what this means.

As he reads, she glances around the room. Even before they moved here, Gladys referred to it as 'the King's Room', making his friends laugh nervously. But she now realises that although it is luxurious, with its ice-machine, refrigerator, TV set, and wall-sized mirror at the foot of the bed, everything in this room is in fact fashioned with darkness in mind. The walls, drapes and furniture are the colour of the night sky. It is like a cave.

Elvis crumples the letter in his fist, then hurls it at the wall.

'We knew it was gonna happen some time,' she says.

'It's all over, Mama.'

'Come here.' She opens her arms and lets him hide his face in her bosom. Stroking his hair, she whispers, 'Nothing's over. You're still here. I'm still here.'

'I'm finished,' he says. 'The fans will forget all about me.'

Knowing he's pouting, she has to will her fingers to finish their path through his hair. 'Oh, baloney! This here's nothing but a temporary setback.'

He looks up, his eyes dark with fear. 'You think the other men are gonna ignore *Elvis Presley*? Treat me like one of the guys? They're gonna make my life hell.'

At this display of more self-pity, she feels herself shrink from him. 'This ain't school, Elvie. Nobody's gonna hide in a ditch and chunk stuff at you, or call you names ...'

He covers his eyes with one hand, as though shielding himself from her.

'None of those men got what you got. You just take anything they say with a smile, and move right along.' She grabs his wrist, tugging his hand from his face. 'Look at me. It's like I always told you: you got the strength of two. And the talent. And you're gonna be even better when you come back, I just know it.'

He sniffs. 'Will you come with me, Mama?'

She smiles. 'Mama's coming with you wherever you go, you know that.'

1: TUPELO

SLEEPWALKING: 1937–1942

1937

There is just a door, big and shiny black. Leaning close, Elvis sees
his own face in the new paint. He pats his hands on the cold wood,
touching his reflection, and it makes a sound like somebody banging
an empty bucket. He pats harder, watching his eyes appear and
disappear beneath his hands, until he is beating on the door.

He is almost three years old, and standing outside Tupelo jailhouse
with his aunt Lillian. It is a Thursday afternoon in winter, and frost
is still on the sidewalk. His daddy is inside the jailhouse, because
the men have taken him and won't give him back, which makes his
mama cry.

He must get in there, after his mama. She has gone, taking with
her all the warmth and light in his world. He cannot hear her voice,
but he is sure she must be calling for him.

The empty-bucket sound grows as he beats on the door. It
vibrates along his arms, past the white cuffs his mother has sewn
onto his shirt, and all the way to his chest.

'Don't be pitching a hissy fit,' says Aunt Lillian, who is bony, and
louder than Mama. 'Your mama's just visitin'. She'll be out soon
enough.'

Elvis yells for his mama.

Aunt Lillian grips his arm and yanks him away from the door. 'Now you better hush up, or the police will come get you, too.'

Elvis yells louder, as loud as he possibly can. But still there is just the black mirror of the door, and his own face, appearing and disappearing.

Then a man comes out.

'What's all this hollering?' he asks. The man has two chins and his breath clouds the air. He's wearing a smart cap with a glinting silver star at the front, and on his hip is a pistol in a holster. Something about the way the man rests a hand there makes Elvis think of Brother Mansell touching his leather Bible.

Elvis stops crying, shocked by this sight.

Aunt Lillian steps back, but Elvis reaches for the pistol.

The man says, 'No, no. That ain't for young 'uns. When you're grown, then you can hold it.'

But when Elvis makes another grab for the holster, the man crouches before him and weighs the pistol in his hands.

'I guess you can touch it,' he says, unlocking the barrel and spinning it around. 'If you keep your mouth shut.'

Golden bullets – Elvis has seen these before, on the table at his grandfather's house – tumble into the man's hand like treasure.

Carefully, Elvis places his fingers on the pistol's wooden handle. It is smooth and solid.

The man smiles. 'That's for protection,' he says, pocketing the bullets and snapping the barrel back in place. 'Yours and mine.'

Now Elvis's attention is caught by the gleaming buttons on the man's cuff. The cuff is stiff, not darned, and absolutely clean.

'You like that, huh? My uniform?'

Standing, the man brushes himself off. His trousers have sharp creases, and his shoulders press at the seams of his dark blue jacket.

Elvis cannot take his eyes from him. For a moment, he forgets that his mama is crying inside the jailhouse with his daddy.

The man puts a hand to Elvis's hair and lets it rest there. 'Poor child,' he says.

Then the door opens, and in the place of Elvis's reflection is his mama. She steps towards him and with one sweep of her arms lifts him away from the man's hand. The lightness in Elvis's body as the sidewalk disappears beneath him is sudden and wonderful. He gazes into her wet eyes and says, 'Mama!'

'Elvis,' she says, pressing her smooth cheek to his. He breathes in her good Mama smell.

She carries him along the sidewalk. Aunt Lillian hurries behind. When Elvis drags his eyes from his mama's face, the man has gone.

Aunt Lillian's kitchen is full of kids making noise. Cousin Billy keeps patting Elvis's hair and saying, 'Still the baby, huh?' Lola Flora lies in the centre of the floor, kicking her heels on the boards and humming a tune. Bobbie rocks back and forth on her chair, pretending it's a horse. Elvis races between his cousins, unsure which is best. He keeps an eye on his mama, who is sitting at the table with Aunt Lillian. Aunt Lillian is talking in a strong voice about how things are, and how they should be, as she pours coffee.

Elvis's mama looks kind of blurry. Her face is redder and her eyes smaller than usual. Her body is folded up in its chair and she dabs at her nose with a handkerchief. It's her best one: she's shown it to Elvis and has told him she used it on her wedding day, because it was the only thing she had with lace on. Watching his mama lift the crumpled, damp cloth to her nose, Elvis suddenly finds it terrible to see that handkerchief getting spoiled. He jumps over Lola Flora's body and whumps his hand down on his mama's knee.

'There, there, baby,' he says in his clearest voice.

His mama stops dabbing her eyes, so he pats her knee again and repeats, 'There, there.'

A smile plays around her mouth.

'Glad, that boy of yours is sure surprising,' says Aunt Lillian, putting down her coffee cup. And everyone in the room looks at Elvis.

His mama laughs, and her face seems to come into focus again. She lifts him to the safety of her knee, squeezing him around the middle, and whispers in his ear, 'There, there, my baby.'

1939

One bright February morning, a truck pulls up in the dirt road outside the house, music blaring from its radio. For days now, Gladys has been talking of Vernon's return from the pen. Thanks to her petition and his good behaviour, he's been pardoned and is coming home after over a year. She grasps her son's shoulder and squeezes, hard. 'Oh,' she gasps. 'Oh, my.'

Elvis studies his mother's pale face. He considers her to be beautiful. Her black hair shines and her skin glows white, but it's not these things that make her special. Uncle Frank and Aunt Leona, whose house they are living in, often talk of her warm and easy way with folks. His mama smiles a lot, and laughs at many things he just can't fathom. She returns his unblinking gaze for a long moment before stating, 'But it can't be. It's too early.' Still, she unbuttons her apron and casts the item aside, revealing her best dress, the pretty green one that he likes. Then Gladys slips on what Elvis knows to be her special shoes. Tiny straps encircle her ankles. She pats her hair and pinches up the blood in her cheeks. Pulling open the front door, she lets the music in.

Elvis rushes to her, grabbing her legs, pushing his face into her thin skirt.

She puts a hand to his head. 'Don't be foolish, baby. Mama ain't going nowhere.'

As he peeks out at the day, cool air hits his face, making him blink. The truck is real fine: army green, with a shining black roof. He'd like to swing himself up into its cab. From its open window comes the voice of his mama's favourite singer: Jimmie Rodgers. Whenever she talks about Jimmie, her eyes brighten, as if she's seeing something that belongs only to her. *I'm gonna buy me a pistol, just as long as I'm tall, I'm gonna shoot poor Thelma, just to see her jump and fall* ...

Gladys walks onto the porch.

The music stops and a man climbs from the truck. He's dressed in a battered leather jacket a little like Vernon's. Although Elvis knows Vernon's jacket is folded into the trunk beneath Uncle Frank's bed – he and Mama are sharing a pallet on the kitchen floor – for a second he wonders if his daddy's hair colour has changed. The man is about Vernon's height. And hasn't Grandma Minnie Mae said that prison will do strange things to even the strongest of fellas? But then his mother's shoulders sag, and he knows this is not his father.

The man tips his hat. 'Good morning, ma'am. Sorry to disturb ...'

His mother sways a little, and lets out a groan.

'Ma'am?'

Gladys puts a hand to her pale face. Elvis runs to join her.

Clasping her son to her side, she says to the man, 'I'm sorry. I – I thought you were my husband.'

'Pardon me, ma'am?'

'I been waiting on my husband's return, after – a long spell.'

The man takes off his hat and holds it to his chest, revealing his dark hair. 'I'm right sorry, Mrs—'

'Presley. Gladys Presley.'

The man clears his throat. 'You want to sit, ma'am? Can I fetch you a chair?'

'No, no. I'm just fine.'

'What about your son here?' The man squints at Elvis. 'Reckon your mama's all right, child?'

'My daddy's coming home today,' says Elvis, in his clearest voice.

Gladys pats his hair. 'That's right, baby. Now, how may I help you, sir?'

'You know where Lake Street is?'

Elvis watches the man nod seriously as Mama gives rambling directions. He feels sure that, soon enough, he will have her back inside, where he can seat her in a chair and fetch her a glass of water, maybe pat her on the knee and say, 'There, there,' and she will touch his cheek and thank him from the bottom of her heart.

When Gladys has finished, the man says, 'OK if I visit your outhouse, ma'am? I been awful long on the road.'

'It's over the back there. Help yourself and welcome.'

As the man rounds the porch, he glances up and says in a slightly lower tone, 'Anything I can do to thank you, lady? Make amends for your disappointment and all?'

Gladys touches her neck and lets out a small, amused noise. 'Oh, no!' she says, her words coming out in a rush. 'Ain't no call for that!'

The man walks on.

Then Gladys pulls herself straight. 'Hold on,' she calls to his back, 'there's one thing you could do.'

Elvis gazes at her, confused. It must be past the hour for his milk and biscuit, now. Why is she encouraging this stranger to linger at their house when his father – his actual, real father – may be home any minute? And what if his daddy finds his mama talking to this man? Elvis already understands this would not please Vernon one bit.

'Would you put the music on, just while you're gone?' Her voice has gone real high and tinkly. 'I don't know why, but I guess I got a hankering for a song this morning.'

'Sure,' says the man, with a wide smile. 'I understand.' He walks back to his truck. 'There you go,' he says and, with a flick of his hand, a song about a train blares out. Gladys and Elvis both know the tune.

The man salutes, then disappears round the back of the house. Once he's gone, Gladys claps her hands. 'Daddy's coming home today!' she says.

Elvis says, 'But that wasn't him, Mama.'

'I know that! But did you see he had a jacket like Daddy's? It's a sign! A sign that Daddy's really coming.'

Elvis had not considered that his father might fail to return.

'But Daddy *is* coming,' he says. 'You promised.'

'Sure he is, baby!' Gladys gives her son a sideways look. 'I love this song! Now, you watch this!'

And she arranges herself on the centre of the porch, arms stretched to either side. The song's chorus begins, and she breaks into a dance.

'Watch your mama, now!'

Her feet pound the boards, moving so fast that he cannot quite fathom what it is they are doing. Her skirt flies this way and that, revealing her long legs. A train whistle blows, and she grins and pretends to pull a cord. When the music becomes more urgent, she frowns in concentration, thumping out the rhythm with her feet, twisting at the waist. He's seen her sway and clap her hands in church; he's heard her sing along with the radio at Uncle Bob's house. But he's never seen his mama dance like this. Her body appears light as air, yet it feels to Elvis that the whole house is shaking. The porch vibrates, sending pleasant tremors through his bare feet and up his legs. Gladys smiles so widely that he spots her tongue, pink and shocking inside her mouth.

She reaches out and he readies himself to be scooped up, but she touches only the air.

This is too much. Sensing that the only way to get her attention is to join in, he grabs her sweaty hands and shouts the words he can make out: 'RUMBLE' and 'ROAR!'

He looks into her laughing face as she sings along. Then she twirls around, losing his hands, so he twirls too, even though he understands that he is getting in the way and she would rather he sat and watched.

Only when the radio announcer's voice comes over the song does Elvis hear the low whistle and the clapping.

The dark-haired man is standing by the oak tree, watching.

'That was mighty fine!' he calls. 'Both of you!'

'Oh, my,' says Gladys, wiping an arm across her brow. 'You weren't meant to see that.'

'You a good dancer, Mrs Presley,' says the man.

'Oh, baloney,' says Gladys, beaming.

The man saunters to his truck. As he slams the door, he says, 'Thank you, ma'am, for the entertainment.'

Back inside, they are both slightly breathless.

'Let me get your butch, baby.'

He sits at the wooden table, on the verge of tears. He doesn't know why he wants to cry, but he knows his mama will be disappointed if he does. This is a happy day. She's told him so, many times. But Mama is strange today. She just won't look at him properly.

She sets a cup of milk on the table and he takes a sip. For once, even though she's added a little molasses, it doesn't taste good. His stomach feels hard and bunched up, as if it's full of marbles.

'Drink your butch, now, Elvie.'

Usually she would sit and drink, too. They would say their words for milk together, *Butch, butchy, yummy creamy butch!* She would stroke his face and they would share some buttered biscuits. But today his mama cannot seem to sit down. She rose early to wash the floors and scrub the porch boards, and now she is fiddling with flour and lard, filling the air with white dust that catches in his throat.

'Gonna make Daddy some dough burgers, just how he likes. And an apple cobbler, too. Then when Uncle Frank and Aunt Leona

23

come home from work, they can sit with you and me and Cousin Corinne and Daddy, and we can all eat as a family.'

Dough burgers are *his* favourite. And she's not looking at him, even now.

He wants to knock over the milk, let it run across the table and drip onto the clean floor.

But instead he asks, as he has done many times, 'Mama, did Daddy do something bad?'

Light and quick, not missing a beat, she rubs fat into flour with the tips of her fingers. 'It's like I said, baby. Daddy made a mistake. And the Christian thing is to forgive. Those men who took him away have forgiven Daddy. They shortened his sentence because he's been so good. That's why he's coming home.'

Elvis focuses so hard on his milk that his vision blurs.

'Will the men come for me, Mama?' he asks, his lower lip trembling.

'Oh!' She swoops to his side. 'No, baby! What made you think that?'

He looks at her troubled face, drinking her in.

'Sometimes ... I make a mistake.'

Like yesterday, when he let Corinne's English bulldog play in the house, and Mama yelled because she'd just got all the sheets clean for Daddy and now she'd have to start over.

'Oh, no! The mistakes you make are only small, baby. Mama's gonna protect you, you know that.'

She pulls him to her chest, and he relaxes against her gratefully.

'I thank the good Lord I have you, baby. I thank Him every day.'

As she has given him this, he offers her something in return. 'Poor Daddy,' he says.

'Poor Daddy!' she agrees.

Prising him from her, she says, 'Elvie, I want you to promise me something.' She grips his shoulders. 'When Daddy comes, we ain't never gonna talk about that place again, OK?'

He reaches up to dust the flour from her hair, but she stops his hand.

'Elvis? You hear what I said?'

He blinks.

'Daddy won't want to keep going over it. So don't go asking him a heap of questions. OK?'

But he has so many questions! What was it like, in jail? Was he chained up, like in the stories? Did he sleep on straw? Was he whipped?

'Daddy won't want to think about all that bad stuff. We're gonna help him do that, ain't we?'

'Yes, Mama. Poor Daddy.'

'That's right. Poor Daddy.'

That afternoon, when Cousin Corinne comes home from school, she and Elvis crawl into the space beneath the porch. There isn't room to stand, but there's enough to play. He likes it here, even though it smells of chicken shit and Mama says to watch out for snakes. It is more sheltered than the yard, and from here he can hear Mama and know she's there without having to check on her. She walks across the porch in her stockinged feet. *Thumpety-thumpety-thumpety.* Much more sedate and measured than this morning's dancing. *Clonk-whoosh.* Dipping the pitcher in the water bucket. *Thumpety-click-clunk.* Going back through the door.

'Elvis!' moans Corinne. 'You ain't playing!'

He studies his cousin's small eyes and clumps of lashes. She is louder and quicker than him in everything.

'I'm playing dead!' he says, lying on the damp ground, letting the dirt brush his cheek. He wonders if this is what it's really like to be dead. Smelling the cool earth. Hearing the living walk over you as you peer out at a thin strip of light.

Corinne thrusts a corn shuck with a scrap of crocheted fabric wrapped round it into his face. 'You be baby.'

'Waah!' says Elvis, automatically. 'Baby hungry!'

'Just you wait now, baby,' says Corinne, arranging herself so she is sitting next to his head. 'Mama's busy. You gotta wait.'

Clinkety-clunk-clunk. And a scrabbling sound. Mama straightening Aunt Leona's furniture, again.

'Don't wanna.'

'Mama knows you a good baby, but you gotta wait,' says Corinne.

Suddenly he can stand it no more.

'TORNADO!' he shouts, sitting up and shaking the corn doll in Corinne's face. 'TORNADO!'

Both children are familiar with this game.

'Hide!' shrieks Corinne, and they throw themselves, face down, in the dirt.

They've heard all about the real tornado that hit Tupelo when Elvis was a baby. Mama loves to tell the story. It lasted just a few minutes but it killed hundreds and destroyed entire streets. God's wrecking ball had come to town, she says, and it shook the house, the yard, the sky itself. The first she'd known of it was the whispering of the newspaper sheets that lined the walls of their house. She'd stood in the yard, Elvis on her hip, and seen something green and scattered in the sky. The clouds billowed into gigantic mushrooms, then flattened. Vernon's uncle Noah had collected the whole family in his school bus and taken them to shelter in his brick house, where Gladys had braced herself against the wall, holding Elvis to her, as the tornado came close. She held him so hard he cried, but still she held him tighter.

'Is it passing?' asks Corinne, her voice subdued.

'It's coming right this way!' shouts Elvis. 'You'd better get on!'

Corinne hauls herself onto Elvis's back. She's almost two years older, and her hot body feels reassuringly heavy. Her hair tickles his neck. The knobbles of her buttons push into his spine.

He can still hear his mother overhead. There's a scratching noise, as if she's cleaning the stove.

'Hold on, now!' he says.

'Reckon it's passing over.'

'No. Stay down.'

As Corinne clings to him, he rocks to and fro, slowly building up speed.

'TORNADO!' he cries. 'Hang on!'

'I can't!' squeals Corinne.

One last jerk and she'll fall into the dirt. He whips himself sideways, but Corinne hangs on, her weight squeezing the breath from him.

'Reckon it's passed,' he whispers.

'Naw,' she says, hopefully. 'Looks like it's coming back.'

There are unfamiliar steps above, now. Heavy and deliberate. They cross the porch and there's a long pause.

Then a shout comes from the house. 'Vernon!'

Summoning all his strength, Elvis gives a single thrust of his body, and Corinne tumbles off.

Above them, the screen door is wrenched open, and there's the sound of running, followed by a long wail. Then he hears nothing at all.

Elvis stays where he is, sweating and slightly dizzy. Looking at Corinne he announces, 'Tornado's over.'

The room seems much smaller with his father in it.

Vernon's face is grey and baggy-looking, and his clothes hang from his bones. He stands by the stove, blinking at Gladys, who has her hands across her mouth, and seems to be propping herself against a chair.

'Glad,' he says, 'you ain't changed?'

'Not one bit!' Mama says, grasping Vernon's hands in hers.

Then Gladys notices Elvis in the doorway. Wiping her eyes she says, 'Baby, come say hello to your daddy.'

Elvis twists his fingers together. That leather jacket in the trunk won't fit this man any more. The man this morning seemed more like his daddy, or, at least, how Elvis imagined his daddy would be when he returned: solid-looking, confident, winking. Driving a loud truck. Perhaps bearing gifts, like the music his mama danced to. This man's eyes shift from spot to spot, not quite focusing. His pants and shoes are covered in dust. And there's a nasty new smell in the room.

'Elvis,' says Gladys, 'come on over, now, and say hello to your daddy.'

Elvis considers crying 'TORNADO!' again. He hears Corinne, still playing beneath the house, singing a lullaby to her corn doll.

'Elvis ...' warns Gladys.

'It's all right,' says Vernon. He walks slowly across the room and crouches down before his son, his knees cracking. Elvis notices a small hole in the thigh of his father's pants and the skin beneath, pink and scaly-looking. The smell grows stronger. 'Hello, son,' Vernon says. 'All right with you if I come live here?'

Elvis glances up at Gladys, who nods, firmly.

'I guess,' he says.

Then his father embraces him, and Elvis feels the hardness of Vernon's collarbone against his cheek.

'Daddy's back,' says Vernon. 'And soon we can get our own place.'

Elvis pats his father's arm. 'Mama'll be real happy now,' he says.

Vernon laughs, uncertainly.

'I brought you something, son.'

He fishes in his pocket and produces a piece of paper. Carefully, he unfolds it to reveal a once-glossy image of a man in a pointy green hat with a quiver of arrows slung across his shoulder.

'I saved it for you. From a movie magazine.'

Elvis takes it in his hands. The paper is soft as cloth, and tatty at the edges, but the colours are bright. The man's hat sweeps across the page and, beneath his moustache, his teeth are milky white.

'Robin Hood here's what you call an outlaw, see? A law-breaker. But he's a good man,' says Vernon.

'Is his moustache real?' asks Elvis.

Vernon frowns. 'I don't know. I guess.'

'Say thank you, Elvis,' says Gladys.

'Thank you, sir.'

Vernon straightens up. He looks at his wife. 'Run along and play now, boy. You could pretend to be Robin Hood!'

Elvis gazes at his mother, but she is too busy smiling at Vernon to notice.

A low growl comes from behind him. He turns to see Corinne on all fours, pretending to be a dog, her corn doll's head jammed between her teeth.

When he looks back, his parents have disappeared into Uncle Frank and Aunt Leona's bedroom.

* * *

As far as Elvis can tell, his daddy sleeps pretty much all the time.

At night, the three of them share a pallet on the kitchen floor, but as soon as Aunt Leona and Uncle Frank have left for work, Vernon makes use of their bed. While his mama is doing laundry in the yard, Elvis sneaks into the bedroom to get a look at this man, his father.

He has the Robin Hood picture in his pocket, not because he loves it but because he wants to keep it safe without having to see it, and he fingers its wilted edges as he stands by the bed, watching the hump beneath the quilt. Mama spent some time trying to get Daddy out of the bedroom this morning. First she talked to him real sweet, offering coffee and biscuits and even fried apple pie. Then she raised her voice and asked how long it was going to be like this. Elvis heard no reply. After that, his mama had let his daddy be.

Elvis moves closer and examines Vernon's face. It's creased into the pillow, and is almost the same yellowy colour as the flour sack from which the case is stitched. Elvis tries to recall what this face used to be like, but can picture only his daddy's dark blonde curls, which are still there. His voice, too, is the same, although Elvis remembers his father singing 'Clementine' and 'I'll Fly Away'. No songs have been sung in the house since Vernon's return. There's that sour smell about him, still. Perhaps he's been sleeping so hard that he hasn't had a chance to wash. Mama says he's tired, after being away so long, and needs to rest.

Then Vernon's eyes flick open. They are gummy and red around the rims. Elvis ducks, too late.

'What you up to, boy?'

Elvis slides his body beneath the bed, and waits.

'Come out and let me look at you.'

Elvis stays where he is, studying the unswept floorboards.

'You like that old picture I got you?'

'Yessir,' says Elvis, from under the bed.

'That's good, son. Did I tell you who it is?'

'Robin Hood.'

'Naw. That's Errol Flynn, pretending to be Robin Hood. For a movie. You seen a movie, right?'

'Yessir.'

Gladys sometimes takes Elvis to see a picture playing on the back of the flat-bed truck that parks outside Uncle Noah's store during the summertime. But he hasn't seen any movie with this man in it.

The mattress judders above, and his father lets out a long sigh.

'Shall I get Mama?' asks Elvis.

'What for?'

Elvis can't think of a reason that would sound good.

'Come out, now,' says his father, gently.

Elvis scoots from beneath the bed but remains sitting on the floor. His father has his hands tucked beneath his head.

'When you getting up, Daddy?'

'When I'm good and ready,' says Vernon, gazing at the ceiling.

'You wanna play some? I got a truck ...'

'Not now, boy.'

'Daddy?'

'Yeah?'

'What did you do?'

Vernon's eyes roll towards Elvis. Slowly, he heaves himself into a sitting position. Before speaking, he takes a long drink from the cup on the nightstand.

'Man name of Orville Bean, owns half of East Tupelo, messed with me. He wrote me a cheque for a hog I sold him, and it said "four dollars". That hog was worth more like forty. So I changed the numbers on the cheque. That's all.'

'You got sent to the pen 'cause you changed some numbers?'

Vernon presses his lips together. 'Uh-huh. But it was wrong of me to do that.'

Elvis nods in what he hopes is an understanding way.

'You been taking care of Mama good, I can tell,' says Vernon.

Then a loud voice comes from the front of the house.

'I gotta talk to my son,' it says.

There's a slam, and his mama's voice is pleading, 'You can't go in there right now, JD ...'

'Son of a bitch,' Vernon mutters. He looks at Elvis. 'Fetch me them pants,' he instructs, nodding at the chair beneath the window. Elvis does as he's told. From the other room comes the sound of boots treading the boards, his mother offering coffee, and chairs scraping. And the voice again.

'Don't he know it's nearly noon? His brain get fried in Parchman, or what?'

Vernon buckles his belt and pushes open the door. Elvis trails behind.

Elvis's granddaddy is sitting in the biggest chair, the one with the fancy cushion Mama made. The sight of this man's bony behind crushing Mama's fine embroidery makes Elvis's breath come quick. The man smooths his hair back with a big hand and blinks through his thick eyeglasses. His eyebrows are black and wiry. Sometimes this man is sitting on the porch when Elvis and Gladys visit Grandma Minnie Mae, but as far as Elvis is aware he has not visited this house before now.

'Daddy,' says Vernon, from the doorway.

'Son.'

Elvis has never seen any look other than a scowl on his grand-daddy's face, and today it is particularly impressive.

'My wife fixed you some coffee?' Vernon asks.

'No need,' says JD. 'This won't take long.'

Elvis makes a break for it and runs to his mother, who is standing by the bucket and dipper with the coffee pot in her hand. He hangs on to her apron.

'What's on your mind, Daddy?' asks Vernon.

JD cocks his head to the side. 'We oughta talk private.'

'Anything you got to say to me you can say in front of my family,' says Vernon.

'If that's how you want it,' says JD.

Gladys puts the coffee pot back on the shelf and presses a hand to Elvis's shoulder.

JD narrows his eyes. 'What I gotta say is this: why ain't you out working a job, boy?'

'Ain't found me one yet, sir.'

'I hear the WPA's looking for men to dig latrines down in town. That sounds like it'd be near perfect for you, with all your experience shovelling pig shit.'

A strange noise comes from Vernon's throat.

'JD,' says Gladys, 'I'll thank you to remember that my son is in the room, and his ears don't need to hear no cursing—'

'You need to get your ass down there,' JD continues. 'You just can't get out the pen and go to bed, boy. Folks is saying you as good as dead in here. You gotta step up. Provide for this family. Your gal here's been doing it long enough. Now it's your turn.'

'Like you did, Daddy?' says Vernon, looking up.

There's a silence. Gladys's fingertips dig into Elvis's shoulders, making him squirm away.

JD pushes back his chair and strolls across to Elvis like he has all the time in the world. Crouching down, he peers at his grandson.

A powerful smell of tobacco comes off him as he pats Elvis on the chest, hard, three times. 'You listen to your granddaddy, boy, and listen good. Don't be like your paw here. You know what he did, don't you? He cheated. Lied. Stole. Took the easy way out. That ain't no way to live.'

'Reckon that's the only way you taught me,' says Vernon.

In a flash, JD is up on his feet. He marches across to his son, draws a hand back, and slaps him across the face.

Elvis pees in his pants, just a little bit.

Vernon stands there, hanging on to his face like it might fall off.

'Get out of this house,' says Gladys, her voice trembling. She goes to the door and holds it open, leaving Elvis standing alone, exposed to these two men, one with his head in his hands, the other breathing hard and opening and closing his fist.

'Get out,' she repeats.

JD picks up his hat. At the door he turns to Gladys and says, 'I feel right sorry for you, woman.'

'You ain't got the faintest idea what he's been through,' says Gladys. 'He don't deserve no more punishment.'

'Naw,' says JD, 'and neither do you, I don't reckon.'

Still scowling, he places his hat on his head, tips it to Elvis, then leaves.

1942

Gladys's body is glued to the bed, sweat oozing beneath the flesh of her breasts as she listens to the sounds of the warm June night: Vernon's breath, shallow and steady as the whirring of the katydids in the trees; the low voices of Vester and Clettes from the neighbouring rooms, quarrelling over how much liquor Vester has consumed. She counts herself lucky that, whatever else he may be, Vernon is not a true drunkard. Unlike her, Vernon will take a drink or two, even though he calls himself Assembly of God; but Gladys has never had cause to drag her husband out of a bar by his hair. There have been times she's convinced herself he will turn to the bottle. After all, he's not as strong as she is. Ever since Vernon returned from Parchman, Gladys has felt her age: as the older one she must carry her husband through.

She hasn't always felt this way, though. Even now, aged thirty, she fears there is something of the devil in her. Had it begun when she'd thrown that ploughshare blade? She can't have been more than ten years old when the farm owner went for her daddy and sisters that day they were working his field. His high-topped boots had glinted like new money in the sun as he steadied his horse and brought

34

back his whip. She'd ripped the sharp end from a ploughshare and chunked it right at his head, shocked by the strength that was suddenly hers; she'd wanted nothing less than to kill that man stone dead. She'd missed; the blade had fallen to the ground not far from her own feet. The man had been so surprised that he'd laughed and spared her daddy the whipping. It had been Gladys who'd been hit, later, by her father's own hand.

She'd felt it dancing, too, on Saturday nights before she was married, when she'd experienced music as something that entered not just her ear, but also her belly.

Vernon had watched her, then. He was a boy who smiled easily and laughed at nothing at all. After the grief of her beloved daddy's early death and her mama's lifelong sickness, meeting Vernon had been like opening a window onto a sunny morning. All the Presleys were handsome but the twenty-one-year-old Gladys had thought Vernon, who was seventeen, too young and too good-looking for her, and she'd tried Vester, his older and more sedate brother, first. But then she'd seen the wanting look in Vernon's cool blue eyes as he'd watched her dance. Unlike other boys, he didn't stare at her body, but at her face; it wasn't until they were alone, around the side of his mama's house, that he'd glanced down at the front of her dress and said, 'Gladys Smith, you look more alive than any girl I ever laid eyes on.' Not two months after that, they eloped to the next county and were married in secret. Vernon added a year to his age to make it legal, and Gladys took three years off hers to make it seem respectable.

The idea that she was pretty had come as a surprise to Gladys, whose physical shortcomings were often remarked upon by her own mother, who was beautiful and petite all her life. Even in her sickbed, Doll Smith had kept a comb and a mirror beneath the pillow, in case visitors came calling. 'Gladys,' she'd say, 'where in the name of all that's holy did you get those shoulders? I swear there's more power there than in your daddy's whole body.' To Gladys, it had never felt powerful to be big. It had felt only shameful and awkward.

But Vernon took away that shame, at least at first. He said he would tell his brother how it was now: he might be younger, but he was smarter than Vester, and had always told him how things were. Gladys had seen no reason to doubt this. Not long after, Vester married Gladys's sister, Clettes, which had been a load off her mind.

Five nights of broken sleep have taken their toll. Gladys's eyelids droop, and, before she knows it, she dreams she's cradling Elvis, the small baby who loved to sleep on her chest. Like a hot rock, he balanced on her sternum. He was never heavy, but when unconscious he was dense, somehow; his limbs fell into her flesh with the weight of sleep. She would clasp both hands around his back, rest her chin on his head, close her eyes, breathe in his warm baby scent, concentrate on his breathing. It was important to hold him there; she was convinced that if he fell from her chest she would roll in her sleep and crush the life from his beautiful limbs.

Now she drifts in and out of a light slumber, just as she did when Elvis was an infant, her body waking her at twenty-minute intervals.

At three in the morning Gladys snaps fully awake. She gropes for her baby, realises there is no baby, and knows there is something more urgently missing. Her son is missing not just from her arms, but from the house. She understands this without looking at Elvis's bed, because the air is cooler now and the sounds of the night – a cat mewing for shelter, the bullfrogs pumping out groans – are louder. The front door must be open.

She springs to her feet. Elvis's collection of funny papers is neatly stacked by the pallet on which he sleeps, but there is no Elvis. There is just his sheet, crumpled on the floor.

Gladys does not waste time by waking Vernon. She pulls on her housecoat, stuffs her bare feet into her shoes, and goes outside.

The weeds in their square of yard are wet with dew and she breathes in the scent of fresh earth. She heads down the track between the handful of other houses which surround hers and towards the road, praying her instinct hasn't failed her and that she has woken before he's gone too far. The first time he sleepwalked out of the house, a neighbour found him wandering down the highway in his nightshirt. She's never asked Mr Vanderholm what he was doing on that stretch of road at two in the morning. Instead she darned the hole in the shoulder of Elvis's nightshirt and vowed to stay half-awake through the night from then on.

Once she's on the gravel road she looks both ways. Faced with the emptiness stretching ahead, her body weakens for a second, but the panic comes again, propelling her down the hill, towards the highway. He has gone way too far. She hears herself muttering it as she runs: *This is way too far! Way too far!* and in some dim part of her mind there is the hope that tomorrow she will be glad she was alone on this road, glad there was nobody else to see her sweating in her housecoat, her shoes gaping from the backs of her naked feet.

She cuts through a small pine wood, calculating that this is the way he came before, and his sleeping legs will somehow remember. The trees' darkness seems absolute and she considers turning back for Vernon, but that would cost her too much time. Her boy may be sleepwalking down the middle of the highway while some truck barrels towards him. So she plunges on, calling his name, stumbling on the rough ground, trying not to picture the snakes that might be slithering towards her feet, scratching her arm on a branch but managing to make her way through the trees to where the street-lamps glow along the empty road.

Then she sees him. He's crouching on the shoulder of the road, swaying back and forth on his haunches. If he were mumbling, folks might take him for feeble-minded. The relief of it almost has her falling to her knees in the ditch, but she must reach her son and remove him from danger before allowing herself any such foolish-ness. And so Gladys sprints along the concrete, yelling for him. But he does not look up, or quit rocking. When she reaches him she kneels down, small stones gritting her knees. She takes his face gently in her hands and says, 'Baby, it's Mama. Get up, now.'

His eyes fall on her without the remotest spark of recognition. She hauls his sleeping body to its feet and drags him down into the wet slipperiness of the ditch, where they collapse against one another. Lord knows what trash is down here – she can smell something rotten, and her feet skid on paper packets reduced to slime. She feels some insect nibbling her bare calf. But they are safe, lying together on the soft dirt. She holds him against her, pressing his face into her shoulder, and she feels the change in him as he wakes. First his fingers clasp her waist, then his breath shortens and he raises his face to hers. 'Mama?' he asks.

'Don't you worry, baby. You was sleepwalking again. Mama's gonna take you home now.'

His eyes go round. 'Where we at?'

She sits up and brushes off her housecoat. Above them, a truck rumbles by, making him cover his ears in fright.

'In a ditch by the highway. We gotta walk back through them trees, OK?' She stands and pulls him upright. He looks around, biting his lip.

'Come on, now. You gotta walk for me.' She scrambles up the bank and holds out a hand. 'It ain't far.'

He hesitates, scanning her face for clues about exactly how and why they have ended up here, and whether this is all right or not. On taking her hand, though, he seems, suddenly, to accept the situation wholly. 'All right,' he says, and he lets his mother guide him.

All the way back to the house, he holds her hand. A tree frog starts up, and another answers. The moon is bright and the black sky swirls above, scattered with stars, and Elvis begins to chatter. 'What time is it?' he asks. 'Is it the very middle of the night?' He looks up at her, his face glowing, and she can't help a smile. 'Look at the stars, Mama!' he says, and she nods. She worries, though, that her husband will have been woken by her absence, and will be wandering the streets, searching for them.

But when they reach home, Vernon is still sleeping. They tiptoe to Elvis's bed. Gladys picks the crumpled sheet from the floor and tucks it around his body. Then she sits beside him. 'You OK, baby?' she whispers.

He nods.

'Now give me your best smile.'

He obliges, stretching his full lips wide and creasing his eyes. Her son has eyes like her, heavy-lidded, slightly slanted. She hopes it won't hold him back to have such foreign-looking eyes.

'Nose squash,' he commands, and she leans in to his face, her nose pressed to his. They stay like this for a few minutes, breathing the same air, whispering to one another.

'Mama?'

'Mm-hmm?'

'I won't do it again.'

'I know, honey.'

'You don't need to worry none.'

'I know, honey.'

'Baby's gonna be all right.'

'I know it.'

'You can sleep now, Mama.'

'You too, baby.'

Back in her own bed, she decides they will go to the cemetery tomorrow.

Thirty-five minutes. On that January night, seven years ago, it had taken thirty-five minutes between death and life.

The dead one came first. His silence, when the midwife lifted and slapped him, seemed to make the world stop. Minnie Mae had to shout at Gladys to make her listen. 'There's another one coming, Glad, you gotta get on with it, gal!'

But Gladys was looking at her dead child, trying to see something other than the blueness around his slack lips, the pallor of his washed-out body. He looked like something pickled. She could hardly breathe, let alone push. She wanted nothing other than sleep.

'Give the other one a chance!' cried Minnie Mae, taking her by the shoulders and shaking her. 'Get on with it!'

As if she had any control over this thing.

Frost on the glass. Her breath and flesh misting the air. She thought of cows in a barn, helpless against the cold, but still steaming. Vernon and his daddy and uncle had built this two-room place for them, right next to her father-in-law's house, and it had felt so homely, with the smell of the new wood and the bright drapes she'd run up on Minnie Mae's machine. Even the oil lamps had seemed quaint. They'd gathered wild roses and honeysuckle from the woods behind and planted them around the place. But now it smelled of blood and urine and fear.

'Glad, I ain't gonna tell you again, gal. Push!'

She'd hollered only twice during the whole thing. Minnie Mae had thought to wrap the dead child – they'd already called him Jesse, after Vernon's father – in a dishcloth and pass him to Vernon, who was in the next room, not in the bar, which is where Gladys wished he was, so he wouldn't have to lay eyes on his dead son. When she imagined Vernon holding the grey lump, she hollered. Then she raised herself from the bed and crouched over the rug for the next contraction, thinking she wanted it over, now, for this baby to be out and done with. It might as well fall to the floor if it was going to be wrapped in a dishcloth and buried in the earth. Minnie Mae hurried to protect the rug with an old sheet, and as she did so Gladys hollered again, so loud and raw that Vernon was knocking on the door to come in and Minnie Mae was yelling, 'She's all right! It's just the other one coming. Don't you dare come in here, Vernon Presley!'

Minnie Mae caught the second child and Gladys collapsed on the rug. And then his sound filled the place, and the door was opening, and Vernon was coming over, pushing his wiry mama out of the way – which Gladys had never seen him do before – but she couldn't look at her husband for long because she was gazing at her boy, who was alive. Minnie Mae cut the cord with a deft snick. When

Gladys had the child in her arms, he quietened and looked at her as if she were the only light in the room. He was, as Minnie Mae said, no bigger than a minute.

'I thought I'd lost you,' Vernon said, his hand trembling on her shoulder.

A spike of rage rose in her. Was that all he'd thought about, in all this? His own loss?

She handed him his son. 'Take him,' she said, 'and quit your crying. We got a son. There ain't nothing to cry about now.'

There was no money for a gravestone, plaque or marker, but still they know exactly where to go. Or, at least, Mama says she knows where her other baby is buried. But sometimes Elvis wonders. Leaves fall, frost covers the ground, new stones are erected every week at Priceville cemetery. The place changes, and all he knows for sure is that his brother lies somewhere between the large tree with the crooked trunk and the line of small, plain graves at the back.

Usually they go on the last Sunday of every month, after church. But today Mama had appeared at the gates after school and said, 'Let's go visit your brother.' Recognising the urgency in her voice, he knew better than to say that he needed to pee. He also knew better than to question the logic of visiting a dead person. In a way, he thinks, Jesse isn't even dead, not truly, because you need to have been alive to be dead. And his brother took not one breath on this earth. His brother was born dead.

Not long ago, as his mama was readying herself for one of their Sunday visits, his daddy said, 'Ain't no need to keep on going there, Glad. Everybody knows you won't forget.'

'I don't go for nobody but my own self,' she'd said, pushing past him and grabbing Elvis's hand.

Vernon caught her arm and said, 'Why's Elvis got to go, every time? He's just a boy.'

Gladys's face softened, a little, and she released her grip on her son.

At the loss of his mama's touch, Elvis panicked. 'But I wanna go, Daddy!' he insisted.

After that, it was impossible to say otherwise.

This morning his daddy left for Japtown, almost two hundred miles away. He is to help build a camp for Japanese prisoners of war. They had all cried, but Elvis was glad it was his father, not his mother, who was leaving, and that his father was doing something for the war. Many East Tupelo men have joined the military, but his daddy cannot become a soldier, because he was in the pen. Elvis knows he must never mention this fact, although sometimes he feels it is not a fact at all, merely a memory. When the other boys ask him what his daddy is doing for the war, Elvis can now say Vernon has special and important work, constructing a prison for the enemy.

The cemetery is a couple of miles from school, and Gladys takes it slow in the July heat. Elvis's limbs prickle with frustration as they make their stately way along the hot highway in silence, past Johnnie's Drive-In, where older boys go for burgers, and, after he got a job with the WPA a few years back, his daddy once took him for the most delicious meal of his life: a dough burger, fries and a cola. There were coloured plates and a bright metal rim around the table. His mama does not suggest they stop, though.

Eventually they turn off and walk up the hill, through the welcome shade of the woods. The dust road which takes them past a few wooden shacks is cool beneath Elvis's bare feet. The leaves of the yellow poplars *tick-tick-tick* above their heads. He stops for a minute to pick some ox-eye daisies from the bank and gives them to his mama to add to the small bunch she has collected for Jesse's grave. She tells him to keep them – he can place them there himself.

It takes them an hour to reach the black gates to the cemetery. He follows his mama beyond the marked family plots to the patch of grass at the back, beneath which Jesse is buried. The grass here is regularly watered and always a vivid green. Gently, he places the flowers down and wipes his hands on his pants. His bladder is now uncomfortably full. They stand side by side in silence, and his mama drops his hand, clasps her own together and bows her head. He stares at the ground and tries to imagine his twin brother, but sees only his own shadow stretching away. He likes to think that Jesse was his identical twin. Mama has said she doesn't know this to be true, but she feels it to be so. If there was another Elvis, would that make him less himself? Or more?

Jesse, he says, in his head. *Jesse, can you hear me?*

No reply.

We're here again, and every time I'm sure you gonna say something! Or give Mama a sign. You make her so sad.

No reply.

Ain't my fault you died, you know.

No reply.

After letting a decent time pass, he wanders off. Maybe he can pee over by the woods. Nobody will see – there's nobody here save him and Mama. He reaches his favourite headstone, the one with the white marble angel on top. Most of the stones are plain, but this one is different. The angel wears fancy armour like the Roman soldier Elvis has seen in a schoolbook; his hair is feathered around his face, his bow pulled taut. His sandals curl around the top of the grave as if he's balancing there, and, when he's sure nobody else is around, Elvis often gives the angel a little shove, as if he could push him from the stone. Below the angel's feet, a sculpted scroll reads, *Let us put on the breastplate of love.* Elvis likes this idea; it reminds him of his favourite superhero, the Phantom, fighting for justice, peace and love.

He glances across to make sure his mama hasn't moved, and, forgetting his bladder, clambers onto the gravestone and pulls himself to where the angel stands. Holding on to the stone legs, he looks over the cemetery and imagines himself flying like the Phantom, shot from the angel's bow into the sky. He closes his eyes.

Jesse. I'm thanking this angel for taking you and not me. Do you hear?

No reply.

You don't do a lot of talking but I know you're listening. And watching, too. Do you see me, putting on the breastplate of love?

Wobbling a little, he stretches his arms to the sky and shoots an imaginary arrow in his brother's direction.

Then, swamped with guilt, Elvis jumps down and hurries back to his mama. She's kneeling now, arranging the daisies on the ground, tidying up her imaginary marker. She's brought a pair of small scissors with her and is snipping the grass so it's even. He watches her for a while, then he starts to rub her back, in case she cries this time. She never cries at the cemetery, although he always expects her to. Would she weep over *his* grave? He's sure she would. It's impossible to hold his body still enough to do the stroking, though, because if he relaxes his muscles he'll pee his pants. So he hops from leg to leg and pats her shoulder. He realises that it's been twenty minutes, at least, since she even looked at him, and he wants her back.

She fusses with the flowers. It won't be long before she'll turn to him, her face set in a blank stare, and say, 'Let's go home, baby.' On the way she will hold him tightly and say things like, 'I got you, ain't I?' and, 'God gave you all of Jesse's strength, you know that?'

He's tempted to try to wrench the flowers and scissors away from her and yell that none of this does any good. Just for a second, he imagines pulling out his peter and pissing right there on the grave.

Take that, Jesse. You won't never know what it's like to grab your peter in your hand and take a long, hard pee.

He backs away from the grave and waits for it to be over, praying for greater muscle control or for some other way to rid himself of this irresistible urge. Eventually, though, he has no choice. Closing his eyes, he releases the pee in a joyous stream down his leg. The liquid settles and glistens on the hot, dry ground, and immediately starts to stink.

When Gladys turns, she gives the puddle a long look. He studies her face for signs of change and a sob rises in his chest, because he knows from her narrowed black eyes, the way her lips are set in a terrifying line, what she will do. It is what his daddy does, sometimes, and what she does, too, on even rarer occasions. But this is one of those occasions for sure. She takes a breath and swats him, hard, on the side of his head.

Pain thrums through his skull, but it's nowhere near as bad as the time his daddy went for him with the dishtowel. Elvis had stolen a strip of chicken from his mama's plate and his daddy called him a *long hungry*, twisted the cloth into a thick rope, and thrashed him about the head, yelling that he should never steal food from his own kin.

Gingerly, Elvis touches the spot that Gladys swiped. There's no blood, just a burning soreness.

Gladys stands, flexing the fingers of the hand that struck her son. She opens her mouth and shuts it again, her face red as a blister. Then she puts the offending hand in her pocket and walks away without looking over her shoulder.

He swallows his tears. She'll look back, soon. In the meantime, he'll just walk on Jesse's grave, see how she likes that. His toes, damp with urine, rub together as he moves in small circles over the grass.

Damn you, undead brother. Damn you, you long hungry. You stole from your own kin. You took her love from me and there ain't one thing you can do with it.

He kicks the flowers that his mother positioned, scattering them. A few land in his pee. With his heel, he grinds them further in, then glances across to see if she is looking. But she is still walking towards the road.

Once she reaches the entrance, she'll look. She won't go through the gates without him.

Jesse, maybe it's just you and me, now.

She's almost at the gates.

I'm sorry, Jesse. I'm sorry it was me and not you.

And then he's running, wet pants slapping his legs, toes squelching.

'Mama! Wait!'

Just beyond the gates, she stops.

'Mama!' Even though he can see she is waiting now, he cannot stop yelling, *Mama, Mama, Mama,* and when he is in her arms he is still saying it.

She strokes his head.

All the way through the woods, he cries as they walk hand in hand. He keeps crying long after the panic and the hurt have left him, because he wants to punish her, and he wants to make her speak. But she just lets him cry until his throat aches and his eyes are hot and grainy.

It's not until they reach home that she says, 'Sorry, baby.' Her face is drawn, her voice flat. 'Mama's sorry.'

The evening has grown dark and she's kneeling before him on their porch. His stomach growls. She touches his face. 'Can you forgive me, baby?'

It's the most he can hope for. He nods, and is embraced.

That night, he sleeps in her bed. When his father was in the pen, he shared his mother's bed, but Elvis has only a dim recollection of this. Since he started sleepwalking, he has sometimes had the luxury of a night in the safety of his mama's arms, but always at the disapproval of his daddy.

This is different. This is every night for the coming few weeks. Although Gladys doesn't say anything to this effect, Elvis knows it. His daddy is far away in Japtown, and his mama's bed is now open to him. He knows better than to climb in without an invitation, though, so he stays awake on his pallet, waiting for her to appear.

When she comes in, she has her white gown on and her hair is brushed, which makes her look like a pretty ghost from a book, perhaps one who is condemned to haunting because she was once wronged by her true love.

She sits on the edge of her bed and sighs.

'You still awake, baby?'

He nods.

'We'll sure miss Daddy while he's gone, won't we?' she says.

'Yes, Mama.'

She's not looking at him, and the fear that she will turn down the lamp without inviting him in rises in his chest. Perhaps peeing on Jesse's grave means he will never be welcome in his mother's bed again. But then she turns to face him. 'It's hot as all get out,' she says. 'Reckon there's a storm coming. Why don't you come in here where we can keep one another safe?' And she holds the sheet up to welcome him.

Elvis scrambles in but remains a few inches from her, just in case she's still sore about him peeing in the cemetery. She turns out the light, then she says, in a low voice, 'You might as well be in the next county. Come on over here.'

The warm scent coming from her lets him know that she has opened her arms. He wastes no time in snuggling as close as he can, so he can smell her properly. His mama's flesh always smells just right. He cannot think what she smells of, only that she smells of Mama. It's like slotting himself into the rightest, sweetest spot in the world; his body fits into the dip beside her, and she envelops him in her strong, smooth arms. The weight of them around his waist anchors him.

Outside, the wind has risen, making the trees creak and moan. The Frisco train gives its long, lonesome wail. The windows and door begin to rattle, and he presses his face deep in her bosom. She murmurs, 'Careful now. Don't block your airways,' as if he could be choked by her closeness. He ignores the warning, breathing his mama in. He is blind in the dark, his face covered by her flesh, and at last he can stop moving; he can almost stop listening to the rushing noise of the trees.

She whispers into his hair, 'Now this is good. We wouldn't want you wandering out there on the highway, you could slip right under the wheels of some truck.' If Mama didn't hold him, would he be helpless to stop himself opening that door and stepping into the night, stumbling into ditches and across ravines and into the jaws of who knows what danger?

'Let's pray to Jesse, now,' she says, and he feels her bow her head. Her chin rests heavily on his crown as she mumbles the words.

'Beloved Jesse, watch over us, dear son, and bless us. We miss you every day, but we try to live as if you were among us. Let us feel your spirit, Jesse, in everything we do. Amen.'

'Amen.'

After a pause, he asks, 'Mama, is Jesse jealous that we're still alive?'

Last Sunday the preacher had spoken of the sin, and asked all those who'd fallen prey to the green-eyed monster to hold up their hands and receive the Lord's forgiveness. His mother's hand had shot right up, and, after a moment, his father had followed suit.

'Oh, no, Jesse don't feel that way. He's happy for us.'

'Does Jesse love me, Mama?'

'He loves all his family, just like a good son ought to.'

Elvis tries to feel his dead brother's spirit. Perhaps it is in the hot fug of his mama's bed. Perhaps Jesse's spirit is right here in this sweet spot. Why else would it feel so good?

Graceland, 23 December 1957

Colonel Tom Parker has announced his intention to visit Graceland, and the house is on alert. As Gladys sits in the dining room, waiting for the Colonel's foghorn voice to blast through her afternoon, she can hear Vernon instructing the maids to dust the bannisters and shine the door knocker one more time, and to make sure there's enough potato salad, in case the Colonel wants to stay and eat. She can also hear Elvis telling his daddy to quit fretting, because the Colonel will be in and out faster than green grass through a goose. His manager rarely visits, and Gladys knows that Tom Parker's reluctance to come to Graceland is her doing: she's made no secret of her dislike of the man.

When the call comes from the gate, the family gathers around the polished dining table, with Elvis sitting at the head, in front of the Christmas tree. His red shirt matches the tinsel with which he and Gladys festooned the tree yesterday. Elvis had helped her in silence, but at least he'd come out of his room for an hour. Vernon is dressed in a stiff suit and tie. When he pours himself coffee from the pot Alberta has left on the table, the doorbell chimes, making him twitch and splash a little on his pale blue pants. Both Gladys and Elvis ignore his curses, because Alberta is already showing Tom Parker in.

It's a cold day, but the Colonel, a stubby man with what hair he has left dragged across the dome of his head, is dressed in a short-sleeved shirt and a lightweight green knitted vest. His stockinged feet are stuffed into a pair of bashed-up-looking sandals. As he marches into the dining room, his round eyes look a little bleary. Gladys wonders if he, too, has had his sleep disturbed by the news of the draft. In one fist he holds a ham as big as his whole arm. Brandishing it before them, he says, 'Why the long faces? Colonel's here, and he's brought you a gift for Christmas!' Then he heaves the meat onto the table with a *whap*. It skids slightly on the surface, leaving a greasy smear.

Gladys knows that Elvis has already given Tom Parker his Christmas gift: a red BMW Isetta. The day after receiving the draft notice, he'd told her the Colonel would fix this army trouble, and had raced off to present his manager with the keys. When he returned, she'd asked him what the Colonel had said, and Elvis had just shaken his head and retreated to his bedroom.

Vernon, holding one hand over the stain on his pants, extends the other. 'Welcome to Graceland, Colonel,' he says. 'Mighty fine to see you again.'

The Colonel pumps Vernon's hand up and down, his tanned face beaming. 'That ham is all the way from my birthplace of West Virginia! I had a friend deliver it to me especially for the Presleys.' He often claims to be from West Virginia, but from the way his voice sometimes becomes sharply guttural, Gladys suspects Tom Parker is actually a Yankee.

'And that's because I am *always* ruminating on how to make the Presleys not only rich but also happy,' the Colonel continues. 'When I wake each morning, my very first thought is of our boy here.'

Breathing audibly through his nose, the Colonel approaches Elvis, who hasn't risen from his seat, and waits. Slowly, Elvis stands and mumbles, 'Hello, sir.'

It's the first time Gladys has seen her son greet his manager with anything less than goggle-eyed enthusiasm.

'Come on, now,' says the Colonel, holding his arms out. 'Ain't you going to say hello to ol' Colonel properly, son?'

Elvis has no choice but to be embraced, briefly, by his manager's fat arms. He submits to several hearty slaps on the back.

Then the Colonel releases him, and looks at Gladys. 'Mrs Presley.'

'Mr Parker.'

'Now don't get up,' he says, although she has made no move. 'Do my eyes deceive me or have you lost a little weight, there? Looks to ol' Colonel like you're doing a whole lot better than me!' He pats his own big belly and grins.

Gladys does not smile.

'You'll understand, Colonel,' says Vernon, who is hovering behind his shoulder, 'that we're more than a little mixed up here today, what with this drafting news.'

'Oh, I understand,' says the Colonel, lighting a cigar, 'and that's why Colonel is visiting. You don't mind if I help myself to a little coffee here?'

Seating himself next to Gladys, he reaches for the pot.

'You folks know I tried my absolute darnedest to keep Elvis out of the army,' he says, sloshing coffee into a cup, 'but, well, in the end, Uncle Sam calls the shots, even with Colonel himself.'

Vernon takes a seat and says, 'We appreciate that, Colonel. We appreciate everything you've done for this family.'

Gladys gazes at the Christmas tree. She can just see the edge of one of the angel's wings, peeking out from the branches. Elvis hadn't noticed where she'd stashed it, yesterday. Or, if he had, he'd kept quiet.

The Colonel is still talking. 'Now, I want to give y'all my personal guarantee that Elvis will be taken good care of. I will see to it that he is quite safe. And I will be working for him – doubling, no, tripling my efforts! – every moment that he's away.'

Gladys is surprised by the sudden squeeze to her hand as, beneath the table, Elvis clasps it in his. She returns the gesture, and feels strong enough to speak up.

'That's just fine, Mr Parker,' she says, relishing how the man blinks, hard, every time she fails to call him Colonel, 'and, well, maybe I'm being a little slow here, but I'm having some trouble understanding how you *can* guarantee Elvis's safety when he's in the army.'

The Colonel puts down his coffee cup. 'Mrs Presley,' he says, narrowing his eyes, 'I appreciate you're concerned about our boy's welfare, but compared with being exposed to thousands of rampant females on some stage, the army is a pretty secure place to be! I mean, that *is* the point of the army—'

'Unless there's a war,' says Gladys.

Vernon coughs. 'Now, Glad—'

'Mama's upset, is all,' says Elvis.

She holds her son's hand tighter.

The Colonel takes a puff on his cigar and fixes Elvis with his bulbous eyes. Gladys feels her son shrink back.

'Sure she is,' says the Colonel. 'Ain't we all? But we gotta make the best of this thing. To my mind, this here's an opportunity! Now, if we can accept this, and if Elvis can do his patriotic duty, and if he behaves himself in the army – which I'm sure he will – then I can give you the Colonel's personal guarantee that when our boy is discharged he will be the biggest star the world has ever seen. Think about it. When Elvis comes home, he won't just be a number-one entertainer, he'll be a bona-fide all-American hero, adored by every patriotic citizen of this great country!'

There's a pause. Elvis and the Colonel are still holding one another's gaze.

'I ain't looked at it that way,' Elvis says. 'But it kinda makes sense now you say it.'

'Son, it's the absolute hundred-per-cent truth,' says the Colonel. 'You're gonna get what you deserve. Not only millions of dollars, but the respect of millions of people the world over.'

Elvis removes his hand from his mother's.

'Mama, you can understand what the Colonel's saying, can't you? I mean, it sounds pretty good.'

Gladys looks towards the tree again, unable to speak.

Clamping his cigar between his lips, the Colonel pushes back his chair.

'Good! Now I just want to take five minutes of Elvis's time alone, and then I will let y'all enjoy a family Christmas,' he says.

'You ain't staying for something to eat?' asks Vernon.

The Colonel stands. 'Heading straight on back to Madison, I'm afraid. I got your son's business to attend to!'

'Do you like our tree, Mr Parker?' Gladys asks.

'It's real pretty,' says the Colonel, placing a hand on Elvis's back to steer him from the room.

Gladys fishes the angel from its hiding place and holds it up. 'Elvis won't let me put the angel he made in elementary school at the top. Don't you think it oughta be there, Mr Parker?'

'Lord, Mama,' says Elvis, smiling for the first time in days. 'What you doing with that old thing?'

The Colonel laughs. 'Mrs Presley, I think anything our boy has made should be right at the very top of the tree. Happy Christmas to you, now!'

'Happy Christmas!' calls Vernon, trailing after the two men.

When the others have left the room, Gladys shoves the angel back into the branches and goes in search of a drink.

SAVED: 1945–1946

1945

Elvis wakes late to the smell of oatmeal and the sound of his father singing. Since he got the job driving a delivery truck for L. P. McCarty's, Vernon often sings around the house when he's home. This morning's rendition of 'Corinne, Corinna' is especially joyful. Vernon's job keeps him away for days at a time. Elvis wonders what his father sees when he's alone out there, on the road. It must feel like freedom, driving for hundreds of miles, counting off the towns, perhaps stopping at some restaurant for a Pepsi and a sandwich, thinking only of the road ahead. He can hardly believe his father gets paid for such a thing.

Elvis jumps from his bed, because it's Saturday, which means he can go to Tupelo town with Mama to look in the windows of Reed's at the clothes and Este's at the jewellery. Perhaps they will even stop by TKE's for some pie.

After he's fed Mama's beloved White Leghorns and collected their eggs, he rushes back into the house, where his daddy is now seated at the table, drinking coffee.

'Hello, son.' Seeing his father's warm smile, Elvis succumbs to his embrace. There's a smell of oil and leather, and the salt-sweat of Vernon's skin.

'Still skinny,' says Vernon, turning him round for an examination. 'You been feeding this boy, Glad?'

'Night and day,' sings Gladys.

'Missed you, boy.'

'I missed you too, Daddy.'

Which is true, although sometimes Elvis prays his daddy won't come home before Saturday morning, so he can stay longer in his mama's arms.

Gladys touches Elvis's head. 'I'll fix you some of them eggs, baby.'

His father pulls out a chair for him, and Elvis sits.

'I'll take some eggs, too, Glad,' says Vernon, blowing on his steaming coffee. 'Got me some big plans today. Me and Elvis are going hunting.'

Elvis's stomach clenches. What about Reed's? What about that pie? Although he's shown him how to kill doves and squirrels with his slingshot, his daddy has never taken him on an actual hunting trip. Vernon isn't keen on shooting. If he has to do something with his hands, he'd rather tinker with an engine or make something from wood. He never tires of describing his plans to build a house for them, soon. Somewhere better than this duplex.

Gladys scrapes her spatula around the skillet. 'I planned to take Elvis to town.'

'He ain't going to town. He's going hunting with his daddy. Ain't that right, son?'

Gladys puts down a plate of eggs, cooked to rock-hard perfection.

Elvis gazes at his mother, willing her to change his daddy's plans.

'Ain't that right?' Vernon says, and he mouths something Elvis cannot read.

'I guess ...' says Elvis, pushing a fork into his food.

'Don't go letting him shoot rabbits. You know he's tender-hearted,' says Gladys.

Vernon only laughs and winks at Elvis. 'We won't shoot no rabbits. I promise.'

* * *

By the time they have walked down Reese Street and headed up the track, it's past ten. It's April, and everything is newly green. The light leaking through the poplar leaves is becoming brighter. The mockingbirds are singing with all their might. His father leads him confidently through the brush, striking the ground with a stick to ward off snakes. Vernon has a spring not just in his step, but in his whole body as he strides along with a hand on his son's shoulder. But Elvis cannot stop thinking of Reed's window. They have a fancy cowboy shirt, which he'd been hoping to get another look at. It would be something just to go in and touch that shirt. He imagines it would feel cool and smooth, like the sides of Mama's best china cup, and soft, too, like her skin.

His father has brought his old leather bag, presumably with his catapult inside, and has his shotgun slung across his shoulder. The grey metal of the gun's snout chimes against the rivets in the bag, keeping time as they walk. Instead of thinking of shirts and pieces of pie, Elvis tries to concentrate on this sound.

It is not that he doesn't want to shoot. When Odell, his friend from church, let him take a shot with his BB gun, Elvis had enjoyed crawling on his belly through the dirt and getting the rabbit in his sights. But he'd found the quiet waiting impossible to endure. He'd tried to let himself become like a stone, as Odell advised. But who would want to be like a stone? When everything else was moving – the grass, the trees, the sky, the birds, the insects, his heartbeat, his breath – why should he remain still? Why play dead when you are alive? What a waste of energy. What a waste of time.

Mama says good things come to those who wait, but he doesn't see that. If you wait, you may as well be asleep.

His father leads him on until they hit the edge of Mud Creek, where men come not to hunt, but to bathe. Elvis has heard the shrieks of joy echoing from this place on hot summer afternoons.

The bathing hole is overhung on three sides by weeping trees. Men and boys fish here for catfish, perch and bass, but this morning Elvis and his father are alone. They stand on the bank, which shelves steeply into the water, looking across to the red mud of the opposite shore.

'I guess you can figure why I brought you here,' says Vernon.

Elvis knows well enough, but he shakes his head.

'You know men come here to wash, and to swim sometimes?'

'Mama says never to come here for that.'

Vernon looks off into the trees. 'She does. The thing you gotta understand, though, is that all men and boys come here, and all mamas tell them not to. But the mamas know they're gonna. And they don't mind one whit.'

Elvis frowns.

'What I mean is, what your mama don't know, won't hurt her.'

'You saying we got to lie to Mama?'

'Ain't lying, as such. More protecting her.'

Elvis licks his lower lip. 'But she says it's dangerous.'

'Sure, there's the odd snake, and them catfish can get pretty big and kinda cross sometimes—'

'What about the boy who drowned?'

Vernon raises his eyebrows. 'That boy lost his wits, is all. Long as you keep your head, you'll be OK.'

There's a pause.

'What if she finds out?'

Vernon removes his gun from his shoulder. 'You gotta learn, son, that there's two worlds. The woman's world, and the man's world. And this here is part of the man's world. Women ain't got jackshit to do with it.'

As his father begins to unbuckle his belt, Elvis can see that he has little choice but to brave the water. He turns hot, then cold, at the thought. He has never liked being naked in front of others. Even with his mama, he will cover himself with his hands when he's getting in or out of his nightshirt.

'Why don't we go cross yonder?' asks Elvis, pointing towards the other side, where the shore shelves more gently.

'Better just to jump straight in deep,' says Vernon.

Elvis can smell the water: cold, muddy, alive. And the gum trees, too, with their gluey punch.

'But the catfish ...'

Vernon drops his pants. 'They ain't gonna bother us.'

'Odell got his finger bit. It went right to the bone. He reckoned that thing was more cat than fish.'

'Get your clothes off, son. We're going in.'

Vernon stands before him, naked from the waist down. He never removes his shirt in front of anybody. Once Elvis had tried to lift it when they were roughhousing, and his father had cuffed him round the head. Gladys explained, later, that Daddy's back was marked, badly. It was an ugly thing that he didn't want Elvis to see, and it had happened when he *went away that time*, which is how she now refers to Vernon's spell in the pen.

Elvis looks into his daddy's light blue eyes. They are dancing.

'You chicken, boy?'

'No.'

'You ain't afraid of them snakes, are you?'

Elvis peers at the fat pink end of his father's penis, poking from beneath his shirt.

'Naw.'

'All you gotta do is jump up and yell, "Here comes Elvis!" Those snakes'll be good as gone.'

Elvis laughs, a little.

'So go on, then,' says Vernon. 'Get 'em off.'

Elvis unbuttons his shirt and pushes down his pants and under-shorts. He wonders if this would feel better if Magdalene Morgan were watching him. Sometimes, in church, he catches her eyes resting on his face, as if she's searching for something there, and it gives him a huge jolt of pleasure to be looked at in that way.

Then he sees something copper-coloured moving in the trees on the other side of the water. Squinting, he realises this is the hair of Noreen Fishbourne, the fourteen-year-old girl whose breasts push against the front of her too-small pinafore. Odell says that Noreen is fast, and most probably will have a baby soon, the way she carries on. Many people in his church believe Noreen to be possessed by a demon.

Elvis stands frozen with shock, unable even to cover himself with his hands, as Noreen, aware that she's been caught, places a finger on her lips and fixes him with a stare. There is a long moment during which neither of them seems to breathe. She keeps staring at him so strong it makes the pit of his gut contract and release as if he were hungry. Then, just as Vernon twists round to see what has caught his son's eye, Noreen slips away into the brush.

'Yeeeeeeeee-hah!'

Vernon jumps into the water, knees tucked to his chest, sending splashes up Elvis's body and ripples across the creek.

Elvis stands dumbly, waiting for his father to emerge, wondering what to do when he does. He cannot tell Vernon about Noreen; he doesn't care that she would get in trouble, but he can't face admitting that she's seen him, naked as Adam. Perhaps her demon has seen him, too.

He considers gathering his clothes and running after her.

Then a few bubbles break the surface, but Vernon does not appear. He's been down there a while now. Elvis inches to the water's edge. Holding his hands to his groin, he leans over, peering into the cloudy pool. His whole body feels burned by the air. He thinks he might explode with shame.

'Daddy?'

His father could be down there, bitten by a deadly cottonmouth, his lungs fighting the muddy water. And it would be Elvis's fault, because Noreen looked at him.

'Daddy!'

The water parts and Vernon emerges, face blood red, eyes streaked with mud, teeth shining white. He lets out a great shout: the long, loud sound of the still living.

Elvis is so relieved that he leaps into the creek. The water takes his body, right up to his shoulders.

Vernon gives another whoop. 'There you go, boy! You in deep now!'

And he is. It's cold and silty, and there is something touching his foot that feels like a branch, or maybe a snake. He swallows, shudders, and concentrates on moving through the water to reach his father's outstretched hands.

'Easy, now,' says Vernon.

Elvis wades further in, then, alarmed at the way the mud is dragging his feet from him, panics and almost goes under. The water jumps to his chin and he gets a tangy mouthful, but he is caught by Vernon, who scoops him to the safety of his chest.

They bob together, Elvis gasping and trying to smile.

'It's OK, son.'

Elvis wipes the silt from his eyes and takes a deep breath.

'I'm gonna tell you something. And you must never tell this to your mama. Understood?'

Elvis can only blink, and scan the bank for a glimpse of Noreen's red hair.

'Fact is, I never learned to swim. But that don't stop me enjoying this creek. You can go under like that, and the water brings you right back up again, long as your feet find the bottom. Understand?'

Elvis shakes his head.

'If you can pretend to swim, then it's like you really can.'

'You just pretend?'

'Hell, yeah. Sometimes I almost convince myself, I'm so good at it.'

At this, Elvis laughs.

'Morning, Vernon.'

Elvis whips his head around. Removing his shoes on the bank is Roy Martin, who owns the grocery store on Lake Street. Elvis glances back at his daddy, unsure if it's all right for another man to be here, and wondering if Mr Martin has seen Noreen. But his daddy is smiling determinedly.

'Morning, Roy. Great day for it.'

Mr Martin tugs his shirt from his head. He is a large man, and although he is much older than Vernon, his shoulders are packed with muscle and his neck is thick. He pushes down his pants and undershorts in one sweep and stands, stretching his naked body towards the sky.

Taking hold of Elvis's chin, Vernon twists his head around. 'Quit staring,' he hisses. In a louder voice he calls, 'Just showing the boy the ropes.'

''Bout time, ain't it,' states Mr Martin.

'Woulda had him down a year ago. But you know Glad.'

There's no reply.

Elvis wonders if Mr Martin will notice that his daddy is still wearing his shirt, and that it's wet through and light brown from the creek water. He's aware that his father is sometimes awkward in the company of other men. Vernon's own father, JD, hasn't visited since that time after Vernon got back from the pen. Mama has warned Elvis that it is their job to protect Daddy from the other townsfolk, who just don't understand what he's been through.

Vernon tries again. 'That woman is awful tender-hearted when it comes to her son.'

Elvis watches his daddy's hopeful face as he waits for Mr Martin's response. But nothing comes.

There's a lot of splashing, and from the way the water is rocking around them, Elvis guesses that Mr Martin is now submerged.

Vernon's face falls. 'Maybe we better haul on out,' he mutters.

Suddenly it seems very important to Elvis that they stay in the water.

'Spin me round first!' he says.

Vernon hesitates, glancing towards Mr Martin.

'Daddy, spin me round! Please!'

Vernon rearranges his hands beneath Elvis's armpits and looks him in the eye. 'A spin you want, is it?'

'Yeah!'

'You asked for it, boy.'

Gripping him hard, his daddy lifts him so his feet no longer touch the bottom and whirls him in a circle. Then he does it again, faster. The water rushes over Elvis's legs, both soft and urgent. The sunshine warms his naked shoulders. Elvis lets out a hoot, and his daddy joins in, still whirling him in the water, until they're spinning so fast and whooping so loud that Elvis doesn't know who is keeping who afloat or where the bottom of the creek has gone. There is just the water, holding them both.

It makes him think of what Brother Mansell says in church about being open to the glory of God, and he is about to shout it out loud, to lift his face to the sun and yell, 'Glory!' when he remembers that Mama isn't here, and doesn't even know what he is doing, and Noreen has seen his peter. He wriggles from his father's clasp, and almost goes under again.

Vernon finds him and lifts him once more. 'You gotta stop doing that,' he says. 'You gotta work on pretending.'

Elvis coughs out a mouthful of gritty water and rests his head on his daddy's shoulder. Together, they watch the ripples they've made run all the way to where Mr Martin stands, looking off towards the trees.

* * *

Grandma Minnie Mae has told him: love'll hit you like a carny truck. When it comes it looks all fancy and colourful and like life itself. But then it just drives on, and you got to keep up, and sometimes ain't nothing you can do but hang on the back and get dragged through the dirt.

Although he has noticed Magdalene Morgan at school and in church before, Elvis doesn't even begin to feel the carny truck until she sings.

Brother Gains Mansell, an uncle of Gladys's, introduces her at the Wednesday evening service, telling the congregation that Magdalene has been practising a solo of 'The Old Rugged Cross'.

Elvis stretches his neck to get a clear view as she walks out wearing a pink dress with a white collar, her head held high. He's sung in church as long as he can recall, but never alone in front of everybody, though he's imagined what it would be like many times. Not for one minute did he think this girl would beat him to it.

Magdalene stands before the congregation, her whipped-up black hair surrounding her face like a dark cloud. Her cheeks are pale saucers, perfectly round. She holds her hands together tightly, and without waiting for Brother Mansell to count her in, she begins.

'On a hill far away stood an old rugged cross ...'

Brother Mansell rushes to catch up on the piano, and the congregation smile indulgently as Magdalene's voice drifts over the pews. Everyone, even Magdalene, is slightly unsure where this voice is headed.

'I will cling to the old rugged cross, and exchange it one day for a crown ...'

Elvis smiles to himself: he could do better. She's pretty good, but his voice is stronger and more beautiful than hers. Grandma Minnie Mae weeps when he sings 'Danny Boy'.

As she reaches the second verse, though, Magdalene's singing grows more confident, and he finds himself imagining joining in. Together, they could fill the room. His sound could sweeten hers. He would tell her to take her cue from him, and her pretty mouth would open at his command.

By the end of the song, he has decided that they will sing together, and that perhaps he will fall in love with Magdalene Morgan. Maybe then he can forget the feeling of Noreen's stare. Whenever he passes Noreen in the street, she doesn't smile or blush or turn her head like other girls. She looks him right in the eye, as if daring him to speak.

That night, he hopes he will dream of Magdalene. But it's Noreen who comes to him. In the dream, he's pushing her down into the creek. As he watches her hair turn dark in the muddy water, he feels relief, because now she won't be able to look at him. But when he wakes, he is hotter than hell, and the blood throbs in every part of his body.

That Sunday, there's a dinner at Brother Mansell's comfortable five-roomed house. Gladys has baked a caramel cake to add to a table already overflowing with the congregation's best offerings: fried pies, chicken and dumplings, stuffed eggs, apple cobblers, potato salads, fried catfish, bean pots, cornbread. There's real coffee, too, and bottles of Big Orange and root beer for the children. The guests spill out onto the porch and the backyard. The other boys from church – Jack, Odell, Kenneth – run off to climb the oak tree while their parents stand and admire Brother Mansell's fiery azaleas.

Elvis has already made up his mind to talk to Magdalene, but first he takes a plate and loads it with chicken and dumplings and collard greens and cornbread. Sunday dinners at the preacher's house are no time to lose your appetite: the food is free. Gladys often points out that Brother Mansell is family, so they should make the most of his kindness, and not feel shy about helping themselves to a second plate.

After consuming one plateful of chicken Elvis resists going back for another and, leaving his parents in the house, slips out into the yard to look for Magdalene.

He doesn't have to go far. She's sitting on a ground rug by the fence, concentrating on peeling an orange. Before he can let himself think better of it, Elvis marches right up to her and announces, not as enthusiastically as he'd hoped, 'I liked your singing.'

She glances at him and nods, then gets back to work on the fruit, pressing her thumb into the skin and releasing a spray of moisture into the air. It smells clean and sweet; nothing like the orange Kool-Aid his mother fixes for a treat sometimes. First wrenching the whole thing apart, Magdalene loosens a segment. She waves it in the air, and, assuming she is offering it to him, Elvis holds out his palm.

Her eyes meet his, then she pops the orange into her mouth and chews, her gaze sliding to the side.

'I guess everybody's been saying you're good,' he says.

She swallows. 'Nuh-uh.'

'Well,' he says, stuffing his hands into his pockets, 'you are. I wasn't sure, at first. But then you really got it.'

She does not look pleased, but it seems to him that her eyes don't often tell the truth, which he finds interesting. When he's caught her staring at him in church, her expression can shift from boredom to interest in a heartbeat. He can always tell what his mama is thinking, and most often Grandma Minnie Mae too; but this girl's thoughts are a mystery to him.

'You wanna go walking?' she asks.

'When?'

'How about Saturday? You can take me to the hatchery. Probably warm enough now.'

The hatchery is where courting couples go for picnics and kissing. There are plenty of low trees and hidden nooks there, and there is no way Mama will allow it. He calculates, though, that she will probably be distracted enough for the next half-hour or so not to notice his absence.

'How about right now?'

She stands. 'OK,' she says, taking his hand and planting what's left of the orange in his palm.

Elvis looks down at the fruit.

Magdalene puts her hands on her hips. 'You wanted it, didn't you?'

He peels off one sticky segment and gives the remaining orange back to her. 'It's yours, Magdalene,' he says. 'I want you to have it.'

It amazes him that it's so easy to escape the preacher's garden and walk away from his family and the members of his church. He and Magdalene simply stroll out, side by side, in silence. Everybody is too busy eating and gossiping to notice.

Once they're on Kelly Street, Magdalene wipes her hands down her front, and he has to stop himself from advising her not to dirty her Sunday clothes. She's wearing a light blue dress with an embroidered trim all along its edge. It's too big for her – probably it was once her sister's – but still he feels proud to be walking with a girl who looks so good. Not that there is anybody around to see them; most folks are at the church dinner. The porch swings hang empty, and the streets are silent on this spring afternoon.

She takes confident strides and walks a little away from him, as if to avoid physical contact, even of the accidental kind.

He must ask her about the singing, but every time he thinks he's going to say something, the words go dry in his mouth.

'Your mama's real nice,' she says. 'You're lucky. My mama don't even notice where I'm at, half the time.'

'Mama frets too much,' he says, unable to hide the pride in his voice.

They're going uphill, and the houses have all but disappeared. On reaching the gum trees of the Old Saltillo Road, Elvis considers showing Magdalene the house where he was born and Jesse died. He can see the two-roomed shack, just a little way along the road. Every time they pass it, his mama points it out, telling him the story of his birth, and how his daddy saw a blue light in the sky that night, and saying it's a shame the folks who live there now don't keep it nicer.

Elvis decides he won't mention his dead brother to Magdalene. Not yet, anyhow. He should get back to the preacher's house. Mama will be worried.

But first he must ask his question.

He takes hold of her arm, stopping her in her tracks.

'We oughta sing together,' he says.

'Say what?' she asks, casting a curious look at his hand on her light blue sleeve.

He holds on. 'We oughta sing together.'

'How come?'

'You sing good. I sing good. Why wouldn't we?'

'Well,' she says, slowly, 'I ain't at all sure what my daddy would say, for one.'

'Why?'

''Cause you are a boy, Elvis. And I am a girl. Or ain't you noticed?'

'But – but I'm clean! And it'd be in church ...'

She looks again at his hand. He is about to remove it from her sleeve when she touches his fingers. 'My daddy might think you're in love with me, or something,' she says, quietly.

'Why would he think that?'

'Oh, I don't know.' She looks at him very intently, as if he should know the answer.

'Well,' he says, 'maybe I am.'

This seems to be the right answer, because she pushes her fingers through his, and he feels her warmth go all the way up his arm and down his spine.

'I could talk to him, I guess,' she adds.

He swallows. 'That'd be real good.'

As they stride back into Brother Mansell's yard, Gladys is nowhere to be seen. Jack and Odell and Kenneth are running around the bottom of the oak, pretending to shoot a possum. Mrs Clarke and Mr Harris and Mrs Stephens are standing by the chicken house watching the boys, but there is no Gladys.

Elvis pushes past the smaller kids and crashes into the house. Is she wandering the streets, hollering and crying his name? If she is, everyone will know his shame, both at having wronged her and at the intensity of her love.

Brother Mansell is leaning on the mantel, talking to Bobby Green. Unable to hear his mother's voice, or even his father's, Elvis stands in the centre of the room, sweating.

'Son,' says the preacher, placing a hand on his shoulder, 'if you're looking for your folks, your father went home a while ago, but your mother's in the kitchen, I believe.'

Elvis charges from the room.

In the kitchen, sitting quietly at the table while Mr Miller stands above her, is his mama. Her hands are spread wide on the lacy cloth.

She doesn't return his gaze, because she is waiting for Mr Miller to conclude his story, seemingly entranced by what's coming from his mouth. It's something about the success of his hogs this year. She smiles and nods, her cheeks and chin shining.

'There you are,' says Magdalene, who has caught up with him. 'What you up to, running in like a scalded haint?'

Grabbing Magdalene's hand, he says, 'Mama!'

It takes Gladys a moment to tear her eyes from Mr Miller, who hasn't quite finished his tale. 'Oh,' she says, 'hello, Elvis. You having a good time?'

He grips Magdalene's hand tighter and swings it to and fro triumphantly, hoping his mama will register what is going on.

'Hello, Magdalene,' she says, turning her gleaming eyes on the girl.

Mr Miller looks at the two of them, his bushy eyebrows raised. 'You kids lovebirds now, huh? That it?'

'Yes, sir,' says Elvis, firmly.

Magdalene lets out a small gasp.

'Girl don't look too sure about it, though!' says Mr Miller.

'We are,' says Elvis. 'Ain't we, Magdalene?'

'Guess so,' says Magdalene.

'Ain't that sweet?' says Mr Miller.

Gladys crosses her arms. Maybe she will jump up and force Elvis home. Or call Magdalene an ugly name.

Instead, she leans towards the girl. 'You two oughta sing together in church. Don't you agree, Mr Miller?'

'Lord, yes! Just think of it: East Tupelo's lovebirds *and* songbirds! Now, wouldn't that be fine?'

Gladys nods at her son. 'Real fine.'

'I already told her that, Mama!'

Gladys gives a tiny smile. 'I reckoned you might have, son.'

* * *

It is late afternoon, before the Wednesday evening service, and Magdalene has come to Elvis's house to sing. It's raining, but there's no wind, so they sit on the porch. Gladys leaves a pitcher of iced tea and some crackers on a tray, then disappears into the house, letting the screen slam behind her.

Elvis looks at the dripping oaks across the street and says, 'We can't sing here.'

'Why not?' Magdalene asks. She's already helped herself to a drink and a cracker.

'The noise.'

'What noise?' says Magdalene, through a mouthful of crumbs.

Elvis points upwards. Water patters unevenly on the roof.

'The rain.'

She gulps down the remains of the cracker and then hides a smile behind her hand. 'Elvis,' she says, 'ain't nobody gonna hear us, anyhow.'

'Mama will,' he says. Because he knows she will be listening intently, even as she scrubs the stove.

Magdalene pats the wooden chair beside her. 'Come on over here,' she says.

He sighs. 'It won't work,' he says. But he sits, anyway.

Magdalene rearranges her skirt over her knees and wraps her cardigan tightly around her. Her cloud of hair looks smaller today. She smells faintly of bacon grease, and also of something sweet, like beer.

Then, without warning, she turns to face him and starts singing 'Joshua Fit the Battle'.

For the first moments, he can do nothing but be almost painfully aware of her physical presence. Her breath touches his face as she lets out the notes. A warm droplet of her spit lands on his hand, and he wipes it, hurriedly, on his pants. Her perfect cheeks become filled with strong colour. But all he can see written on her face is effort, which he knows is wrong. Elvis has studied the best singers at church, and they all shut their eyes and contort their faces only when they reach the best parts, and even then they wear a look not of effort, exactly. It's more like real intensity. It seems to him that this must be the way to let the Spirit in. Brother Mansell often says it. *Let God in. Put your own self to one side, and make space for the Holy Spirit!*

Wanting to show Magdalene how it should be done, Elvis tries it now. Closing his eyes, he sings, *'You may talk about your men of Gideon'* and pretends he's at the front of the church, with the whole congregation watching his expressive yet mysterious face, witnessing him letting God in.

As he sings, he doesn't swoon, or see the blinding light of the Holy Spirit. What he experiences is intense concentration on hitting the notes. It feels comfortable, and happy, and right. It feels easeful.

He also forgets all about Magdalene. When he opens his eyes, close to the end of the song, he's almost surprised to see her there, smiling at him.

The rain falls harder, hammering on the porch roof, bouncing off the steps, forming brown puddles in the road. Wet chickens squawk and retreat beneath the house. But Elvis and Magdalene keep singing. When they make a particularly good noise together, Magdalene puts a hand on Elvis's knee and keeps it there. He closes his eyes again, and finds himself pretending the hand is Noreen Fishbourne's.

* * *

The travelling preacher is a skinny man with a nose shaped like a turnip. He stalks the aisle of the Assembly of God church, the light coming through the altar window making his shoes gleam. Every Sunday morning Mama buffs the family shoes as best she can, but Preacher Brown's shoes are something else. They are black, without any discernible laces, and they shine like glass. They make Elvis think of Cinderella's slippers. Gorgeous, painful, improbable.

The room falls silent. People cease their fanning, despite the humidity in the small wooden building. The preacher takes his time, allowing the congregation to get a good look at him. He runs a hand along the polished pews as he walks, his fingers catching the sleeves of several women's blouses, the click of his shoes resounding on the swept boards. At the front of the church, he stops but does not look at anybody. Not yet. Instead he takes a seat to the side, first brushing it with a crisp handkerchief, so he can watch Brother Mansell open the service.

The congregation shift and settle.

For weeks, everybody has been talking of Preacher Brown's visit. Elvis has heard his mama whispering to her friends Faye Harris and Novie Clark that Noreen Fishbourne will finally be free of her demon. For didn't Preacher Brown deliver little Frank last time? He may be a small-bodied man, but he has the biggest spirit in Lee County. Miss Novie said she saw a strange green ball of light shoot down the aisle, right out the door. And hasn't little Frank been an angel ever since?

The church is busier than Elvis has ever seen it: anybody who hasn't found a seat is standing at the back. Magdalene Morgan, who has held his hand every day after school all semester and sometimes goes to the front of the church to sing with him, is sitting in the row behind, but her attention is all on the preacher.

Elvis scans the room for Noreen and spots her red hair easily. It has been parted precisely down the middle like a split loaf; the two sides are plaited and pinned tightly around her ears.

Brother Mansell starts by welcoming them on this special day, and leading them in 'Leaning on the Everlasting Arms'. They stand and sway, and Elvis tries to lose himself in the song, but he cannot stop gazing at the back of Noreen's head. Perhaps that red hair will catch fire when she is delivered. Maybe blood and flames and pillars of smoke will rise from her, just like it says in the Bible. That would teach her to go sneaking up on naked boys. His mama says redheads have hot blood, and this shows itself in their hair. No wonder

Noreen's parents can't control the girl. It must've been easy for the devil to take hold.

There are only two testimonials today. Billy Clarke stands and says he has quit taking tobacco. Vona Newell has, with God's help, persuaded her youngest and most difficult child to stop spilling his milk. Everybody claps. Brother Mansell congratulates them both and calls for more. There's a shuffling of feet. Many congregation members focus on the ceiling or the floor, eager to get past the testimonials.

Brother Mansell mops his brow and finally introduces Preacher Brown.

There's a round of applause, together with loud shouts of 'Hallelujah!' Elvis finds himself jumping to his feet with his mama and yelling, "Praise!' She turns to him and beams, and he claps louder.

Preacher Brown stands and looks directly at the congregation. Every face in the church is lifted towards him, and he seems to spend five minutes just making sure he has seen everybody, and everybody has seen him. Then, slowly, he raises both hands and hangs his head.

He starts low.

'Brothers and sisters. I know there's not one among you here today who is without sin.' His voice is soft and fluid as he lifts his heels and stretches his hands higher. 'But I'm asking you now, who here is ready to be saved?'

A murmur ripples round the room.

Preacher Brown snaps his head up. His eyes are as bright as his shoes.

'Because you'd better be ready. You may be thinking, "Tomorrow I'll begin living a holy life."' He strides back and forth along the front of the church, his voice hushed. '"Tomorrow I'll pray to the Lord Jesus. Tomorrow I'll help my neighbour. Tomorrow I won't take that liquor."' He stops and looks at Annabelle Wiston in the front row. '"Tomorrow I'll wipe that paint from my face."'

Miss Wiston gasps audibly, and has to be consoled by her sister.

Preacher Brown points a finger at the crowd. 'I'm here to tell you, tomorrow ain't soon enough!'

'Tell it!' somebody says.

'Tomorrow ain't no time! You gotta be ready today! And not just today, but right now!'

A few 'Amen's rise into the sticky air.

Preacher Brown removes his jacket and lays it carefully on his chair, revealing its delicate pink lining. Carefully, he unbuttons his cuffs and rolls up the sleeves of his white shirt to reveal the thick hair on his forearms, and an enormous gold watch. He reaches for the ceiling and says in a quiet voice, 'Are you ready, brothers and sisters?'

'Yes, Lord!'

'I said, are you ready?'

Elvis sneaks a look at his mama. Patches of her cream blouse have stuck to her back, revealing the outline of the various and unfathomable straps and clasps of her underclothes. He clutches her hand, wanting to distract her from what he suspects she will do next, but she gives him only a brief glance before returning all her attention to the preacher.

'Then I say to you, as Mark said, "In God's name I will drive out demons!"'

It won't be long before his mama will start: the sweat patches and the visible underwear are a sure sign. Elvis chews his nails and tells himself it will be over soon. There is no need for him to shake, or cry. His daddy has often told him there is no need for any of that stuff, because he has nothing to shake or cry about.

'I will drive out demons and let God's light in!'

Sure enough, as Preacher Brown talks, Gladys leans forward, gripping the pew and closing her eyes, to receive the Spirit. Then the sound comes from her. It is pitched somewhere between a moan of terror and a recitation of a multiplication table. It has the regularity of something learned, and yet it is completely without sense.

Vernon looks on, unconcerned. They have both witnessed it before. Elvis bites his thumb, hard.

'For did not Mark say that the Christians would grasp snakes with their bare hands?'

Gladys rocks back and forth and it is all Elvis can do not to grab his mama and yank her back into her seat. He tries again to grasp her hand and make her still, but her fingers slip from his.

Preacher Brown is advancing down the aisle. As he passes, men and women emulate his mother, clutching whatever is nearest to them – pews, prayer books, children's heads – and chanting their strange language. They whisper and grunt. Some collapse to their knees, or are caught in the arms of their neighbours.

To Elvis's relief, Gladys slides back into her seat, but still her mouth moves and the sounds come out. He touches her damp shoulder. When she doesn't respond, he takes her face in his hands and whispers in her ear, 'Mama, Mama, Mama!'

'Let her be,' hisses Vernon.

'Now,' says Preacher Brown, who has reached the front of the church once more. 'Who among you requires deliverance from evil?'

Gladys ceases her noise, and opens her eyes. They are brilliant with tears, and he is flooded with relief. It is the happiest she has looked for many months, and, more importantly, she is seeing him once again.

Preacher Brown is beckoning the congregation forth. 'All those who seek freedom from demons, come on up.'

People clamber from their pews to form a line long enough to reach the door. At the front is Noreen, flanked by her parents. Preacher Brown, who isn't much taller than the girl, squares up to her but addresses Noreen's father.

'Brother,' he says, 'is this your daughter?'

'Yes, sir.'

There is a pause as Preacher Brown looks the girl over. Fans click in the thick air. A ripe, sweet smell of overheated bodies and warm wood fills the church.

'And does your daughter have the Devil in her?'

'Noreen has had the Devil ever since she was but eight years old, sir.'

'And how does this evil spirit manifest itself, brother?'

'She won't abide by no rules at all. Not mine, not the church's. She runs around like a fully grown girl. Makes her mama and me ashamed.'

'Noreen, is this the truth?'

The girl bows her head.

'I see the Demon has your tongue.'

'He surely does, sir,' says Noreen's father. 'He has every part of this girl—'

'Noreen, do you want to be saved?' asks Preacher Brown.

The girl does not look up.

'Noreen. I ask you. Do you desire to be saved today?'

'She wants it so bad, sir!' says her father.

'I am going to order this Demon out of you,' says the preacher. 'It will be hard, but it will be worth it. For when this Demon sees God's light, he will fly out the door, and you will be filled with the spirit of Jesus.'

Elvis and Gladys look towards the door. Right at the top, there is a crack large enough for a small bird to fly through.

The preacher takes the girl's shoulders and spins her round to face the congregation. Her freckled chin quivers. It's rare for a girl this young to be delivered, and Elvis glances at his daddy, thinking perhaps he will run to the front and put a stop to it. Vernon wasn't Assembly of God until he met Gladys, and although he's been saved, he often misses services. He's also told Elvis that he doesn't believe in evil spirits. Once, when they were walking through Priceville cemetery at dusk, Elvis had hidden his face in his father's shirt, scared of the shadows. Vernon had informed him confidently that there was no such thing as ghosts, demons or spirits. It was real people who could hurt you, he said; his advice was to fear the living, not the dead.

But now Vernon stares straight ahead, riveted.

The preacher lays his hands on Noreen's head. 'Brothers,' he says, 'I need some volunteers here.'

Mr Martin, Mr Newgate and Mr Miller rush to the front.

Noreen lets out a yelp as Mr Martin grabs her shoulders. Kneeling before her, Mr Newgate clasps her wrists in his hands, and Mr Miller stands behind to take hold of her waist. Preacher Brown spreads his fingers wide and presses them along her white parting.

'I must warn each and every one of you in this room to keep your eyes good and closed now. For if you look at this Demon, it will see a way into your soul.'

Noreen has turned pale. Gladys puts her arm around Elvis and draws him to her. 'Shut your eyes, baby,' she whispers. 'The men will put things right. It's a happy day.'

He half-closes his eyelids, and through the slit he sees Noreen squirm and gasp as the men tighten their hold.

'If she struggles,' says Preacher Brown, 'remember it is the Demon fighting the Holy Spirit, and you must hold her tighter.'

They do so, and Noreen hollers loud enough to make Elvis's skin rise.

Gladys puts a hand over his eyes, and he smells the greasy animal-scent of her lanolin cream.

Then all he knows are the sounds. 'BE GONE!' shouts Preacher Brown. 'FEEL THE MIGHT OF THE LORD! LEAVE THIS HELPLESS CHILD! LET HER BECOME PURE AGAIN!'

And her shoes scrabbling on the wooden floor. And men grunting. And something ripping.

He gnaws on his fingers, desperately trying to find enough nail to get a good bite.

The wordless language comes again from somebody's mouth – not his mother's.

And Noreen keeps on screaming. It is now a high, almost triumphant, scream. It rips around the church so wildly that a few children begin to weep in fear. And at this moment Elvis tastes his own blood

79

and believes the Demon is truly in Noreen. This sound must come from the Devil. He thinks of his dream of holding her in the water, and wonders if it was God's way of telling him that Noreen needed to be cleansed.

'WE WILL NOT GIVE IN, DEMON!' shouts Preacher Brown. 'WE WILL DEFEAT YOU WITH THE POWER OF THE HOLY SPIRIT!'

The congregation pray. But Noreen – or perhaps the Demon – is still screaming. There is an almighty whack, which could be her foot kicking the floorboards. Or somebody hitting the ground.

'IN GOD'S NAME I DRIVE YOU OUT!'

The preacher is hoarse now.

'OUT, I SAY! OUT!'

Then the scream falters. And there's quiet.

When Elvis opens his eyes, Noreen lies limp in her father's arms, her face slack. Elvis cannot stop looking at Preacher Brown, whose scant hair is now sticking up from his head as if he's been hit by a lightning bolt. His damp shirt is creased, and his collar has come undone, revealing a neck shining with sweat. He plants himself in front of Noreen, spreading his legs and his arms wide.

'She is saved!' he says, lifting his hands.

'Saved!' everybody, including Elvis, chants.

Preacher Brown sweeps an arm over the crowd and points to the ceiling. 'Thank you, Sweet Jesus!'

'Hallelujah!' cries Gladys.

The preacher shakes his head, as if in disbelief at his own powers. Then he gestures for quiet. He starts to pray. 'Blessed Father, we thank You for Your grace ...'

The congregation close their eyes and follow his words. Elvis sneaks a look around the room at the bowed heads. He senses that, right now, everyone in the church would do anything this man asked.

Then the preacher catches Elvis's eye. Elvis starts, alarmed, but before he can look away, the preacher smiles widely, right at him. 'Praise the Lord!' he says.

'Praise the Lord!' shouts Elvis, in response, and Preacher Brown nods.

'Take her home, brother. Today the Demon was no match for the Holy Spirit!'

As Noreen's father carries her down the aisle, women touch the ripped hem of her pinafore and gasp, 'Glory!' Noreen's hair has burst from its pins and it springs from her head like flames. Seeing her limp, helpless body, Elvis wants to slap her face to waken her. He wants her, he realises, to fix him with that look again.

But she does not. He is free to look at her face, now, for as long as he likes.

The preacher checks his gold watch. 'Who is next?' he asks.

Afterwards, on the walk to Brother Mansell's house for refreshments, everything goes a little wonky. The gum trees along the road seem to bend with the midsummer heat, their thick leaves gathering dust, and the sun seems to have got right inside Elvis's skull. His mama walks ahead with the rest of the congregation. The occasional 'Amen!' or 'Glory!' still rises from the crowd, and the women's voices chatter and swoop around him like birds. Keeping his head down, Elvis tries to catch up with the others, but his legs feel strangely heavy, as though the road is sticking to his feet. It's been hours since he had anything to drink, and his tongue feels as dry as a scrap of old newspaper. He tells himself that he just has to make it to Brother Mansell's, where there will be iced water. It is less than half a mile away, though it seems as distant as the moon.

To ease his journey, Elvis imagines, as he often does, Jesse walking beside him. His brother is nimble, and better at getting along this hot dirt. He doesn't fuss about the flies or the dust or the stray dog who sometimes sleeps in the road. Nothing ever makes Jesse afraid, and nothing can slow him down. As he skips along, he giggles and swings his arms.

In an effort to distract his brother, Elvis tries talking to him, saying, *You know, Jesse, Mama says I'm a miracle.*

And Jesse's voice comes right back. *Huh! Wouldn't be no you without me, boy.*

Jesse is older by only a matter of minutes. Yet here he is, talking as if he is grown, and knows things other boys do not.

It does not seem strange to Elvis that Jesse has chosen, for the first time, to make himself heard. Not compared to the way the road is warping before him, or the way his body feels so loose with heat that it might come apart.

You see what happened with Noreen? Elvis asks.

Kinda fun, wasn't it?

It was God's work.

Looked like Preacher Brown's work to me.

They have reached Brother Mansell's house, and the congregation have gathered in the shade of the wide porch. Elvis takes the steps one at a time. They seem to wobble beneath his feet. Once he's at the top, he stops, and immediately becomes bathed in so much sweat that he can taste it.

'Elvis?' His mama looms up. 'You feeling all right?'

Elvis opens his mouth to reply, but his heart seems to be there instead of his tongue, and his lips won't move. Everything is pulsing, and he has no breath. Then his limbs go liquid, and the daylight disappears.

When he comes to, he is lying on the cool wooden floor of the living room, next to the piano. His mama is kneeling beside him, squeezing his hand to her bosom, and Preacher Brown is behind her saying, 'Child's all right. Just overwhelmed by the Spirit. Sometimes it's like that, when God melts your heart.'

Elvis's eyes hurt.

Jesse, he whispers. *Now I know.*

Know what, boy?

I know God.

Say what?

He blinks and sees that Preacher Brown is praying now, and the rest of the congregation are joining him in an ecstatic hum.

You crazy, says Jesse.

I'm saved, says Elvis.

1946

Elvis and Gladys are on their way out of the house, headed for town, when Vernon says, 'Watch your spending, Glad. You keep goin' over that Beauty School and we ain't gonna make it.'

Vernon is out of work again and frequently at home. The payments on their new four-roomed house on Berry Street are expensive, but when he signed the deed he'd promised her that they had enough to keep their heads above water, just so long as the water didn't get too high.

Gladys pauses on the porch and stares at her husband, who is leaning on the screen door. Elvis, sensing that he should remove himself from the situation, slopes off down the steps and waits for her in the road. He has the guitar she recently bought for him strapped to his back. He's yet to play an actual tune on it, but he likes to wear it.

'You said you liked my hair,' she says.

'I love your hair, Glad. What I don't love is how much it costs.'

'The apprentice fixes it. I get it discount.'

'Just don't go buying that boy more stuff in town. He's had more than enough lately.'

He turns to go back into the house, but Gladys reaches for his wrist. 'He deserved that guitar. He's been so good.'

'Least he's gotten over that goddamn Bible fever,' Vernon mumbles.

After Preacher Brown came to church last year, Elvis did act strange – he'd look dreamily off into the distance while she spoke, and prayed at the oddest moments. Once, hearing the call of a mockingbird, he fell to his knees in their yard and said God had told him to give away all his funny books. But then, last fall, he'd entered the talent contest at the Mississippi–Alabama Fair, standing on a chair to sing 'Old Shep'. He'd won fifth place. Ever since, instead of praying under his breath, he's been singing.

Gladys says, 'We ain't shopping, anyhow. I'm taking him over the courthouse, for the Saturday Jamboree.'

'That don't cost nothing?'

'Not one cent. What'll you do while we're gone?' she asks, keeping her eyes on him.

'That ain't decided yet.'

'Uh-huh.'

Gladys knows Vernon will go fishing, and maybe on to a bar, but she doesn't want to get into that right now. She's promised Elvis they'll be at the courthouse for two o'clock, and from the corner of her eye she can see him jogging on the spot with impatience. She'd heard him early this morning, feeding the chickens in the yard, probably with that guitar strapped on, before she or Vernon had risen from their bed.

She turns on her heel and descends the stairs. On reaching the bottom, Gladys can't help but look back and admire the new paint on the porch, the bright green drapes she's made, and the door knocker, shiny as a new coin.

Vernon calls out, 'Elvis! Keep an eye on your mama for me.'

Every Saturday afternoon they tune in to WELO together to listen to the Jamboree hosted by Mississippi Slim. It's broadcast live from the Lee County courthouse, and for weeks Elvis has been asking Gladys if he can go see it in person.

The heat of the early September afternoon comes at them like a wall, and neither can find much energy for talking as they make their way down the Old Saltillo Road towards the highway. Elvis is wearing his best pants and a good shirt, one Gladys made. She notes with irritation that his wrists are already showing beyond the cuffs. As he walks, the guitar slaps his back.

At the bottom of the road, she stops and removes her straw hat so she can wipe her brow with her handkerchief.

Elvis says, 'I coulda caught a ride with Miss Mertice. She works at the Black and White—'

Mertice Finlay is a new neighbour of theirs. She lives with her mother and three mean-eyed cats.

'Not on your own you couldn't.'

'Miss Mertice woulda been there.'

'But she's got to work. Then you'd be alone all morning in town, waiting.'

'I coulda gone to the movies.'

'You think we got money to waste on that? Didn't you hear what Daddy said?'

They start walking again. To one side are yellow fields and tall, spindly trees. To the other is the wide highway with its trickle of traffic. Gladys clutches her purse close to her hip and ploughs on, across the sizzling forecourt of the Savings filling station, ignoring Elvis's longing look towards the swinging Pepsi sign.

'When I'm grown, I'm gonna buy you a car just like that one.' He's pointing to a big, sparkling vehicle with tyres blacker than tar. She stops and watches it pull up to the pumps, the sun bouncing off its windows.

'Won't that be fine?' she says.

'And a house for you and me,' he says, 'and Daddy.'

'We gonna have five rooms, or six?' she asks.

'We're gonna have at least eight! And I'll buy you dresses, Mama. Real pretty ones. What kind do you want?'

'Oh, anything in lavender crêpe will be wonderful.'

'And you can get your hair fixed in a fancy place every week.'

She laughs at this new addition to their often-repeated fantasy.

'Daddy won't say nothing,' he adds, quietly, ''cause I'll be the one working.'

They walk in silence for a while, crossing the levee and reaching the town. When they hit East Main, Elvis asks, 'Mama, you reckon Slim will look as good as he sounds?'

'He sure looks good in the newspaper.'

'Reckon he'll have that cowboy shirt on?'

'He'll have everything on: the shirt, the hat, the tie.'

'Bet he's got ten rooms in his house,' says Elvis.

'I doubt that, son,' says Gladys, smiling.

'Maybe six, then.'

'Maybe so. You gonna enter the WELO talent contest?'

'No way, Mama!'

'You oughta. You sing real nice.'

'Maybe one day.'

'You and Magdalene could go on.'

'I don't know, Mama. I don't reckon Magdalene is ready for that,' says Elvis, solemnly. 'She might mess up.'

The courthouse is a large, fine old building which makes Gladys think of a wedding cake. Its golden-domed clock tower, long windows and ivory-coloured stone speak of some glorious past that she figures must have been real for a handful of folks round here.

A line of people stretches all the way from the courthouse steps, down the tree-lined white path, to the corner of the sidewalk. Gladys and Elvis cross the leafy square, and she feels him begin to pull away from her.

'Keep close,' she warns. 'There's a lot of folks here.'

They join the back of the line and Elvis removes his arm from hers but stays near. Out of habit she reaches to straighten his collar, but then draws back, realising he has already done it himself.

The sun presses on her head. In front of them is a woman with two girls of about Elvis's age, and an older boy. The girls turn cart-wheels on the lush lawn of the courthouse while the boy, who is a little heavy, crosses his arms and scowls. He is taking up a lot of the sidewalk – if he were to move up a little, Gladys could stand in the shade afforded by the cherry tree.

'Excuse me, ma'am,' says Gladys, catching the woman's eye, 'you got any notion when they might let us in?'

The woman is wearing a yellow hat and carrying a matching purse. 'They usually open the doors round one-thirty,' she says.

'Oh, thank goodness! It's awful hot out here. I'm about fit to melt!'

Gladys glances at the boy, who stares at the ground.

'Byron, honey,' the woman says, 'move on over so this lady and her son can step into the shade.'

Byron scowls but does as he's asked. The woman in the yellow hat holds out a hand and says, 'I'm Patty Wren. This your first time at the Jamboree?'

'Gladys Presley. Is it that obvious?'

Mrs Wren laughs. 'Not at all.'

'My boy's been itching to get here for weeks! He loves Mississippi Slim.'

'Does he want to go in with my kids?'

Gladys and Elvis look at one another. He grins, then pinches his nose to hide it, and says nothing.

'Byron here can keep an eye on him, can't you, Byron?'

Byron scratches at the acne on his chin. 'Mama ...' he whines.

'Course he can! And Pearl and Louise here, too,' says Mrs Wren. The girls, who are dressed identically in shorts and blouses printed with strawberries, gawp at Elvis in silence.

'You could do your shopping while he's in there,' says Mrs Wren. 'Whole thing won't last no more than a half-hour.'

Gladys puts a hand on Elvis's shoulder. 'It's awful kind of you, but I don't think—'

'I'll be all right, Mama,' says Elvis, patting her hand and standing straight. 'You go on and get your shopping done.'

He flashes a smile at Mrs Wren, who says to Gladys, 'There you go, dear. Your son has spoken.'

Gladys ambles down the neat, wide sidewalk on Main without a clue of what to do or where to go. Stopping to look in the windows of Reed's department store, she tries to lose herself in the details of the fabric of the dress that's before her: cream ruffles at the neck, a wide satin sash about the waist, a scalloped hem. But her mind slips to her son, who must be sitting in the courthouse now, close to Pearl, or maybe Louise, swaying to some crooner tearing the heart out of 'I'll Forgive You But I Can't Forget' or 'Paper Doll'. She puts a finger to the glass and traces the outline of the sash, leaving a smear. Then she hurries back to the courthouse.

On a bench near the steps, she sits to watch the wide double doors. There's clapping and cheering, followed by a long break in the noise, during which, she guesses, Slim must be introducing the next act. Feeling closer to her son now, she relaxes a little, tapping her foot in time to the music, and allows herself to picture him at the front, singing. Whenever he sings alone in church, her gut flips over and her eyes become wet. She is fiercely proud, and also afraid, of how good he is. She feels, sometimes, as if she cannot stand it, and must leave the room. It is difficult to make herself sit there, listening, because she knows he has talent, and she also knows that when he sings he goes someplace else, someplace beyond her reach. And in that place she cannot rescue him from failure.

The music stops, and Gladys perches expectantly on the edge of the bench.

When Elvis appears, he walks directly to her, head down, guitar on his back. She pats the space beside her. 'How was it, baby? Tell me boocups.'

'Mama,' he begins, his cheeks flushed, 'it was ... I don't know what it was ...' He shakes his head, searching for a word. 'It was ... real good.'

She nods, encouragingly.

'Slim was so fine! Cracking jokes, you know. And he sang one song real well.'

'What did he sing?'

'"Try Doin' Right". And he had a great guitar, like I never seen, much better than mine, and he kinda laughed all the time, just like on the radio, you know?'

'That's good, baby.'

'And this kid sang, too, he tried to do "Pistol Packin' Mama" and made a real fist of it! I tell you, I know I'd be better than him!'

'Ain't nobody better than you.'

'Can I come again next week, Mama?'

'Next week?'

'Mrs Wren said I could go in with Byron and Pearl and Louise and them again.'

Elvis swings his guitar to his chest and starts fiddling with the strings. 'You don't have to come, Mama,' he says, keeping his eyes on the guitar. 'I could go alone.'

He tries to strum a chord. It doesn't sound good to her.

'Maybe I could catch that ride next time!' he adds, changing chords.

Gladys grabs her purse and rises from the bench. 'We'd better get on home,' she says.

He clutches at her sleeve, but she pulls away, unable to look at him.

As they walk back along the highway, Gladys marches a couple of steps ahead, swinging her purse, and Elvis trails behind, humming and strumming and occasionally breaking into song. She has to stop herself from swinging round and yelling at him to hush up.

Gladys knows she is being unreasonable. She knows that she must let him do this, alone. But she can't help but punish him for it.

By the time they've hit the Old Saltillo Road, she has no choice but to pause for breath. Elvis catches up with her and reaches for her hand.

'Mama,' he says, 'you ain't mad, are you?'

She studies his anxious face. 'I guess I can't stop you, if you want to go.'

'I'll stay home if you want,' he says, pouting a little.

'No, you won't.'

'I don't wanna go without you.'

'Yes, you do.' She takes his hot face in her hands and kisses him firmly on the cheek. Then she pushes him forward. 'Now get on home. And I don't wanna hear one whit more about it.'

Graceland, 24 December 1957

Gladys sits in her favourite chair by the kitchen window, sipping at her grapefruit juice with a little vodka stirred in, wishing the sky would blacken enough for snow so Elvis could have a proper Christmas before he leaves for the army. Once, back in Tupelo, he'd been so excited by the snow that he'd eaten it until he turned a pasty shade of blue; she'd had to bring him inside and feed him whiskey to warm him.

The phone rings.

Nobody answers. Reluctantly, Gladys puts down her drink, heaves her big body from the seat, then crosses the kitchen. Pain prickles through her legs and into her back. She hopes it is not Mr Parker calling. After his manager left yesterday, Elvis had seemed resigned to his fate, and had refused to discuss it further.

'Hello?'

'Mama?'

She always forgets that her son has had this new internal phone system installed, to make it easy for him to find out who is in his house before he leaves his room, or to order food to be taken upstairs.

'I'm coming down,' he says. 'Tell Alberta to fix breakfast for me.'

'I can fix it, son.'

There's a pause.

'I'm coming down,' he repeats. Then the line goes dead.

It is barely midday – early for Elvis, who often won't get up until mid-afternoon when he's home. Much of the household will still be asleep, aside from Minnie Mae, whose TV set provides a constant background murmur to each morning at Graceland. As soon as the news spreads that Elvis has risen, though, the mansion will spring to life. Cliff and Lamar, who have been staying with them for months now, will emerge from the basement and grab themselves Pepsis. George will arrive. Nickels will be fed into the jukebox. All the TV sets will be flicked on. The girls, selected by Cliff, will come up the drive, most of them doing their very best not to break into a sprint, although there is usually one who lags behind, her footsteps a little unsure. Whenever she spots such a girl, Gladys wants to rush out and welcome her into the mansion. She cannot imagine what the parents of these girls are doing, letting them hang around the gate of a stranger. But, for now, Graceland is quiet, and Gladys may be able to snatch fifteen minutes alone with her son.

That is, unless he decides to use the main staircase. She's seen him descend like Scarlett O'Hara, letting the mirrors on either wall get a good look at him. When he glides down those stairs, he is already Elvis Presley: fully coiffed, immaculately dressed, eye make-up and powder applied, and the rest of the house is sure to come running. If he chooses the back staircase, which leads directly into the kitchen, there's a chance he might still be her boy, sleep in his eyes, hair sticking up at the crown of his head.

Gladys waits at the foot of the stairs, tapping her foot, hoping. On hearing his heavy tread, she ignores the pain in her legs and rushes to the refrigerator. She finds the peeled onion she keeps in the crisper and bites down on it, hard. It makes her gag, but there's nothing like it for masking the smell of alcohol. Then she begins crashing skillets, fetching bacon and cracking eggs.

Elvis appears behind her, stretching and letting out a loud groan. His kiss on her cheek is soft and wet. There's a whiff of last night's cigars about him. He puts his arms around her waist and nuzzles his face into her shoulder.

'You still eating onions for breakfast, Mama?' he asks, drawing back.

'Got me a craving for them, I guess,' says Gladys. 'Sleep well, son?'

'Like a baby. You?'

'Not so well.'

'You take them pills I give you?'

'I don't like to take them every night.'

'The doc says they're safe. You oughta take them.' He leans over the stove. 'Smells good.'

She selects a grapefruit from the bowl on the counter, then realises, with a stab of shame and irritation, that she still doesn't know this kitchen well enough to be able to locate a sharp knife.

'Why don't you make yourself comfortable in the dining room?' she says, hoping to buy herself time to root around in the drawers. 'I'll bring it over.'

Elvis runs his hands through his hair. She knows it is not looking as he would like: she can see where he's slept on it.

'I'll sit at the counter. But let me call Daddy first.'

While he's on the phone, Gladys hunts for a knife. Opening and closing all the metallic drawers, she finds a whole tray of bone-handled blades of various shapes and sizes, some of which look big enough for hunting. There's even a cleaver. She's not sure who bought these items. She doesn't recall them being on the list she sent to Goldsmith's.

Elvis settles himself on a stool. 'You know Alberta can do that, Mama.'

'I like to do some little things for you.'

'You've had a lifetime of little things. You oughta rest. Take the weight off.'

At the mention of weight, she slams the grapefruit on the counter.

'I didn't mean nothing!' There is panic in her son's face, but also anger.

She tries to calm herself, but it's hard to catch a full breath. Her legs throb. The skin there is hot and tight, as if ready to split. Lately her stomach feels hard and swollen, too. It reminds Gladys of when she was expecting Elvis and Jesse and her body had ballooned and every part of her had pulsed with pressure.

Elvis stands and takes her by the shoulders, as if, she thinks, to keep her at arm's length. 'You ain't – sad, are you, Mama?'

Gladys focuses on the grapefruit, unable to speak.

'It's Christmas, and I'm home now. Ain't no call to be sad.'

Her vision blurs to a yellow smear. It'll be easier on him if she weeps instead of getting mad. 'I miss you, Elvie.'

She's said it so many times these last three years that even she has come to hate the words.

'And now you're going away ...'

'You can come visit. As soon as I know where I'm headed, I'll bring you and Daddy along.'

'The army might not allow that, son.'

'Colonel will fix it. Trust me.' He smiles. 'Don't he always fix everything?'

She can only blink at him.

'You make me worried, Mama.'

'I'm sorry.'

'I can't sleep some nights, fretting over you.'

'I don't want you to do that, son.'

'I got enough on my mind.'

'I know it.'

He sighs, and lets his hands drop. 'You seen Doctor Evans again?'

'More tests. That's all he ever says.'

'What they testing for?'

'Seems like everything under the sun.'

Doctor Evans has asked a couple of times about her alcohol intake, and both times Gladys has managed to laugh and say, 'No more than's ladylike, doctor,' which has been enough to stop him pressing her on the subject.

She sniffs. 'I figure the more tests they do, the less they know.'

'If it was something serious, they woulda found it by now.'

She wipes her eyes, even though tears have actually evaded her. 'Let me fix this breakfast,' she says, eager to get him off the subject of her health.

As soon as Elvis's food – four eggs, six rashers of bacon, sliced tomatoes, freshly squeezed grapefruit juice and coffee – is on the counter, Vernon appears. Although his hair is prematurely grey, and he's put on a little weight, he seems to Gladys to be getting younger. Today he's wearing an open-necked pastel-yellow shirt with a blue fleck – she's seen Elvis in something similar. Vernon favours pale clothes, not caring one whit about how easy they are to stain. Gladys wanted to slap him when he admitted that he enjoyed having his laundry done by the maids. But at least he doesn't throw his clothes away, like Elvis. Several times, Gladys has rescued her son's barely soiled shirts from the trash.

Vernon pours himself some coffee with the air of a man too busy to take a break. In his office next to the car porch, he has filing cabinets, two telephone lines, pinboards, a desk calculator and a swivelling leather chair, but what he does in there Gladys cannot fathom.

He drops onto the stool next to his son. 'You wanted to speak with me?'

'Let me get through eating first,' says Elvis. 'You want some?'

Vernon shakes his head.

Gladys sits opposite the men, taking a chair by the window. She eyes the sky, but there's still no sign of snow.

'Who's coming to eat tomorrow, son? 'Cause I need to fix things up ...'

'I don't know, Mama. Just do enough for ten.'

'Ten?' asks Vernon. 'Seems like a lot.'

'Ten's fine. I can manage ten,' says Gladys.

When he's finished eating, Elvis wipes his mouth on a napkin and says, 'Daddy, I need twenty-five thousand dollars, cash. Can you go get it for me?'

Vernon lets out a loud, mirthless laugh. 'What in the world for?'

Elvis smiles. 'It's Christmas.'

'What happened to yesterday's thousand?'

'I need more.'

Vernon sits forward, clenching his coffee cup. 'Tell me what it's for, then I'll go get it.'

Elvis glances at Gladys. 'Why is Daddy questioning me, Mama?'

Before she can reply, Vernon raises his voice. 'I am trying to do what's right. I am trying to help you.'

Elvis's knee has begun to jog up and down, making the counter shake. 'It's my money, and you can help by getting it for me.' He shows his father his palms, as if this is obvious.

'What you gotta understand, son, is if you keep spending, there won't be no money left.'

'What *you* gotta understand is, I can always make another movie.'

Vernon leaves a pause before saying, softly, 'Not now you've been drafted you can't.'

Gladys rushes to her son's side. Placing a hand on his sleeve, she says, 'What Daddy means is, it's better to be careful. We know you're gonna be even more popular when you come out of the army, but a little caution never hurt nobody.'

Elvis shrugs her off. He pauses for a second, as if considering an appropriate reaction to this outrage, then, with one swoop of his arm, sends his dirty plate crashing to the floor.

'Now, hold on a minute!' cries Gladys. 'You better clean that up!'

'Get Alberta to do it.' Kicking the plate out of his way, Elvis pushes past her to the staircase. Then he turns and glares at his father. 'That money is mine. You are gonna get it for me. And you ain't gonna lecture me about my career ever again, 'cause you know jackshit about it.'

When he's gone, Gladys gathers the scattered cutlery and the greasy plate.

Vernon watches her without moving. 'I'd like to whip his sorry ass,' he mutters.

From the sink, she says, 'You better go get it for him.'

'He oughta be happy!' Vernon snaps. 'I woulda given anything to serve my country.'

Gladys is so surprised by this statement that she freezes. Then she manages to say, 'You woulda made a good solider. And so will Elvis.'

But her husband has already left the room, slamming the door behind him.

Perhaps it's the beers she had at supper – a feast of honey-dipped ham, fried chicken, potato salad, cornbread and three types of chocolate pudding – but by the time Gladys has retired to her bedroom to wrap gifts, her mood has lifted. She presumes Vernon gave in about the money, because Elvis was back to his best at the dining-room table, joking with the boys about getting his army haircut, singing the occasional snatch of 'Silent Night' to his grandmother, nuzzling up to Anita. Anita is dazzlingly blonde, pert and pretty as a peach. She shines so cleanly that Elvis must see his own face when he looks at her. Anita has even promised to help with the cooking tomorrow, as Alberta and Daisy will be with their own families for Christmas.

As she sits on the bed to begin her task, Gladys's mind slips back to the worry of whether the oven will be large enough to accommodate the bird, and her breath comes quick and her head feels as though a heavy hand is pressing upon it. She reaches for her brandy nightcap, and instructs herself to keep focused on Elvis's gift.

For weeks she has been wondering what to give him. There is, of course, little that he cannot buy for himself, and since all her money comes from him, it feels strange to buy her boy a gift at all. So, eventually, she decided to make him something.

When he was a child, she'd regularly made clothes for him and herself, but Gladys hasn't used her sewing machine since the move to Audubon Drive. Elvis and Vernon laughed at her when she insisted on bringing it to Graceland too, asking why she would choose to sweat for hours over that noisy machine. Didn't she realise she could just *buy* something? In many ways, she agrees with them: it is a kind of madness to want to run her needle over cloth when she can order anything she wants from Goldsmith's, but all her adult life Gladys has known the joy of stitching a well-fitted sleeve into a shirt, finishing a collar, choosing buttons. She's no longer sure, though, if her fingers are up to the task. They tend to slide on any small, smooth object; sometimes she finds it difficult to keep hold of her cutlery. Even this wrapping paper is slipping through her fingers.

And so, with the help of *McCall's* magazine, she has made Elvis a washbag. Although she selected it because it had seemed a manageable task, one she could definitely finish in the time she'd allowed herself, it wasn't easy to sew: gripping the needle made her fingers ache, and the close work had her eyes smarting. She has fashioned it from thick black velvet, lined with gold satin, and embroidered his initials on the front in gold thread. Monogrammed objects have always pleased him; he has been writing his name on his possessions ever since he was a boy.

She slices through the thick silver paper and places the washbag in its centre. Looking at it now, she is alarmed by its amateurish appearance. The letters are slightly askew, the upper loop of the 'E' not quite matching the lower, and the drawstring doesn't pull as tight as it should, but, she reassures herself, it is a private item that he can use without fear of judgement from others.

And she has the snowballs in the deep freeze.

They'd had a heavy fall in November, while Elvis was away in Hawaii. Flakes had whirled and dived past the kitchen window, gently patting the glass, and as she'd watched Gladys had felt a deep contentment settle within her. She'd sat for a good hour, witnessing the world turning white. The tips of the fence, the angles of the car porch, the spikes of the oak branches all became blunted with snow. She'd wondered how she could share this comfort with her son. Calling him was out of the question, because he'd be working, getting ready for his show, and it would be almost impossible, anyway, to communicate how it felt to be in the middle of a snowfall when he was under a burning Hawaiian sun. She'd pictured him rolling down the white bank of the hill towards the gates of his mansion, snow sticking to his hair and coat, leaving a green trail as he tumbled, hugging himself, all the way to the bottom.

Then it came to her. She had rushed out in her housecoat and scooped up what she could. First being careful to remove any stray grass, mud or stones, she squeezed the snow into six neat balls, then held up the hem of her dress so it made a bowl, dropped the snow-balls in it, and carried them to the house. She placed them carefully in a pan, and hurried to the deep freeze, where she stashed her bounty. After letting the heavy lid drop with a great whoosh of freezing air, she turned to see Vernon watching her. He stared at her hot cheeks, wet hands, and house shoes soaked with snow.

'You done lost your mind, woman?' he asked.

Gladys did not feel the need to answer him.

She hasn't planned how she will present her son with the gift of snow just yet, but the thought of it glows within her as she puts the final piece of sticky tape in place. Perhaps she will keep it in reserve, in case he doesn't respond well to the washbag.

She's been asleep for less than an hour when she's woken by an almighty bang, and she's right back in the Tupelo tornado, a green sky above, the walls of her house shivering from the blast. Groping blindly for her son, she pulls only the silk coverlet towards her. Another explosion has Gladys fully awake and sitting up, heart racing, and realising that she's not at home, but in the mansion, alone in her huge bed. Vernon chooses the guest bedroom more and more now, saying he can't stand his wife's night-time wanderings.

As she pulls on her housecoat, she's calling for Elvis. Maybe he's still safely in the basement, where he'd gone after supper with Gene and Junior and Lamar and Cliff and Anita and the rest of the girls – she's given up trying to learn their names. Gladys peers down the steps. Though the lights are burning and the TV sets are on, there are no voices.

Suddenly there's a boom and a flash. The hallway lights up, and she ducks and cries out his name again, but nobody comes running. Guns. There must be guns. Just months ago, there was an attack on Liberace's mother at the star's home, and ever since, Elvis has been careful that Gladys should never be alone in the house. He has surrounded his family with more men; he never calls them body-guards, but they certainly look ready for a fight.

In the kitchen, she calls for him again and is answered by another explosion; the windows go blue and green. When she sees fire falling through the sky, she understands what is happening and sinks into a chair, all the strength in her legs gone. There is no shooting. There are no intruders. Elvis is letting off fireworks.

Now she understands why he needed so much cash: he'll have driven over the state line to buy boxes of the things. It's not the first time.

Boom. The window glows pink. Squinting through the glass, she makes out bodies rushing around the back lawn. There are squeals and shouts of 'Over here!' and 'Come on!' and 'Now!' Then another crack, and a series of Roman candles illuminate the sky, fizzing above the fields and plummeting back to earth. She sighs. She won't inter-fere. It's important for Elvis to blow off steam, especially after the news of the drafting.

But where is Vernon? Surely the noise must have woken him. For a second she considers knocking on the guest bedroom door, then thinks better of it. Some nights he crawls in even later than Elvis, and if this is one of those nights she'd really rather not know.

Resolving to pour herself a beer and find her pills, she rises and, from the corner of her eye, she spots a glowing figure running towards the house. As it gets closer, she realises it's Cliff, and there are flames coming from his coat.

She rushes to open the back door and peer out. Her nephew Gene, who Vernon calls 'that idiot boy', throws himself at Cliff, bundling him to the ground.

'Aunt Gladys!' he shouts. 'Get water!'

She grabs the nearest pan from a shelf and runs to the faucet, ignoring the ache in her legs. As she does so, she remembers the snow in the deep freeze, but rejects the idea of using it: that is for her son, for Christmas.

By the time she's reached them, the fire is out, and Cliff is sitting on the grass, grasping his forearm and moaning, his coat smoking in his lap.

'What in the world are you boys up to?' Gladys demands.

'He's OK. Ain't you, Cliff? Ain't you OK?' says Gene, whose freckled face is smeared with soot.

Gladys crouches next to Cliff. The sleeve of his shirt is in tatters.

'Put your arm in this, if you can,' she instructs, placing the pan of water by his side. He does as he's told, and lets out a yelp. Now that she's outside, Gladys can hear, between the explosions, the sound of her son's laughter as it climbs from amused chuckles to wild barks. Usually, on hearing this delirious sound, Gladys cannot help but laugh in response. But not tonight.

'We got to get you to a doctor,' she says.

'Noooooo!' sings Gene, jogging on the spot. 'Noooooo doctor!'

'Ain't no need,' says Cliff, through jagged breath. 'I'm OK.'

'Where's Elvis?'

Cliff and Gene exchange a glance. The laughter is becoming louder.

'Over yonder, in them trees,' says Gene.

'Well, go find him and tell him to quit. I want an end to this.'

'It's a game of war, Aunt Gladys!' says Gene, clenching a fist and punching the air. 'Elvis is the captain!'

'War?'

'Battles! Fighting! Real fun stuff!'

'And what you fighting with, Gene?'

Gene looks at the ground, then at Cliff, then at the ground again. 'Not the fireworks. Noooo, ma'am! Noooo!'

Gladys hauls herself to her feet. 'You fetch Elvis, right now!'

'But it's safe, Aunt Gladys! Elvis says so! He told us, didn't he, Cliff? He said, nooooo aiming for the face—'

'Gene,' says Cliff. 'Go get the boss.'

Another explosion. Green fire drips through the sky.

'*Get Elvis!*' Gladys cries.

Gene scampers away.

'Let's go inside and patch you up,' Gladys says to Cliff, helping him to his feet.

As they walk to the house, she asks, 'How can a game be called war?' and Cliff replies, 'Guess it ain't really much of a game, Miss Gladys.'

TROMBONE: 1947–1948

1947

As Aunt Lillian often remarks, Vernon seems to make a habit of losing jobs and houses. It isn't long before he falls behind with the payments on their new place and Elvis and his family have to move again, first to Tupelo's poorest coloured neighbourhood, Shake Rag, and then, when Gladys gets a job with Aunt Lillian at Long's Laundry by the railway tracks, on to a house on North Green Street. Grandma Minnie Mae, who Elvis has recently nicknamed 'Dodger' on account of her ducking out of the path of a ball he threw across the yard, moved in with them after her husband shocked the whole of East Tupelo by filing for divorce. Vernon calls his daddy a no-good liar, and worse. But Dodger looks to Elvis like she's happy to be free of that old man. From the way she swings her long, stringy body around their rooms, humming a little tune, sweeping corners that only she can reach, her ankle-length skirts whispering along with her breath, it seems to him that she's dodged another ball.

They are still in a coloured neighbourhood, though Vernon often points out that theirs is a whites-only rental, and is on the very edge of what he calls Dark Town. They have no call to feel ashamed, he says. The Presleys can hold their heads up, even on the neat streets of Tupelo. Gladys says nothing, but her rage is obvious to Elvis. When his daddy is home, it's there in her every movement, even in the way she holds her son: her arms are stiffer than they used to be, and her embrace sometimes threatens to squeeze the breath from him.

It is early summer. Elvis is out in the small backyard – so small there was no room for Mama's chickens, who have been left with Uncle Noah – standing on an empty crate. A chinaberry tree growing in the neighbour's garden casts its umbrella-shaped shadow across him as he practises his line for a school play.

'My name is FEAR! People tremble and shake when I am near!'

He pretends not to know that he's being watched through a hole in the wooden fence by the coloured boy who lives in the house behind his. If he admits he knows this, then he might have to feel ashamed.

'My name is FEAR! People tremble and shake when I am near!'

It's important to scowl, and to make himself bigger as he says the line. He breathes in, expanding his chest. Miss Camp has instructed him to imagine he is the Devil himself as he speaks the words. 'But only,' she has warned, her string of pearls trembling, 'for the duration of your performance.' It's actually near impossible even to open his mouth at his new school. Most of the other kids at Milam wear pants and sweaters, not overalls, every day of the week. Not one of them lives near Dark Town. Miss Camp likes Elvis's singing, though, especially 'Barbara Allen', which Grandma Dodger taught him. Miss Camp says that's a sweet, sad song, and she's right. When he sings it he doesn't have to worry about sounding hillbilly. Sometimes his eyes well up when he gets to the bit about the mother digging the grave long and narrow, and Miss Camp looks at him like he's as good as those kids in pants and sweaters, if not better.

Elvis knows his face is right, but he's struggling with his voice. He tries again. 'My name is FEAR!' Then he stops and looks around, in case the boy reacts. But there's just the warm breeze in the china-berry leaves, and the low buzz of flies.

'My name is FEAR!' Louder. 'People tremble and shake when I am near!' No. He rushed that last bit, and barely whispered it.

He jumps down, rubs his hands roughly over his sweating face, then, without thinking too much, leaps onto the crate once more.

'My name is FEAR!' The whole thing shouted now, and his body as big as he can make it. 'People tremble and shake when I am near!' Perhaps a little pause after 'tremble' and more emphasis on 'I'.

This time he imagines he's up on the screen at the Strand, a bad guy in a sharp suit in a Gene Autry picture. Balancing his imaginary pistol on the shining hood of his brand new automobile, he narrows his eyes and recalls Miss Camp's words. *The Devil himself.* His suit is black and his car is deep red and his aim is deadly. He says the line once more and twirls around, still brandishing the pistol, being careful not to look towards the gap in the fence, where he hopes the eyes of the boy will be widening in awe. He's almost singing the line now. He's not sure what he's doing with his body; it's something between acting and dancing; something, perhaps, like the Devil himself. Closing his eyes, Elvis thrusts his hands in the air and yells, 'My name is FEAR! FEAR, I tell you!' He almost laughs at himself, but not quite. 'My name is FEAR and people tremble and shake and damn near piss their pants when I come around!'

Then he fires off a round of imaginary bullets, his groin juddering as the pistol explodes.

To his great surprise, a finger appears through the hole in the fence.

'BAM-BAM-BAM!'

Elvis stops and stares. The finger remains where it is.

'BAM!' says Elvis.

'BAM!' says the finger.

Gladys has told him to be polite to his neighbours but not to get involved with coloureds, because these things have a way of not turning out for the best. And, mostly, it's easy to follow her instructions.

When he walks along the street, few people look him in the eye, even though he cannot help but stare at everybody he sees. Here on the Hill it's not like in Shake Rag, where the women wore feathers and paint in the daytime, but there are still preachers dressed in shining suits and chunky jewellery, women in fancy hats like toy buildings, and music coming from the most unlikely places – Mr Ulysses Mayhorn's store, for one. He's heard that trombone moaning, and he wants to hear it again, soon.

But Mama is working over at Long's, and is not here to watch over what he hears or sees.

When Elvis approaches the fence, the finger disappears. He looks through the gap and there's no sign of the boy, but his garden is a paradise. There's not only a large watermelon patch, but also a fig tree, a peanut patch, and an orchard of peach and apple trees with a couple of matted-looking mules standing beneath. Everything is glowing in the afternoon sun, as if waiting to be taken. Elvis stares through the gap, trying to drink it all in before it disappears. He knew the people on the Hill were respectable coloureds – ones with jobs in the finest houses in Tupelo – but he had no idea they might have gardens like this. This garden is almost as good as his uncle Bob's, and Uncle Bob has one of the best gardens in East Tupelo, with enough produce to feed half their church. Surely Mama could have no objection to him talking to a boy with such a garden. A boy with such a garden would be, in her eyes, a clean and deserving kind of coloured boy.

Then Elvis hears breathing, and realises the boy is pressed up against the fence, just out of his eye-line but real close. He shifts round so he can see the side of the boy's face.

'Bam!' Elvis says again, softly.

The boy jolts away from the fence. He's tall and well built and neat-looking. He has a long face and eyes that slant slightly as they stare at Elvis. He doesn't smile, but he doesn't look afraid, either.

'I'm Elvis Presley,' says Elvis.

'That's funny,' says the boy. 'I reckoned your name was Fear.'

After a moment, Elvis breaks out laughing.

'I'm Sam Bell,' says the boy.

For days, the performance on the crate becomes a ritual. Elvis climbs up, does his line, does it again, and Sam watches through the gap in the fence. Sometimes Sam laughs, and his laugh is like somebody falling down the stairs: a long, loud series of bumpy noises. When he laughs, Elvis gets mad, and tries the line a different way, telling himself no coloured boy will laugh like that at him. It always ends in them both firing their finger-pistols.

Then Elvis says, through the fence, 'Your garden sure looks good.'

Sam crosses his arms tightly and stands very still.

'You got peanuts back there?' asks Elvis.

Sam sighs and tilts his head.

'Them mules look like they could use riding.'

Sam lets out a small laugh. 'They's good for nothing but petting.'

There's a pause.

'You good at saying that thing of yours,' Sam says. Elvis notices Sam has a way of not opening his mouth very wide when he speaks, as if he's unsure whether he should make any sound at all. But when he does, his voice is low and serious. It makes Elvis want to speak in the same way as Sam: with measured, thoughtful authority.

Elvis grins. '*You* good at firing that gun of yours.'

'You could maybe come over,' Sam says, 'but I gotta ask Mama first.'

This is all the invitation Elvis needs. In a flash, he's crawled beneath the fence and is standing next to Sam. From here, the garden doesn't look as big as it did from the other side, and Sam, too, looks smaller. The two boys blink at one another. Sam's overalls are newer than Elvis's, but he, too, is barefoot. He smells a little spicy. Perhaps he has something in his hair, which is cropped close to his head and shines in the sun, as if it's oiled.

'I'll go ask her, then,' Sam says.

'I'll come with you,' says Elvis.

Sam looks hard at him. Then he shakes his head and mumbles, 'I guess.'

All his life, Gladys has warned Elvis: *Don't go in other people's houses and dirty their floors. When you play with a friend, stay in the yard. If it's wet, play on the porch, or beneath the house, so long as you've checked for snakes.* Back in East Tupelo, he'd spent hours with Guy and Odell, playing trucks beneath the floorboards of his own house. The fine dirt there made a good racetrack.

As Sam leads him through the orchard to the porch, Elvis smells the ripe peaches on the tree and tells himself that perhaps the rule about playing in the yard doesn't apply with coloured folks. So many rules are different, when it comes to them. And, as a white boy, doesn't he have the right to go in that house if he pleases?

On the porch, they hesitate.

'I don't know what she'll say,' Sam warns.

'Won't know till we ask her,' Elvis assures him. Usually, if he's polite enough, and smiles at the right moments, older folks say yes to him.

Sam pulls open the screen door and Elvis follows him over the threshold and into the aroma of freshly baked biscuits. His stomach growls. The floor of the living room is so polished it gleams, and in the corner of the room is a piano with the lid up. The keys are all intact, and there's music on the stand. It looks as though it will play good, exactly like the one in church. He could sit there, and let his fingers run over the smooth keys, turning his hand so his knuckles catch each one. Sometimes he can pick out a tune in church, when the preacher lets him. He's much better at playing the piano than the guitar.

When they reach the kitchen doorway, Sam's mother stands before them. She is wearing a flowered dress and a checked apron, and she's as tall and thin as Dodger. She seems to fill the entrance, stretching her arms from one side of the door frame to the other, blocking their progress.

Seeing Elvis, she draws in a breath. And stares. At first her stare is openly surprised, as if she might laugh. Then her eyes dart suspiciously from Sam to Elvis and back again.

Suddenly Elvis knows with absolute certainty that he should not be here, that his mama will be disappointed and his daddy mad enough to whip him. But it is too late to back out.

Sam, who stood so straight and still before, is quivering. His hands keep fluttering around his body, as if to chase away some phantom. Is this what *he* looks like, Elvis wonders, when Miss Camp tells him to please hold still, for heaven's sake?

'Who,' Mrs Bell asks Sam, 'is this?'

Mother and son consider Elvis as if he's a curious and perhaps dangerous pet that's just been delivered to them by mistake.

'Elvis,' Sam manages. 'This here's Elvis.'

'What kind of name is that?'

'His name,' Sam states, simply.

She keeps her hands on the door frame. 'And is *Elvis* a friend of yours?'

Just in time, Elvis stops himself from answering the question for Sam. Instead he focuses on Mrs Bell's hair, considering its depth and texture, imagining how it might feel beneath his fingers. Would it be like wire wool? Or soft, like a lamb's coat?

'Samuel? Is this boy a friend of yours?'

'Yes, Mama,' Sam mutters.

She breathes deeply through her nostrils.

'Your mother know you here, Elvis?'

'Yes, ma'am,' says Elvis, scratching at his neck.

She lets her hands drop. 'Well,' she says, stepping back so they can pass, 'I guess you'd better come on through. Sit down there. I'll fetch you both some biscuits.'

'Thank you, ma'am, that sounds real good,' says Elvis.

Mrs Bell gestures towards a wooden chair at the table by the back door.

Before he sits, he cannot stop himself from adding, 'You have it real nice here, ma'am.' It's what his mama would say, in this situation. She might add a question, too, about which talented lady did the pretty embroidery on the cushions in the living room.

Mrs Bell stares at him as though she might laugh again, then gathers herself and nods, sternly.

Also at the table is an older woman. Her hair is tied up in a purple scarf which tugs at the skin on her forehead. After watching Elvis settle his dusty behind on the chair, she turns slowly to Mrs Bell, who is standing at the counter, putting biscuits onto a plate. 'Lorene,' she says, 'what's this white boy doing in my house?'

Mrs Bell places the plate on the table, together with a pitcher of milk and some cups. 'He's a friend of Sam's, Mama.'

The old woman looks at Sam. 'That right, Samuel?'

'Yes, Grandma.'

There's a pause while the old woman's frown deepens. 'Tell me something,' she says, slowly. 'How can that be, son?'

Beneath the table, Sam's hands begin to flutter again. Elvis wants to reach out and hold them down for him. But he's not sure, yet, whether it would be OK to touch Sam. He looks clean enough, but he's been warned by Dodger to watch out for nasty coloured diseases.

Mrs Bell touches her son on the shoulder. 'Take a biscuit, Sam,' she says. She pours milk for both boys. Elvis drinks his down, putting his lips to the side of the cup, right near the handle, so as not to swallow anybody else's germs.

'I asked you a question, Samuel,' the old woman says, fixing her eyes not on Sam but on Elvis. 'I said, how can that be?'

Sam has yet to touch his biscuit. 'He lives on over the back. I saw him through the fence.'

'And that makes him your friend.'

Sam's mouth moves but no sound comes out.

'How old are you, Elvis?' asks Mrs Bell.

'Twelve, ma'am.'

'There. He's just a boy,' she tells her mother.

The old woman beckons Elvis with one finger. 'Come here, boy, and let me look at you good.'

The woman's dark eyes shine. Perhaps she has voodoo powers, like the gypsy back in East Tupelo, who sometimes used to call to Elvis from her porch. Folks said she'd cursed the man who'd wronged her in love, and that he'd never walked again. His mama told him not to look at her, and Elvis had no trouble obeying that particular instruction.

Sam kicks at Elvis's chair and hisses, 'You heard her!'

Mrs Bell says, gently, 'Go on, Elvis. My mother can't see too well, is all.'

He senses he will not get a biscuit until the old woman has examined him, and so he does as he is told.

She keeps beckoning until Elvis is almost touching her. The skin on her face looks both soft and tough, like the cover of an old book. Her nose quivers as she lets out a long breath onto his face. It smells of violet-flavoured candy. 'What you up to, boy?' she asks.

'Nothing, ma'am.'

'Who your kin?'

'The Presleys, ma'am. My daddy is Vernon Presley. And my mother is Gladys.'

'Ain't never heard of them.'

'My uncle, Noah, is mayor of East Tupelo.'

The old woman's lips curl into a smile. 'You an Above-the-Highway boy!'

'I was, ma'am. But now my family lives right here in Tupelo.'

'Your mama know you here in this house?'

Elvis does not hesitate to tell the lie again. 'Yes, ma'am.'

She studies his face for a long moment, and he manages to keep looking right back at her.

'You a good friend of my Samuel's?'

'Yes, ma'am.'

'For how long?'

'About a week.'

She clicks her tongue.

'You hungry, Elvis?'

'I could eat something, ma'am.'

'I bet you could. You looks hungry, like most of them Above-the-Highway boys.' She laughs. 'Lean and white and right squirrelly.'

'Mama—' Mrs Bell warns.

She nods towards Elvis. 'You can sit.'

He hurries to his seat, almost knocking it over in his haste.

Mrs Bell offers Elvis the plate. There are three left. He considers Dodger's words about coloured diseases, but he cannot refuse this hospitality. He knows his mama wouldn't want him to. And he's so hungry he could eat the biscuits and the table, both.

'Thank you, ma'am.'

As he reaches for the food, the old woman leans over and whispers in his ear, 'Don't you ever cross our boy, you hear?'

He nods, his mouth already full of delicious dough.

* * *

With the summer vacation started and the play done (Elvis thinks he didn't give as good a performance as he'd managed in the yard), they are in Sam's tree house, arguing about whether to go to Mayhorn's store. The pitcher of lemonade and the plate of peanut crackers provided by Mrs Bell have been hungrily consumed. They have stroked the mules, led them around the orchard and attempted riding them until the animals protested, loudly; they have crawled around the peanut patch, pretending to be snipers. Elvis did such a good impersonation of being wounded that Sam rushed to his side, almost in tears.

Now Elvis wants to listen to Mr Ulysses Mayhorn play his trombone. He's cycled slowly past the store on a few occasions, lured closer each time by the music coming from inside. He has never dared to stop, but with Sam as cover, perhaps he could linger a while. Perhaps he could learn more about this music, which seems to speak of secret, thrilling, terrifying things. He knows people call it the blues. How sound can be a colour, he doesn't yet understand.

'You crazy,' says Sam. 'Mama'll never let me go over there alone.'

'You won't be alone. You'll be with me.'

'You understand what kinda music they play, don't you?'

'Uh-huh.'

'Mama wouldn't like it one bit,' says Sam. 'She says that music ain't holy.'

Elvis can hear the rattle of pans in Mrs Bell's kitchen, the cardinals in the dusty trees, somebody laughing on North Green. He wants to hear the trombone again. That trombone moaned like somebody getting the spirit. But Mrs Bell may have a point: whether that spirit is good or evil, he's not sure.

'She ain't gonna know. It won't take long.'

And then, another time, it was like crying. Crying with joy, like his mama did after he sang in that talent show. Or crying in pain, like Mama does now, when his daddy fails to come home nights.

Never, never, never, wailed the trombone.

'We can't go over there,' says Sam. But then he looks at Elvis, head tilted, a tiny smile playing on his lips. 'Can we?'

'We got my bike. We'd be there and back in twenty.'

The used bike was a gift from his daddy to make amends for having to move again. These days, with his mother and father both working, more things are appearing in the house. Not long ago, Vernon came home with a Victrola. Dodger says Vernon should make the rent before buying such things. Vernon tells his mama to hush up, but he says it low enough for her to miss.

Sam flops backwards and lets out a heavy breath. 'It's too hot to bother.'

Which is always Sam's excuse for not doing what Elvis wants.

'You sound like an old man, boy.'

'We ain't got no money!'

Elvis grins. 'That's where you wrong, Samuel Bell.' He produces a nickel from his pocket and drops it on Sam's chest, where it clatters on the rivets of his overalls.

Sam sits up. 'Where d'you get that?'

'Earned it. Doing deliveries for Mr Harris.'

Sam laughs. 'You too much.'

'Come on,' says Elvis, jumping to his feet. 'Get your ass moving.'

Cycling along the street, Elvis thinks about how he looks. He is careful to sit upright and let what breeze there is blow his hair straight back, to steer the handlebars loosely yet confidently, to look generally as though he is in absolute command of his bike, even though Sam is giggling and swaying as he balances on the crossbar. Elvis tries not to think too much about being a white boy with a coloured passenger. Despite Vernon's disapproval, Gladys has said it's all right to go play in Sam's yard; but she hasn't suggested he bring Sam over to the house, and Elvis knows that if Vernon catches him with Sam on his bike there'll be hell.

It's near five-thirty, and people are beginning to spill onto the sidewalk, making their way home from work or braving the slightly gentler heat of the late afternoon. One woman stops and looks at Elvis and Sam and says something to her pretty daughter. Elvis considers waving at the two of them, then thinks better of it. Folks will sometimes make allowances for kids when it comes to colour, but not that many allowances, especially when the kids are twelve already. Sam is tall, too, and with his serious, long face, looks more like fourteen. Which is another good reason to take him to Mayhorn's.

Elvis stares straight ahead, set on making it to the store before Sam changes his mind. From the crumbling, dark alleyways of Shake Rag come the cries of babies and the raised voices of women, but they must pass quickly to find the real music. Sticky heat blasts their faces and dust kicks up behind the bike as Elvis gets up speed. Sam holds on tight, wobbling but not protesting.

Outside the store there are brooms, aprons, washtubs, cans of gasoline, kerosene lamps, matches, rope, hoes, watering cans, spades of all sizes, copper kettles, buckets and dippers, dishcloths and men. Four of them are sitting on the porch steps, listening to Mr Mayhorn tuning up inside the store. Elvis is aware the men will have seen him hanging round here before, and must think him a curious, hungry-looking, dog-like boy who has no business at a coloured store, listening to coloured music.

Suddenly losing his nerve, Elvis pedals harder and cycles straight past.

'You missed it!' Sam hollers. 'Elvis! You missed it!'

As if in echo, the trombone calls out, long and loud. *Never, never, never.*

Elvis skids to a halt, breathing hard.

'What's wrong?' asks Sam. 'You blind?'

Sam is his cover. With Sam here, it will be all right.

Elvis swerves the bike around and pedals back to Mayhorn's.

Spine straight, he brakes sharply, causing Sam to tumble from the crossbar. Elvis drops the bike, wipes a hand through his hair, then looks up at the men on the porch. The men look back at him. A long moment passes. The one on the lowest step looks the hardest. His brow is beaded with sweat and his white shirt clings to his chest. He wears a wide gold chain around his neck and his hair is oiled into waves; he looks strong and protected.

Slowly, he says, 'Evening, boys.'

'Sir,' says Elvis.

The man looks through him and addresses Sam. 'You Lorene Bell's boy?' he asks.

'Yessir.'

'You got her eyes. Those pools of sorrow, just the same.' He raises his chin. 'And this boy's with you?'

Sam glances at Elvis, hands fluttering. 'He's a friend of mine, sir.'

The man nods.

A long note blasts from the store, and Elvis shifts from foot to foot, eager to move closer to its source.

'Your mama's a good woman,' says the man. 'She still working over that house on Highland Circle?'

'Yessir,' Sam replies.

The man shakes his head. 'Then she still tolerating a whole crock of shit. 'Scuse my language, boys.'

'That's OK,' says Elvis. Vernon would curse from dawn to dusk if Gladys let him.

The man ignores him. 'Tell your mama Joe says hello, you hear?' he says to Sam.

Hearing a few notes strung together, Elvis walks forward and puts his foot on the step.

Joe holds up his hand. 'If you boys is figuring on buying candy, you'd better come back tomorrow. Store's closed for today. Mr Mayhorn's practising with his band.'

'We'll come back—' Sam says.

Elvis cuts him off. 'Actually, sir, we came to hear the music.'

For the first time, Joe looks Elvis in the eye. He lets out a long whistle.

The man sitting on the top step quits puffing on his cigarillo. 'Then we oughta charge you, boy,' he says, in a surprisingly squeaky voice. 'Doncha think, Joe?'

'Sure 'nuff, Willie.'

'But, sir,' stammers Elvis, 'I don't—'

'Now,' says Joe, 'I wonder. What's the going rate to hear Ulysses and his band down Vaughan's?'

''Bout fifty cents, I reckon,' says Willie.

Sam digs Elvis in the ribs. 'You got that nickel,' he mutters.

Elvis digs in his pockets. He produces the coin and holds it up to Joe, hopefully.

Joe throws back his head, and from somewhere deep inside his gut, a laugh escapes. 'I's messing with you!' he roars, batting Elvis's hand away. 'Y'all can sit over there, by ol' Henry. He won't pay you no mind.'

Henry, who is leaning on a stick as he chews tobacco, looks to be the oldest of the men. First spitting to the side, he nods to the boys.

Elvis and Sam huddle together on the step, as far from Henry as they can.

Willie is still laughing. 'What a skinny white boy like you want to listen to ol' Mayhorn for?' he asks. 'Thought you white boys liked Perry Como and that Sinatra fool.'

'I can't stand that shit,' says Joe, with a look over at Sam.

Elvis clears his throat. 'Actual fact, sir, I like the Ink Spots best, I reckon.'

Willie sniggers. 'Ink Spots is minstrel music.'

'Naw!' says Joe. 'I can stand a little Ink Spots.'

'The Ink Spots are very great musicians,' Henry suddenly states, rolling his tobacco from cheek to cheek. 'Very great indeed.'

Everyone is quiet for a moment, as if waiting for the old man to go on. But he just settles himself on his stick once more.

'I like "My Prayer",' says Elvis. 'Reckon that's my favourite ...'

'Hush up now,' says Joe. 'Show's about to start.'

Elvis grips his knees to keep them from moving. The men shift around him, clearing their throats, arranging their legs. Sam whispers, 'We can't stay long,' and Elvis nods, impatiently.

Then the trombone sounds. Gently, it climbs from a growl to a wail to the sweetest note he's ever heard. It reminds him of Magdalene Morgan's singing: it has something of that same purity. But the most delicious thing about it is that he can already feel it's going to be sullied. The trombone climbs and climbs, then swoops low, and the double bass cuts in, anchoring the brass with its regular beat. A man begins to sing. His voice sounds as though it's been dredged from the bottom of a creek.

'*Call my baby*

Call her quick ...'

Sam's hands have stilled now. Elvis can tell he's listening, too.

'*She's been rolling in the dark ...*'

Every man on the steps wears the same look. It's the one his mama gets when Brother Mansell brings the congregation down after they've sung an energetic, upbeat tune. He reminds them to feel the Spirit, to let it in, because God's love is there, if only they'll accept it. They'll be richly rewarded, oh, yes, perhaps not now, but in the hereafter, when no matter what hardships they have suffered in this life, they'll all be welcomed in that place of ease and peace. And yet, it's not exactly an easeful look his mama gets. There's that slight lift of the eyebrows, an opening of the mouth that suggests some great, barely controlled longing. All the men have that look, now.

'Rolling in the dark
My baby's been out rolling in the dark ...'

The song goes on for over ten minutes, and during that time, the world around Elvis slips away. He stops thinking about the men on the steps, or Brother Mansell, or his mama. Everything but the song quietens. It's like a long, cool, sweet drink on a blistering day. It's better than that. Better, even, than his mama's embrace. It's better than anything he knows.

He sits and he listens, the dusk gathering around him.

Five songs later, when the musicians break and Elvis finally turns to Sam, he's so ecstatic that he cannot speak. He can only grin.

Sam says, 'We gotta get back.'

Elvis stares at him, stupefied.

'Mama will fret,' Sam says. 'She'll already be fretting.'

It is growing dark. Gladys will be home from work, and his supper will be cold. But, at this moment, these facts do not seem very significant to Elvis.

Joe and the other men have gone inside, and the sounds of laughing and back-slapping drift from the store.

Getting to his feet, Elvis tries to peer through the screen. He chases the delicious scent of cigarette smoke with his nose. There's a flash of brass, and a white handkerchief raised to a sweating fore-head. He ducks back out of the light.

'They ain't through yet,' he says.

Somehow, all thoughts of what his own mother will say about him being out after dark – and there's no way on this earth he'll admit where he actually was, but he'll consider that later – have disappeared.

Sam stands up. 'I gotta get back.'

'Just ten more minutes.'

'I gotta get home right now!'

Joe unhooks the screen and looks out. 'What's going on?'

'Nothing, sir,' says Elvis, before Sam can speak.

'Ain't you boys gotta get home? Your mamas will be waitin' on you,' says Joe, looking at Sam.

Sam nods solemnly.

'Goddamnit!' Elvis explodes.

Joe gives him a long, steady look. 'What's the problem, son?'

'I want to listen, sir. That's all.'

'How am I gonna get home?' asks Sam, almost in tears.

Joe places a hand on Sam's shoulder. 'Here's what we're gonna do. This boy here – what's your name, son?'

'Elvis. Elvis Presley.'

'Elvis is gonna take you home.'

'But—'

Joe holds up a hand. 'But nothing. Listen. I let you stay, and tomorrow I got a whole heap of trouble in my lap, courtesy of your daddy, or your brother, or your uncles. And that's trouble I can do without. Understand me?'

Elvis hangs his head.

'This way, you go, my hide is safe, and y'all can come back next week, long as you promise to go on home when you supposed to.'

'Come on,' says Sam, plucking at Elvis's sleeve.

'Listen to your young friend here, Elvis,' says Joe. 'He talks a lot of sense.'

But Elvis is not listening. He can hear only the trombone, which is sliding out into the evening again.

He's not listening, either, to the shouts from the pool hall, the slamming of the huge door to the Elks' Club, or even to the singing inside the church as he cycles home along North Green Street with Sam on the crossbar. He sees lights from the houses, the swaying of porch swings, the flutter of women's skirts as they step out with their young men, the black glint of the electricity wires scoring the sky. He sees it all, but he doesn't hear a thing, because Ulysses Mayhorn's trombone is still exploding gently in his mind.

After he's dropped off Sam – and neither boy utters a word of goodbye – Elvis lets himself into the house. At the table, Vernon, Gladys and Dodger are waiting. The glare of the overhead light gives their faces a greenish tinge. Vernon is eating his corn and does not look up, but Gladys jumps to her feet and, before Elvis can duck, swipes him across the head with the back of her hand.

It's not a hard blow, but it does reduce the volume of that trombone.

Dodger says, in a low voice, 'Boy don't deserve that.'

Gladys rubs at her hand.

'Sit down, Glad,' Vernon orders, licking his buttery fingers.

Gladys ignores him. 'Where you been all this time?' she demands.

A place has been set for Elvis, so he pulls up a chair and sits, calculating that this will buy him some time to think of a reply.

'Answer your mother,' says Vernon.

'Sorry I'm late, Mama,' Elvis mumbles, eyes on the table.

'I was out later than this when I wasn't much older—' Vernon begins.

Gladys cuts him off. 'Times was different then. And you wasn't raised round here. Lord knows who's out in them streets.'

'Glad's right,' says Dodger. 'Gotta be real careful out there.'

'Where you been, son?' asks Vernon.

'You might wanna eat that chicken, fore it gets cold as a witch's titty,' whispers Dodger, patting Elvis's knee.

'Don't you dare touch that plate till you told me where you been, Elvis Presley!' His mother is standing over him, close enough for her spittle to land on his cheek. He can't find that trombone, now.

So he faces her. 'Listening to some music,' he says, slowly.

'Boy's always loved music!' says Dodger.

'Where you been listening to some music?'

He hesitates, then recovers. 'Church.'

'You been all the way over East Tupelo?'

'Naw. Church on North Green.'

There's a pause.

'The nigger church?' asks Vernon, pushing his empty plate away.

'Not inside! Just outside, listening.'

Dodger chuckles and shakes her head. 'Well, butter my behind and call me a biscuit,' she says.

'What for?' asks Vernon.

'I told you. I was listening. To the music.'

'You sure that's all you was doing?' asks Gladys. By the softer tone of her voice, he can tell that she is ready to believe him.

'I told you, Mama. I couldn't lie to you, you know that.'

'You weren't round one of them juke joints, were you?'

'Course not!'

'Bad things happen in them places.' Gladys sits down, apparently relieved. 'A juke joint's no place for a young boy like you.' She touches his hair.

'What was you doing listening to a bunch of niggers?' Vernon asks.

'They sing pretty, Vernon. You got to admit that,' says Gladys.

'Pretty crazy,' says Vernon. He widens his eyes and waggles his hands.

'At least it's holy music,' says Gladys. 'Who was with you, Elvie?'

'Couple of boys from school. It's kinda a thing with some of the Milam fellas.'

'Their mamas know they was at the coloured church?'

'Sure.'

Gladys sighs. Then she takes up a spoon and ladles mashed potato onto her son's plate.

'Well, I hope you was careful on the way back, and didn't talk to nobody.'

'I was, Mama.'

'Maybe I could come meet you, next time.'

'Ain't no need. I got the bicycle now.'

'Boy's all right, Glad,' says Vernon, rising and stretching. 'He don't need you to watch over his every move.'

Gladys serves Elvis a helping of greens. 'Just tell me next time, you hear?'

He nods and starts in on his food, wondering how long he can keep this wonderful thing a secret from his mama.

* * *

Elvis goes to Mayhorn's store whenever he can, with or without Sam. He takes his guitar with him, and somehow it seems protection enough. As the summer goes by, Sam comes less often, and by the end of August, Elvis is going to the store alone.

One evening, the music is so good that he stays long after the sun goes down. It's not that he thinks it's better than the music in church. It's more that he's discovered it's possible to like both kinds equally; that both kinds rub along in a funny sort of way. He knows other folks find Mr Mayhorn's playing ungodly, but he can't see that. It seems to him that this music gives him everything he needs, everything he didn't even know he wanted. God must be in it somewhere! So why should he move? How can it be important to be home, even if Mama is waiting? He stays so long that more men arrive, some with women on their arms. The women stand off to the side and chatter when the music stops, their dark, painted lips moving quick.

'Fine-lookin' ladies over there, ain't they?' says Joe.

Elvis ducks his head.

'Don't let their menfolk catch you gaping.'

'No, sir.'

'You got a little girl?'

'Yeah,' says Elvis, sitting up straight. 'Name of Magdalene.'

'Magdalene? As in Mary Magdalene?'

'I guess.'

He's familiar with the story of the fallen woman. How she used her long hair to cover her nakedness in the desert. How she washed Jesus's feet and wept at the crucifixion.

Joe laughs. 'Boy, you don't need to look for trouble, do you? It finds you!'

'She's a good little girl, sir. Real fine.'

Joe shakes his head. 'Sure she is.'

Elvis scowls, feeling he ought to make some kind of stand for Magdalene's honour.

'Anyways,' says Joe. 'Mr Mayhorn wants to meet you.'

'Pardon me?'

'I done told him, 'bout this funny white boy who keeps hanging round, and he says he wants to get a look at you.'

Elvis has imagined many times what Ulysses Mayhorn might look like. Sometimes he's pictured him as a huge figure with a handsome head as large as the room and hands that can reach you, wherever you are. Other times, he's figured him to be nothing more than an old coloured shopkeeper with a limp.

'When?' Elvis asks, unable to keep the urgency from his voice.

Joe touches him on the shoulder. 'Soon.'

On his next visit to the store, Elvis imagines Magdalene sitting next to him, listening. Instead of perching on the splintered wood of the Mayhorn steps, he's in a fancy auditorium, and he can feel the warm skin of her forearm against his own. She's wearing her best lace collar and cuffs, and her skirt rests easy on her pure white knees. Lately, they've been sneaking to the woods behind Priceville cemetery to lie side by side. He takes her there to see Jesse's grave, and she doesn't complain when he suggests they rest beneath the pines on the way back. It reminds him of the tornado game he used to play with Corinne beneath his cousin's house, but so far he hasn't asked Magdalene if she will lie on top of him. Her moods are unpredictable, and if he hasn't praised her performance in church highly enough she's capable of ignoring him for an entire week. If he could bring her here to the store, maybe she would understand his longing to feel her whole body pressed down on his, her soft hair falling about his ears, covering his head like water.

But there is no way he could bring an eleven-year-old white girl to this place. He hasn't even told her that he comes here.

Joe taps him on the shoulder. 'Come on. Now's the time.'

Elvis scrambles to his feet, happy, for once, to leave his daydream.

Inside the store, the air is thick with cigarette smoke, sweat, and the tang of moonshine. This is what it must feel like, he thinks, to walk into a juke joint. He is glad to be wearing his good pair of tan pants and the white cotton jacket given to him by his new friend James. James also attends Milam but isn't as highfalutin as some of the other kids. After the school play, he'd told Elvis he'd done a good job. And, more importantly, James's brother is Mississippi Slim of WELO. Every Saturday, Elvis still goes along to the courthouse for the Jamboree, and hopes to be noticed by Slim, but now James goes with him. Elvis believes the jacket was once Slim's own – James swears that it was.

The other men watch Elvis as he follows Joe deeper inside, beneath the large scales hanging from the ceiling, past the sacks of meal and maize, the barrel of mash for hogs, the shelves groaning with canned greens, beans and pork. Beneath the long counter at the back of the store are boxes of matches, candles, Hay-Po hair oil, leather rollers, combs, razors. But the place is transformed in this light. Two oil lamps cast long shadows and make even the empty crates, which have been shoved to the side to make way for the musicians, glow warmly. The guitarist sits on an upturned box, his instrument resting on his lap like a sleeping child. He's twisted to the side, deep in conversation with another man, but Elvis notices the crisp creases along the sleeves of his lime-coloured shirt. His guitar is dark red, and much bigger than Elvis's. It shines even more deeply than Mississippi Slim's guitar. Elvis is so distracted by the instrument that he jumps when Joe grabs his arm and spins him round. Before he's had time to take a breath, he's looking into a pair of big yellowy eyes.

'Elvis. This here's Mr Ulysees Mayhorn.'

He is not much taller than Elvis. The top of his head is bald, and the hair around his temples is grey and stands out like wings. Sweat is lodged in the wide wrinkles of his forehead. His black silky shirt is embroidered on the shoulders with unicorns. He is squat and solid, and when he opens his mouth the men around him stop talking.

Mr Mayhorn sticks out a meaty hand. Taking it, Elvis feels the bones in his fingers grind together, and gets a strong whiff of alcohol. He cannot tell if this is liquor, or cologne.

'You interested in the blues, Elvis?'

'Yessir!'

'You friends with Lorene Bell's boy, I hear.'

'Yessir.'

'Where is he?'

Elvis looks round the room, then at Joe, who shrugs.

'Truth is, sir, I don't reckon Sam loves the music the way I do.'

Mr Mayhorn fingers a button on his silky chest.

'You live in this neighbourhood, Elvis?'

'Yessir. Up on North Green.'

Mr Mayhorn places a hot hand on Elvis's shoulder. 'OK, boy. You good.' Then he turns back to his musicians.

Joe moves forward, ready to take Elvis back to the steps, but Elvis stays where he is. 'Mr Mayhorn, sir?' he asks, quickly. 'Will you show me your trombone?'

Without looking at him, Mr Mayhorn replies, 'That depends, Elvis. Will you show me yours?'

The store explodes with laughter. Elvis's skin burns. For a second he stares at the wooden floor. But then he gathers himself and says, 'I would, if I had one.'

He'd hoped that would bring more laughter – and it does, a little.

Mr Mayhorn looks over his shoulder and flicks his eyes over Elvis's white jacket. 'Kinda busy now, son. Come by the store some time when I ain't practising.'

At lunchtime the following day, Elvis walks out of school. He grabs his guitar from the space between the stationery cupboard and the blackboard, and heads for the bathroom, but instead of going in he ducks around the side and pushes open the door to the schoolyard. Behind him are the sounds and smells of the canteen: steel on steel, boiling meat, hundreds of young voices raised in excited conversation. Without looking back, Elvis straps on the guitar and hurries to the gate which leads to the eastern sidewalk.

He crosses onto Allen Street, sprinting away from the bright red school buildings. He doesn't think about his growling stomach. If he can get to Mr Mayhorn on his lunch hour, he has a chance of being introduced to the trombone.

It feels wrong to be out on the heat-blasted sidewalk when everyone else is inside, or resting in the shade of a porch. Hitting North Green, he slows to a jog. The sun burns the back of his neck, and he wishes he'd worn the white jacket so he could turn up the collar. Most places – the pool hall, the juke joint, Mr Harris's store – are closed, with the blinds pulled down. He gets the feeling that nobody in the world is outside at this moment. He is free to do exactly as he wishes, without fear of another soul witnessing his actions.

He hopes Mr Mayhorn will ask if he can play, so he can show him the chords he's mastered, and maybe sing some, too. The guitar doesn't yield to him as he would like: it's hard to learn, and has none of the instant joy of singing. His fingers become thick and creaky on the strings. But wearing it has become a uniform, a shield. If nothing else, he can use it to beat time.

When he reaches the store, he's pleased to find the blinds closed and the door shut. A sign says, *Back at 2pm!* RC Cola and fruit crates are stacked high in the front yard. He can smell chicken's feet – he knows the aroma from Sam's house – and it sets his mouth to watering.

He picks his way round to the back, then climbs the steps to the door, guessing this leads to the Mayhorn living quarters, and Jesse is suddenly there.

You can't knock on a nigger's door.

Why not?

'Cause you ain't got the balls. You should turn round and run right back to Miss Camp. You love her.

I don't. I love Magdalene.

Sure. She ain't never gonna give you an inch, boy.

I just gotta find a way to get to her—

You gonna knock on that door?

Elvis stares at the rusty curlicues of the screen, and wishes he'd been able to bring Sam with him.

Got any money on you? 'Cause you know the nigger's gonna need paying.

I got my lunch money—

Knock it, then.

He knocks, and immediately there is barking from what sounds like at least a dozen dogs.

A girl no more than a few years older than Elvis opens the door and squints through the screen. Her apron is covered in roses and her bangs are in rollers. Over the rest of her hair is a net, like the one Dodger wears in bed. She pulls the collar of her dress tight.

The dogs – Elvis can see three – gather around her legs and sniff at the screen. They are large and beautiful, with silky hair and long ears.

He realises she is waiting for him to speak.

'Howdy, miss,' he begins. 'I'm here to see Mr Mayhorn.'

She peers at him quizzically, then calls back over her shoulder, 'Daddy! Somebody here for a visit.'

'Hope I haven't called at a bad time,' Elvis says.

'Who's there, Dinah?' Mr Mayhorn's voice.

'Tell him it's Elvis Presley,' says Elvis.

'Say what?'

'Elvis. Elvis Presley.'

'It's Ellis Presley, Daddy.'

There's a short pause, then Mr Mayhorn calls, 'Bring him in here.'

'He says come in,' says Dinah, wrenching the screen back.

The dogs jump at Elvis's legs, barking.

'Don't pay them no mind,' she says, walking through the living room. 'They's hungry but they can't eat till Daddy finished.'

He stumbles after her, his legs hindered by swishing dog tails. Crates from the store are piled up in here, too, and there's a threadbare easy chair with another dog, smaller than the rest, curled on its seat. Dinah opens a door and points him into the kitchen.

The walls are painted a dark, flaking green. At a wooden table sits Mr Mayhorn, wearing his undershirt.

'You'll have to wait for me to get through eating,' he says. His hair is flatter than it was the other evening, and he has on a pair of wire-rimmed spectacles which look tiny on his heavy face.

The dogs immediately lie at Mr Mayhorn's feet, looking up at him expectantly. He ignores them, and continues to scoop rice from his plastic plate and into his mouth with swift precision. Not a grain is spilled from his fork.

'Sit down, boy.'

Elvis does as he's told, taking the chair opposite Mr Mayhorn. He props his guitar against the wall, but Mr Mayhorn doesn't seem to notice it.

'You hungry?'

'No, sir,' says Elvis, but his eyes won't move from Mr Mayhorn's food.

'Dinah, fix Elvis a plate.'

Dinah, who has been standing in the doorway, watching, turns to the stove and fishes a couple of fried claws from the skillet, then heaps the plate with rice.

Mr Mayhorn has a claw in his hand, so Elvis copies him, closing his eyes and biting into the skin, his teeth grazing the bone. It's chewier and denser than his mama's fried chicken, but it has a deep savoury flavour that he likes.

'That was mighty good,' says Mr Mayhorn, finishing up. 'Thank you, girl.' He gestures to Dinah to come over, and whispers something in her ear. She giggles, glances at Elvis, who smiles his best smile at her. Then she slips from the room. Elvis wonders if she is old enough to be married, and whether he can ask Mr Mayhorn such a thing. Perhaps he can say something about her making somebody a fine wife one day.

He thinks better of it.

Mr Mayhorn wipes his big fingers on a napkin, taking care to clean each one thoroughly. 'Now. What was so urgent you got to interrupt my food?'

Elvis swallows. 'You said to come by when you ain't working, sir.'

'Ain't you s'posed to be in school?'

'We had library hour this afternoon. So that's, you know, kinda optional.'

'Ain't no school I know that's kinda optional.'

'I figured this was more important,' says Elvis, through a mouthful of rice.

Mr Mayhorn pulls his shoulders back. 'Don't you know how goddamn lucky you is in that school?' He jabs his glasses at Elvis's chest; the tips of the arms are furry from chewing. 'You got books over there, I guess? Enough for one each? And that fancy new brick building. Look at yourself, boy. You eating chicken feet with Ulysees Mayhorn when you could be studying to be a lawyer or something.'

Elvis cannot bear to meet the man's stare, so he looks at the wall behind him instead. There's a faded calendar from a paper-products supplier, and a framed picture of Christ with a lamp – the same one his mama has hung on their bedroom wall.

Mr Mayhorn pushes the screen open and shoos the dogs into the backyard. For a second, Elvis considers bolting after them into the brightness of the afternoon.

'You wasting time, boy,' Mr Mayhorn says, quietly.

Elvis pushes away his half-finished plate of food, not caring, now, if his action causes offence. 'I'm just more interested in the music, is all.'

Mr Mayhorn pours himself a cup of water from the pitcher on the table, then takes a long drink. 'How come?'

'I don't know.'

'Not good enough.'

'I love it, sir.'

'Why?'

Elvis looks at Christ's glowing lamp. 'It's like God.'

Mr Mayhorn puts down his cup. 'You blaspheming now?'

'I don't – I didn't—'

'You want to be a gospel singer, that it? Go round praising God and wearing greasepaint? Singing holy and living dirty?'

'No, sir.' Although he has thought about it.

'Hillbilly singing, then? Twanging your guitar there and crying your guts onto your spangled shirt?'

'Not really, sir.' He's pictured this, too.

Mr Mayhorn glances at the guitar. 'Can you even play that thing?' he asks.

'I can play some. But it's hard.'

'It ought to be.'

'Is playing the trombone hard?'

'It's so hard, it hurts. Every time, it's pain. But a good sort of pain.' He waves a hand in front of his face. 'You too young to understand.'

'Can I see it?'

Drumming his fingers on the table, Mr Mayhorn says, 'You don't let up. I give you that.' He sighs. 'Stay there. I keep her in the bedroom.'

He stands and walks gracefully from the room, taking his time. Elvis waits, trying to keep his knees from jogging up and down.

You got what you wanted, says Jesse. *Good job, boy.*

When Mr Mayhorn comes back, he's carrying a battered leather case. He rests it on the floor, then kneels before it. His thumbs click the locks back and a whiff of polish escapes. Elvis doesn't dare to lean across, sensing that he must be patient, and let Mr Mayhorn ease the trombone from its velvet bed.

'First, we got to put her together. She ain't nothing till we make her. And it must be done tenderly.' Still kneeling, Mr Mayhorn points first to the half of the trombone that's shaped like the head of a lily, then to the long thin tube. 'Bell and slide,' he says, removing both halves from the case.

He gets to his feet and, holding the slide in his left hand, balances one end of it on the floor before gently connecting it with the bell.

Elvis stands to get a closer look.

'You gotta treat her real nice,' Mr Mayhorn says, twisting in the mouthpiece. His big fingers hold the instrument firmly yet lightly.

'Step back, boy.' He waves Elvis out of the way. 'One dent in her and she's dead.'

Elvis does as he's told.

Grinning, Mr Mayhorn holds the trombone up and turns it in the air.

'She's real pretty, sir,' says Elvis.

'As a picture!' agrees Mr Mayhorn. He holds the mouthpiece to his lips and blows a long note, sliding it into a tune which Elvis recognises as the opening to 'Basin Street Blues'.

'Now,' says Mr Mayhorn. 'Your turn.'

Elvis stares at him, astonished.

'That's what you came for, ain't it?' Mr Mayhorn asks. 'Hold her here,' he says, taking Elvis's trembling hand and placing it beneath the warm mouthpiece. 'And here.' He fastens Elvis's other hand on the slider, showing him how to hold it between two fingers and thumb. It feels cool and dangerous, like holding his daddy's shotgun.

'Now stand up straight. Get the air into your lungs.'

Elvis does as he is told.

'And quit twitching your leg. You got to pucker up your mouth, real firm at the sides, bit looser in the centre. Like this.'

He presses his lips together, and Elvis tries to copy him.

'Good. Now. Keep your lips shut and blow air through them, real fast, so you buzzing.'

Mr Mayhorn demonstrates, making a high farting noise. Elvis giggles, but Mr Mayhorn ignores him and keeps forcing the air noisily through his lips, so Elvis gives it a try. It tickles, and he wishes he could do it without spitting everywhere.

'Not bad. Lips on the mouthpiece,' says Mr Mayhorn.

When Elvis lifts it to his mouth, the instrument is damp with Mr Mayhorn's spit, but he doesn't care.

'Not too firm,' says Mr Mayhorn. 'Now blow, and remember you want her to come to you, not blast her away. She won't sing without you. You got to show her who's making the music. Now do your buzz.'

Elvis blows, and the kind of sound a dying dog might make comes out.

Mr Mayhorn maintains a straight face. 'Nice try,' he says. 'Go again.'

Elvis blows, and the sound is no better.

'Again.'

Elvis closes his eyes and tries to feel Magdalene beside him, like when he sings in church and that beautiful sound comes from deep within his body. But all that emerges from the trombone is a thin whine.

Mr Mayhorn takes out a handkerchief and mops his brow. 'Hand her over.'

'I could give it another try.'

Mr Mayhorn puts one hand on Elvis's shoulder and the other on the instrument. Gently, he pulls the trombone away and starts packing it back in its case. 'Maybe the horn just ain't your thing.'

A lump comes to Elvis's throat.

'Maybe you oughta stick to your old guitar.'

'I sing some.'

'There you go, then.' Mr Mayhorn clicks shut the locks on the case. 'Now, I gotta get back in the store ...'

'Sir?' says Elvis. 'How did you know you was good?'

'I don't.'

Elvis laughs.

'I'm serious,' says Mr Mayhorn, putting his eyeglasses back on. 'I mean, other people tell me I'm good. And that's real nice. But all I know is, I got to do it. Seem to me that the minute I start thinking I'm good is the minute I start to stink real bad.' He opens the door and gestures towards the glaring afternoon. 'Now get on back to school.'

1948

His mama and daddy go out into the yard to argue, which is almost worse than doing it in the house. Any passing stranger could listen to them out there, and Sam and his family, who Elvis has never heard shouting, will certainly witness every word. At least inside it would be only Dodger who'd know. But after supper is finished and the crockery washed, and Elvis has slipped into the bedroom to be alone with his funny papers, Gladys takes Vernon out under the branches of the chinaberry tree to list his failures.

As her voice rises through the night air, Elvis lies in his bed, having given up trying to focus on Zorro. Gladys explains, almost patiently, the ways in which her husband fails to live up to her expectations. Since he's regained his job driving for McCarty's, these ways have become more numerous and grave. Now he's not only failing his family and his church, but he's betraying them, and she knows it. She'd have to be a fool not to notice the way he smells when he comes home! Does he think these flattened burger buns he's brought home from his delivery round will put her off that unholy scent? Does he truly believe that damaged goods can make amends for what he's up to?

Vernon interrupts his wife with a shout. 'I don't wanna hear this shit again, woman!'

Elvis leaps up and rushes to the door. He imagines himself bursting into the yard, to the rescue. He even has his hand on the door handle, ready for action. But which one to save? He knows it should be Mama, but at the moment it's Daddy he feels for. Gladys warms to her theme. Her eyes will be darker than the night sky now.

'Don't you curse at me, Vernon Presley! You think I don't know what you get up to? I guess you forget to mention your wife and child to them *ladies* in the pig-stands. You're as bad as your own daddy! He spent more time with them whores down Goose Hollow than he did in his own home.'

At this insult, Elvis scoots back across the floor and slides beneath his parents' bed, pulling the dusty rug over his body. There is a deadly silence. Nobody should mention JD Presley, who everybody in town knows to be a swaggering, no-good drunkard, in Vernon's presence, let alone make a comparison between father and son.

Elvis knows that his mama usually starts these arguments, and always gives as good as she gets. Once she left Vernon with a bruise on his cheek the size and colour of a plum. But there is no denying his daddy is the stronger of the two, and Mama will come off worse if the argument becomes a physical fight.

There's nothing but silence, for the moment. Elvis imagines the wrinkles in his father's forehead deepening as he shifts from foot to foot. Elvis used to think of his daddy as a lined man. His clothes were scrupulously ironed, his hair carefully combed, but his face was lined even when he wasn't yet thirty, and he seemed to have trouble standing straight. He often made himself smaller by pointing his shoulders towards the floor and complaining of pain in his back. When he did that, Gladys seemed to tower over him, the breadth of her shoulders matching his, and Elvis liked to believe that his mother's sturdy body was bigger and stronger than his daddy's.

Since he's been on the road, though, Vernon has been standing straighter.

His mama starts again.

'You're good for nothing and always have been! To think I used to watch the door for you to come home! I shoulda known by the way you slouched your old self in, always late, always tired, too doggone lazy to lift a finger—'

Elvis focuses on the mattress above. It swells between the springs like something infected. He wishes he could escape to Mayhorn's, but there is no way out while his parents are in the yard.

'Lazy! My mama always said you was a no-good son of a gun, and she was right!'

The pattern just above Elvis's nose is so faded, the roses look like pink stains. There are no thorns, just petals. He lets his vision blur, and wishes his ears could do the same. Why can't you let your hearing go just out of range, like you can let your eyes slide slightly out of focus? He always hears too much. Even now, he's aware of the slow sweep of Dodger's broom on the kitchen floor. *Whoosh, pat. Whoosh, pat.* No doubt she's listening, too.

'Gladys. Enough, now.'

There's a warning in his daddy's voice, but he's not really mad. Not yet. Sometimes his mama will relent, and then she won't get hit. If his daddy can handle this right, they both might come out unscathed. Elvis wills his father to be smart this time. If he can just hang in there without defending himself too much, Gladys will run out of steam.

'Don't you "Gladys" me!'

'Honey, I understand you're mad, but you got to trust me. I ain't been with nobody but you. I couldn't. You know that.'

'You was before.'

'That was one time! It was a mistake. I was drunk. And I'm sorry. You're my only one, Glad.'

'I don't want to hear it.'

It could go either way. If his father continues in this vein, it could end with the two of them making up in bed.

'Glad.'

'I can't stand it, Vernon. I just can't.'

The worst of her anger has passed. Elvis can hear the difference in her voice. The relenting. Her words not exactly softening, but ready to bend to his daddy's will, if he plays it right.

There's a long stretch of quiet. Dodger's broom stops. Then Elvis hears the weeping, and he slides out from beneath the springs and crawls into the chill of his own pallet. He might be able to sleep now, because he is used to the sound of his mother weeping. And weeping is a lot better than bruising.

* * *

Vernon tells a story about their neighbours.

'Don't go saying too much,' Gladys warns.

'Boy's old enough to hear it.'

A week has gone by since their last big row, and they are sitting at the kitchen table with Minnie Mae and Elvis, having finished a good supper of cornbread, greens and pork chops. Vernon brought the meat home with him, saying it would help Elvis to take in the news. Gladys has told her husband that he can break it. Not one iota of this has been her decision, so she won't be the one to tell her son.

'You know old McCrumb,' Vernon says, 'drives that taxicab?'

Elvis nods.

Vernon leans close to him. 'Turns out he killed his wife. In cold blood.'

'Vernon!'

'Elvis wants to hear this, don't you, boy?'

'Sure I do.'

Gladys covers her mouth with a hand.

'I done heard it with my own ears!' Vernon declares. 'The other night. A scream and then a whump, you know? I tell you, it was like God's own wrath coming down.'

'I didn't hear nothing,' says Elvis, sitting up straight.

'You was out. At that nigger church, most likely.'

'You hear this, Mama?'

To hide her face, Gladys stands to clear the plates. 'I coulda heard something . . .'

'Anyways. Then there's this silence – went on real long – a loud sort of silence, wasn't it, Glad?'

'Musta been him dropping something,' says Minnie Mae, joining Gladys at the sink. 'He always was clumsy as an ox.'

'Naw. Wasn't that at all.'

Minnie Mae takes up the dishtowel. In the window, the women's eyes meet. Gladys raises hers to heaven, and her mother-in-law slowly shakes her head.

'You ain't *seen* nothing, though,' Minnie Mae tells her son.

'I tell you what I seen! I seen old McCrumb putting something in a sack in the trunk of his taxicab! Then driving off real quick!'

'Probably his dinner,' says Minnie Mae, in a low voice.

Gladys stifles a laugh.

'In the middle of the night? I tell you, that weren't no dinner. Unless McCrumb makes a habit of eating his wife's head.'

Gladys crashes a bowl onto the drainer. 'Now you going too far!'

'That's what it was, Glad,' Vernon says, evenly. 'I swear on my mother's life.'

'Careful, now,' says Minnie Mae. 'I'm standing right here, and I'm still breathing.'

Elvis's mouth is hanging open. 'Was there blood, Daddy?'

'Some,' says Vernon, going to the icebox for a beer. 'There was some blood.'

He saunters back to the table and pops the bottle open. 'Word round the neighbourhood is, he drove round all day with his wife's head in the trunk. Imagine that! All them folks getting a ride with the head of a murdered woman!'

'They'da smelled it,' says Dodger.

'Not necessarily. Not at that point. Not if it was still fresh.'

Gladys squeezes her dishcloth dry and stares at the grimy suds in the sink.

'Long and the short of it,' says Vernon, taking a swig from the bottle, 'is the police came by this afternoon and hauled McCrumb off.'

'That don't mean he killed his wife,' says Minnie Mae, gently prising the cloth from Gladys's grip and pushing her out of the way so she can finish the dishes.

'But let me ask you this: where in the wide world has Mrs McCrumb gone?'

'Maybe she's visiting her relatives over Pontotoc.'

'You crazy?'

Gladys has had enough. She crosses the room and places a hand over her son's. 'What Daddy's trying to say is, we gotta pack up and leave. It's for the best.'

'I was getting to that—'

'Like Daddy's saying, it ain't safe here,' says Gladys, being careful to keep her tone flat. 'So we gotta leave.'

Elvis stares at her. Something has shifted in his face, and he looks five years old again.

'Yeah,' says Vernon. 'Your mama here's petrified. Done made her all jittery. This neighbourhood's never been the best, but this – well, it's just too bad. So we're moving to the city. Making a fresh start.'

'The city?' asks Elvis.

'That's right, boy! Just picture it: bright lights! Movie theatres bigger than you've ever imagined! We're gonna make our futures!'

'Daddy says there's more work in Memphis. Jobs with prospects,' says Gladys, glancing at Vernon.

'We're moving to *Memphis*?'

'That's right.'

Elvis swallows. 'That's real far—'

'We leave tomorrow night,' says Vernon. 'We've decided, so why wait?'

At this, Elvis jumps from his seat.

Gladys grasps her son's fingers, but he yanks them away.

'No,' he says. 'I just can't!'

'Why not, son?' asks Vernon.

Elvis is clutching at the back of his neck and bending over as if he might vomit.

'Son,' says Gladys, softly. 'We got to go.'

'But you said the police have taken McCrumb.'

'This morning,' says Vernon.

'Then there ain't nothing to be afraid of, is there, Mama? If he's gone, it's all right.'

Gladys looks to the floor.

Vernon spreads his hands on the table. He seems to be considering his skin's every mark and line as he says, 'We gotta go, son. That's all there is to it.'

Her fists itch to upend the table and send the beer, Elvis's glass of milk, even her beloved hen and rooster salt and pepper shakers – a wedding present from the church – flying into her husband's lap. She's aware that Vernon's story is a fiction, and is pretty sure of the real reason they have to leave. He's been driving somewhere every night for the past month, and, most mornings, he smells of the still. After all, when they were first married, Vernon was warned by the police for making moonshine.

'I know what it is,' says Vernon. 'You don't wanna leave that little girl of yours.'

This is enough to bring a stricken look to Elvis's face, though Gladys doesn't think this is necessarily on Magdalene's account. When Elvis is with Magdalene in church, Gladys can see her son watching the girl not for herself, but for her voice. When he sings alone, she knows he's nervous as all get out, but he puts his whole self into the song. When he sings with Magdalene, any fool can see his frustration in the way he holds his shoulders high as Magdalene misses a note. He wouldn't do that, she thinks, if he were truly smitten with this girl. He might see the mistake, but he'd let it go. He'd forgive her trespasses, just as she has Vernon's. Most of them, anyhow.

'She's gonna be mighty impressed you're leaving for Memphis,' says Vernon, drawing his son into his arms. 'Bet she ain't never been there!'

In fact, Magdalene has been, on the same church trip as Elvis and Gladys. Uncle Noah drove them to the city once in his school bus, to visit the Zoological Gardens. When Gladys thinks of Memphis, she thinks of polar bears and tigers and Odell being sick in a bucket, of the big park where the animals were and how that green space was contained by well-kept paths and signs telling you where and where not to go. Perhaps the whole city is as ordered and neat as this, despite what folks say about the low-down, unholy goings-on there.

Vernon holds Elvis at arm's length and says, 'You gonna be a big city boy.'

Gladys cannot sleep that night. As she often does when her own mind keeps her awake, she goes to Elvis's pallet and gazes on her boy. Sometimes the sight of his slumbering body, so warm and at ease, will enable her to relax into sleep.

When she kneels by the side of his bed and peers into his face, his eyes flick open.

Instead of speaking, she simply peels back the sheet and heaves herself in beside him. He nuzzles into her side, and she kisses his damp forehead.

'We can come back,' she whispers, 'to visit.'

'We can come together,' he says.

'We'll do that.'

'I'll drive you.'

'OK, baby.'

'We'll be together.'

'Always.'

'I ain't letting go of you, Mama.'

'I know it, son.'

'There, there.'

'There, there.'

* * *

145

Mr Mayhorn is counting up the takings when Elvis crashes through the door. He looks up for a second, nods, then goes back to his money.

Elvis stands, panting.

'Show don't start for another two hours,' says Mr Mayhorn, cupping his hand at the edge of the counter and scooping coins into it.

'I'm leaving!' Elvis blurts. 'I came to tell you I won't be coming no more. Not ever again.'

Mr Mayhorn drops the coins into a cotton bag and draws the string tight. He rests it on the counter and takes off his eyeglasses to focus on Elvis.

'Sounds serious,' he says.

'We're going to Memphis. Tonight. Daddy decided just yesterday. Mama's real upset. We gotta leave Grandma behind, too – for now, anyway ... And I won't see you or Sam! Or my girl, Magdalene! She's gonna be broken-hearted. I can't believe it, Mr Mayhorn, I just can't.'

Mr Mayhorn lets him run on, then he slaps a hand down, hard. Elvis watches the counter tremble, and almost expects it to let out a note of grief in response.

'Boy,' Mr Mayhorn says, quietly, 'you lucky. You getting out of here. You escaping! You getting free!'

Elvis looks at him, bewildered.

Mr Mayhorn raises his eyes to the ceiling. 'Don't tell me you ain't dreamed of going someplace else.'

Of course he has. So many of the songs he loves speak of hitting the road, cutting loose, going over the rainbow, way out west.

'You want to stay here and do what your daddy does? That it?'

But there's also no place like home. His mama likes to sing that one, sometimes, and she sounds like she means it.

'I just don't wanna leave.'

'Bullshit. You wanna leave so bad I can smell it coming off you. Man can't hide a thing like that.'

'But, Mr Mayhorn, I came to say goodbye, and that I'll miss this place, and you ...'

Mr Mayhorn removes his eyeglasses and wipes a hand over his face. 'Go on, now,' he says. When Elvis doesn't move, Mr Mayhorn crosses the room, places a hand on his shoulder and shoves him gently towards the door. 'Get going. And don't come back.'

At home, Elvis sits on the back step and weeps. Tracing a line in the soil with his shoe, he thinks about his loss, and it seems limitless.

Then he remembers somebody who will be sad to see him go.

He is just about to cycle all the way to Magdalene's when he has an idea. She won't ever forget him if he can make it clear how much he loves her.

Vernon is busy packing up the Plymouth – a recent purchase – and Gladys is washing the dishes when Elvis slips into the bedroom. Clothes and papers are spread across the mattress, and a suitcase lies open on the floor. Peering beneath the bed frame, Elvis is relieved to discover that his mama's shoebox is still there. He reaches in and slides it across the boards. Gladys has shown him the contents of this box many times. Hastily, he opens it and removes the ivory comb that belonged to Doll, the grandmother he never knew, the paste brooch in the shape of a robin with a cut-glass eye and a broken wing, the piece of lace from a great-aunt's wedding dress, the report cards from every year he's been at school, and finally finds what he's looking for: his parents' marriage licence. He shoves the other items back in the box and slides it beneath the bed. Then he pockets the licence, together with a pencil, and makes for the door.

Once he's cycled down the hill, across town and onto the shoulder of the highway, he stops and leans the document on a lamp post. On the back, he does the best he can to copy the official seal of Pontotoc County, and writes, in script he wishes was neater and more suitably cursive, MARRIAGE LICENSE AND CERTIFICATE of *Magdline Morgan* (he has never known her middle name) and *Elvis Aron Presley*. He also writes the date: *September 11th, 1948*.

The sun is getting lower as he crosses the levee, and the insects start to sing in the long grass. He pedals faster. Vernon has told him they will leave after dark because driving at night is the best way to travel. As he cycles, Elvis prepares what he will say to Magdalene. *I got to leave for the city, but I want you to know that I'll always love you, and here's the proof.* He'll hand her the licence and she'll gaze on it, a little puzzled. Then he'll say, *Maybe we'll be married some day, when the time is right.*

He cycles uphill towards East Tupelo, standing on the pedals to gain more momentum. Her eyes will fill with tears but he'll hold her hand and say, *Can you wait for me, Magdalene? Can you be pure and true?* She'll nod, silently, and he'll kiss the top of her head, and then they'll cry together. Or perhaps he won't cry. She might not appreciate that.

He finds her house in darkness. The porch is empty, and there's no truck outside, so he creeps around the back to try to get a look in the windows, but with all the lights out he can't see much. He sits on her porch steps, thinking he'll wait it out. It'll be more romantic this way; she can find him sitting alone in the evening gloom. He curses himself for not having brought his guitar – he could've strummed a sad tune to welcome her home.

The train's whistle tears through the evening and the sky turns deep orange. Lights start to come on in the neighbouring houses. He hopes somebody will come out and spot him waiting patiently, so they can tell Magdalene what she missed, later.

But nobody comes. From the look of the sky Elvis guesses it must be past nine by now, and his mama will be frantic. He stands and takes a last look at Magdalene's house. Perhaps he should post the licence through her door. He could write her a note about his leaving on the bottom. Then he imagines his mama's reaction to her marriage licence going missing, and he slips the paper back into his pocket, picks up his bike, and makes his way down the dirt road. The girl will never know what he did, but it feels good to have done it.

Graceland, January 1958

Pink, white and blue.

In the warm gloom of the kitchen, Gladys has laid three pretty pills on the counter before her. One is pink and no larger than a pinhead, one is a blue capsule that puts her in mind of ammunition, and the other is a thin white disc. The colours would look good on a spring coat of the kind Elvis's girls often wear: light-weight, high-collared, cropped at the waist and of little use against a March wind. Placing each pill on her tongue, she allows herself a moment to taste the dead chalk of the drugs, then takes a swig of beer, closes her eyes, swallows, and manages not to gag. Doctor's orders. She knows the pink pill is for her weight, but exactly which problems the others are supposed to tackle is a little fuzzier in her mind. She hopes they will at least deaden the throb in her ankles.

It is midnight, and the mansion is quiet. Her husband turned in an hour ago; even Minnie Mae's television is silent. And this morning her son left for Hollywood. The army has granted him a deferment until 24 March, leaving him free to work on the New Orleans movie. He says this picture will be better than the others. He has high hopes. The script, every line of which he memorised before leaving, is based on a popular novel, and the songwriters he likes are working on the music.

Perched on her stool, Gladys feels cocooned by the pastel appliances and thick drapes. She undoes the top button of her pink housecoat. The kitchen – low-ceilinged and without a sufficient through draught – has always been the warmest spot in the house, and the only one that's ever felt homely. For the first time since Elvis left, Gladys's body feels, if not at ease, at least fairly comfortable. She has taken her medication, she has poured her beer, and she has sent Daisy home, because she wants to drink in peace while she waits for her boy to call.

Taking another gulp, she thinks, as she often does at this hour, of that night a couple of summers ago when Elvis's pink Cadillac burned up on the highway. She'd been dreaming that Elvis was in a fire before she woke to the phone ringing and his excited voice telling her there'd been an accident but he was just fine; she should've heard the horn as his car went up in smoke, though! It had sounded, he'd said, like a dying cow. Then, as now, she could clearly picture the flames, feel their heat and glare, the way they must have made Elvis shield his eyes as he stood on the ridge, watching his beautiful car burn. Gladys presses her fingers to her lips, worried that horn sound may be the kind of noise she is making now. Sometimes she hardly knows what's coming from her mouth.

Partly to hide her own sounds, and partly from habit, she reaches for the portable record player. Her son keeps several portables in the house, so he can hear what his songs sound like to his fans when they play them in their bedrooms. Gladys runs a hand across the papered ridges of its surface before clicking the clasps open and propping up the lid. Then she twists the knob and lowers the needle.

She'll play it just once.

Her son's voice begins, at once familiar and strange. It's 'Don't Be Cruel'. She has always loved the upbeat rhythm, the way the song is so happy to plead for love, so exuberant in the face of loss. It's been her favourite ever since Elvis recorded it, but these days it never fails to bring a lump to her throat.

To Gladys it feels as though her son has already become a soldier. While he was an entertainer, or even a movie star, it seemed he might still become what she wanted him to be: settled, married, a father. She didn't have much influence, but at least she had some. What influence can she have over a soldier? A soldier is no longer a boy, but a man. A man with a gun, or driving a tank; a man capable of killing; a man who has seen things no woman has witnessed. He will become one of them, now.

She turns down the volume. Her husband is a light sleeper, and will be mad if he knows she has stayed up again, crying. Vernon hates what he calls her goddamn dismals. She hasn't once reminded him of his own intense melancholy all those years ago when he returned from the state penitentiary, although she has come very close.

The sudden pulse of the phone's ring goes through her. She switches the record player off, then picks up the receiver.

'Mama?'

'Baby! You at the Wilshire?'

'Safe and sound. We got the suite.'

'It's a beautiful hotel.'

'It's nice. But it ain't home.'

'How was the journey?'

'Long. Is Anita there, Mama?'

Gladys hesitates. He'd wanted Anita to sleep in his room while he was gone. But this morning, after his family and friends had said goodbye to Elvis at the train station, Anita had headed back to her apartment before Gladys could speak with her.

'Mama? Can you put Anita on?'

'She ain't here, son.'

There's a pause. Over the line, she hears a woman's voice, and a door slamming.

'I told that girl I wanted her home when I called.'

Gladys reaches for her beer. Holding her hand over the receiver, she takes a drink.

'Mama?'

'I'm here.'

'Can you call her, get her over?'

'It's late here, Elvis. You might could try her apartment.'

'Call her in the morning, then. Tell her I want her to stay with you while I'm gone.'

'I think she had some work to do—'

'She says that, but what she gotta do? I don't want you being alone.'

'Daddy's here.'

There's a noise like static, and he disappears for a minute. Gladys can just make out other men's voices, calling his name.

'Baby? You there?' she says.

She hears him say, 'Wait a minute,' and laugh. 'I gotta go, Mama.'

'I miss you, Elvie.'

'I miss you too. I'll call tomorrow, OK? And get Anita to come.'

He hangs up.

Gladys spends a moment listening to the dead line. He's told her nothing. She's waited up, and all she has received are her son's instructions to call his girl. Her heart knocks at her chest, and despite the usual ache in her legs she has an urgent need to move, fast. To go someplace. Anyplace. The doctor always said the diet pills would give her extra energy. Maybe she should use it.

She replaces the receiver, then goes to her bedroom. She slips on her big fur coat and low-heeled pumps, cursing as she discovers the shoes are a little tight on her swollen feet. There's no time to change, though; she must act now if she's going to do this. If she waits, the pain will set a fire in her ankles and she will change her mind.

Holding her breath, she tiptoes to the front door. She pulls back two locks and she's out, standing beneath the glass lantern. Humming Jimmie Rodgers's 'Blue Yodel', she hurries down the steps, into the night.

2: MEMPHIS

THE COURTS: 1949–1953

1949

At three-thirty in the afternoon, Gladys sits down for the first time that day. Miss Richardson from the Housing Authority is coming at four to interview her about Vernon's application for public housing, and she has been working hard to set their room on Poplar Avenue straight. She gazes at the still-stained door, which she spent the best part of an hour rubbing with sugar soap this morning, and sighs. She's washed and ironed the drapes, as well as the old quilt that covers the easy chair, and retrieved her best tablecloth from the trunk. Their pallet bed is leaning against the wall and the bedding is folded neatly. She's polished the window with vinegar and newspaper and has propped it open to air the place. The whole rooming house smells of damp and cigarette butts and blocked drains.

None of them has slept well since moving to Memphis. There are sixteen families in this building, crammed into as many rooms, and the slamming of doors is a constant interruption. After eleven p.m., the cries from the street seem to grow louder and more frantic, and, even now, Gladys can hear the sound of radios from the rooms above and the crying of babies from those below.

She'd heard the stories, of course. Back in Tupelo, Mr Martin, the butcher, regularly told Gladys that Memphis was a wicked city. He was fond of saying that Beale Street made Harlem look like a kindergarten. Gladys had little knowledge of Harlem, but she understood what Mr Martin meant: Memphis was the kind of place where Goose Hollow whores and their customers would be welcome.

Nothing had prepared her, though, for their new neighbourhood of Little Mississippi. There is a smell here that still makes her draw breath. Even in January, she's aware of the aroma of greasy hotplates, automobile fumes and liquor. As they'd driven through the outskirts of town for the first time on that warm September night, she'd taken in the lights of the juke joints, gas stations, cafeterias and car dealerships, and not one of them seemed in any way connected to the other. It was as though these places had sprung up, at random, and nobody cared enough to move or tidy them into some understandable pattern. It was nothing like the Zoological Gardens, after all. To Gladys, Memphis did not look like a city; it looked like a mess. In downtown Tupelo, there was order to the streets and leafy squares, but she couldn't discern any here. As they approached the centre of town, the streets became narrower and the buildings taller and more frequent, but there was the same feeling of things being thrown down, of the city being made up as it went along.

And the lights! Even at one o'clock in the morning, bulbs burned in houses, bars and restaurants. Signs for drive-ins, liquor stores and movie theatres glowed. And everywhere was concrete. Stepping from the car to look up at the large rooming house – from outside, it appeared faintly grand, with a turreted roof and a pillared porch set well back from the road – she was surprised to hear the insects still whirring, and to feel the warm intimacy of the night air. That, at least, was the same.

Every night since they arrived, Gladys has begged Vernon to take her home, and Vernon has accused Gladys of having no faith in his ability to take care of his family. His mother, along with Gladys's sister Clettes, Vester and their kids, will be coming out here soon enough, he keeps saying. Lillian has said she and Charlie want to come. And maybe Gladys's younger sister, Levalle, with little Junior and Gene. She won't be lonesome long! They'll get a better place. His contact in Memphis, who found them this room, has explained it to him: they just have to wait a few months, then the public-housing people will give them an apartment. A brand new place, probably, with low rent and decent neighbours.

Elvis arrives home, and Gladys rises from her chair.

On his first day at Humes High School, he came back within the hour, saying it was too big, there were too many kids; he couldn't even find his homeroom. Despite his tears, Gladys forced herself to march him back, and she has threatened to do so again if he ever tries another trick like that. She figures that he doesn't yet know enough about the city to have the nerve to cut school.

She kisses him on the hair. He looks paler and thinner than ever. 'Miss Richardson's coming any minute,' she says, 'so wash your hands and face good.'

He bends over the basin she's prepared for him. Their bathroom and kitchen are on the ground floor, shared with the rest of the building, but there is a tap by the door, and a hotplate.

'How was school?' she asks.

'Good,' he replies, unconvincingly. He reaches for a graham cracker and she slaps his hand.

'Wait till she comes. I'll get your butch.'

'I can get it.'

He pours himself a glass of milk from the carton on the window ledge and sits at the table to drink.

There's a knock at the door.

Elvis lets her wipe his mouth with a dishtowel, then she pats him on the shoulder and whispers, 'This is it, baby. Do your best, now.'

When Gladys opens the door, a woman younger than her stands with her hand already extended in greeting. She has a flat face and copper-coloured hair, and is carrying a woven shopping bag full of papers.

'Mrs Presley,' she says, clasping Gladys's fingers and giving them a single squeeze. 'I'm Miss Richardson.'

Before Gladys can answer, Miss Richardson is inside the room. Elvis scrambles to his feet.

'Sit down, son,' says Miss Richardson. 'You must be Elvis.'

'Yes, ma'am.'

She stands on the rug, taking a good look around. 'Yes,' she says, nodding. 'I can quite see why you've applied to us, Mrs Presley.'

'Can I take your coat?' asks Gladys.

Miss Richardson eyes the window and says, 'No need. I won't be too long. Is it all right if I sit at the table here and ask you both some questions?'

'Of course,' says Gladys. She pulls at her collar. She's worn her best dress, one with yellow roses embroidered at the breast, and she suddenly realises it might have been better to look more ragged.

'Now,' Mrs Richardson says, once Gladys has taken the chair opposite, 'tell me how long you've lived at this address.'

'About four months. We moved from Mississippi.'

'Oh? Whereabouts?'

'Tupelo.'

'Charming. What made your family come to the city?'

Gladys and Elvis exchange a glance but Gladys doesn't falter. 'My husband wanted better work. He was here during the war, in the munitions factory—'

'He's found it, I hope?'

'Oh, yes, ma'am. But it doesn't pay so good, and it's a little unpredictable.'

'I see. Your husband has stated in his application that he earns fifteen dollars a week. Is that right?'

'I think so, ma'am.'

'And your rent here is thirty-five dollars a month?'

'That's right. Can I offer you a cup of something, Miss Richardson?'

'No, thank you. Is this your only room here, Mrs Presley?'

It's all too brisk for Gladys, who has faced Miss Richardson's kind before. She didn't get Vernon his pardon from Parchman by rushing things and not taking time with folks. It had taken many afternoons, and a whole lot of listening to other people's troubles, to get enough signatures on that petition. She smiles and pats Miss Richardson's forearm, just lightly.

'I hope you won't mind me saying so, but you look like you could eat something, honey. Won't you take a cracker?'

Gladys holds up the plate determinedly.

Miss Richardson's face softens. 'It's very kind of you, Mrs Presley, but I'm fine. Really.'

'We sure appreciate you coming, don't we, Elvis?'

'Yes, Mama.'

'It's my job,' says Miss Richardson. 'How old are you, Elvis?'

'Just turned fourteen, ma'am.'

Miss Richardson leans back and studies his face. Elvis looks down at the tablecloth.

'And what do you think you'll do when you're grown, Elvis?'

Gladys watches her son. During his God-fearing phase, they used to talk, a little, about him becoming a preacher. But she's unsure if Miss Richardson would be impressed by this ambition. Big-city folks can be peculiar about God. Her own preference would be for him to become a businessman of some kind – perhaps running his own store. He loves pretty things as much as she does.

'I'd maybe like to drive a truck, ma'am. My daddy used to do that, back in Tupelo.'

'That's a good, honest job,' says Miss Richardson. 'But maybe if you apply yourself at school you could get yourself a real trade.'

'That would be wonderful, wouldn't it?' says Gladys.

'It must be difficult to get your homework done with just this one room for your whole family, Elvis.'

Elvis nods gravely. Gladys blinks. The thought has never occurred to her before now. He has a table, and a chair, and pencil. Surely that's enough.

'It can be kinda ... distracting,' says Elvis.

Miss Richardson makes a note.

'But Mama helps me,' he adds, reaching over to squeeze her hand. 'She helps me all the time.'

For the first time, Miss Richardson smiles at them both. 'This boy's a credit to you, Mrs Presley,' she says. 'I think I have all the information I need for now.'

Hope rises in Gladys's heart.

1950

It is spring. Elvis's mama rolls in to his bedroom, smiling. Ever since the family got approval for public housing a year ago, and moved to this apartment in Lauderdale Courts, Gladys is often rolling and smiling about the place. Within the large, modern, red-brick complex, they have not only a living room, but also a separate kitchen, two bedrooms and a private bathroom. The biggest bedroom is his, and his alone, and from the window he can watch the other kids playing on the lawn or listen to the adults talking in the apartments below. From this window he can hear all kinds of things. Music snaking from car radios. Couples fighting or making love. Girls giggling about their sweethearts. Young men making deals. More music from the church across the street. The rattle of the streetcar a few blocks over. The honking of horns on the Mississippi riverboats. He can also climb out – he's tried it a couple of times, but so far he hasn't cut out for Beale Street, or the river. He senses the whole of the city is there, just beyond this window.

Gladys likes to tour all the rooms of their apartment, stopping in each one to exclaim at their luck. Every inch of the place is clean and almost brand new. Of all the rooms, Elvis loves the bathroom the best. Not only does it have a shower and a bath, it also has a lock on the door.

'Baby,' she says, holding out her pale arms. He closes his funny paper and goes to her, and is enfolded in her soft steadiness. She kisses the top of his head, right where he's tried to shape his hair so it lifts from his forehead, and he has to stop himself from pulling away to put it right. She smells of grease from Britling's, where she's now working as a waitress, and there's the sweet vinegar of her own sweat, too, which is sometimes more than he can take, although he knows it's not her fault; it's hard work and hot in that place and there's only so much a tiny bottle of lilac cologne can do.

'Elvis,' she says into his hair, 'I want you to come visit Mrs King with me later on. She's doing one of her Stanley Products hostess parties. Your daddy's working and I don't want you here all alone.'

He is fifteen years old. All the other boys he knows are often left alone. But none of them have a mother like his.

'I know it's a trial, baby, all those brushes and polishes and stuff, but that's what the ladies of Lauderdale love, I guess.' She giggles delightedly.

He has no idea what a Stanley Products party is, but all he says is, 'Yes, Mama. Baby's coming with you wherever you go, you know that.'

Mrs King's apartment is on the next floor up. Elvis likes the shapes of the railings on the stairway: diamonds and stars stretched in shiny wrought iron. The whole building smells of laundry and polish and new paint, and the thick linoleum deadens the sound of their footsteps. Coming to Lauderdale was like entering another galaxy. Even Mama said that, in the end, Daddy was right: everything has been better since they moved to Memphis.

There's a mat announcing *Welcome* outside Mrs King's door. Recently it seems that his life has become one long succession of wiping: wiping his feet on the carpet tiles at the Courts' main entranceway, then again on the mat outside his own front door, wiping his hands so they're clean, but remembering not to use his pants because nobody here in Lauderdale wants to know trash.

'Oh,' says Mrs King as she opens the door. 'You've brought your son!'

'Say hello to Mrs King, Elvis.' A firm pressure on his shoulder.

'Hello, Mrs King, ma'am.'

Mrs King studies him as if she cannot quite believe in his existence. 'I'm afraid he won't have any other kids to talk to—'

'I hope it ain't a bother to you, Mrs King. I couldn't leave him home. His daddy's working tonight.'

Mrs King smiles weakly. 'Go right on through, then, the two of you.'

She smells good, like the flower beds that surround the Courts. She's wearing a large skirt covered with some kind of pattern in green, and Elvis can't keep his eyes off it because it looks like somebody has splashed bright paint all over the material by mistake.

Gladys is studying it, too.

Noticing their stares, Mrs King stops in the hallway and twirls. 'Do you like my skirt?' she asks. 'I picked it up downtown. It was on sale. Frank hates it. He says he has a headache just being in the same room as me!'

Elvis watches his mother smooth down the faded yellow roses on her dress. 'It's awful striking,' she says, and suddenly he hates those roses; he hates the way they look so muted, as if they're covered with dust.

Mrs King guides them into the living room.

'All the ladies are here,' she says, gesturing towards each of them in turn: 'Mrs Nolan, Mrs Pratt, Mrs Lankers, Mrs Ericson – do y'all know Mrs Presley?'

The small living room – exactly the same size and shape as his own – is a mess of colour and perfume and creamy arms folded into laps and hair lifted and curled into fascinating shapes. And there is so much lipstick – lipstick the colour of oranges, the colour of sugar mice, the colour of blood.

The ladies nod and lift their painted lips in smiles.

'And she's brought her son along, too – it's Elvis, right?'

'Yes, ma'am.'

'Isn't that ... adorable?'

There's a short silence while all the women get a good look at him. He fixes his eyes on the low table in the centre of the room. Multicoloured washing-up brushes and dishcloths, cookie cutters, plastic food boxes, rubber gloves, and packets of dusters spill across it like treasure. He'd like to plunge his hands in there and touch all those new surfaces.

'Take a seat, please, Mrs Presley,' says Mrs King, 'and help your-self to potato chips.'

Gladys sits on a chair below the window, and Elvis sinks onto the rug at her feet, resting his back on her legs. He is used to the company of women, but there are a lot of females crammed into this room, and many of them are staring right at him. He retrieves the funny paper from his back pocket and tries to read. The Phantom, still his favourite superhero, is swearing once again to devote his life to the destruction of piracy, greed, cruelty and injustice, but Elvis can't lose himself in the colours and danger of the jungle because he's sitting so close to the calves of Mrs Nolan and, damn, they are fine. He notices that her nylons have no wrinkles; it's as if the woman were born wearing stockings. He can't take his eyes from the elegant dip and slide of her ankle as it meets her magnolia-coloured shoe.

His mama nudges his shoulder with her knee. 'Elvis,' she says, 'Mrs King asked if you want an iced tea, honey.'

The way the ankle becomes foot and the foot becomes shoe. The whole thing a pretty mystery.

'Yes, ma'am, I'd appreciate that,' he says, and feels the women's approval. His mama often gives him reports of how the other fam-ilies in the Courts view him: as a nice boy, clean, well mannered, quiet. Unlike in the rooming house on Poplar Avenue, he's heard nobody at Lauderdale call his family hillbillies, cornballs, rubes, rednecks, clodhoppers or hicks. Not, at least, to his face.

After handing round the drinks, Mrs King begins to display her wares. The women examine and exclaim over each item in minute detail, and Elvis admires them too: the sheen and crackle of the cellophane wrapping on the lavender pomander is particularly pleasing to him. As each woman speaks, Elvis imagines their words flowing to the tune of 'You Call Everybody Darlin'', and pictures how they would look singing it. Mrs King is speaking now, and he likes the colour of her lips. Once, when his mama was late coming home from work, he tried her new Coral Rose lipstick. He blushes to think of how good the waxy cream had felt on his mouth, how he'd gazed in his mama's looking glass and seen a stranger there. When he'd opened his mouth to sing with that colour on his face he could've sworn the sound was better; his voice was richer, fuller, lonelier.

'And this little beauty is – well, can anybody guess?' Mrs King is holding up a plastic box in the shape of a butterfly. It has a hook where the head should be, and is punctured with small circular holes.

His mama says, 'Why, it must be a little insect house or some such!'

The ladies laugh, and so does Elvis.

'Nice guess, Mrs Presley, but it's actually a container for mothballs!' Mrs King turns the box around and reveals the clasp.

Elvis wonders what his mama will buy tonight. His daddy has already told her that she can't spend anything; they haven't money to waste on boxes and brushes and towels, even though times are better. She'd kissed his cheek and said, 'It ain't about the buying, Vernon.' But Elvis knows that it is, and that his mama will come away with at least one item, which she will hide for a while in a drawer before bringing it out and telling Vernon that it's old. Whatever it is, it will be enough to keep her smiling well into the next day.

Mrs King is passing around the order form along with a compli-mentary Stanley Products pen. 'Ladies,' she says, 'these prices are one time only, but don't even touch your pocketbooks right now. Just order whatever you want, and if you change your mind when it comes next week, well, that's absolutely all right. I won't ask for a dime.'

The room hushes as the women tick boxes and print their names and addresses. His mama straightens the paper on her lap and clicks the pen's nib up and down. He daren't turn to look at her; to do so would give the game away entirely.

He feels, rather than hears, her sigh, and it's the kind he knows well: resigned, gentle. Her lap shakes a little as she writes her name.

'I'm gonna get me the pink pitcher and matching cups,' she says, to no one in particular.

He edges closer to her, resting his head on her knee to let her know that he has witnessed this transgression but he understands, and will not tell. She touches his head in recognition of their pact.

* * *

When Betty McMahon appears, Elvis is sitting on the front steps of the Courts with his new friends, Buzzy and Paul, who also live in his apartment block and attend Humes High School. It is a good moment to see Betty, Elvis thinks, because it is evening. Cardinals flit and whoop among the young cherry trees which edge the Courts' square lawn. The dusk settles around them and in the half-light he can think about singing. Usually he would sit here alone, picking out a sweet, sad tune to sing softly to himself. Tonight, though, he's asked Buzzy and Paul to listen, and they're already bored with having to be quiet as Elvis readies himself, and having to pretend not to notice when he misses a note and starts over.

Most importantly, the cool darkness masks the acne which first appeared on his face a few weeks ago. His hands are often feeling for those sore little lumps beneath the skin that signify the start of another pustule. His fingers check the progress of each one as they gather around his chin and nose, leaving a spray of marks. He touches his jaw and feels a tender place. It will be red in the morning, but in this light it's probably not so bad.

'Hey, Betty,' Buzzy says, and she stops on the steps beside them. Looking down at her feet, she turns one ankle this way and that, pointing her toes first at Elvis, then at Buzzy. Betty seems always to be moving, even when she's still. She's spoken to Gladys – sometimes they sit and talk animatedly on the lawn chairs her parents set up outside the Courts – but never directly to Elvis.

Both Buzzy and Paul are better than Elvis at talking to girls. Buzzy is already broad-chested and has the beginnings of a moustache. Paul is skinny and blonde, but taller than Elvis. Buzzy and Paul are also better at football, fighting, talking about the girls they're going to go with and even, recently, the girls they have been with. Buzzy says he's kissed Betty McMahon and she let him cup her titties. That's the word he used, 'cup'. As if he were a container for her. Elvis thinks of Buzzy and Betty and wants to hurt them both for not including him in this act of containment. He's never properly kissed a girl – he'd always got Magdalene's cheek, never her lips – but he has imagined kissing Betty many times.

'Hi,' Betty says, looking at none of them in particular. She tucks her hair, which is the colour of sand on the kind of beaches he's only dreamed about, behind her ear. Almost immediately, it slides back to touch the side of her face.

'I'm going up to the Incurables tomorrow, Betty, if you wanna come?' says Buzzy.

Her eyes widen. 'You're going *where*?'

'Up to the Home for Incurables on McLemore.'

'Is that lepers and stuff?' She pulls a disgusted face, but it doesn't wholly convince Elvis. It's the kind of face a girl might pull when talking about roaches. The kind of face she's expected to pull.

'Sounds scary,' she says.

'It ain't scary, Betty.' Buzzy narrows his eyes and strokes his baby moustache. 'Sad is what it is. Matter of fact I go up there quite a bit, you know, what with my charity work with the Oddfellows.'

'That's real caring of you, Buzzy, but I'm kinda busy tomorrow.' Paul sniggers.

Buzzy gives a theatrical shrug. 'Just doing my bit. Paying my dues.'

'You going too, Elvis?' Betty turns towards him suddenly, her skirt swinging. The light coming from the recess behind them shines on her legs, making her ankle socks appear luminous.

Buzzy and Paul are looking at him too. Elvis shifts his guitar and mumbles, 'Ain't reckoned on it.'

'Know what I reckon?' says Betty, a little smile dimpling her cheeks. 'I reckon them old Incurables would just love to hear you sing.'

This makes Buzzy burst out laughing.

Betty fixes Elvis with a stare. 'I'm serious. I've heard your singing and it's real nice.'

He ducks his head, wishing he could stop smiling.

'I heard you,' Betty continues, 'even though you sing so low the crickets drown you out.'

Buzzy laughs again, mirthlessly this time, then makes a grab for the girl's hand. 'Come on, Betty,' he says, putting on his Clark Gable voice. 'Sit beside me here so we can discuss our future together.'

She doesn't move.

'You look real pretty tonight,' Buzzy says, and Betty's face softens.

'Elvis, can't you control your friend?' she says, freeing her hand.

'Oh, Presley's a nice boy,' says Buzzy, 'but he can't control nobody. He can't even control his own face.'

'Come on, now ...' Paul says. They often tease Elvis about his shyness, but until now it's been just between the three of them.

'One time,' Buzzy continues, 'his mama was calling on him, you know, in that way she does? Sort of like, "Elvie, *baby* ..."' Betty grins, a little bit. 'And we all joined in, and poor old Presley – his lip just about dropped to the ground.'

Elvis looks at Betty, hoping the darkness is hiding the worst of his acne.

'Picked it right up, though,' he says.

'Say what?' asks Betty.

'My lip,' he says. 'I picked it right up off the ground.'

She laughs then, and it's surprisingly low and belly-like, and it makes him want to take her in his arms.

'Well,' she says, moving on up the steps, 'see you, boys.'

The next day, straight after school, Elvis boards the Oddfellows' bus with Buzzy and Paul. As they travel through town, he hardly notices the department stores, movie theatres and cafeterias. Instead, he sits on his hands and thinks about Betty and that movement she makes, tucking her hair behind her ear only for it to slide back again. Having learned all about love from Eddy Arnold, Kay Starr and Bing Crosby, he longs to experience for himself that yearning for another, special human being, and he's decided that human being should now be Betty McMahon. Magdalene Morgan was, he tells himself, somebody special, but she was not special like Betty. All night he relived the moment when Betty said, *I've heard your singing*. She has his voice in her head! She must have heard him sing 'My Happiness' in the dusk of the Courts. Was she alone then? He hopes so. Maybe she was sitting at her window, a hand in her beach-coloured hair. Or maybe his song made her stop whatever she was doing – reading her romance novel or fighting with her sister – and pause, take a breath, and wonder, *Who is this, singing so soft and low and tender?*

His mama has said it's a fine thing, going to the Home for Incurables. Elvis is more than a little worried, though, that he'll catch something, or that the sadness of the place will be unbearable. Gladys has warned him that, though they are not contagious, the Incurables might look scary. He imagines himself telling Betty about it, afterwards: 'Such poor folks, without hope,' he'll say, and perhaps she'll squeeze his hand.

The Home for Incurables is in a large old house; they spot its turret from the end of the street. The porch is pristine white, the drive long and curved. The bus slows to a halt and everybody goes quiet. As they disembark, the boys stop chattering and laughing and let the elder Oddfellows lead the way to the door. They are a small group, about ten in all. Elvis, Buzzy and Paul hang back and are the last to step inside.

Once he's over the threshold, Elvis's instinct is to turn around and get right back on the bus. It's not the look of the place. It's grand, opulent, even: there are thick carpets, an antique clock ticking louder than his heart, a sweeping oak staircase of the kind Bette Davis might descend. There's only the occasional, muted sound of somebody coughing. But there is a smell. A greenish, antiseptic odour fills the air, making him think of the nurse in the school medical room, stainless-steel kidney dish to hand and bony fingers prodding his stomach for signs of some terrible inner disease.

A woman who has introduced herself only as 'the matron' is leading them down a corridor. Her starched skirt stands proud of her knees like a pegged tent as she shows them into a room with the word *Solarium* stuck on the door. High-backed chairs are arranged before the long windows, and in the chairs are the Incurables themselves. The bright heat of the place sets Elvis sweating. He cannot look at any of these people, and fears he'll puke if he has to breathe that smell for a minute longer.

Paul says, 'You OK? You don't look so good.'

Elvis says nothing. Somebody is coughing again, more urgently.

Paul thrusts a tray of milk and cookies at Elvis. 'We got to hand these round.'

Elvis nods, and his feet move across the carpet. In the first chair is a boy, younger than him, with yellow skin and patchy hair. He refuses a cookie and Elvis, relieved, is about to move on when the boy grasps the arms of the chair, displaying the flaking skin on his knuckles, and asks, 'Can you play that thing?' so loudly that everyone in the room turns to look.

Elvis had almost forgotten about the guitar slung across his back. He still doesn't play so well, but lately he's started taking it not just to school but everywhere he goes, even though he has yet to admit that he wants people to listen, that this is the reason he has it on him at all times. Performing is still more pain than pleasure for him. He's been singing before an audience in church for years now, but in any other setting he can get seriously spooked. At his cousin's party he'd insisted Aunt Lillian – whose family have recently made the move to Memphis – turn off all the lights before he would sing.

'Cat got your tongue? Can you play guitar, or what?' the boy asks.

'He always carries that old thing around,' says Buzzy who, Elvis now notices, is sitting next to the prettiest Incurable in the room. 'He's kinda shy about playing it. He ain't bad, though. Not *good*, but not bad.'

An old man seated near the window, legs wrapped in plaid blankets, begins to moan softly. Elvis throws a look at the matron, who is standing by the door. She nods. 'Sing something for us, son. I think we'd all appreciate that.'

Here there are no lights to turn off. There is only the sun, flooding the air around him, making his eyes water. He wipes the sweat from his brow, clears his throat, laughs a little, hangs his head. And everyone is still looking at him, waiting.

Jesse, can you see me now?

The old habit of talking silently to Jesse comes back, completely unbidden. It's a shock, and a relief.

'Sing, then!' demands the boy.

Old dead brother, where have you been?

The boy rises from his chair and turns to face the other Incurables. 'He can't play,' he sneers. 'I can play one of them things. Who wants to hear *me* play?'

'Lee,' the matron warns. 'We've all heard you play, and you're real good. Everybody knows it. Sit down.'

Reckon I oughta hit him, Jesse? One push and he'd be over.

Lee sits, and gives Elvis a defiant stare. Buzzy begins whispering to the pretty Incurable, and Paul starts the rounds with the cookies once more. But Elvis can't let the moment slide. He clears his throat.

'Might I sing right now, ma'am?' he asks the matron.

'Only if you want to,' she says, smiling.

'Oh, *now* he's gonna sing!' Lee says.

Watch me, Jesse.

So Elvis swings his guitar to his front and takes hold of its neck. Then he closes his eyes and begins to strum. The man in the blankets moans louder as Elvis begins in on 'My Happiness', the song he's most comfortable with. He gets it wrong, though, and has to start over.

Are you with me?

He fears his body might melt, here in the solarium with ten pairs of Incurable eyes upon him. His fingers feel like rubber and he has little control over the chords, yet he carries on, because, despite everything, the room is listening. He can feel them listening, all of them. Even Buzzy has stopped chewing on his cookie. Elvis dares to open his eyes but cannot look at their faces yet, only at the picture on the wall of wheat fields, the clouds behind them yellow and splitting. He focuses on the edge of the largest cloud and keeps singing. His voice is not as good as he wants it to be. It doesn't vibrate with sadness or swoop with longing. Sometimes, when he's singing on his own in the darkness, he feels his voice beginning to do both those things. It's like it lifts from his body and goes someplace else.

He gets through the song. Nobody moves, smiles, or claps. He wonders how he can escape the room without anybody noticing.

Then he hears the matron's voice. 'Young man, that was real pretty. Sing us another.'

And so he does as she asks. He sings the same song again, and this time he lets his eyes rest for a few moments on Lee, who cannot look back at him, and then on the pretty girl next to Buzzy, who cannot take her eyes from him.

Back at the Courts, his mama asks him to go to the laundry room to check if the wash is done.

He likes it down here; it's warm and hushed, it smells good, and it feels hidden. He makes a mental note that it would be good to come here at night, to sit alone among the pressing irons and airing racks, the washtubs and spin dryers, and practise singing.

Several machines are humming. He watches the top of a washtub as it vibrates and steams. Together the water and the motor make a regular *slosh-thud-slosh-tick-tick-slosh-thud-slosh* rhythm. Shifting his focus to his own reflection in the shining metal front of the machine, he puts down the basket and tries to replicate the way he stood as he sang in the Home for Incurables. He thinks he had his right foot forward, and maybe rocked a little on his heels.

'Hi, Elvis Presley.'

Betty McMahon is standing in the doorway, cradling a plastic basket similar to his. She walks over to a tub and places her laundry on the floor. She takes her time, swaying her hips as she moves.

'Let me help you with that,' he says.

'Thanks, but I oughta take care of my own dirty clothes, I reckon,' she says, bundling items into the machine.

Elvis laughs, too loud. He's about to turn away and hide his embarrassment by checking his own laundry when she says, 'So did you go sing to them Incurables?'

'Uh-huh.'

'You did?' Betty turns to face him, her eyes alight. 'How was it?'

'It was a real old place, but the patients didn't look too sick, and there was this smell—'

'I meant, how did the singing go?'

'Oh!' He laughs again. 'They liked me, Betty. They really liked me.'

She pours out a cupful of detergent, tips it into the drum, slams the lid, then sets the dial. 'Well, sure they did.'

A great churning noise starts up as the machine gets going, and she has to raise her voice. 'I knew they would.'

Leaning on the machine, she looks him over. It suddenly strikes him that if he can be that person who sang this afternoon, he can be a person who kisses Betty McMahon.

'They really liked me!' he repeats.

She shrugs. 'That's because you sing nice.'

From the way she studies his face – as if there is something about him that she finds both amusing and sweet – he senses he can move closer to her now.

He walks to where she is and leans next to her. The washtub's vibrations run along his spine.

'I like your hair,' he says.

'Say what?' she asks, tipping her head towards him.

There she is, so close that he can smell apple shampoo.

When he puts his mouth next to her ear, she doesn't draw back.

'I said, I'd like to kiss you,' he whispers.

She looks at him hard. Then she places a hand on his shoulder and pulls him in.

It is a short, dry kiss, but to Elvis it seems to make everything stop, apart from the rhythm of the laundry as it tumbles from side to side in the drum.

1952

He spends his summer vacation doing four things: working at Loew's State movie theater as an usher (he loves the uniform), kissing Betty in the laundry room (he wouldn't say they're *dating*, even though they've stolen the occasional kiss over the last two years), trying to persuade Gladys that he should quit Humes High, and growing his hair.

On Wednesday – his first day back at school – nobody notices his hair, and Gladys is still insistent on him getting his High School Diploma. And so on Thursday morning, as he stands studying his reflection in the bathroom mirror, Elvis decides to make a change. If nothing else, *he* is going to be different. His hair is long enough, now, to style into a pompadour, like Tony Curtis wears. He applies a good wodge of Vaseline to the sides of his head and drags his comb through the goo, slicking it back. It stays in place well enough, and shows off his sideburns, which have also grown over the summer. Then he tries to pile what's left on the top, curling it with his fingers. But his hair is fine, and won't do anything but flop, so he shakes a few drops of Fitch's rose hair oil onto his palm and tries again. He manages a wave of sorts, and while it's not long enough to hang in his eyes, it is longer than any other boy's at Humes. He isn't entirely happy with the result, but it's better than before.

As he's leaving the apartment, Gladys stops him.

'Don't forget your lunch money,' she says, holding out fifty cents.

'That's OK,' he says, patting his pocket. 'I got it.' Working at Loew's, he has his own money.

She grabs his shoulders and pulls him close so she can examine his hair.

'What you done here?' she asks, peering all around his head.

He ducks away from her. 'Just trying something out,' he says.

She steps back and folds her arms. 'It looks different,' she says. 'If different's what you want.'

'I kinda had Tony Curtis in mind.'

Gladys snorts. 'You and a hundred thousand girls.'

He reaches past her for the door.

'Come over here.' She holds her arms open, and Elvis relents, settling himself in the familiar space between them.

'Mama's so proud of you,' she whispers. 'You gonna to be the first in this family to finish high school.'

She releases him, looks his hair over again and says, 'I could put a permanent on there when you're home. Give it some *whump*. I got a home kit somewhere.'

He thinks this sounds like a good idea.

All morning, Elvis's stomach fizzes with something between fear and excitement. He meets Buzzy and Paul, and they look at his hair quizzically, but don't say anything about it. He's decided, anyway, that one of the things that should be different about Senior Year is the company he keeps. Buzzy and Paul are fun but, he thinks, pretty ordinary. And they don't care about music in the way he does. When he starts talking about the latest record he's heard on WDIA, they look bored.

By lunchtime, Elvis has waited so long for somebody to say something about his hairstyle, that he begins to wonder if it isn't actually that noticeable. He heads for the bathroom, because he doesn't want to spend his lunch money. He wants to save every cent for records, and perhaps even a new shirt. With all the hours he's put in at Loew's he might even be able to afford one he's seen in the window at Lansky's Tailors, so long as he can get credit.

As he pushes open the greasy door, a wall of cigarette smoke sets his eyes watering. It billows over the tops of the stalls and obscures the mirror – not that he could get close to it, with all the other boys crowded around. He produces his comb from his pocket and becomes aware of them nudging each other as they watch him in the glass. Every one of them sports a fierce crew cut. The word *faggot* is whispered. He manages to ignore it, but his hand shakes a little as he tries to sculpt his pompadour.

Jerry Bryson, who is famous for going all the way with the leggiest girl in the nearby Catholic school, calls out, 'How about I give you a haircut, Presley?'

The other boys step towards him, hemming him close to the basins. Then there's the sound of flushing, and they all look towards the end stall. Red West, a star football player who is known for his bright orange hair and his willingness to take on anybody in a fight, emerges. Elvis lets out a small whimper. If Red joins in, he may as well say his prayers.

'We're gonna give Presley here a haircut,' Jerry says to Red, 'seeing's how he forgot to get one for himself.'

Red concentrates on washing his hands, tipping up the chrome soap dispenser and cursing softly when nothing comes out. 'Why would you do that?' he asks.

'Just take a look at it!' says Jerry.

Red's pale face is like a paving stone: flat, white, speckled with brown dabs of colour. Even his eyes are pale, framed with light lashes that give him an unreadable, slightly lizard-like appearance. He glances at Elvis then turns to Jerry.

'You do that, you got to cut mine, too.' He keeps his voice low and his hands in his pockets. Such cool menace reminds Elvis of his grandpa JD. 'And then I'd kill you dead.'

Jerry holds up his hands. 'It was just a joke,' he says.

'Get out,' says Red, nodding towards the door.

Jerry manages an unconvincing grin before hurrying off, followed by the others.

When they've gone, Elvis finds himself leaning over, grasping his knees with his hands and taking big gulps of air.

Red clicks his tongue. 'You asked for that. Your hair is weird, man!'

Elvis manages to straighten up. 'I was going for a Tony Curtis kinda thing. I didn't know it would upset those guys so bad.'

At this, Red looks interested. 'You seen *The Prince Who Was a Thief*?'

''Bout fifteen times.'

Red gives a short laugh.

'I can get you in Loew's State, for nothing,' says Elvis. 'I work there.'

'You from Lauderdale, ain't you?'

This is the first time somebody from Humes High hasn't accused him of coming from the country.

'Yeah.'

'That's pretty close to me.'

Elvis nods. Everyone knows that Red is from Hurt Village, which has a reputation for being the toughest housing project in Memphis.

'OK, so. See you around,' says Red, opening the door.

'Wait,' says Elvis. 'I oughta thank you.'

'Damn right.'

'Thank you, man. Really. And I wanna do something for you, in return.'

Red shakes his head, then seems to change his mind. 'You like music, don't you?' he says. 'I seen you with your guitar. And I heard you sing pretty good.'

Elvis nods.

'Wanna come to the Midnight Ramble with me tonight?'

The Midnight Ramble at the Palace on Beale is where white folks go to hear black musicians and singers. It's also where white men go to see black girls do shake-dances of all kinds. Elvis has heard plenty about it, but has only fantasised about going there.

'Hell, yeah,' he says, unsure of how he'll square it with his mama.

'OK, then,' says Red. 'Meet you at the corner of Winchester and North Main, round ten.'

* * *

Since she's started work as a nurse's aide at St Joseph's Hospital, Gladys's feet are sore every night. She spends much of her day mopping blood from floors, cleaning up vomit, emptying bedpans and changing soiled sheets, but she'll tell anybody who'll listen that she loves her job. Doesn't she have the cutest pea-green uniform, complete with little white cap? And while the doctors rarely look her way, the nurses are mighty appreciative of her work. The St Joseph's building puts Gladys in mind of a high-class hotel, with its rust-coloured towers and pointed windows, its elaborate carved doors and potted palms in the sun room.

It's half past four and she's with her last patient of the day, Mr Bertleman, who is recovering from pleurisy. As one of the wealthier patients, he has his own room on the fifth floor. Gladys has been washing and dressing Mr Bertleman for the last two weeks, and has come to enjoy his company. He tells her long stories of his family, who hail from Central Gardens, and have connections to Boss Crump himself.

He's well enough to sit in the chair by the window, which is where Gladys is combing his receding hair. She takes her time, being careful not to catch his ears with the sharp ends of the plastic teeth. Pausing to clean the comb, she glances out of the window and stops still.

The most astonishing car is pulling up right outside. Vernon and Elvis cannot walk down the street without remarking upon the make, model, engine or year of some vehicle or other, but Gladys has never been particularly interested in such things. This car, though, is different. It is the palest pink, and glows like a pearl in the soft September sunshine. She almost drops her comb as she watches it park up, intent on discovering who will climb out of such a vehicle.

'What are you gawping at?' asks Mr Bertleman, rising from his chair. He clutches the sill.

'Just a car,' says Gladys, 'you oughta sit down, Mr Bertleman.'

He lets out a soft whistle. 'That's not just a car. That's a Cadillac. Series Sixty-two Fleetwood.'

'I ain't never seen a car that colour before.'

'Must be a customised model,' says Mr Bertleman. 'Folks who know no better are always making a ham-fisted job of these things.'

'Ain't it the prettiest thing?' says Gladys.

The driver door opens and out steps a woman, not young, but slim and expensive-looking, wearing a cream outfit which matches the shade of the tyres.

'Will you look at that,' says Mr Bertleman. 'The lady drives herself!'

He starts to cough, doubling over with the effort, but it takes Gladys a moment to tear her eyes from the car and suggest he should get back to bed.

When he's reclined on the pillows, she takes up the comb again. She cannot stop thinking of the car, though, and keeps glancing at the window.

Mr Bertleman says, 'Gladys, last night I nearly threw myself clean out of that window you keep ogling.'

She lays the comb on the nightstand.

'I thought about it,' he says, shaking his head. 'I pondered, long and hard.'

'But you're all well now, honey,' she says, plumping up Mr Bertleman's pillows, not looking into his face. 'You can go home tomorrow.'

'That's just the problem.' He grasps her hand. 'I can't face it, Gladys. That's the truth.'

'Come on, now,' she says, squeezing his fingers. 'You gonna go home and see your family.'

'Gladys,' he says. 'Please. Listen to me.'

She smooths down her uniform and finally looks him in the face. His cheeks are thin, and she can see the tiny blue veins threaded around his nostrils.

'I'm no good to them!' He lets out a moan that Gladys can only consider childish. It's the kind of sound Elvis used to make as a very young boy whenever she refused him something in a store.

She sits on the edge of the bed. 'Why you talking this way, Mr Bertleman?'

'I can tell you, can't I?' he asks. 'I feel sure you'll understand. You're a country woman.'

Gladys isn't certain what this has to do with anything, but she answers, 'Yes, sir, and proud of it.'

He squeezes his eyes shut. 'I been with the whores down on Beale, more times than I care to recall.'

Gladys draws in her breath. 'The Lord forgives us, if we truly repent.'

'My wife won't, though. She doesn't understand it. But you do, don't you, Gladys? You know that men have needs. I can tell just by looking at you.'

Gladys stares at him, unable to quite take in what he's saying.

'And those women down there ... it's an awful temptation to any man, so I figure it's better to go there than betray my wife with another white woman.'

After a moment, Gladys dares to say, very quietly, 'Women have needs too, Mr Bertleman.'

She thinks of her own passion for the young Vernon. Back then, he'd often said she was too much, and she'd known it was true. With him, she was too much. She clung to his arm wherever they went, kissed him right in front of whoever was watching, wanted everyone to know that handsome Vernon Presley was hers. But that kind of love cannot last, and has not been part of her life for many years.

'Not like men do,' he says.

Gladys rises from the bed. 'You just gotta show your wife you're real sorry.'

Vernon said he was sorry, when she found out about the woman on the road back when he drove a truck in East Tupelo, and she'd mouthed the words of forgiveness. Since they moved to Memphis, she has learned that it's better to turn a blind eye to any evidence of his betrayals. It's not that she wants to let him off the hook. It's that she wants to spare herself the pain.

Turning to face Mr Bertleman, she places a hand on his bony shoulder and pushes down harder than she should. 'You take care, now,' she says, smiling the best she can.

When she steps out onto the street, the Cadillac has gone.

Trying to forget Mr Bertleman's words, she slips into the drugstore on her way home and buys the most expensive home-permanent kit on the shelf. She also promises herself a beer once she's home, if Elvis isn't already there. Her son disapproves of alcohol, having been brought up Assembly of God and witnessing the way it's made his granddaddy JD mean and no good. But since Elvis has been working at Loew's and staying out late, Gladys has been accompanying Vernon to bars, despite her previous distaste for drinking. At first, Vernon was reluctant to take her, saying she should go to church instead, even though his own churchgoing days were behind him. When they first moved to Memphis, Gladys had tried their neighbourhood Pentecostal, but it just wasn't the same as back home, so her attendance dwindled to Sunday-morning services with Elvis. Which left a lot of her evenings empty and lonesome.

Once she'd convinced Vernon to let her join him at the bar, he'd insisted that she at least take a real drink. Now Gladys looks forward to her first beer of the day. The fuzzy kind of lightness it brings is a totally new experience for her. With a few drinks inside her, she doesn't have to think of what Vernon is up to when he stays out all night, or ponder upon her son's happiness. All she has to think about is whether to drink another beer.

On reaching her apartment, she hears music and realises Elvis is already home. He has his own radio in his bedroom now, and as soon as she slams the front door the volume is reduced. He doesn't appear, but she's glad. Her head feels tight after her hot walk along Winchester; there's grit in her eyes and her feet are sore, but before removing her shoes and pantyhose and splashing her face with water she wants to hide the kit in her bedroom.

When she's done so, she knocks on Elvis's door, and enters without waiting for a response.

He's sitting on the sill, looking out at the parched grass, listening to some mournful song. Probably on WDIA, the coloured station.

'How was school, son?' she asks.

'Fine, Mama,' he says, smiling faintly.

'Bet it feels good, being a Senior and all.'

'Uh-huh.'

'Supper in an hour,' she says, backing out.

'I been thinking, can you do that thing to my hair?'

She smiles to herself. 'Sure,' she says, 'if I can find the kit ...'

Gladys trots to her own room, where she spends a few minutes opening and closing drawers so that he'll think she's having to hunt. She finds her basket of rollers, then removes the kit from the paper sack and picks off the price tag.

'You'd better come in here, baby. It can get a little messy,' she calls, dragging a chair from the kitchen to the bathroom. She places it in front of the sink. 'And fetch us both a cool drink,' she instructs. 'You can leave the radio on, if you want.'

He comes in with two bottles of Pepsi and an enamel bowl full of cold water for her feet.

'What would I do without you, baby?' she asks, sitting on the rim of the tub and plunging her feet into the bowl. They both take a long drink. Then Elvis reaches for the box.

'Lilt,' he reads. '*New Miracle Mist!*' He grins. 'Sounds pretty good.' He turns the box over. The woman on the back looks like Rita Hayworth. 'I don't wanna look like that,' he says, 'though I understand why she would.'

'You just need to sit and relax,' she says, removing her feet from the bowl. 'I'll do the rest.'

'I only want the bit on the top done, where it's long. I don't want it curly all over, like some piccaninny doll.'

Standing behind the chair, she surveys him in the mirror. Despite his acne, Gladys can clearly see her son has grown into a fine-looking young man. He's like Vernon was at seventeen, but she notes with pleasure that Elvis also has something of her own darkly handsome daddy about him.

She runs her fingers through his sticky hair. 'Got a whole heap of mess in it, ain't it?'

'I guess it can't hurt ... can it?' he says.

Ignoring him, she unscrews the bottle of lotion, and the heavy scent of ammonia fills the room.

'Damn, Mama!' Elvis clamps his hand over his nose. 'What is that stuff?'

'Don't curse.' Gladys reads the side of the bottle. '*Cream oil cold wave lotion ... contains ammonium thi ...* something. I can't read that word.' She hands the box to him.

'Thio–gly–colate,' he reads.

'Now ain't you glad you stayed on at school?'

She snaps on the pink rubber gloves and gets to work, gathering up a small section of hair with her comb before squeezing on a blob of lotion, combing it through, winding it onto the roller and securing it with a rubber band.

'Ow!'

'You gotta be a man about this,' warns Gladys.

She works her way around his scalp, combing, lotioning, winding.

'You think I oughta dye it black?' Elvis asks, studying his reflection. 'All the best-looking actors have dark hair. Valentino. Robert Mitchum. Tony Curtis.'

At the sound of the key in the lock, they exchange a glance.

'Thought he was working late,' says Elvis.

'What's that goddamned stink?' shouts Vernon.

Elvis rises from his chair, but Gladys pushes him down.

'Daddy can't see me like this,' he hisses.

'Too late,' says Gladys. Then she calls out, 'We're in the bathroom!'

They are both still for a minute, listening to Vernon huffing and puffing, removing his shoes in the living room, turning off the radio, and opening the refrigerator.

When he leans on the door frame, dangling his beer bottle from one hand, he's quiet for a while. Elvis keeps his eyes on the floor tiles.

'I'm helping Elvis with his hair,' says Gladys.

'I see that,' says Vernon.

'How was work?' she asks. 'No overtime today?'

'Didn't need me.'

She picks up another roller. 'That's a shame. You missed all last week.'

'I was sick. And I'm just about fit to die in this heat. Don't know how much longer I can keep hauling goddamn paint cans.'

His complaints about his back have increased since he took the job at United Paint two years ago.

'Why don't you rest up in the living room? Put the fan on.'

'Can a man expect supper round here any time soon? Or is this here beauty parlour keeping you too busy?'

She snaps the roller into place. 'There's some cold chicken in the refrigerator.'

He grunts but doesn't move from the doorway.

'You know,' says Gladys, brightly, 'I saw the most adorable automobile today. Y'all would've gone crazy for it.'

'Ain't like you to notice such a thing,' says Vernon.

'It was a Cadillac. Series Sixty-two Fleetwood.'

Elvis says, 'How do you know that, Mama?'

'Mr Bertleman at the hospital told me. And it was pink as a rose.'

Vernon sniggers. 'A rose? How can a car look like a flower?'

'Something about it made me think of them wild ones we used to have at home.'

She twists the last roller into place. Elvis looks so strange with the top of his head covered in plastic that she has to stifle a giggle. 'You're done!' she says, peeling off her gloves and throwing them into the sink.

'Talking of flowers,' says Vernon, sauntering across to his son and staring at his reflection in the mirror, 'ain't you got nothing to say for yourself about all this ... *women's* stuff?'

'Now don't get mad, Vernon,' warns Gladys. 'Won't do a man in your condition no good.'

'I ain't never seen nothing like it! The girls won't like a boy who gives himself a permanent wave.'

Elvis laughs. 'What do you know about girls, Daddy?'

'Enough,' says Gladys, in a low voice.

Vernon ignores this. 'All the Presley men are handsome, and Lord knows you ain't no different. But not one of them would've given a thing like this a second's thought.'

'What harm can it do?' asks Gladys.

'It's vanity, Glad. Worse than that.'

'Maybe I just wanna look like you, Daddy,' says Elvis.

Vernon grins. 'You can dream, son,' he says, running a hand through his own thatch.

'You got great hair,' says Elvis.

'Just don't let nobody else know about this,' sighs Vernon. 'That's my advice.'

When he's gone, Elvis whispers, 'I'll buy you one of them cars, Mama.'

'You will?'

'Uh-huh. Just as soon as I've made my fortune.'

It's been a while since they had one of these fantastical conversations. This is the first time since they moved to Memphis that she can recall him saying such things.

'I'd love that, son,' says Gladys, sitting on the edge of the tub to finish her Pepsi. 'But it'd be wasted on me. I can't drive.'

'You're forgetting. I can hire somebody to drive it for you.'

Gladys imagines herself sitting in the back, watching the high collar of a coloured man in a cap.

'I'd like to sit up front while *you* drive,' she says.

'Sure,' he says. 'Long as you don't keep griping about my speed.'

She kisses him on the cheek, and he grabs her hand and holds it tight.

'Thank you, Mama,' he says.

She smiles. 'Now, I gotta fix supper, and you gotta do the impossible, Elvie. You gotta sit still for an hour.'

'An *hour*?'

She laughs. 'It needs to develop. And then we gotta neutralise you ... but that don't take nearly so long.'

As she's leaving the room, he says, 'How much do I owe you, Mama? For the hairdo?'

'Just a pink Cadillac,' she replies.

At ten-fifteen, Elvis meets Red to walk to Beale. They march along North Main in silence, both concentrating hard on smoking their cigarettes. Red walks fast, head down, shoulders bunched, but Elvis is glad he doesn't suggest riding the streetcar, because he needs every cent he has in his pocket for this evening.

They're over halfway along before Elvis comes up with, 'What music do you like?'

'Anything Dewey Phillips spins is all right by me,' says Red.

'Dewey's crazy,' says Elvis. '*Dee-gaw!* Never miss a show. You hear it just now?'

'Sure.' Red launches into his own impression. '*I'm as nervous as a cotton-pickin' frog on the freeway with his hopper busted!*'

Elvis laughs. 'You ever go up to that coloured church in East Trigg to hear ol' Reverend Brewster?'

'Ain't too keen on churches.'

'Music there's supposed to be real fine, though. Back in Tupelo, I used to hang round this coloured store. Heard a cat named Ulysses Mayhorn play his trombone.' Elvis has never before used the word *cat* in this way – the way that Dewey uses it – and it feels good. Red flicks his cigarette butt into the road. 'That right?'

'He kinda liked me, too, you know? Showed me how to play, a little,' says Elvis. 'I miss ol' Mayhorn.'

It's not his first time on Beale, but it is the first time he's been here after dark. As they walk, Elvis is tempted to pause and look in the windows and doorways of every pawnshop, drugstore, bar, restaurant and pool room, but he senses Red won't stand for it, so he keeps walking, head down, until they get to Lansky's, when he is compelled to look up. Slowing his feet, he takes in the lighted display: an electric-blue suit teamed with a pair of crocodile shoes, the colour of canaries. He almost expects to see the face of Mr Lansky peering out, inch tape curled about his neck, pristine shirt-sleeves rolled neatly to the elbow; but, of course, it's way after hours. The last time Elvis walked past, Mr Lansky noticed him gazing in the window and nodded in acknowledgement. After that, Elvis had felt an inch taller. Maybe next time, he can actually go in the store.

The sidewalk near the Palace is thronging with white people, all here to see the Midnight Ramble. Cars crawl along, some honking their horns. Most of the crowd are men, and almost all of them drunk. They holler to one another, daring their friends to risk going into the club known as 'the Castle of Missing Men'. Elvis has heard the stories of shootings there. A few women in towering heels and bright lipstick cling to their men, and there's a smell of lilac perfume, liquor, barbecued meat, and the fresh fish that was sold earlier in the day from the sidewalk. A warm wind blows up from the Mississippi, causing the women to clutch their companions tighter, and Elvis to reach once more for the comb in his pocket.

As they wait in line, Red talks in a low voice about the girls round the back of the Palace.

'These girls are famous for popping white boys' cherries.'

'How do you know?'

'Guy I know went there and blacked out cold, right between a hooker's thighs! She brought him round at her chest, like she was nursing him, and he went and fainted again at the sight of her big brown titties.'

'That's crazy,' says Elvis, looking over his shoulder to check if anybody has heard.

'Plumb wasted five dollars!' Red sighs. Then he leans close and whispers, 'Could be you tonight, E.'

'I ain't got five dollars.'

'She'll do it by hand for one-fifty. Or, you know, the other way' – Red opens and closes his mouth, like a fish – 'for three.'

Elvis snorts.

'Ain't it about time you got broke in?' says Red. 'You seventeen now, ain't you? That's a man, near about.'

'How you know I ain't already broke in?'

Red draws back and smiles widely. 'You ain't.'

'Maybe I wanna keep myself clean for a white girl.'

'Man,' says Red, 'don't you know nothing? These coloured girls are for practising on. They love it. And no white girl will mind you knowing a few things. In fact, she'll thank you for it.'

'Move it along, boys,' says a voice from behind, and they follow the pack into the theatre.

Inside, Chinese lanterns hang from the smoke-stained ceilings. There's a smell of roasted peanuts and whiskey, and the purple carpet sticks to Elvis's shoes.

They take their seats – the cheapest, at the back of the balcony, behind a group of guys who are passing a flask of something along the row and already whooping, even though the lights are still up. Taking a look around, Elvis sees that he and Red are the youngest there. Red's orange crew cut stands out from the crowd, as always, but everyone is too excited to pay them much mind.

Red says, 'So what you done to your hair now?'

'Nothing,' says Elvis.

'Looks different to this morning.'

'Just fixed it up again, is all.'

'Lookin' good for the ladies, after.'

'Them ain't no ladies.'

The lights go down and a drum roll starts.

A stout black man wearing thick eyeglasses and a green velvet tux strides out. 'Well, yeeeessir-eee, it's Nat Dee!' he announces, and a great cheer goes up.

'That the guy from the radio?' Elvis asks Red, who nods, not taking his eyes from the stage.

'... and have we got a show for you tonight! A Midnight Ramble to end all rambles and all midnights! Now let's warm y'all up with a taste of those Vampiiiiiin' Babies!' He leaves the stage, clapping, and the band launches into 'Beale Street Blues'.

The curtain draws back to reveal a line of black women wearing silver skullcaps decorated with bursts of feathers. Through their short silver gowns, the outlines of their underclothes are visible. For the first few bars of the song, they do nothing but stand on their silver heels, one stockinged leg in front of the other, hands on their hips, smiling knowingly.

The theatre erupts into whistling.

Then, as the singer begins, the whistling subsides and the audience grows focused.

At first, Red nudges Elvis's knee repeatedly, sniggering as one of the girls shakes her ass at the band. But he soon settles into silence, and, like everyone else, leans forward in his seat, clutching his thighs. Elvis does the same, trying not to blink. One of the girls, the tallest one whose ironed hair hangs to her shoulders, seems to be looking right at him as she comes to the edge of the stage, dips her knees, winks and blows a kiss. Joining the rest of the line, her hips fly this way and that and her shoulders shimmy towards the audience, as if she is longing to touch them, or perhaps to be touched by them.

When the girls remove their gowns, throwing them into the pit in one swoop, the men around Elvis stand and make barking noises. Elvis stands too, his eyes glued to the tall girl, noting the way she holds one hand elegantly aloft before swinging it in a circle, while somehow managing to unclasp her bra with the other hand. Then, as one, the girls turn their backs to the audience and, casting a glance over their shoulders, let their brassieres fall to the floor.

Unable to bear the tension, Elvis begins to laugh.

The barking and whistling becomes louder; so loud that he can't hear the music.

When the girls finally turn around, ten pairs of black nipples bob into view, like a line of cherries on a one-armed bandit.

At this, Elvis doubles over, absolutely hysterical.

1953

One Saturday afternoon in spring, a loud honking coming from the street has Elvis rushing to the window of his family's new apartment on Alabama Avenue. An old car draws up and the horn sounds again in four short bursts.

'What's going on down there?' asks Gladys, without moving from the couch.

But Elvis is already out of the door.

He's been borrowing Vernon's car for a while now, using it to go across town with Red to McKellar Lake or K's Drive-in. He's saving for his own automobile, but so far he's managed to amass only ten dollars.

'Daddy!' he calls, bursting onto the sidewalk. 'Daddy!'

Vernon is leaning against the driver's door, arms folded. 'What do you reckon to her, son?'

Elvis skips around the car, letting his fingers trace its smooth outlines. It is pale green, with rounded fenders and lamps like bug's eyes, and not a little rust around the doors and hubcaps.

'She's just about the best-looking automobile I ever laid eyes on,' he announces.

Vernon opens the door. 'Hop in,' he says, sliding across to the passenger side. 'Let's take her for a spin.'

Elvis glances up at the apartment. From the window, Gladys stares down without waving.

'What about Mama?' he asks.

'What about her?' says Vernon, tossing him the keys.

Since they moved to Alabama Avenue, his mama hasn't seemed eager to leave the apartment. She didn't want to move again, but because their combined incomes were over the limit set by the Housing Authority, the family had no choice. The apartment is older and shabbier than the one at the Courts; the kitchen is tiny, the bathroom has no shower, and each night Elvis takes the couch. But their landlord, Rabbi Fruchter, who lives downstairs, is friendly enough and doesn't seem to mind when they use his telephone. Elvis knows this private apartment is, in fact, an important step up for their family, even though Gladys does not appear to care that they have escaped the public-housing system.

The car smells of tobacco and oil. He guns the engine.

'Hear that?' says Vernon. 'That's a Lincoln engine all right. Real low and smooth.'

It sounds pretty growly to Elvis. He rests his elbow in the place where the side window should be. Seeing him looking at the hole, Vernon says, 'We can get her fixed up with some cardboard there.'

The steering wheel is slippery beneath Elvis's fingers as he guides the car along the street.

'You think Mama's OK, Daddy?'

'She took the move hard, is all.'

'She can quit her job just as soon as I graduate.'

'Amen.'

They turn onto Poplar Avenue. Vernon and Elvis both notice two pretty girls on the sidewalk, their hair scraped back into identical swinging ponytails, but it is Vernon who leans over to sound the horn. The girls give the car a glance but offer no other reaction.

'So you got your own car,' says Vernon, grinning.

'Say what?'

'She's all yours, son.'

Elvis gapes at his father. 'Are you serious?'

'Keep your eyes on the road. It's high time you got your own vehicle. A young man needs his own mode of transportation.'

'I'll give you the money I got saved—'

'You bet you will. Now all you need's a girl to go in it, huh? Got anybody of special interest at the moment?'

During his last months at Lauderdale, Betty McMahon stopped showing up in the laundry room, leaving Elvis to watch his own reflection in the washtub and run through his expanding repertoire of songs about lost love.

'No, sir,' he says.

'Well, good. Play the field, that's my advice. And never fall for an older woman, 'cause they never, ever get any younger.'

Elvis steps on the gas.

It's not a girl he wants in the car, though. It's Red.

That evening, Elvis is determined to take his friend with him on a journey. After his shift at Loew's Theater, he removes his uniform, puts on his green shirt and blue jacket (which he feels complement the car), re-sculpts his hair, and drives to K's in the hope of finding him.

It's busy on the lot, with car-hops weaving in and out of vehicles and groups of kids sitting on their hoods to talk loud and drink colas. Elvis spots Red with a gang of football guys. He has one foot up on the fender of Jerry Bryson's car, which, Elvis notes, is newer and shinier than his own. Driving up as close as he can, Elvis sounds the horn and yells Red's name. He has to yell several times before Red screws up his burger wrapper, tosses it to the asphalt, and saunters over.

'Nice wheels, E. You pay extra for the rust?'

'Get in. We're taking us a little trip.'

'Kinda late, ain't it?'

'I wanna show you something.'

Red laughs. 'You oughta take a date, boy.'

'That's for tomorrow night,' says Elvis.

'You ain't gonna to sing to me, are you?'

'You coming or not?'

Red glances back at the group, who have stopped talking and are watching Elvis's car. Then he opens the door and climbs in.

The moon is full, hanging heavy and golden in the sky. It looks to Elvis like it might burst. They drive along Lamar Avenue towards the highway. From the sidewalk comes the occasional laughter of girls, the shouts of men, the smell of fried chicken, and the sound of music as they pass the juke joints that become wilder towards the edge of town. Elvis steers with one hand, a faint smile on his face, remembering how he'd longed, as a boy, to have the freedom his daddy had, driving that truck through the darkness from one mysterious place to the next. Now he is on the road for real, with a friend beside him, and a journey to complete.

Red is talking about a girl named Wendy Snipes.

'Swear to God, E, she's the best-looking gal I ever seen.'

'Even better than them Vampin' Babies?' asks Elvis.

'Funny guy,' says Red. 'Your cherry popped yet?'

There's a short silence.

'Now, you gotta give me more information than that,' says Red.

Elvis flicks a look over at his friend. 'I'm working on it.'

To distract Red from this conversation, Elvis turns on the radio. They're out of town now, and the highway stretches blackly ahead. They pass water towers, cattle farms, grain silos, pine forests, churches. He relaxes into his seat. Driving into the night with Kay Starr's voice coming over the airwaves is much better than trying to sleep on the couch, especially after a shift at Loew's, when the pictures from the screen seem to flicker across the insides of his closed eyelids. Those times he can't turn off the pictures, he'll slip out of the apartment and sit on the porch, gazing up at the windows of the buildings across the street. There's always a light on somewhere, and Elvis finds it comforting to imagine the folks behind the glass, still awake, living their lives after dark.

'We could just keep going,' he says, 'all the way to the end of the road.'

'Where we headed, anyways?' asks Red.

'Tupelo, Mississippi.'

Red sits up straight. 'What in the hell for?'

'It's where I'm from.'

'Jesus, E! I figured you was taking me to some roadhouse—'

'Don't you wanna see where I was born?'

'—reckoned on shooting some pool, maybe scoring us a couple of hot gals.'

'It's a shotgun shack. Two rooms. My twin brother died in there.'

Silence. The signposts along the highway seem to have run out. On either side of the car, thick forest rises up.

'E, that's real tragic and all,' says Red in a low voice, 'but it's Friday night, man. Don't you wanna get a little fun?'

'I figured you'd wanna see it. It'd mean a lot to me.'

Red sighs, and, resting his forehead on the dashboard, pretends to sleep.

Elvis slaps him across the back of the neck. 'Wake up, man!'

Red continues to snore theatrically.

'Suit yourself,' mutters Elvis. 'But we are going to Tupelo.'

Red lifts his head and settles back into his seat. 'If you say so,' he says, before going to sleep for real.

The road gets rough around Pontotoc and Red stirs but doesn't wake. It's two in the morning before they reach Tupelo. As he drives along North Green, Elvis finds his fingers tapping at the wheel with increasing speed. After they first moved to Memphis, he and his mama would regularly ride the bus here to visit friends and family, but he hasn't been back to town in a couple of years, and he's suddenly afraid that the whole place will have changed. Perhaps he'll look around and recognise nothing and nobody.

Then he spots Mayhorn's store, and his old house, and Sam's place, and the goods train lets out a long wail almost as if to greet him. He cruises down a deserted Main Street just to check off the stores: the Black and White, Hall's Café, Weiner's Jewelry, TKE's. Crossing the tracks, he points the Lincoln towards East Tupelo. Here the night is blacker than in Memphis, and louder, too: the bullfrogs, cicadas and katydids all welcome him with rising chants as the car rumbles slowly along the Old Saltillo Road.

Elvis pulls up beside the house where he was born. Closing his eyes, he breathes in the air, smelling the damp earth, listening to the night music.

Red stretches and yawns. 'Where we at?' he mumbles.

'East Tupelo, Mississippi,' says Elvis.

Red rubs his eyes. 'Son of a bitch,' he says. 'Guess you weren't kidding, then.'

'Nope.'

'I gotta piss.'

Elvis stays in the car while Red stumbles out to the nearest tree.

Using the rear-view mirror, Elvis straightens his hair and sport coat. He can ignore Red pissing beneath the oak, he tells himself. This can still be something good. Something meaningful.

Jesse, he says, silently. *You here?*

The insects sing their reply.

Red slaps the car's roof. 'You gonna sit there all night?'

'Hush up,' hisses Elvis, climbing out. 'Folks here are sleeping.'

'No kidding,' says Red, casting a glance over the dirt road, the tiny wooden shacks, the raked yards, the woods behind. 'Must've been something, growing up out here,' he adds. 'What the hell did y'all *do*?'

Elvis leans back on the hood and smiles. 'Played in the creek and them woods. Went to church.'

'Sounds swell.'

'See that house, there? That's where I was born. My daddy says there was a blue light in the sky that night. My twin brother was born first. He was dead already, though. They buried him in the cemetery over that hill. Damn near killed my mama. But I was alive.'

'A blue light?'

'That's what Daddy says.'

'You sure you ain't getting it mixed up with that photography place on Beale?'

'This ain't no joke,' says Elvis.

'I have no idea how I got born,' Red muses. 'Apart from the usual way.'

'Your mama never tell you nothing about it?'

'Not one thing.'

They stare at the house in silence. Above the roof, the sky is prickling with stars. The paint is peeling from the walls and one of the porch steps is broken. In the yard, a bicycle frame lies rusting among the weeds. The truth is that Elvis remembers nothing about living in this house. But his mama has told him the story of how they had to leave when Daddy went to jail. He sat on the porch while she piled up their belongings around him: a table, two wooden chairs, a trunk, one bed, a washbowl, a couple of buckets. Those salt and pepper shakers she loves so much. But he cannot mention these things, even to Red, so he says, 'Can you picture it? My brother, dead in a shoebox, and me, bawling and alive. Poor Mama.'

'It's real sad, E.'

'What do you think it means, Red?'

'Means?'

'Why did it happen that way?'

After a while, Red ventures, 'God's will, I guess.'

Elvis has to stop himself grabbing his friend by the lapels. 'That's what I think! But what does that *mean*?'

Red's pale eyes avoid Elvis's. 'Well, I guess there ain't no sense to it.'

'I think about it a lot, you know? I think: why did I live, when he died?'

Red gives a shiver. 'I ain't got no answer for you, E.'

'Why was it Jesse, and not me?'

Red peers at him, frowning. Then he puts a hand on his shoulder. 'I reckon you oughta just be damn grateful it was you,' he says, quietly. 'Now can we please get out of here?'

On the drive back to Memphis, Red doesn't complain when Elvis sings 'Old Shep' three times, followed by two renditions of 'The Old Rugged Cross'. By the time they reach the city limits, they are harmonising on 'Farther Along', leaning together to hit the notes, their own sweet noise accompanied by the rumble of the car's wheels on the bumpy concrete as they head for home.

Mama has waited up.

She's asleep on the couch, her head resting on a cushion, her legs drawn up beneath her. Her stockings have been discarded on the coffee table, like shed skin.

He tiptoes over and watches her for a few seconds. It crosses his mind that he could lift her and carry her to bed, but he decides she probably wouldn't want that, so he kisses her cheek instead.

She wakes.

'I took Red to Tupelo, Mama.'

She yawns. 'You did? That's good, son.'

'I figured if he's gonna be a good friend then he oughta see where I'm from.'

She stretches out her arms and pats the couch. 'Tell me boocups.'

'It's late.'

'Don't matter. What did the house look like?'

He thinks of the rusting bicycle frame in the yard. 'The same.'

'I loved that place when your daddy first built it for us.'

'Mama, you ever wish we still lived there?'

She looks at him for a long moment. 'Do you?'

He wonders what she'd like him to say. 'I like Memphis. But Tupelo will always be home.'

She nods. 'That's just about the way I feel, son.'

He rests his head on her arm, and she strokes his hair.

'I prayed to Jesse,' he says.

'I'm glad to hear that.'

'You don't think I'm crazy, Mama?'

She sighs. 'No more crazy than me.'

Graceland, January 1958

As Gladys strides away from the house, taking delicious lungfuls of cold night air, she congratulates herself on making it this far. Her shoes are pinching but she can bear it. She is going out! This is her house, and she is free to leave it. The blue lights illuminate the way to the gate, and Gladys almost giggles, imagining herself yodelling and skipping down the yellow brick road in *The Wizard of Oz*. She'd seen the picture for a birthday treat with Elvis and Vernon at the Lyric, back in Tupelo. Stepping into the Lyric was not unlike stepping into Oz itself. There were plush red carpets, tubes of coloured lights seemed to drip down the walls, and huge swags of blue velvet framed the screen on three sides. What had made them all gasp was not the moment when the land turned technicoloured. After all, they were used to seeing the world in colour. It was the moment towards the end of the film, when it dawned on them that the faces around the bed were not only the faces of Dorothy's loving family, but also of her fantastical friends. Her journey to Oz had been a dream and real, all at the same time. She'd been through the tornado and followed the yellow brick road, but she'd never left her loving family. Gladys had wept and wept.

The night is starlit and still, and the trees make no sound as she rounds the bend. She looks up at the bright moon, and understands why her son chooses to go out at night and sleep during the day.

The darkness gives him freedom. In the dark, he is detached from the daily lives of others, and at liberty to do as he pleases.

Of course, Elvis would go plumb crazy if he knew his mama was planning to walk out of Graceland alone at this hour. And until this moment, Gladys hadn't realised that she'd wanted to. Seeing the fans almost rip him clean in two, and hearing the stories of all the folks who consider her son one step away from the Devil, she'd been glad of the wall, the fence, the security gate and the length of their driveway. But right now she wants something else: to feel the grass beneath her feet; to have her hair curl in the damp night air; to walk along the street alone, without any notion of where she is headed.

Her nephew Harold's light is burning in the gatehouse. He's taken over from Vester for the night shift.

'Howdy, Harold,' calls Gladys, clip-clopping to his window.

Harold's head jerks back, and he blinks at her, his swollen eyes a little pink.

She raps on the glass. 'Open up so I can talk to you.'

Harold scrapes his hair into place, then slides the glass across.

'Hi, Aunt Gladys,' he says, with a sheepish grin, 'Golly! Musta dropped off there.'

'That's OK, Harold. I just wanna go out the gate here. Can you open up for me, please?'

Harold's smile falls. He scratches his cheek. 'Why, Aunt Gladys, I ain't too sure—'

'Only, I'm having trouble sleeping, and I figure a little walk to that paddock over yonder is just the thing I need. I got a hankering to see the horses there. Seeing horses always eases my mind. You know what a country girl your old aunt is, don't you?'

'Does Uncle Vernon know about this?'

Gladys taps her foot. The leather of her pumps bites at her toes. 'Sure he does, honey.'

Harold looks a little doubtful. 'I ain't certain Elvis would want you wandering out there all alone, ma'am.'

'Elvis ain't here. And you know he'd want his mama to be happy, don't you? Now open up. I won't be but fifteen minutes.'

With that, she steps back from the window, crosses her arms, and eyes the gates expectantly. It takes a few moments, and she can hear Harold muttering to himself, but eventually they swing open, and she trots through, head held high, waving at the gatehouse as she goes.

The empty highway is wide and black, the air faintly stained with the smell of gasoline. The electricity wires strung along the street give off a gentle hum, but otherwise there is no noise at all. Once she's walked a little way along the grassy shoulder, away from Harold's sight, Gladys pauses. Her shoes are rubbing badly now, and her initial burst of energy is wearing off, but she is still elated to have escaped. A single truck rumbles along the other side of the road, and she gazes after it, wondering what it would be like to hitch a ride across the state line. It's been a while since she went back to East Tupelo. Lately Vernon doesn't want to drive there, asking why in the world they would go visit some one-horse town when they live in the best mansion in Memphis.

She walks further, and the light dims. The highway stretches ahead, the dots of its lamps strung out for miles into the darkness. She knows the paddock is at the next turning in the road, but she can't recall how far that is, having only been driven from the house by her son or her husband. She supposes it would all have been different if she'd learned to drive; she has the pink Cadillac that Elvis gave her, but she's never dared to get herself behind the wheel. If she had, she might not be stumbling along the shoulder of the highway in these torturous shoes.

The cold air sneaks beneath the hem of her coat, and she pulls her collar tighter. She doesn't care about seeing a horse, but if she can make it to the paddock then she'll have proved something to herself. That she can walk alone. That she can do something more than sit and wait for Elvis to call.

She's beyond the Graceland grounds now, and the trees to one side of her are thicker, the air damper. In an effort to keep her feet from freezing, she steps from the grass onto the edge of the highway, and remembers those nights back in East Tupelo, running along the shoulder after her sleepwalking boy.

Then she hears the rumble of an engine. A car is coming towards her, its headlights illuminating the trees, the rich texture of her coat, the crust of mud on her shoes. She puts a hand up to shield her eyes from the glare, and in the sudden brightness she imagines, just for a second, that her son is driving this car, that somehow he's made it home from California already. The vehicle slows as it passes her, then pulls in a little way down the road.

Gladys stares at the tail lights, unsure whether to turn and run or to approach the car. The engine is still growling when the driver pokes his head out of the window.

'You OK back there, ma'am?' he calls.

In the gloom, she can't make out much about him, but his voice sounds young.

'Just fine, thank you,' she calls back, not moving.

There's a pause, then the tail lights turn white, and, with a high-pitched whine, the car reverses.

The man kills the engine and peers at her through the open window. He is thin and curly-haired, and holds a cigarette between his fingertips.

'What you doing, wandering around out here at this hour, ma'am?'

'Oh,' says Gladys, trying to sound flippant, 'just taking me some air, I guess!'

Glancing back, she can see the glow of blue light from her house. If this man means her harm, will Harold come running? Or has she gone too far for him to hear her scream?

'You oughta be careful,' says the man. 'Can I offer you a ride someplace? Take you home, maybe?'

She judges him to be in his late thirties; younger than her. He's unshaven but he looks clean enough. Bright-eyed, too, like the young Vernon.

'Where you headed?' she asks.

'To work,' he states. 'Night shift. Don't usually see nobody walking here, though.'

By the way his words slow as he leans across to get a better look at her, she suspects that he is beginning to realise who she is.

She giggles and removes her hands from her collar, so her coat slides open to the cool night. 'Well,' she says, smiling, 'now you have.'

'I sure have,' he agrees, taking a drag on his cigarette. Then he thumps a hand on the dash. 'Shoot! You ain't out here looking for Elvis, are you, ma'am?'

Gladys freezes.

'Like all them gals that line up outside those godawful gates down there?' The man lets out a hoot of laughter. 'You seen 'em? He's got his own self on his own goddamn gates! I swear, you can take the boy out of Hicksville, but you sure can't take Hicksville outta the boy. Still, maybe the army will knock some sense into him.'

Gladys draws her coat around her and drops her eyes.

The man shakes his head. 'Naw. Course you ain't. 'Scuse me, ma'am. I'm just foolin'.'

She tries to smile.

The man clears his throat. 'Well, if you're sure you gonna be all right ...'

'I live just over yonder,' she says, pointing in the direction of the paddock.

'Somebody waiting on you there?'

'My husband.'

'So long, then,' he says, flicking his cigarette from the window. And he pulls away, leaving her to watch the red smears of the tail lights shrink to nothing.

When she arrives back at the mansion, Harold is standing between the open gates, shining his flashlight up and down the highway and exclaiming squeakily about all the terrible things that could have happened to his aunt.

Gladys pats him weakly on the arm. 'Your aunt's just a holy fool, is all.'

Then she takes off her shoes and limps up the driveway. With every step it's as if another layer of skin has been stripped from her feet, and she looks back, almost expecting to see a trail of bloody footprints. But the driveway is clear, and Gladys continues her silent path back to the kitchen.

DIXIE: 1953–1954

1953

It's late summer, and way too hot to wear the black bolero jacket he's recently bought, so Elvis has settled for his thick dress pants and best red shirt for his visit to the Memphis Recording Service. With his guitar strapped to his back, he walks past the shining windows of the car showrooms towards the intersection of Union and Marshal avenues. Each time he's imagined this moment – which is every day for the past six months – he has pictured himself in a similar outfit. In his mind, his hair is always precisely the right shape. But now it's hot enough to melt the asphalt, let alone Vaseline, and a greasy lock keeps falling into his eye, along with dust from the cars cruising down the wide street.

He's seen a picture of the owner of the Recording Service, Mr Sam Phillips, in the *Memphis Press-Scimitar* and has admired his classy suit and hairstyle. In that photo, Mr Phillips looked a bit like a dark-haired Ashley Wilkes in *Gone with the Wind*, but better than that. More manly.

Elvis likes the hit record that Mr Phillips brought out on his Sun label, the Prisonaires' 'Just Walkin' in the Rain', but he's got something different in mind for his recording. He wants something smoother. Something more Perry Como. Something he can do in a bow tie and imagine singing to a girl who will be much better-looking and more loyal than Betty McMahon. Something that will make grown men weep.

At the sight of his own reflection in the glass door of the studio, his spine weakens. He's struck by the idea that Jesse is looking back at him, and feels suddenly exposed. He's told nobody he is coming here today, not even Mama. Though he wanted to tell her, he couldn't help imagining how unbearable it would be to admit that nothing had come of his walking through this door, and he'd decided it was better to keep quiet than face her disappointment.

He's actually a little shocked that his own feet have carried him all the way to number 706. Perhaps he'll just duck in to Miss Taylor's restaurant next door. In his pocket there's more than enough for a soda and a hamburger. Now he's graduated and is working five days a week at M. B. Parker's machinists, it's easy to have some left over.

He pushes the door open.

Taking off his guitar and grasping it by the neck, he stands on the chequered tiles and looks at the woman behind the desk.

'Well, good afternoon!' she says.

He nods, but can't seem to remember how to speak.

To his relief, she rises from her chair and guides him in, shutting the door. When the air from her rotating fan hits him he gets a whiff of his own body: sweat, and maybe some oil from his car.

'May I help you, young man?' she asks.

With her golden hair and brightly patterned dress, she looks like a lady from one of his mama's magazines. Her glasses have sparkles in the rims. Standing behind her typewriter, she beams.

'I'm Miss Keisker,' she says. 'What can I do for you, son?'

He gestures vaguely to his guitar and manages to clear his throat. 'I heard you could make a record here, ma'am.'

'A two-sided acetate will be three dollars ninety-five plus tax. Is it for yourself?'

'Ma'am?'

'You want to do the recording yourself?'

'Yes, ma'am.'

'When?' She flicks through the ledger.

'Uh ...'

'You want to do it right now?'

'I guess.'

'I think we can manage that.' She glances at her watch. 'I'll just see if Mr Phillips has a moment. Wait here, please.'

First smoothing her dress, she opens the door at the back of the room and Elvis gets a glimpse of what's beyond: a microphone, a piano, and empty space.

Seeing this, he doesn't know if he can keep standing. While Miss Keisker is gone, he fights the urge to save himself the shame of it all and escape onto the bright street by reminding himself that he'd managed to sing at the Humes High Minstrel Show before gradu-ating. The moment his homeroom teacher, Miss Scrivener, had called him out as the winner had made his whole school career worth enduring. When he'd told his mother, she'd shrieked with happiness.

Miss Keisker slides back into the room.

'Take a seat, son. Mr Phillips will be ready for you in just a moment.'

Elvis does as she asks. She makes a note of his name and address, then takes his money. The bills are sweaty and limp from his pocket, but she doesn't seem to mind. As she checks the amount, he seizes his chance.

'You know anybody who's looking for a singer, ma'am?'

This is actually what he's come here for. Not to cut a record – although he's burning to find out what his own voice really sounds like – but to reach other musicians, and to figure out how he might get himself up on a proper stage somewhere.

Miss Keisker leans back in her chair and considers him, clearly surprised that he's found it in himself to ask a direct question.

'Let me see, now ... What kind of singer are you?'

'I sing all kinds,' he says.

She smiles. 'Let me put it another way. Who do you sound like?'

And he replies, quite honestly, 'I don't sound like nobody.'

'Is that so?' she says, raising an eyebrow.

Mr Phillips puts his head around the door. 'Ready?' he asks.

Elvis leaps up and jabs his hand in the man's direction. 'It sure is a pleasure to meet you, sir.'

Mr Phillips nods. He's even more groomed than his picture suggested, and his hand is cool. Holding the door open, he says, 'Come in, son.'

It's a plain room, a little bigger than Elvis's own front yard, tiled white from floor to ceiling. In the centre stands the mike, as lonely as an abandoned child. There is no sound and, it seems to Elvis, no air, in this room. Just a hot vacuum that he cannot possibly fill.

Mr Phillips climbs into the safety of his booth and shuts the door. He's looking not at Elvis but at the knobs and sliders on the desk, so it's a shock when the man's voice, suddenly loud, crackles over the speaker in the corner of the room.

'What are you going to sing?'

Elvis can see his own reflection in the glass and, through that, Mr Phillip's perfect hair. He attempts to sculpt his own back into shape without success.

The voice comes again. 'Son? Do you know what you're going to sing today?'

Only now does he make up his mind which song to perform. '"My Happiness".'

Mr Phillips looks up. 'All right. Are you ready now?'

Elvis nods.

'You see that green light over there? When it comes on, you can start. Just relax and take your time.'

Elvis tries to feel Jesse's presence, to address him silently, but nothing comes. It's as though his brain is stuck on the dial between radio stations, and all he can get is static.

The light flashes on. He positions his slippery fingers on the guitar strings. Then he closes his eyes and tries to imagine he is not in this studio but sitting in the laundry room at the Courts in the warm semi-darkness, singing to Betty with the washtubs for accompaniment.

The guitar doesn't sound good. It's hollow and barely melodic. His voice is not as good as it can be, but maybe it's good enough. And he was wrong about this room. Once he's started to sing, it vibrates with sound. At first it's discomfiting, this new noise. The room makes his voice different. He's sung the song so many times and it has never been quite like this before. Realising that it sounds better – rounder, smoother, and yet more alive – he is able to push through to the end of the song.

Mr Phillips looks impassively through the glass.

What did you think of that, Jesse? Pretty good, huh? You couldn't do no better, anyhow.

Mr Phillips checks his watch. 'All right. I got that. And you're doing a two-sided?'

Not even a smile or a 'well done'. What had he imagined? That the man would come rushing out to shake him by the hand? That he would stand and clap? Well, yes. He'd imagined both those things.

'I'm gonna do "That's When your Heartaches Begin".'

'Go ahead.'

The green light comes again. He tries to find the song and sing it as it should be sung, as he knows he can. He tries to use the room to help him. But his eyes won't close; they flick back and forth from the green light to Mr Phillip's perfect, unmoving hair. Then the expensive-looking crispness of the man's shirt. Then the reflection of his own ugly pockmarked skin. Elvis doesn't make it to the end. Instead he stumbles, ducks his head, and says, 'That's the end.'

The green light turns red.

Mr Phillips frowns at the deck. 'Take a seat with Miss Keisker. Your recording will be ready in just a moment.'

Elvis stands, looking into the booth, desperate for something else. Even some disappointment, a sigh, or a 'That didn't go so well, how about we try it again?' from Mr Phillips would be better than this brisk efficiency.

What the fuck are you laughing at, Jesse?

Mr Phillips looks up. 'Something I can help you with, son?'

'No, sir. I guess not.'

'Go take a seat, then.'

'Thank you, sir.'

Because there is nothing else he can do, Elvis leaves the room.

1954

At the Rainbow Rollerdrome, he leans on the railing and watches the skaters. Packs of girls glide and swish across the floor, their skirts flying like trash at the side of the highway. Other boys from Humes also stand and watch, but Elvis keeps his distance. Even he fears he may have overdone it tonight, a little. If he were to join them – and he wants to – they might ask where the bullfight is, or when he's going to break into a Spanish dance. Earlier on, at home, he'd felt powerful and ready in his pegged pants and bolero jacket. He tries to hold on to that feeling as he scans the floor for Dixie Locke, who is fifteen and has dark eyebrows and a pointed chin, which she likes to lift in his direction.

Dixie is the reason he has started attending the Bible-study group at the First Assembly of God on McLemore. He's been going to services there for a while now, mainly to hear the singing of the Blackwood Brothers, the gospel quartet who form part of the congregation. During Bible-study, the younger members sit in a circle in the stuffy, carpeted room off the church to discuss the meanings of the parables and try to relate them to their own lives. Dixie says little, and Elvis even less. It seems a long time since he was saved on the porch of Brother Mansell's house, and he dislikes the church's list of things he shouldn't do. These days, music is where he feels closest to God.

When he was within earshot Dixie had said – was it deliberately loud? – that she was going to be here tonight. It's warm in the Rollerdrome, which makes the scent of teenage sweat and popcorn stronger. Elvis doesn't want to smell these things. He wants to smell her, Dixie. He thinks perhaps she smells like fresh milk with a little molasses. She might taste like that, too, if he can get her in his mouth. Red claims it drives the chicks wild when you suck their earlobes. You've got to nibble on an earlobe, as if it's too cold to take a bite, as if it's a Popsicle, he says.

They're playing Teresa Brewer now, and Elvis straightens his body to let the music in. Sometimes it feels as if the music enters his spine and enables him to stand taller. Miss Keisker hasn't called to say she's heard of somebody looking for a singer, even though he keeps stopping by the studio, just to say hello. Maybe next time he could mention that to her. *It's like it goes into my spine, you know? Right up my back.* She might understand that. She might even tell Mr Phillips that he said it.

Then he spies Dixie, skating alone at the edge of the rink. In her white pantyhose and a little pink skirt, her hair set in the usual neat waves that fall to her shoulders, she weaves in and out of the other kids. Watching her, he comes to the conclusion that she's not the best skater on the rink, but she is, unlike many of the others, utterly confident in her abilities. As she pushes off, she half-closes her eyes and leans into the air as if reaching for something. She never wobbles, or pulls a self-conscious face. Then she sees him and, just for a second, her arms flail, but she continues to skate, completing another lap before allowing herself to look again. He raises his hand and she smiles, showing the gap between her front teeth, then glides over to where he is.

All at once, her boots are hitting the barrier with a whack, and she's holding on to the railing, her hands close to his, and she's talking, too. 'I know you from church, don't I?'

Wrong-footed by her being the one to speak first, Elvis can only nod.

'You're Elvis, aren't you? I'm Dixie, Dixie Locke,' she says, and laughs brightly. When her eyelids flutter, he relaxes a little. She is nervous, too.

'I know who you are,' he says. 'Wanna get a Pepsi?'

'Sure.' Her voice is not so bright, but it is warmer, now.

He fetches two drinks as Dixie waits at a plastic table, skates lined up neatly beside her chair, chin resting on both hands. Before setting the cups down, he wipes the table with a serviette, then, unsure what to do with it, lets it drop to the floor, hoping she hasn't noticed.

He sits opposite her. The sweet stickiness of the drink is sublime in his mouth and he feels so revived that he's able to say, 'I've noticed you. In church.'

'What did you notice?' she asks, chewing on her straw.

'Your hair, mostly.'

She looks off towards the rink. 'Oh,' she says, 'that.'

'It's the same colour as my mama's,' he says, then wishes he hadn't.

'Uh-huh.'

'Real black, I mean.'

She lets the straw drop from her mouth into her empty paper cup and says nothing.

'Sure hope I ain't offended you,' he says, because it is something to say.

'Lord, no,' she says, studying the cup. 'Why would you think that?'

'Some girls are easily offended.'

She nods, holding a hand over her mouth.

There's a pause.

'What's your mama like?' she asks.

He brushes a hand across the ruffles of his shirt. Each one is deep red, soft as a rose petal. Where can he begin? 'She's real nice,' he says. 'Everyone thinks so.' Then he adds, because he senses he should,

'But she always wants to know what I'm up to!' and feels immediately as though he has betrayed Gladys.

'Mine too!'

'Which is good, I guess.'

'Kind of irritating, sometimes, though.'

He nods. 'What about your folks?'

Her daddy is as tall as a tree and says about as much. Her mama is sweet but never misses a chance to read her the riot act. Her sisters get in the way but are cute, mostly. Her uncle is a tease and sometimes takes it too far. Elvis absorbs it all, amazed that Dixie feels easy enough to share this with him, and he wants to share something back, so they are even. But, when she's finished, he just asks if she can stay for the next session. She says she can call her folks, they'll be fine. And so they sit for another hour, talking about her family and his, about the church and the people they know there; Dixie makes it clear who she likes and who she doesn't, and they discover a shared passion for the Statesmen. They've both seen the quartet at the all-night gospel singings at the Ellis Auditorium.

'Those guys don't just sing, they *perform!*' he tells her, leaning back and hooking his hands behind his head.

'I just love Jake Hess,' she says. 'The way he moves.'

He looks at her intently. 'That right?' he asks.

She giggles. 'Oh, not like *that!*'

But he knows she's lying.

'We oughta go together next time,' he says. 'So I can keep an eye on you.'

'I'd like that,' she says.

Encouraged, he suggests they drive up to K's for a hamburger, even though it's ten-thirty and this will be the last of his money for the whole week. There isn't a hint of hesitation in her voice as she accepts.

As he opens the door to the Lincoln, he says, 'The car's not mine.'

Red swears some girls will go with any guy who has a car, and Elvis doesn't want Dixie to be one of those girls.

She pauses, studying his face. He's not good at lying, never has been; he feels himself wanting to laugh and tell her it was all a joke, but then she says, 'You can drive it, though, right?' and he grins.

It feels like nothing on earth, driving the Lincoln with Dixie beside him. It's January, and cold in the car. The old engine rattles as they cruise along Lamar. She sits close enough for him to be aware of her shivering. He still has a piece of board fixed where his side window should be, so he rests his arm on the back of the seat, close to her shoulders. Dixie edges a little closer. They're both silent as the lights rush to greet them on the dark and lonely road.

What is the right thing to say to a girl as you drive into the star-clustering night? Perhaps it would be better to say nothing at all, but she's opening her mouth to talk again and so he gets in first with, 'I like to sing.'

Because he wants her to know that. He wants her to know how important it is, and how he means to be as good as, or even better than, Jake Hess.

'I heard that,' she says.

'You did? Who told you?'

Is he *known* for this thing, even beyond his immediate friends? His scalp tingles with joy.

'Oh, you know. Folks.'

'I'm gonna try out for the Songfellows.' Something he hadn't quite decided upon until this moment.

'That's wonderful, Elvis,' she says. 'I'd love to hear you sing.'

And only then can his hand let go of the seat and find her knee. It's warm and thrillingly alive beneath his fingers. 'You will,' he says. 'I promise.'

When they arrive at the drive-in, it's still cold in the car, even though he leaves the engine running, but nothing can stand in the way of his enjoyment of K's hamburgers. They are the most delicious food he knows. In fact, he finds it hard to think about anything else while he is eating this burger. Dixie, the late hour, the music coming from the car radio (it's Dean Martin, and he loves Dean's smoothness, just as he loves the roughness of Muddy Waters), all fade as he sinks his teeth into the sweet and giving bread, tastes the sour smack of gherkin and tomato and the salty depth of the meat itself. He can hardly believe that now he's out of school and in a job it's possible to afford such things on a regular basis. There is only this: the chewing and swallowing, and the next mouthful. Elvis tries not to gobble, for the girl's sake. His mama is always saying, *Slow up, baby, it'll still be there one minute from now.* But it's never felt that way to him. He must get it in his mouth, all of it, right now. And with each mouthful there is that small pang of regret that this one brings him closer to the last, closer to the moment when the hamburger will be no more.

He chases crumbs and drips of sauce round the wax paper with a finger until he notices that Dixie has left half her burger untouched. He stares at what's left on her tray as she chatters. Noticing his eyes on her food, she offers him what's left. While he finishes up her burger, she's jittery. She keeps glancing at her watch and laughing and saying it doesn't matter, they won't mind.

His mama will mind, but she won't say anything. Gladys will be sitting up, looking at the clock, listening to the radio, unable to sleep until he is home. But, tonight, that is her problem.

As Elvis hands their empty tray to the car-hop, Dixie fiddles with her hair, waiting. The stiff set of her waves reminds him of a corrugated fence, but he chases this thought from his mind, and reaches for them anyway, finding he can push his fingers right in and touch her unguarded neck. Her collar is high but not high enough to protect her earlobe, which he takes between his finger and thumb. She shivers and pulls slightly away, and, knowing he's risking losing her, but not caring, he moves closer, as he's seen it done in countless movies. Once he watched Red necking with Wendy Snipes and it seemed that their faces were so deeply connected one of them would consume the other soon enough. More than anything, it looked like hard work – Red's body was tense and absolutely still while his jaw did everything for him, and Wendy was pushed back, her head crushed against the wall of the schoolyard. He senses this is not what Dixie wants. She doesn't want to be squashed against concrete and have her jaw overworked, as if she's chewing through a piece of gristly meat.

And so he chooses her hot cheek first, letting his lips brush against it; then he moves to her jawline, which is unmistakably tense. Her breathing is quick and shallow. As he finds her lips, he tastes malts and lipstick – he recognises the flavour from his own experiments with his mama's make-up – and thinking of this urges him on until he has her mouth open to his own.

'When can I see you again?' he asks, drawing back.

'Tomorrow.' There is something new in her eyes, a kind of triumph. It reminds him of his mama's look, the first time he brought a real wage home. Excitement and gratitude. But mostly gratitude. *Finally*, her eyes say. *Finally, here it is: what I was waiting for. What only you can give me.*

And it's this look, rather than the kiss, nice though it was, that makes him forget he is even driving as takes Dixie home. It's like the engine is him; his foot part of the accelerator, his hand melded to the steering wheel. He has only to make the smallest gesture for the car to take him exactly where he wants to go.

* * *

In the kitchen, Gladys stands above her son, watching him shovel egg into his mouth. She's risen early, so she can catch him before he leaves for work. Often, now, she won't see him in the mornings, and only briefly in the evenings. He likes his new job, driving a truck for Crown Electric, and she never has to prise him from his bed to get him there on time. Sometimes he borrows the truck on weekends to take her to church with him, and they're both proud to sit up front and watch the road disappear so far beneath their feet.

'Dixie?' she asks. 'That's her name?'

'Yes, Mama. That's her name. Miss Dixie Locke.'

She's known for over a month that something's been going on. She knew as soon as he came in so late that night from the Rollerdrome, not because it was past midnight – he's always going to listen to music being played somewhere, and she would never tell him not to do that; he's been going alone to radio stations since he was eleven years old, after all – but because he's been so distracted, so reluctant to sit down and talk to her when he comes in. They used to talk for hours sometimes, he always had *boocups* to tell her about his day, his hopes and his fears. Then, suddenly, this past month, it seems he's had nothing to say at all.

'It's a nice name, son.'

She imagines her: trim, neat, a touch conceited. Over the past year, Gladys has put on forty pounds and can't stop noticing the way her skin puckers and sags around her mouth. Every window she passes, she tries not to look at her reflection, but in the end it always catches up with her. And when it does, it's a shock to see her forty-two-year-old self. She knows it's herself looking right back at her, but it's not a self she quite recognises. There are too many shadows on that face. Too often, it looks gloomy or plain afraid, even when Gladys has reckoned her mind to be empty.

Elvis forks in another mouthful. Will this girl, Dixie, fix his eggs in the way that he likes – well fried, not turned, left on a low flame until they're absolutely solid?

He wipes cornbread around his plate. It's often disgusted Gladys to see Vernon eating. The glugging and slurping like plumbing, the way his saliva escapes his mouth and beads his lips. But she finds the spectacle of her son eating nothing but charming. Few things give her greater pleasure than to see Elvis enjoy something she's made for him. She remembers baking a pound cake for his fourth birthday; she'd saved up the ingredients specially, and had found herself going teary at the sight of him putting it in his mouth, chewing, swallowing, asking for more.

'You want more, baby?'

The sun shines through the window, covering her son's knees in brightness. He pushes back his chair.

'No, thanks, Mama.'

'So when you gonna bring Miss Dixie to meet your family?'

'Soon,' he says, pecking her cheek.

'A girl won't reckon you're worth too much if you don't let her meet your folks.'

He blows her a kiss before stepping out of the apartment and into the crisp February morning.

In the event, he gives her little time to prepare. 'Dixie's coming tomorrow,' he announces on Friday night, before heading downtown with Red.

On Saturday, Gladys rises early to polish the kitchen linoleum and scrub out the sink. She runs her cloth over every surface of the apartment, then considers washing the covers on the couch, but decides it's too late to get them dry. She bakes a pound cake, remembering still that birthday treat that Elvis liked so much, and thinking that it wouldn't be nice to come across too fancy, anyway. A pound cake is good enough. It'd be even better with some cool cream, but she won't send Vernon to the store, even though they can afford such small luxuries now that Elvis brings home more than his daddy each week.

In the mirror on the back of the pantry door she yanks some grey hairs from her temples. She has on her second-best dress, blue wool with a pink belt. She doesn't want the girl to think she's tried too hard.

She means to love Dixie, as Elvis loves her. She doesn't know the Lockes, but she's managed to prise some information from her son about his meeting with them: Dixie's mother was kind and pretty, Dixie's father didn't say much of anything. Gladys appreciates that Elvis's appearance has become surprising, and could, to other families, be kind of alarming. She tries to imagine how it would feel if it were the other way around, if Dixie were her daughter, bringing Elvis for a visit. But she can only imagine seeing beyond Elvis's long hair and interesting clothes – others might call them flashy, or worse; she wouldn't – to his impeccable manners and softly spoken charm. How could any mother not be impressed by that?

She goes to the sink and rinses her hands, which are damp with sweat. She wipes the table once more, and peers out of the window. It's started to rain lightly, and a couple of kids are jumping on and off the sidewalk with their hands held over their heads. Vernon is also out there, waxing the car in preparation for the girl's arrival, despite the weather. He stretches himself across the windshield, all his back trouble forgotten.

Elvis's car pulls up and Gladys inches away from the window. She removes her housecoat, scanning the apartment for anything out of place. She hears Vernon say, 'Well, just look at *you*!' and the sound of a girl's laughter. Then their voices are echoing up the stairwell, Vernon's taking the lead as he says Elvis ought to give Dixie a ride in the Crown Electric truck some time.

In order to look as though she hasn't been eavesdropping, Gladys retreats to the kitchen and starts spooning coffee into the pot. Even when she hears the door open and their voices in the living room, she doesn't turn around, wanting her son to come find her.

'Mama! We're here!'

The two of them stand in the kitchen doorway, both flushed and slightly damp, breathing quick and blinking. Elvis has a hand on Dixie's shoulder. She barely comes up to his chest, and the black curls of her hair rest on her shoulders like jewels.

'Welcome, dear, to our home,' says Gladys, stepping forward and taking both of Dixie's hands in hers. 'I want you to treat it as your own.'

Dixie smiles. 'It's sure good to meet you at last, Mrs Presley! Elvis has told me so much about you!'

'Call me Gladys, honey.'

'Is the coffee ready, Mama?' says Elvis, eyeing the cake on the table.

'You two go sit and I'll bring it on through,' Gladys says, waving them out of the kitchen.

When she has the cake and the coffee served, she tells Elvis to scoot along the couch so she can sit next to his girl. Sandwiching herself between them, she says, 'What do you reckon to our television set over there, Dixie? Elvis got it for us.'

'It's real fine, Mrs Presley.'

'We love *Candid Camera*.'

'Never miss it,' says Vernon.

'And did you see our piano, too?' asks Gladys. 'Since he's been working, Elvis just keeps coming back with these little surprises! But I'm sure he spoils you as much.'

The truth is that Gladys frets over her son running up debts, but his joy at bringing such treasures home prevents her from mentioning it.

Dixie shifts forward on the cushions so she can look directly at Elvis. 'And you call call *me* high class? When you have a TV and a piano both?'

Elvis slaps her leg playfully and she returns the gesture with a delighted squeal, prompting him to slap her again. This goes back and forth for a full minute, leaving Gladys with nothing to do but sit in the middle and witness the flirtation.

When their game is over, Elvis says, 'Dixie's Assembly of God, Mama.'

'That's real encouraging to hear, Dixie. We all need a little guidance in our lives, don't you think? Especially when we're young and all. What do you make of our Pastor Hamill?'

'He's neat,' says Dixie. 'Real *dramatic*.'

Elvis launches into a long tale of how they met at Bible-study class. As he talks, Dixie follows his every move, nodding, smiling and laughing a bit too loud at all the correct moments. Gladys watches her, thinking that she looks like a little doll. She decides that Dixie must have lived a sheltered life, with a father going out to the same job every day in a smart suit and tie, and a mother who has never had to dirty her hands in a laundry, hospital ward or field.

How else could her brow be so smooth and her eyes so bright? How else could she sit there and smile and smile and eat up all that cake and drink in Elvis's every word and glance like it was nothing at all?

After they've finished their coffee, Vernon suggests that Elvis help him finish up waxing the car. Dixie shoots a look at Elvis, clearly alarmed, but the two men rise and leave the room, leaving Gladys alone with the girl.

Dixie turns to Gladys and shrugs. 'They won't be too long, I guess!'

'Don't bank on it, honey. Takes those men the whole afternoon to polish up one car sometimes. I swear they love them old automobiles more than anything in this world.'

Dixie swallows and looks at her shoes.

'Anyway,' says Gladys, stretching her legs and leaning back on the couch, 'this gives us girls a chance for a real good talk, don't it?'

Dixie nods and makes a small noise that sounds like agreement. Glancing at the piano, she says, 'Does Elvis play that thing?'

'He sure does. Taught himself on my brother-in-law's piano, not long after we moved to Memphis. He never played for you?'

'Oh, he sings a lot. And plays guitar, of course.'

'Ain't that a beautiful thing?'

'Do you sing too, Mrs Presley?'

'A little. But Elvis's daddy is a better singer than me. He used to serenade me some when we was dating.' Keeping her eyes on her coffee cup, she continues, 'Do you love Elvis, Dixie?'

Dixie lets out a high-pitched giggle.

'I hope you don't mind me asking you that question. You see, I know my son is a very loving boy, he's always been that way. And I know he loves *you*.'

'He does?'

'Why, ain't he told you so?'

Dixie plays with one of her curls. 'Not in so many words.'

'Well, you know how boys can be, Dixie. Some of them find it a little hard to say these things.'

'I do love him awful, Mrs Presley!' Dixie blurts, kneading her fingers together in her lap.

Gladys takes her hand, which is warm and slightly sticky, and pats it. 'I could tell the minute I saw you, dear.'

'You could?' says Dixie, blushing.

'Oh, sure. But then, who *wouldn't* love him?'

Dixie laughs uncertainly.

'Now,' says Gladys, 'tell me. Are you a dancer?'

'I have done a little ballet—'

'I thought so! Your head sits in just exactly the right place on those pretty little shoulders.'

'You're too kind.'

'Oh, Dixie, I always hoped Elvis would marry somebody just like you.'

Dixie stares at Gladys, her eyes brighter than ever.

★ ★ ★

It has been six months since Elvis and Dixie started dating and, at Gladys's suggestion, the girl has agreed to join her in cooking a celebratory lunch. In the Piggly Wiggly, Dixie had suggested buying the ingredients for a fish gumbo and a baked Alaska, but Gladys managed to steer the first course back to meat loaf and mashed potatoes.

They arrive home from the supermarket before the men, who have gone to pick up Vernon's car from the repair shop. While Dixie sets the table, Gladys focuses on the meat loaf. Once she's got it in the oven, she takes the weight off, sitting on a chair to watch Dixie whip the egg whites for the dessert.

Gladys points to the spotted scarf Dixie is wearing to hold back her hair. 'I wish I could wear a something like that!' she says. 'It looks so … carefree.'

Dixie stops beating the eggs and pulls the scarf from her hair. First shaking it out, she hands it to Gladys. 'It's yours,' she says. 'Why don't you try it?'

'Oh, I'm too long in the tooth for that kind of stuff,' says Gladys, but she strokes the scarf, feeling its milky texture.

'Come on,' says Dixie. And, leaning close to Gladys, she loops it around her head, tying it on top, then steps back to admire her work. 'It looks cute,' she states.

Gladys touches her hair and lets out a giggle. The doctor has prescribed her some pills to help her reduce her weight, and they make her giddy with energy one minute, exhausted the next.

Dixie resumes her beating.

After a moment, Gladys says, 'I ain't sure if this is something you wanna hear, Dixie, but I want you to know that there are things you can do to make sure you don't have a baby until you're married.'

The beater stills, egg dripping from its wire.

'I don't mean to pry,' Gladys continues, 'but I do know how men can be.' She believes Elvis to be different to his daddy, but she doesn't want him shamed by this girl's pregnancy.

Dixie starts up whipping again, even harder than before. 'Elvis ain't like that!'

'I'm sure glad to hear it, honey, but if you're ever worried about anything, you can talk to me, you hear?'

Just then, Vernon and Elvis burst in. Perhaps for Dixie's benefit, Vernon has started wearing cologne, which makes the apartment smell like a hairdresser's shop. Elvis shouts for his mama and rushes into the kitchen with his face all lit up, saying he's got news, but, seeing Dixie with the wire whip in her hand, he pauses in the middle of the room.

Gladys says, 'Congratulations on your six-month anniversary, son. Dixie here wanted to celebrate with a special family meal.'

'I'm making baked Alaska,' says Dixie, her cheeks still flushed.

Elvis doesn't move towards either of them. Instead, he swallows and says, 'What in the world is that?'

'You're gonna love it,' says Dixie.

'Well, what are y'all standing there for?' says Gladys. 'You men get washed up so we can enjoy our lunch.'

Vernon looks at Elvis, who blurts, 'I got a call, Mama! From Sun Recording! They want me down there!'

'What?'

'Rabbi Fruchter downstairs just told me Miss Keisker telephoned—'

'Miss who?'

'She works with Mr Phillips, the owner ... I didn't tell you, 'cause I wanted it to be a surprise, but I went over there for a sort of audition—'

Gladys's heart leaps as she begins to understand what he is telling her. 'You did?'

'And now Mr Phillips has a song he wants me to try!'

She jumps to her feet, nearly knocking Dixie's bowl of eggs from the table. 'Then you gotta get over there!'

'I gotta change first.'

She gives her son a little push on the arm. 'You look great! Get going!'

Elvis looks back at Dixie. The wire whip is still suspended in the air.

'Sorry, honey,' he says.

Dixie nods, but says nothing.

After he's gone, Gladys beams at her husband and says, 'We'll just have to eat lunch at suppertime, won't we?'

'Just relax, and let me hear a song that really means something to you, now.'

Mr Phillips expects something from him, but Elvis isn't at all sure what that something might be. The song Mr Phillips asked him to sing first – 'Without You' – hasn't gone so well. It's the kind of heartbroken ballad that Elvis loves, but he couldn't get behind it, somehow. It just didn't have the yearning that it needed, and it remained little more than a wheedling complaint. When the song was over, Mr Phillips had rubbed at his ear, as if the sound had been an irritation to him, and he wanted to wipe it away.

'Sing something that comes from your own experience,' he suggests now. 'Anything at all.'

Elvis stands, hanging on to the microphone stand, rocking back and forth on his heels.

'Elvis?'

He doesn't think Mr Phillips wants to hear a gospel song, not even 'The Old Rugged Cross', or 'Milky White Way'. He'd like to sing 'My Happiness', but it took Mr Phillips a year to call him back the last time he tried that one on him.

'You're doing just fine. Sing anything you want.'

'Anything, sir?'

'Anything that's special to you.'

Knowing this may be his only chance to impress somebody within this thing called the record industry, Elvis panics. There are so many songs that are special, and he cannot seem to recall a single one right now. He pinches his nose, laughs, shakes his head.

'I just can't think of a song, sir.'

'Sure you can,' says Mr Phillips.

It has to be a ballad. A ballad was what Mr Phillips called him in for, and ballads are what Elvis has always liked the most, ever since he sang 'Barbara Allen' in class, ever since he heard his daddy singing 'Clementine'. Ballads are sweet, and sad; they express the best emotions.

He clears his throat, then starts in on 'Tomorrow Night', which he sometimes sings to Dixie on her front porch. He tries to picture her pretty little face as she drinks his voice down and gazes at him as if she's still thirsty, but Mr Phillips's shiny chin keeps interrupting the image.

When he's finished, Mr Phillips tilts his head and rubs his ear again.

'OK, son. Thanks for coming in. Thank you very much.'

The green light goes off. Nothing more is said.

Elvis doesn't go straight home, despite the celebratory meal waiting there. Instead, he drives the Lincoln too fast along Riverside Drive, making the engine growl and cough. Keeping the radio switched off because he cannot stand to hear anybody's voice right now, he considers how he could murder Mr Phillips and Miss Keisker, both. Maybe he could smash his car through the front window of the studio, straight into her neat desk, cleaving it in two. Maybe he could keep going, through that wall behind her and into the glass of the booth and right through Mr Phillips's shining chin. Finish them both off.

He parks up and stares at the big brown river. He can smell its claggy dirt. Maybe he should drive down the muddy bank and into the water, let the river swamp the car, seep into his clothes and hair, fill up his mouth and lungs and ears. There'd be hardly any sound down there, beneath the surface. He wouldn't be able to hear one voice, not even his own. He remembers the time at the swimming hole with his daddy, when he panicked that Vernon wouldn't resurface. But Vernon always seems to come back up, to keep on going, no matter how tough things get. Many times, Elvis has been sure that his father was broken – after the pen, after Mama found out about the woman on the road back in Tupelo, after they first moved to Memphis and they were so poor Vernon had lined his shoes with cardboard. But Vernon has a habit of rising again. It's something that Elvis knows he must learn if he's to be any kind of man.

He remembers, too, Noreen's red hair through the trees, and how he covered himself in shame. If Noreen saw him now, she'd laugh in his face. And Vernon would, too. *You think you got it hard? You oughta try my life, boy.*

Elvis decides that the best thing to do is not mention any of it to a living soul. He can just refuse to discuss it. Mama will press him, because she is used to him telling her everything, but he thinks maybe this time he can resist. He can keep this entirely to himself. After all, that's what his daddy would do.

Feeling a little better, he guns the engine and drives home.

All week, Elvis relives Mr Phillips rubbing his ear and saying, 'Thank you very much.' Whenever his mama asks what happened, he holds up a hand and tells her he doesn't want to talk about it. He does the same to Dixie, and she stops asking much quicker than Gladys.

Then there's a phone call.

He's in the Suzore Number 2 movie theatre, eating popcorn and watching an interestingly brunette Lana Turner in *Flame and the Flesh* when Gladys battles her way down the aisle.

'Get yourself home,' she hisses. 'Rabbi Fruchter got another call from a Sun Records man.' Then she glances up at the screen and says, 'And what you doing watching nasty movies, anyhow?'

Standing in Rabbi Fruchter's hallway, Elvis twists the telephone's cord around his fingers and hardly dares breathe. The man on the line, whose name is Scotty Moore, tells him to come to his house on Belz on Sunday to run through some songs with him and a friend.

'We're in a group called the Starlite Wranglers,' he says. 'You probably heard of us.'

'Oh, sure,' says Elvis, trying to recall if he's seen them anyplace. 'You're real good.'

'So we'll see you around three.'

'What did Mr Phillips say about me, again?'

'He said you sang.'

Elvis waits for more, but nothing comes. So he asks, 'Want me to bring my guitar?'

'If you want.'

'Mr Phillips didn't say nothing about me?'

'He just asked me to listen to you, and tell him what I thought.'

'So it's a try-out?'

'See you Sunday.'

By the time Elvis arrives on Belz, he's found out from Mr Cuoghi, who owns Pop Tunes, that the Starlite Wranglers are about as far backwoods hillbilly as they come, but Scotty Moore is respected in the clubs around the city for his guitar playing. He also learns that

Mr Moore has a cute second wife named Bobbie, and that his first wife is living out in Washington with their kids. Elvis decides not to mention this part to his mama.

The sidewalk by Scotty's new one-storey house is clean and dotted with young trees. Up the street, a couple of kids are sitting on the kerb, too hot to do anything but suck on their Popsicles. It must be at least a hundred degrees out here. A man stops washing his car to watch Elvis as he walks up to the porch in his pink pants and white lacy shirt, which is sticking to his back. He carries his guitar in one hand, unsure whether he's done the right thing in bringing it. It's old now, and too small for him, and is covered in scratches. In the mirror at home, he'd held the guitar to his chest and practised what he'd say to Mr Moore: *It sure is a pleasure to meet such a great musician, sir. I've admired the Starlite Wranglers a long time. I hope we can work together real well.*

A skinny woman with short dark hair opens the door. She's wearing a pair of pedal pushers and has nothing on her feet. Putting a hand to her cheek, she inspects Elvis with what he takes to be alarm.

'Sorry to trouble you, ma'am ...'

'Scotty!' she calls back into the house, fixing Elvis with bug eyes. 'The kid with the sideburns is here!'

As she ushers him in, Elvis is careful to wipe his feet on the doormat, but he doesn't apologise when his hand brushes her arm.

The living room is so tidy it's like nobody lives there. It's bigger than his parents' entire apartment, and the shelves are lined with stacks of magazines and records. There's no TV, but there's a record player on the table by the window, and a double bass propped against the wall.

'I'm Bobbie,' says the woman, using her hand to wipe some imaginary dust from the couch. 'Can I get you something? A beer or ...'

'A Pepsi, if you have it, ma'am.'

She nods towards his pants. 'Where in the world did you pick those up?'

'Lansky's Tailors. They're the best on Beale.'

'That right? I might get myself a pair.'

'You must be Elvis.' A short man with a neat face is striding towards him. The man's hair sits respectfully flat on his head and his jeans look very clean and new. He can't be more than a few years older than Elvis but something about him makes Elvis feel childish by comparison. Slipping an arm around Bobbie's waist and pulling her in close, the man says, 'I see you've met my wife.'

Elvis touches his nose. 'She's made me feel right at home, sir.'

'Scotty Moore,' says the man, holding out a hand. His nails look manicured, and his shake is surprisingly strong.

'I'm a real fan,' says Elvis, having forgotten the rest of his speech.

'Bobbie got you something?' Scotty asks.

She frees herself from his arm. 'I'm on it,' she says.

When she's gone, Scotty grins, just briefly, and then looks serious again. 'Sam said we might play around a little, see what happens. I got Bill coming over, too. He plays bass.'

'I know. He's real good.'

'You seen us, then?'

'Thousands of times, man.'

To avoid Scotty's penetrating eyes, Elvis leans his guitar on the couch and walks across the room to look out at the yard. The yellow grass is patchy and could do with straightening out round the edges. 'You make a living out of performing?' he asks.

'Not yet.'

Elvis turns to him. 'But you mean to, right?'

Scotty takes up his guitar, which has a good sheen on it and looks like it means business, just like him. 'Sure.'

'Me too,' says Elvis, having just decided this.

Scotty strums a few chords and says nothing.

'I mean,' says Elvis, stalking the room as he speaks, 'Mr Phillips told me I could.' He selects a few records from the shelf and flips through them, doing his best to appear careless. The Coasters. Muddy Waters. The Dominoes. The Platters. Hank Snow. Rudi Richardson. Coming across a Lowell Fulson, Elvis holds it up and says, 'I love this guy.'

'You do?'

'I love all of these.'

'Marion – Miss Keisker – said you're a good ballad singer.'

Elvis cannot stop a big smile springing to his face. 'Well,' he says, slowly, 'Mr Phillips said I could make it, if I hooked up with you guys.'

Scotty studies him for a long moment. Elvis goes back to flipping through the records.

Then Bobbie calls out that Bill has arrived, and Scotty leaves Elvis alone in the living room. There's a lot of noise from the hallway. Bobbie's laughing, Scotty and Bill are both talking about the show they did last night, how crazy it was and what time they made it home and what time they woke up, and how it's hot as all get out. There's a resounding slap, which Elvis takes to be Bill's hand landing on Scotty's back.

The door opens.

'So this is the kid!' says Bill, putting his big, grinning face up close to Elvis's and grabbing his hand. He's older than Scotty. His eye bags seem to be stained brown, like ashtrays.

'I'm a big fan ...' Elvis begins.

'Sure you are! Why wouldn't you be? What's your name, again?'

'Presley, sir. Elvis Presley.'

'Your mama give you that name?'

'It was my daddy's middle name.'

'And he let you have it, all the same?'

Elvis looks to Scotty, and then back to Bill, who's grinning broadly.

'Elvis here says Sam told him he could make it,' says Scotty.

'With your help,' says Elvis, ducking his head.

Bill bursts out laughing. 'Sure he did, kid!' he says, slapping Elvis on the back.

'So are we getting down to this thing or what?' Scotty asks.

Suddenly unable to stay in the room with these two men, one who seems just too big and loud to fit in the place, and the other so neat and contained that it's downright spooky, Elvis excuses himself to the bathroom. As he rushes out, he hears Scotty mutter to Bill, 'This won't take long.'

In the hallway, Elvis takes a deep breath. Maybe if he can just get his bearings, keep smiling, he can do this thing. *My name is FEAR!* he whispers to himself. *People tremble and shake when I am near!*

He bursts back into the room. 'What do you want me to sing?'

'Up to you,' says Scotty.

'You know "I Love You Because"?'

'Sure,' says Scotty, leaning over his guitar and strumming it, making a deep and lovely sound which Elvis judges to be about ten times better than anything he's managed to produce from his own instrument.

'You can start,' Scotty instructs.

'You ain't playing?' Elvis asks Bill.

'I don't play on Sundays,' says Bill, cracking open a beer. 'It's against my religion.'

'He's my second pair of ears,' Scotty explains.

Elvis tries to strum the intro, gets it wrong, apologises, starts again. His hands are sweating madly. Scotty and Bill's eyes are on him, so he fixes his own gaze on the drapes, which are blue and covered in cream swirls that look like ice cream, and he tries to start singing, but he misses his cue, apologises, and has to start over.

'Just relax, man,' says Bill. 'Everything's cool.'

Elvis manages to start singing this time, but just as he gets into the second line, and is beginning to feel as though he might be able to make it through the song, Scotty starts fingerpicking notes, so that his guitar sounds like it's singing a completely different tune from the one coming from Elvis's mouth.

Elvis stops. 'How'd you do that?' he asks.

Scotty shrugs. 'Practice. We starting over?'

Elvis begins the song once more, focusing on his own voice this time, determined not to be out-sung by a guitar. He tries to wring some emotion from the words, but he knows what he's doing isn't impressing Scotty or Bill too much. Even though he plays as though he has electricity coming from his fingers, Scotty's face remains flat as an iron. Bill just stares and drinks, as if he's got better things to do on a Sunday afternoon.

They run through a few more ballads, and with each one, Elvis's voice becomes weaker, and his heart sinks lower. After an hour, Scotty looks at his watch and announces that it's been a real pleasure, and that they'll be in touch.

Elvis leaves without saying goodbye. He climbs into his car and races over to Krystal Burgers.

After he's got his order, Elvis drives straight back to Scotty's, one sweaty hand on the wheel, the other on his paper package of food, and parks in front of the house. While waiting for his burgers, he had an idea that he could change their minds, that they could try again and it would all be different, but now he can hear music coming from the house. Unsure what to do, he starts in on the food. The afternoon has become even hotter. The sky seems to be pressing on everything. Nobody is out on the sidewalk, now. As he chews and swallows, he listens to the song drifting from the windows, and it sounds much better than anything they'd managed that afternoon. It's a country song, 'Bumming Around', and although it's fun, it's got pump in it, and it sounds like Scotty and Bill are enjoying themselves plenty without him.

Elvis grabs the door handle, ready to run up the path, hammer on the door and announce his intention to sing something else, something with a good beat behind it, just like the one they're doing now, if only they'll let him. They have to listen! But then they begin their version of Hank Williams's 'Kaw-Liga', and Elvis lets his hand drop. Hank died just a few months ago, OD-ing on drugs in the back of his Cadillac, having drunk up all that money and fame. Mama loved Hank, and so did he. The thought of the country star stops Elvis from running up that path. What would Hank do? He wouldn't go back to beg. He'd move on, find another opportunity.

Elvis knows he ought to go home and tell Gladys everything. Perhaps they could cry together over Hank, and sing 'I Saw the Light', like they did back in January. But instead he starts the engine and drives a little way down the road, parks the Lincoln beneath the trees, and keeps listening to the music, banging his head over and over on the burning steering wheel.

That night, he drives around downtown, calling in to the Green Owl where somebody is singing 'Fool, Fool, Fool', which makes him leave again.

But the next evening, when he arrives home from work, Gladys and Dixie are waiting for him on the couch with the news that he's had another call from Sun. Mr Phillips wants him back over there.

This time, Elvis changes his clothes and shines his shoes before saying goodbye.

The temperature is higher in the studio, and it seems to Elvis that he and Scotty and Bill are making heat and moisture more than music. Scotty is a little friendlier, patting Elvis on the shoulder and telling him to just relax and do it like they did at his house. For the first couple of hours, Elvis suggests songs endlessly, trying all his favourite ballads, putting everything he has into it, sometimes even breaking off in the middle of one to start another. Occasionally Mr Phillips tells Scotty not to make his guitar part too darn complicated. Other than that, he just rubs at his ear and looks impassively through the glass, like he did before.

It's almost midnight when they reach the end of 'Harbour Lights'. Mr Phillips sighs and says they might take a break, then disappears to fetch them some Pepsis.

When he's gone, they look at one another in silence. Bill's eye bags are bigger and browner than yesterday afternoon, and even Scotty's shirt is creased and has become unhooked from the back of his pants. His hair, though, is still absolutely flat.

'What I gotta do to make that man like me?' Elvis asks.

Bill and Scotty sit on the floor, Scotty leaning back on the piano and Bill using his bass as a prop for his elbow. Neither of them has an answer, so Elvis stays on his feet, and starts suggesting songs again. He's used to being awake at this hour; he sometimes thinks he feels most awake between midnight and three in the morning. If he was home he'd be watching the street from his window, wishing he was out there. Now that he is out, not on the streets but in this studio, making music, he means to hang on to every moment of it, even if it's not the kind of music that Mr Phillips wants to hear.

'You know that ol' Arthur Crudup song? "That's All Right"?' Elvis asks, and when they ignore him he launches into it, just goofing off, imitating Arthur's raspy voice and leaping around as he sings, dipping his knees, tipping his head back and shouting the song to the ceiling as a way of releasing all his frustration while Mr Phillips is out of the room. He imagines he's one of the Vampin' Babies on the stage at the Midnight Ramble, and starts wiggling his ass and his shoulders in time. Soon Bill is laughing and joining in, getting up to slap the bass as if it needs punishing, twirling it around on the spot and crouching to wiggle his own behind. Then Scotty is standing and making his guitar sing along in its own peculiar fashion, and for the first time that evening, all three of them are smiling at one another. Elvis sings louder, stretching to some ridiculously high notes, swinging his arm in a slow circle in time to Bill's bass, imagining now that he's in Ulysees Mayhorn's band, among the mops and lamps and upturned vegetable crates of the store.

'What the hell is that?'

Elvis stops, abruptly.

Mr Phillips is back behind the glass. He's staring at Elvis hard, but he doesn't look mad. He looks as if he has a thousand questions.

'Elvis, I didn't think you'd know that song.'

'We was just fooling around ...' says Scotty.

'Well, do it again!' says Mr Phillips. 'Back up, find a place, and let me get something of that.'

Elvis glances at Scotty, who shrugs.

'Come on!' says Mr Phillips. 'You had something there! I don't know what it was, but it was *something*.'

They start over.

* * *

The day after Dewey Phillips played her son's record on the radio – not just played it, but damn near wore it out (she heard it fifteen times: she counted), Gladys puts on her good shoes and informs Vernon that she needs to go downtown to pick up some special things for a cake to celebrate Elvis's success. Vernon gives her a look which tells her he knows that what she really wants is to hear Elvis's song over the radio in a shop or a cafeteria somewhere, so she can tell somebody that voice is her son's. But he drives her anyway.

On the way to the Piggly Wiggly, it crosses Gladys's mind that she might see somebody she knows, perhaps Mrs King from her Lauderdale days, and Mrs King might even have heard the broadcast and be thrilled, not to mention envious. Even if she hasn't heard it, Gladys will be able to announce the news. *Oh, didn't you hear? Dewey Phillips played Elvis's record – yes, he has a record out – and apparently the phone lines at the station lit up like a fairground! And Dewey interviewed him, right there on the show!*

It's mid-morning, and the heat in the car is so intense she has to close her eyes and concentrate on breathing steady. Vernon just frowns against the glare. They've both been up the whole night with Elvis, going over it all. Elvis made her repeat exactly what she heard on the radio during his interview. He was so excited and nervous that he had no idea what he was saying. Gladys suggested they get Dixie over, but Elvis told her that Dixie had left town last night, on a family vacation.

'You know,' Gladys says to Vernon as they drive down Poplar Avenue, 'we can't let this go to Elvis's head.'

'Aw, Glad. Let the boy have a little fun.'

'We want him to get his electrician's certificate, don't we? All this could be kinda distracting.'

'Our son is on the radio all night – he's interviewed by *Dewey Phillips* – and all you can talk about is *certificates*?' asks Vernon.

Gladys giggles. 'I loved it when I heard his name. *Elvis Presley*. I couldn't believe I was hearing those words.'

'I know,' says Vernon. Then he launches into his Dewey impression. '*That was Elvis Presley with "That's All Right, Mama"!*'

'Think he'll be in the *Scimitar*?'

'I don't doubt it, gal.'

She checks the money in her change-purse. 'What do you figure they'll ask?'

'How should I know?'

'I guess they'll wanna know about where he's from, what he likes to do … Do you think they'll ask about his folks?'

'He can make all that up.'

'Vernon!'

'That's what the movie stars do.'

Gladys giggles again. 'I'm still hearing Dewey say his name.'

'*Elvis Presley!*' Vernon hoots.

She doesn't mention it, but hearing Elvis's name on the radio had actually felt exposing – dangerous, even; to Gladys's mind, hearing your full name in public usually means trouble. The last time

Vernon's full name was uttered out loud before an audience was, after all, when he was sentenced at the Lee County courthouse.

As she walks to the store, leaving Vernon in the cafeteria down the street, a thick wave of July heat rises from the sidewalk, making Gladys feel as though her body is seeping into her clothes. Her dress goes limp, flapping against her thighs, and she becomes aware of her own odour. But none of it matters, because soon she will be in the air-conditioned Piggly Wiggly, and she might even hear her son's voice coming over the tannoy.

Of course, Mrs King isn't in the store. Gladys doesn't bother with a cart. She takes the aisles slowly, her ears keenly aware that the radio is in fact playing Perry Como's latest. When she reaches the refrigerator, she stands before it, basking in the cool air coming from the metal shelves as she decides which margarine to buy. She'd like butter, but it's so much more expensive. She wonders if they will have more money soon. Elvis has said that, if he sells records, there could be more coming to them. Vernon says he's never met a guitar player worth a damn, and that guitars never mean cash, only liquor and loneliness. He says that's why most country songs are sad songs. But Elvis's song isn't sad. As she listened to it last night, she understood that it was a song full of energy and youth and hope, and she noticed something in it that she hadn't heard in her son's voice before then, something she couldn't quite put her finger on, but standing here in the cool air it comes to her: her son's song sounded like money.

She chooses the Oleo and goes to the cash register. The girl doesn't look at Gladys as she states the amount owed. Gladys has the change ready, but she hesitates, because the Perry Como song has finished now.

The girl repeats the amount and Gladys almost holds up a hand to shush her, but then realises that the next song is also not her son's. Snatching up her goods, she leaves the money on the counter and hurries through the doors.

* * *

She tells Vernon that it's too hot to be downtown and she wants to go home directly. Recognising her mood, he complies without comment.

When they reach their apartment, Gladys spots her sister Lillian waiting on the porch.

Since she moved to Memphis, Lillian has dropped by occasionally, but has been too busy with her own family to come regularly, which Gladys hasn't much minded. Lillian has never been shy about letting Gladys know all the ways in which she is more knowledgeable, experienced and sensible than her little sister. And as they've grown, these ways seem to have become more numerous.

Gladys almost tells Vernon to turn the car around, but then Lillian waves, and she has no choice but to wave back.

'I guess y'all have been out celebrating!' Lillian calls.

Beneath the midday sun, Gladys walks slowly towards her sister.

'Guess y'all are too grand to stay home, now!' Lillian continues.

Gladys leans in to kiss Lillian's cheek, and she notices something nervous in her sister's expression, as if she is expecting Gladys to make some sudden, unexpected move.

'Come on in,' says Vernon, holding the door open.

'Ain't seen you in a while,' says Gladys, when they reach the apartment.

Lillian plops herself in the easy chair and kicks off her shoes. 'You know how it is,' she says. 'There's always something.'

'Let me fix you gals a cool drink,' says Vernon, disappearing into the kitchen. The only time Vernon makes refreshments is when Gladys has a female visitor.

Gladys sits on the couch and mops her brow with a handkerchief. 'If it gets any hotter my feet will just explode!'

'How you been, Glad?' asks Lillian.

'Oh, you know,' says Gladys. 'We're getting along. How are you all?'

'Charlie ain't been so good,' says Lillian. 'Heart trouble. He can't work, as a matter of fact.'

'I'm right sorry to hear that.'

'Billy's working, but you know hard it can be to stretch one wage to a whole family.'

'I sure do.'

'But I didn't come here to tell you my troubles!' says Lillian, leaning forward. 'You better tell me everything. We didn't know Elvis had a *record*.'

Gladys allows herself a smile. 'Well, I hardly knew myself—'

'And then Bobbie comes running in from Lord-knows-where last night and says to turn on the radio 'cause her cousin's on it! Charlie told her not to be so darned foolish, but when we tuned in, there he was! We couldn't credit it! How come you kept all this a secret from your family, Gladys?'

'Like I said, I didn't know myself.'

'But Elvis tells you *everything*, don't he?'

Ignoring this barb, Gladys says, 'Elvis didn't realise, till yesterday, that Mr Phillips – that's the man who owns Sun Records – was going to take the song to the radio station. And then he didn't want anybody else to know, in case Dewey didn't play it, or folks didn't like it.'

'But he did play it!'

Gladys nods. 'He played it fifteen times. *Fifteen!*'

Lillian stares at her sister. 'What he do that for?'

'Folks was calling the station, asking for it. Didn't you hear Elvis being interviewed?'

'I turned in early.'

'Dewey asked Elvis all kinds of questions. Poor Elvie, he was so jumpy! Not that it showed, of course, but I could tell. We was up all night, we was that excited! Isn't it just the most wonderful – the most astonishing – thing you ever heard?'

Vernon comes in with the iced tea and a plate of crackers. He sets the glasses on the coffee table, then stands back and beams.

'Glad telling you all about our boy's success, Lillian? Ain't it something?'

Lillian casts a look around the room, then, glancing down at her hands, says, 'Bobbie told me some folks thought maybe Elvis was a negro.'

Vernon, still standing, folds his arms. 'What the hell are you talking about?'

'Well, I guess it was the way he sang the song.'

'*Who* thought Elvis was a negro?' asks Gladys.

'I don't know! But Bobbie said Dewey made a point of asking Elvis which school he was at, so folks would know he was white.'

'But it's *obvious* he's white!' Gladys says, her voice rising.

'Obvious to us, maybe,' says Lillian, dabbing at her mouth with a handkerchief. 'But that Dewey Phillips, he plays mostly race records, don't he?'

Sitting on the arm of the easy chair, Vernon places a hand on Gladys's shoulder. 'Well, what does it matter?' he asks. 'Elvis was on the radio.'

Lillian helps herself to a glass of iced tea and takes a long drink. 'Oh, it don't matter none, I guess.' She nibbles on a cracker, then adds, 'Good to get it straight, though. A mix-up like that could lead to all kinds of trouble.'

Vernon raises his voice. 'Elvis was on the radio, and people all over Memphis liked what they heard. That's what counts.'

'That's right,' says Gladys, reaching for her husband's hand.

Lillian slaps Vernon's knee. 'Now don't go getting ornery on your sister-in-law, Vernon Presley!'

'Vernon's just proud of his son,' says Gladys.

'We all are!' says Lillian. 'And it sure is good to see you two again. This family ain't been together nearly enough, lately. I want y'all to come visit just as soon as you can.'

They drink their tea, and smile.

After Lillian has left, Gladys and Vernon share a couple of beers.

'We gotta watch her,' says Vernon. 'And all the others, too. I mean, it's nice to share good fortune and all. But we oughta be careful.'

Gladys laughs it off, telling her husband not to be so suspicious. But it takes a few more beers to settle her nerves.

Graceland, 24 March 1958

When Elvis returns from a night at the Rollerdrome with his friends, Gladys is waiting for him.

It is four a.m. He must report to the Memphis draft board for induction into the army at seven. Gladys has been awake all night, listening for the sound of his car coming up the driveway. Around three she gave up trying to sleep in her bed and decided to wait it out on the huge white couch, custom-built and not long installed in the living room. Although she thinks the couch ludicrous, she likes this room. The ivory drapes and the blue of the walls were her choices; she finds them restful. The colour of the walls makes her think of a bird's egg, although Mr Golden, who helped them with the decor, called it Dresden blue.

Now Elvis stands in the doorway, looking at her from under his brow, a hopeful smile playing around his mouth. The others, seeing her there, stop their babbling and shuffle downstairs to the den. She hears Cliff say, 'Army's gonna be a breeze compared to facing your mama, boy,' and one of the girls giggling in response.

Elvis sniffs and composes his face. 'Mama.'

'Elvis.'

She glances at the clock.

He takes the opportunity to stretch out on the couch beside her, placing his head heavily in her lap and closing his eyes. He smells strongly of cigarettes and perfume. Whether it's Anita's or his own, Gladys cannot tell.

'Mama, can you do something for me?'

She doesn't answer.

'Can you keep your eye on Anita? Truth is, I ain't sure how much I can trust that girl.'

'Any fool can see she's devoted to you.'

He frowns. 'But how do I know she really loves me?'

He's asked this question before, of other girls. Usually Gladys would provide him with comforting words, saying that of course the girl can see the real him, and loves him not for his money and his fame but for his own self. But she's no longer sure if this is true. Anita wants a career in entertainment, and does a good job of almost outshining her son whenever they are seen in public. So Gladys says, 'Well, why don't you just ask her?'

He sighs. 'I'm dog tired.'

'You oughta've gone to your own bed instead of out on the town.'

'Mama,' he murmurs, 'it's my last night in Memphis.'

'Looks like morning time to me, son.'

He covers his eyes with one hand, as if he might drop off to sleep, which prompts her to shove him from her lap. He yelps and laughs, but Gladys isn't smiling.

'Now you listen. I want you to go and eat good,' she says. 'Then wash up and get yourself ready for the US Army. As if this thing ain't bad enough without you showing up at the draft station looking like some alley cat just dragged itself in off Beale.'

'I was at the Rollerdrome!'

'But where was you after that?'

He throws himself back on the cushions and lets out a great huff of indignation.

She stands. 'If I were you, I'd worry less about Anita loving you and more about how you're gonna make it through today,' she says, wrapping her housecoat tightly around her. 'I'm gonna go fix you some breakfast.'

'Daisy can do it,' he mumbles. 'You oughta take the weight off—'

'Not this morning,' she warns, turning for the door. 'This morning I am fixing you breakfast.'

She's sitting on her bed in her underclothes, staring blindly at the new pink dress laid out beside her, when Vernon comes in.

'Glad. I sure hate to rush you, but we gotta leave soon.'

Her husband looks fresh and well ironed. He always enjoys having his picture taken for the papers; being before the camera seems to increase his brightness, as if a switch has been flicked and his lights have come on. It's the same with Elvis. Vernon's suit is new, a sombre shade of grey, and his shoes squeak as he crosses the room to sit beside her.

'I can't wear this one,' she says, pushing the dress away.

'But you bought it specially.'

'It don't feel right. It looks like a wedding outfit, when this here's more like a damn funeral.'

'Don't start with the dismals, Glad.'

'Why did I go and yell at him this morning, of all mornings?'

'You was upset. We all are.'

'Just fetch me the blue one, will you?'

Vernon goes to the closet and rakes through the dresses, holding them up for her 'yes' or 'no', tossing the unwanted ones on the carpet as he goes. She doesn't have the energy to tell him to pick them up.

He holds up a dark blue one with a slash of cream silk at the chest.

'That's it.'

'Put it on, then,' he says, softly. He checks his watch. 'Lord! It's past six already.'

She snatches the dress away. 'I'm losing my son today, and all you can think of is the time!'

'You ain't losing him, Glad. He's going in the army, is all.'

'He could be fighting in a war soon!'

253

'Honey,' says Vernon, looking into her face. 'They won't harm a hair on his precious head. Colonel will take care of that.'

'Colonel?' She almost spits. 'If he could take care of anything at all, Elvis would never have got that draft letter!'

Vernon hangs his head. 'You gotta get a hold of yourself. Boy's gonna serve his country. Ain't nothing we can do about it.'

'I already lost one. I can't lose another.'

He sits beside her and, to her surprise, takes her hands in his.

'I lost him too,' he says, quietly.

For a moment, she thinks about laying her head on his shoulder. But then she straightens her spine. 'Give me a minute to get this thing on,' she says, removing her hands from his and shaking out the dress with a crack.

Vernon stands and wipes his face. 'Wear the diamond earrings,' he instructs, before closing the door.

At the drafting office, Gladys tries to focus on following her son into the building without getting distracted by the crowds of reporters and fans on the sidewalk, but even inside there are camera bulbs flashing and people yelling his name. The Colonel seems to be herding them to and fro, chewing on his cigar and grinning like an alligator as he hands out balloons with the name of Elvis's new movie, *KING CREOLE*, stamped on the side. Elvis somehow looks well scrubbed and rested, smiling and talking fast to anybody who asks him a question as if he's had a solid ten hours in bed. Gladys knows he takes a little medication sometimes, when he's on the road or working long hours in Hollywood. When she asked him about it, he told her all the stars take something to help them through, even Judy Garland, and that he would use the washbag she made him to keep his pills safe while he was gone. The studios arrange for doctors to prescribe medication especially, he said, which she'd thought very generous of them. But this morning, as Elvis signs papers and poses for picture after picture, Gladys notices his hand twitches even more than usual. The blue of his eyes has all but disappeared, replaced by the wide blackness of his pupils.

Vernon holds her arm tighter than is comfortable, keeping her as upright as him. They follow the crowd back into the cars and over to the Kennedy Veterans Hospital, where Elvis is stripped and weighed and measured and has all his fingers dipped in ink and rolled across a page as if he's about to be taken to the state pen. The Colonel pats Gladys's arm and whispers in her ear, 'Your son is worth his weight in gold.'

More photos. More documents. Elvis eats an army sandwich, but Gladys can't face any food at all. Then he holds up his right hand, managing to control the twitching for a minute, and says the words, *I, Elvis Presley, do solemnly swear that I will have true faith and allegiance to the United States of America.*

More photos, and suddenly everyone is leaving. She must say goodbye, now, and Elvis is there, right up close, still smiling although his eyes are all wrong, but she can't smile back as he hugs and kisses her and whispers in her ear, 'I'll send for you and Daddy just as soon as I can.'

And as the reporters push closer to Gladys, calling her name now as her son boards the bus, she finds herself uncomfortably aware of how it would look if she *were* to smile and wave with the others when the newspapers have made such a great deal of her being a devoted Christian mother whose special bond with her boy has granted him the strength to become the star he is today. She wipes her cheek, and lets her mouth fall into a silent howl of dismay, just as though she were attending the funeral of her only son, and the flashbulbs blaze around her.

3: MANSION

MANSION

THE ROAD: 1955

1955

When Elvis drives into the outskirts of Tupelo town with his mama beside him, a few heads turn to take a look at his car. Cutting his speed to allow people to appreciate the quality of the used Lincoln, he glances at his mama, half-expecting her to wave like the Queen of England.

Instead, she beams and says, 'Sure is good to be back.'

It's a grey Thursday in early February, and they're both hunched up against the cold. The car's heating system isn't working as it should, and Gladys has her hands folded inside the cuffs of her new winter coat.

'What you gonna do in town while I visit with Novie?' she asks.

'I'll figure it out.'

'You might get yourself over to Reed's. Buy a little something for Daddy. They have some high-class neckties there. He's gonna need a few of those, with all the fine folks we're meeting.'

'I could get you something,' Elvis suggests.

He's already bought her two Mixmasters, one for either end of the kitchen, so she doesn't have to walk so far.

'Now don't you go spending any more on me!' says Gladys, rubbing his shoulder.

This is the first time Elvis has been back to Tupelo since 'That's All Right, Mama' came out, and what he most wants to do is drive down Main Street as his new self. He wants to walk outside the courthouse in his new striped pink sport coat from Lansky's and see if anybody recognises him both as the Elvis he once was and the Elvis he's now become: the rising star of the *Louisiana Hayride*, the singer making his mark on the regional country-and-western charts with three records, the young man the local newspapers are calling 'the Hillbilly Cat' (he's not sure about being called a hillbilly of any kind, but Miss Keisker started that one, and she says it's great). Most of all, he wants to meet somebody from the old days, so he can tell them what he says to anybody who'll listen: *It's all happening so fast, I just can't believe it. One minute I'm driving a truck, the next my record is on the radio!*

What he really can't believe, though he would never admit it to anybody, is how quickly he has come to expect success. With every good notice in the local press, every new booking, every promise from Mr Phillips that the next record will be bigger, he expects more. Mr Phillips has told him: there's no standing still in this business. You got to keep climbing, or you'll be sliding right back down that greasy pole.

He's certainly climbing. And there are few things more joyous to him than telling his mother exactly how he's getting higher.

'Mama,' he says, lowering his voice. He's been saving up this piece of news for a while. 'I got a promoter interested in me. A real big one. Mr Neal says this guy knows everybody, even folks out in Hollywood. He's booked me on a tour he runs, with Hank Snow, and Mother Maybelle and the Carter Sisters, Slim Whitman, all of them.'

Gladys gives a little shriek. 'Hank Snow! Son, that's news!'

He can't help but let his voice rise with excitement. 'Sure is!'

'And Mr Neal reckons this man knows folks in Hollywood?'

His mama likes Mr Neal, the local disc jockey who Mr Phillips has brought in to manage Elvis's live appearances. He's built like a bear, is always laughing, and seems just as excited by Elvis's success as they are. Elvis thinks of him as the kind of smart, well-dressed, smooth-talking uncle he wishes he actually had.

'Mr Neal thinks real highly of him. Reckons he knows exactly what's what in the entertainment business. He used to be Eddy Arnold's manager.'

'What's this man's name, son?'

'Colonel Tom Parker.'

'You met him yet?'

'Sunday. After the first show at the Ellis. It's all fixed up.'

Although he's not yet spoken to the man, he's spotted Tom Parker at a couple of his shows. Elvis was doing his spot at the *Hayride* when he first noticed the short fat guy with the cigar clamped between his jaws. What was strange was that instead of watching the show he was looking right at the audience. Elvis dismissed the man as a goof until he saw him again, the next Saturday night, doing exactly the same thing, only the girls were on their feet and really yelling this time. Every few moments Tom Parker would tear his eyes from them, glance back at Elvis, nod, then go back to watching the audience. Elvis thought maybe the man got off on looking at the girls until Mr Neal told him who he was, and that it wasn't the girls who interested him.

'Well,' says Gladys, 'when you meet him, be sure to mind your manners. I don't want none of these big business folks saying I ain't raised you right.'

'Nobody could say that, Mama,' says Elvis, and he plants a kiss on her cheek.

He drops his mother at Novie's house, then cruises down Main. It's two-thirty in the afternoon, and the sidewalk is peppered with shoppers. The store windows reflect his car's streak of cream metal as he glides down the wide street, the radio turned up now that Mama's not here to complain. Several shoppers turn to look, but he doesn't recognise their faces.

Then, outside the TKE drugstore, Elvis's prayers are answered by a cloud of black hair.

He toots the horn and pulls in at the kerb. For a moment he sits, watching her in his side mirror. Magdalene Morgan is taller, slimmer, and her saucer cheeks have become more defined since he last saw her, seven years ago. But she still walks with her eyes fixed dead ahead, as if she knows exactly where she's going and means to waste no time getting there. He notices that her coat is a little shabby about the hem.

He opens the door and steps out.

'Hi, Magdalene.'

She has to skitter to the side to avoid colliding with him. Then she squints at his face.

'Don't you recognise me?' he asks, pouting, unsure whether he's thrilled or appalled.

She continues to squint, so he starts to sing, *'You may talk about your men of Jericho ...'*

'Elvis? Is that you?'

'Wanna grab a shake, honey?'

She blinks. 'Is this your *car*?'

He strokes the hood, which is still warm. 'Uh-huh.'

She folds her arms. 'Well, I'll be doggone! Elvis Presley! Ain't seen you in a while!'

'Come on inside, and I'll tell you all the news.'

Her mouth is working as if she's about to make some excuse.

'I'll buy you a piece of pie,' he says, grabbing her hand. It's cold, and he can feel her bones move beneath his grip.

Tugging her hand free, she says, 'It sure is good to see you, but—'

'I owe you, Magdalene. For leaving town and not saying goodbye and all.'

She looks at him sideways. 'That's the truth.'

'So are you coming?'

She sighs. 'Sure.'

As they walk through the glass door, he resists placing a hand between her shoulders to guide her to the counter. With lunch recently over, only two other people are sitting there: one old lady who is nursing a coffee and smoking a cigarette very intently, and a suited man eating a cheeseburger over his newspaper. On seeing the menu chalked up behind the soda fountain, Elvis's mouth waters. He could have anything he wants. He could have two of everything. But he informs the unsmiling waitress that they'll take a couple of chocolate shakes and a large slice of apple pie to share, and then he tells Magdalene he'll be back in just one second.

On the other side of the room, he drops a nickel into the jukebox and the coloured tubes light up. He chooses 'Blue Moon of Kentucky'. Leaning over the humming glass dome, he watches his record slide and click into place and the needle rest in the groove. Then he closes his eyes and waits for the first verse to finish before turning to face the counter.

Magdalene is watching him, looking curious but not particularly impressed.

'Who's that?' he calls across the room. 'Who's that, Magdalene?' She looks blank, so he strides over to her, arms open wide. 'You know who that is, don't you?' he says.

By this time, the other diners and the waitress have looked up.

Magdalene's eyes slide to the jukebox, then back to Elvis. 'It ain't ...' she says. 'It can't be!'

He nods.

Her cheeks fill with colour, and she claps her hands together twice, as if applauding him.

Elvis sits on the stool and basks in her astonishment. For a full minute, all they can do is laugh together. The man tuts and returns to his newspaper, and the old woman lights another cigarette.

'Gosh dang!' gasps Magdalene. 'I heard you was singing some, but I had no idea!'

'I've cut three records! And they're playing them all over the South. They even buy them in Texas, Magdalene! Don't you listen to the *Louisiana Hayride*?'

She shakes her head. 'My mother don't like it.'

'Well, tell your mother I'm on it! Every Saturday! I'm the star attraction! I tell you, it's all happened so fast I can't keep up.'

The waitress pushes their drinks and pie across the counter.

'Thank you, ma'am,' says Elvis, grinning at her.

'That your record?' she asks. She's a little older than him, has blonde hair screwed into a bun, small shoulders, and a greasy sheen to her forehead.

'Uh-huh. I was just playing it to my old girlfriend here,' says Elvis.

'I like that one,' says the waitress. 'It's real different.'

'Got another one coming out soon, even better.'

'He never was one to hide his light under a bushel,' says Magdalene, rolling her eyes.

The waitress touches her hair. 'I don't guess he oughta hide anything at all.'

Magdalene looks at the waitress, then back at Elvis. 'Well,' she says, pushing back her stool, 'it sure was nice to catch up! But I'd best be getting along.'

'You just got here!' he says, hanging on to her sleeve. 'We used to sing together, didn't we, Magdalene? I reckon this gal here started this whole thing.'

Magdalene waves a hand across her face. 'Oh, now.'

'Ain't that precious,' says the waitress. She turns her back on them, and begins polishing the sundae dishes.

Elvis grins. Magdalene grins back. They share the pie, and Elvis orders another slice. Leaning her chin on one hand, Magdalene watches him eat the lot, then says, in a small voice, 'So how come you never wrote me?'

He swallows. Should he tell her about the marriage licence? About how he sat on her porch steps for the longest time with his declaration of everlasting love in his pocket?

She sucks up the last of her shake. 'You plumb broke my heart.'

'Magdalene,' he says, solemnly, 'I never meant to hurt you.'

She lets out a loud laugh and slaps his hand so hard he winces. 'I'm just kidding!' she says. 'Guess I can forgive you now, anyway, huh? I see you had plans, all along.'

Recovering himself, he announces, 'I got great plans, Magdalene. Like you wouldn't believe.'

She smiles and nods, apparently ready to hear more.

What can he say? His plan is just to keep going. To sell more records. To go all the way. The word 'Hollywood' has been firmly planted in his head by Mr Neal's talk of Colonel Parker's contacts, but sitting here in TKE's with Magdalene Morgan that word seems impossible to say. She might laugh at him again, and he couldn't bear that.

The song comes to an end. 'Want me to play it again?' says Elvis, jumping up.

They listen to it five times in a row, and share another shake. When Magdalene leaves, saying she has to go fetch her cousin from school, Elvis tries to make her promise she will come visit him in Memphis. 'But you're a big star now, Elvis,' she says, buttoning up her coat. 'Why would you want to bother with *me*?' And she strides down the sidewalk before he can reply.

* * *

After performing their first Sunday-afternoon spot at the Ellis Auditorium in Memphis, Elvis, Scotty and Bill are delayed by the line of girls seeking autographs, and, worried about being late for their meeting with Colonel Parker, they have to race down the wet steps and out into the rainy street. They are all still steaming from the show.

An approaching car slows, tyres hissing on wet asphalt, and sounds its horn, making Bill hold up his hand like a traffic cop. 'This here's Memphis's own Elvis Presley!' he bellows through the rain. 'You can't run him down! He just played the Ellis with the Blue Moon Boys!'

When they reach the other side, Elvis asks Scotty if what he's heard about the Colonel is true.

'What you heard?' asks Scotty, setting a brisk pace.

'That he knows Hollywood folks.'

'Oh, that,' says Scotty. 'I guess that's true. I thought you meant about him being a carny and all. 'Cause every bit of that *is* true.'

'Colonel Tom Parker has toured the nation with bearded ladies, performing bears, and men encased in ice. Not to mention dancing chickens and psychic dwarves,' Bill cuts in.

'Some of that ain't true,' says Scotty. 'Far as I can fathom.'

Having reached the canopy of Palumbo's restaurant, they stand beneath it for a moment, each catching their breath. Elvis adjusts his necktie and brushes the rain from his shoulders. Bill combs his hair. Scotty checks his watch, informs them they're ten minutes late, and puts his hand to the door.

Before they go in, Elvis asks, 'Do you reckon this could be, you know, real big for us?'

Scotty keeps his hand steady. 'Depends what Sam says, I guess.'

'We're already big!' Bill pats Elvis on the back. 'He's booked us on that tour of his, ain't he? That's us and the goddamn gorgeous Carter Sisters, Elvis! Now let's get in there and hear all about it.'

It's warm, hushed, and almost empty inside. Elvis can see five men arranged around a table beneath a low, multicoloured glass shade at the back of the restaurant. On one side are Mr Phillips and Mr Neal, and on the other are Oscar Davis, Colonel Tom Parker and a man Elvis doesn't recognise. Mr Davis has been handling the promotion on a couple of their shows, and, as always, looks a real gentleman: fresh flower in his lapel (today's is a purple carnation), immaculate suit, shining silver hair. The Colonel has on a faded tan jacket, no necktie, and his unruly eyebrows are bunched together as he talks to Mr Phillips, who is leaning back in his chair, arms tightly crossed.

For a second, Elvis considers ducking right back out the door. What could he possibly add to this conversation? He knows Mr Phillips means well by introducing him to all these fellas, but he'd really rather be back across the street in the auditorium. His mama and Dixie are coming to the next show, and he wants to make sure they get their seats right at the front.

But then a waiter in a long white apron appears, and Scotty introduces himself. The waiter smiles and ushers the three of them across the patterned carpet to the table at the back of the room.

None of the men looks up. They are too busy listening to the Colonel, who is in the middle of a speech. His voice is relaxed, as if he's merely stating the obvious.

'... boy can't come to nothing while he's on Sun Records. He needs a national stage. That's the fact of it.'

Mr Phillips has his mouth set in a thin line, but his eyes are popping with disbelief.

Mr Davis holds up a hand. 'Now, what Tom means to say, Sam, is that you've got a great act here' – he gestures towards Elvis, Scotty and Bill – 'a *great* act, and it would be a shame to waste such potential when you've already done so much.' He smiles broadly. 'Welcome, boys! Don't pay us no mind! We're just having a little discussion here ... Take a seat, why don't you? No call for formalities.'

Mr Davis offers Elvis a seat next to Colonel Parker.

Scotty and Bill drag chairs from the next empty table, and perch close to Mr Phillips, who is still scowling at the Colonel.

Mr Davis does the introductions. Colonel Parker nods at Scotty and Bill, then turns to Elvis and shakes his hand with warm, meaty fingers.

'So you're the sexy hillbilly singer, huh?' He fixes Elvis with a clear stare. 'My wife tells me you got all the gals in a spin!' There's something boiled-looking about his face: his cheeks are pink and shiny, like a doll's. Elvis almost laughs, seeing the man up close. But the Colonel's voice is deadly serious. 'I was just telling Mr Phillips here that if you really want to make it, you gotta go national,' he continues. 'You look to me like a boy who really wants to make it. Am I right?'

'Yessir,' says Elvis.

'There you go!' barks the younger man next to Colonel Parker.

'That's Mr Diskin,' says the Colonel. 'He's my lieutenant.'

Mr Diskin performs a goofy salute.

Elvis smiles, and looks to Mr Phillips for guidance, but Mr Phillips is staring at the Colonel and asking, 'May I speak, now?'

'Mr Phillips, you may speak whenever you like,' says the Colonel.

'I find your attitude a little hard to take, Mr Parker. You stroll into my town and tell me my label ain't worth a damn—'

'Colonel didn't say that,' Mr Davis cuts in. 'What he said was—'

'What he said was, my artist won't get nowhere if he sticks with me. Least, that's what I heard.'

Elvis has seen Mr Phillips's chin jut out at this kind of angle before, when he's feeling something real good about a song, and he's heard him when his words start running off in all directions, either from excitement or frustration, but he's never seen him get real mad. It makes Elvis's gut shrink, because there's nothing he can say to make this any better, and, without ever meaning to, he seems to have caused the whole thing. He wishes he could leave, right now. He doesn't really see why he's needed here, anyway. The businessmen could deal with all this stuff without him.

'Who are you to tell me my business, anyway, Mr Parker?' says Mr Phillips, whose voice has gone a little squeaky. 'I make the decisions about my artists! I'm the label man, here! Last time I checked, you were just bookings and promotion!'

Scattered on the cloth before Colonel Parker are numerous emptied sugar packets. He reaches for another from the dish at the centre of the table, rips off the corner with his teeth, empties the contents into the dregs of his coffee, and flicks the packet onto the pile. Quietly, he says, 'You're taking this way too personal, Mr Phillips. My concern is to help these boys get to where they want to be. Where they rightly should be. Which is on a national stage, just like I said. I think that's what everyone around this table wants.' He sups the last of his drink. 'And, last time I checked, these boys don't belong to nobody.'

Mr Phillips can only glare at him.

Mr Davis says, 'Maybe we ought to move on to the details of this tour.'

Mr Neal, who, until now, has been silently studying the edge of his napkin, says, 'Yes! Great idea. Tom, you were telling me, weren't you, about that big resort hotel in Nevada you're talking to …'

Elvis manages to sit for a while as the talk turns to dates, towns, venues, promotional activities. Mr Phillips glowers in the corner, not uttering another word. Elvis is so distracted by Mr Phillips's mood that he doesn't really hear what's said. Scotty and Bill seem at ease; they help themselves to coffee from the pot on the table and even throw in their own suggestions for venues. Unable to stand it any longer, Elvis rises from his chair.

'I'm right sorry, gents,' he says, 'but we gotta get back for the next show. It was a real pleasure to meet you, Colonel Parker, and you, Mr Diskin.'

Holding out his hand, he realises it's trembling, but he's unsure whether it's with outrage on Mr Phillips's behalf, or with excitement at Colonel Parker's words: *a national stage.*

Colonel Parker looks surprised. 'Leaving us already, son?'

'I'm sorry, sir, but I like to be ready, you know, for a show.'

Colonel Parker sits back in his chair and folds his arms. 'That's a good attitude. But you do realise this is *your* future we're discussing here?'

'And I'm real grateful to you, Colonel Parker, it's just—'

The Colonel holds up a hand. 'Call me Colonel. And save your gratitude,' he says, 'for when I've made you a real star.'

Elvis lets out a laugh, but the Colonel keeps a straight face.

There's a pause, and then the Colonel waves him away. 'Off you go, then, fellas! I like to see entertainers committed to punctuality! See you on the tour!'

As Elvis turns to leave, Mr Phillips glances at him and Elvis flinches, expecting to see blame of some kind in his eyes. But all he sees is sorrow.

* * *

The lights in the Big Creek High School gym are down, but Elvis can see the girls up front, screaming, crying, beating their fists on their knees and shaking their heads as if in grief. Ever since he became a regular act on the *Hayride*, his shows have gotten crazier, but this is the craziest yet. He's got pretty good at knowing which flick of the wrist or hip, which special kind of sneer, will have the girls leaping from their seats. At first, Mr Neal paid a few of them to scream, at least that's what Bill said, but tonight it doesn't look like any girl here has much control over what her body is doing.

Scotty hides his amazement behind an ironic smile, but Bill looks like a schoolboy who just got told there are no more lessons, ever. They've all quit their day jobs, and after every performance Bill tells Elvis how he just can't believe it. All this money. All this music. All these *girls*! There are always girls waiting after a show, and they are ready and willing for just about anything. The ones Elvis doesn't want, Scotty and Bill can scrap over.

He drops to his knees at the edge of the stage as he finishes 'I Got a Woman', knowing that it will get them on their feet, and looks out at the front row. Instead of standing to clap, they are lifting their skirts and showing him everything they've got. Some of them are wearing underclothes, but not all. One girl with blonde curls falling in her eyes has her checked skirt bunched around her waist and her legs wide apart. She's bellowing like some animal. He pauses, seeing the darkness between her thighs, and almost points his finger – but then remembers who he is now, and that he's on stage, and if he points at this little girl, who knows what will happen to her? She could go to jail.

He shakes his head and laughs at the delicious insanity of it, and hopes his mother and father, who are watching the show from a couple of rows back, haven't noticed what's going on. Gladys and Vernon regularly come along if it isn't too far to travel, and he likes that they are there to see how popular he is, and how good he's become at putting on a show. He doesn't hold back for his parents' sake. His mama says how an audience reacts to him is a special thing, so why should he put the brakes on? If anything, he wants to push the audience further, so his mama can see how much they adore him, and how hard he works to be worthy of their love.

He's into 'Baby Let's Play House', pumping his legs to the beat, singing about how he'd rather see his baby dead than with another, when he realises that the audience can't hear him. They're covering their ears and yelling and whistling so loud he fears he may lose the song, or the dusty curtain above the stage might fall on his head. He can no longer feel the thump of Bill's bass. The floorboards are vibrating, not with music but with screams. The sound rips through Elvis, making him think of the tornado that went through Tupelo when he was a baby. The Baptist church across the street was razed to the ground, but Uncle Noah's house, where they'd sheltered, escaped unscathed. Gladys has told him, over and over: *Sometimes I think we survived because of you, son. Because God wanted to spare you.* She'd held him so close that he'd screamed to be set free, and the tornado had passed by.

If he can survive that, he can deal with this, easy. He can keep singing as the noise rises up and around him like deep water. He can keep moving, going up on his toes and bumping his hips, turning to face Scotty as he jiggles his ass, which makes them even crazier; and he'll keep pinching his nose and laughing, because now the whole thing's a big joke – the girls, the moves, even the song. And if he laughs first, then nobody else can.

It's a joke only for a moment before he's back in the music, though he senses it's not the song that counts so much as the way he sings it, the way he moves to it. His lungs taking their air and his mouth making these sounds. Nothing can stop what's inside him from coming out. Beneath his satin shirt, his chest expands. His flecked jacket is soaked with sweat. Even his hair seems to have its own rhythm. He feels like that angel back in Priceville cemetery, firing his arrows of love to the mere mortals on the ground. He *does* have Jesse's power. Here it is, coming out of every pore.

Elvis sticks his right arm out and brings it down slow to signal to Scotty and Bill that they should take this last part easy. He slides to his knees again to finish the number, pleading with his baby to come back, and the girls roar and weep their desire to do so, if only he'd let them.

Then they rush towards the stage, hungry for anything he can give, screaming, *ELVIS ELVIS ELVIS*, and he hears his name and recognises it. Yes. Here I am. I was waiting for you, and now I'm here.

Raising his arms in triumph, he says, 'Thank you, you're a great audience,' and then he bows low, straightens up, waves, bows again, thanks them again.

When he finally turns around, Scotty is gesturing to him to get off, and Elvis spots something in his friend's face he hasn't seen before. It takes him a second to recognise the emotion as fear. He glances over his shoulder and realises that dozens of girls are climbing towards him, their skirts hitched about their waists as they haul their legs onto the stage, standing on each other's hands and pushing one another down in their fight to be the first to reach him. Although he has felt something come loose in an audience before now, this is the first time the stage has been stormed.

Scotty has already fled, holding his beloved Gibson guitar above his head, and Bill is on the top step yelling, 'For God's sake, Elvis! Get off!' But Elvis doesn't move. He's fascinated by these girls, the way they have broken all the rules. It dawns on him that the stage is a special place where he and they are free to do what they want.

Together, they can make up their own rules. And he is sure they won't hurt him. They love him too much for that.

But they are coming at him now, a swathe of females panting and screaming his name, their fingernails snatching the air. A girl in a tight yellow sweater is beckoning to him with both hands, her painted mouth hanging open. Another is making a strange grunting noise as she stares at him, slowly shaking her head. A brunette stands in the centre of it all, one hand at the back of her neck, her eyes glassy, as if she's about to faint. Instinctively, he ducks, covering his head with his hands, and is instantly squeezed on all sides by girls. The sweet scent of laundry detergent and hairspray mingles with the sharp musk of their bodies. Somebody grabs at his jacket, somebody else goes for his pants. It becomes a little hard to breathe. He tries to laugh, to say, 'Easy, ladies, give a fella a break,' but finds he has no voice.

'Elvis! I'll love you for ever and ever!'

'Sing to us one more time!'

'I'm yours, Elvis!'

'Please, Elvis! *Please!*'

Then he hears his mother yelling, 'Why are you hurting my boy?'

And his father's voice: 'Get offa him! Go home!'

His parents must be picking them off, because, astonishingly, the hands fall away, the roar in his ears subsides, and he can breathe again. Then his father grips him beneath the armpits, lifting him from the crowd, and his mama takes hold of his legs. To his surprise, she doesn't falter at the weight of him. She anchors his ankles at her hips, as if he is a cart she must pull, and pushes on through the girls, yelling at them to move aside. As Gladys and Vernon carry him to safety, Elvis turns his head and gives the girls a grin.

Backstage, his daddy's shirt is crumpled and his hair is so sweaty it sticks up from his forehead in what looks to be a bad parody of his son's style. His mama dabs at her brow with a handkerchief while

Vernon fetches her a chair, then hands her his hip flask and instructs her to drink. Elvis flinches as, without protest, she takes a good few gulps and wipes her mouth with the back of her hand.

Now he's in the safety of the locker room, Elvis realises his legs are weak, and he takes a chair next to his mother. For a while they both pant and sweat and shake their heads and say, 'Lord have mercy.' Each time Gladys says it, it sounds more desperate, but each time Elvis does, a little laughter creeps in around the edges of the words.

'They didn't wanna hurt me none, Mama.'

Gladys's hand trembles at her mouth.

'They just wanna get close to me, is all.'

Gladys fixes him with a black stare and says, 'Looked to me like they was gonna kill you. They coulda ripped you clean in two.'

Elvis glances at his daddy, who is leaning on the bolted door. He has nothing to say. 'Get that fan on,' Elvis instructs, and Vernon does as he is told.

Thick, stale air moves around them. Elvis takes his mother's damp hand. Gently, he presses it between his own until the trembling stops, and whispers, 'There, there, baby. Elvis is still right here.'

Gladys leans forward so their foreheads touch. Her skin is sticky on his, and he can smell liquor on her breath.

'They just had me so scared,' she says.

'Shh. It's OK, baby.'

'Elvie.'

'Mama.'

'I can't stand to see you hurt.'

'I know it.'

'I keep getting these dreams. They're tearing you apart, and there ain't nothing I can do about it.'

The fan shudders. Outside, they are squealing his name. Elvis tries not to smile, for his mother's sake.

Gladys balls her handkerchief in her fist. She takes a deep breath, shakes her head, then says, 'Maybe you oughta limit these shows, son.'

Elvis leans back in his chair. 'What do you mean, limit?'

Gladys reaches for her new crocodile-skin purse, which is big enough to hold a small cat, drops the handkerchief into it, and clicks it shut. 'I mean, ain't the records enough? All of this – I can't fathom it, son. Seems to me like you ain't thinking straight.'

Elvis jumps to his feet. 'I'm thinking real straight, Mama. I'm building my career here. Tell her, Daddy. The shows are how I sell records.'

Vernon folds his arms. 'Boy's right, Glad. It's all part of it.'

Gladys tightens her grip on her purse. 'But do you have to do so many?'

Elvis paces the length of the room. The cement floor is gritty beneath his delicate shoes. 'I gotta keep selling records!' He manages not to kick a locker door for emphasis. 'So I gotta keep doing the shows. It's like Colonel Parker says, I gotta break out of being a regional star. I gotta go national!'

Gladys clicks the clasps on her purse open, then shut, then open, then shut.

'But you're on stage almost every night, making them girls lose their minds. It scares me half to death to watch it.'

'Mama,' says Elvis, pausing before her, 'you know I'm doing it all for you and Daddy, don't you? Pretty soon I can buy you a house. And a new car. Anything you want—'

'But I can't see why in the world you'd take such risks!'

'I'll be able to buy you anything at all. So you gotta quit asking me to limit stuff.'

'And see you wind up dead?'

She looks at him with such rage that he thinks he might be in for a whipping. That palm might draw back and swat him across the legs. He takes a step away from her, in readiness.

But all Gladys does is snatch the flask from Vernon's hand.

Elvis steels himself. He keeps his voice steady. 'I'm sorry, Mama, but if you can't stand to watch, then I reckon you oughta stay home. Ain't that right, Daddy?'

Vernon nods, silently.

Gladys takes another drink, and Vernon announces that it's time they hit the road.

* * *

In May, he goes to Lowenstein's on Main to buy Dixie a pink playsuit. The assistant looks down her nose at his wad of bills, which prompts him to buy three silk dresses for his mama, too. He hands much of every week's gains over to Gladys for safekeeping, but the truth is there's so much cash around he finds it difficult, and frankly unnecessary, to keep track. There's more than enough for the family to rent a new two-bedroom brick bungalow in a better neighbourhood, and for his father to quit looking for work. Elvis wasn't sure this was such a good idea, but Vernon told him it was simple: he could work for his son, sorting out all the little things Elvis no longer had time for. Answering fan mail, for example. Hell, he was already doing it!

Elvis hasn't seen Dixie in three weeks. He has a short break in his touring schedule, and they have a date arranged for this evening, but as he drives home from Lowenstein's, he wonders if he can present the gift to her sooner than that, and perhaps even get her to let him watch her put it on. But where? If he takes her into his bedroom, his mother will be knocking on the door, and Dixie shares her room with her sisters. Perhaps he could persuade her to try it in the car. The thought of Dixie easing up those little shorts on the back seat of his new Cadillac – which he's had painted pink and white, remembering that car his mother saw parked outside St Joseph's – has him turning the vehicle around and heading straight for her house.

She lives in a one-storey place on a leafy avenue over the south side of the city. He parks the Caddy, throws it a loving look, then races up Dixie's porch steps.

Luckily for him, her father's car isn't in the drive. Mr Locke has made it clear that he's not entirely sure about Elvis. He's always asking about the shows, about how Elvis stands the odd hours, and whether he ever thinks of taking up something a little more steady. Elvis tells him that he's just no good at anything else.

Dixie's mother is more amenable, but even she's no pushover.

'Well,' she says, keeping him on the porch, 'Dixie isn't expecting you right now. I don't think she's ready yet.'

'That's an awful shame, Mrs Locke. I know she'd flip for this movie—'

Then a voice comes from the hallway. 'Elvis? Is that you?'

Elvis smiles. 'Why, there she is, ma'am. And she looks good and ready to me.'

Dixie pushes past her mother, bounces onto the porch, and flings her arms around his neck.

'Hi, sweetheart.' He pecks his girl on the cheek, then turns to Mrs Locke. 'I'll have her back by ten-thirty, ma'am. I promise.'

Dixie tugs him down the steps.

When he has her in the car and they've pulled away from her house, he gestures towards the back seat. 'I got you something,' he says. 'But you can't look at it yet.'

She reaches over to lift the paper, and spots the pink fabric. 'Ooh!' she says. 'Is it for the prom?'

He'd forgotten about Dixie's goddamn High School prom. He'd promised to take her, months ago.

''Cause I already got my dress and all—'

'It's better than that,' he says, 'but you got to wait.'

Dixie moves up close to him. 'You're still taking me to the prom tomorrow night, right?'

'Course I am, baby!' He grasps her hand and kisses her fingers.

'When can I open it?'

'When we get to Riverside Park.'

'I thought we were going to the movies.'

'Are you kidding? I need to see you in it first.'

She gazes at him, wide-eyed. 'Elvis. What in the world are you suggesting?'

'That you try it on for me.'

'And where am I supposed to do that in Riverside Park?'

He drops his voice. 'In the back of the car, honey.'

She slaps his thigh. 'You're crazy! I am not undressing in this car!'

'I won't look,' he says. 'I'll keep my eyes right on the lake. I'll just be taking in the glorious view, baby. I swear.'

She folds her arms. 'I want you to turn this vehicle around and take me straight back home.'

'Aw, you don't mean that,' he says. 'I ain't seen you in weeks! So now I want to see as much of you as I can.'

She's quiet for a few minutes. He keeps driving, sneaking little looks in her direction. She frowns, and starts to fiddle with the hem of her dress, which is white, printed with birdcages, and sits just past her knee.

'Don't you wanna know what's going on with the tour and all?' he asks.

'Sure,' she says, but she doesn't look at him.

'I don't wanna bore you with it.'

'No,' she says. 'Tell me.'

He's called her every night with an update, but he can't seem to tell her the details often enough. Telling Dixie makes it all seem real.

'I'm top of the bill, now. Colonel Parker's real pleased. I think he might wanna be my manager, Dixie! He's told Mr Neal he wants to keep working with me. Did I mention he knows people in Hollywood?'

'You sure did,' says Dixie, glancing at the package on the back seat.

'And the last four shows were total sell-outs!'

'Uh-huh.'

'But I missed you every minute.'

'That's why you bought me a gift?'

'Sure, baby,' he says. They're approaching the park now. 'How about I stop somewhere real quiet, then step out of the car while you … you know.'

'You'll wait outside?'

'You can lock all the doors.'

She says nothing, but she doesn't object when he puts his arm around her shoulder and draws her closer so he can kiss her ear.

He drives towards McKellar Lake, away from the noise of the teen canteen and the dancing pavilion. Finding the quietest spot he can, right out on the far side, he stops beneath the pines. At six o'clock on a Friday, there are a few mothers with young kids packing up picnics and making for home, but nobody else is in this part of the park. He cuts the engine, and the sound of the geese burbling on the water floats through the windows. He fiddles with the radio dial, trying to find some appropriate song, something romantic and passionate without being too suggestive. They both like Mario Lanza, but he can't find anything of that kind. In the end, Dixie reaches over and flicks the switch, killing the music.

'Are you getting out so I can do this?' she says.

'Can't I at least see you open it?' he asks, stroking her shoulder and gazing into her eyes.

She sighs.

He places the package in her lap. Pouting at it, she says, 'You didn't oughta've gotten this for me.'

'I want you to know you're still my girl.'

'But I'm not sure I can give you what you want – what I know you *really* want – in return,' she says, blinking up at him with her eyes all blurry and pleading.

Irritation flashes through him. Is she going to spoil this with her soul-searching? He's already told her he can wait until they're married. Sometimes he wonders why she has to bring the subject up so often. It's not as if he's tried to push her into it. And how does she know what he really wants, anyway? He can get laid, any time he likes. He can take his pick of girls after a show, and he often does, though he's always careful not to get one of them pregnant. Mama has warned him about that, over and over. The first time he'd sealed the deal, the rubber bust and, on her instruction, he took the girl – she was pretty enough, a few years older, and experienced – to the emergency room in Shreveport to get a douche. The whole thing had been more of a relief than anything. Since then, he's been more relaxed about it, but he's gone all the way only with girls who've been round the block a few times, although there's been plenty of fooling around with all sorts of females.

He almost says, *All I want is to see you in the fucking playsuit. Period.*

Instead, he calms himself and says, 'I ain't expecting nothing in return, honest.'

Her pale fingers slide beneath the paper and tease off the tape. Holding up the playsuit, she doesn't gasp in wonder, as he'd hoped. 'It matches your car,' is all she says.

'I can take it right back to the store if you don't like it,' he snaps.

'Don't be like that! I love it,' she says, covering his cheek in quick little kisses.

'Try it on, then,' he whispers, outlining her chin with one finger.

She points to the door. 'Out!'

Sitting on the hood with his back to the windshield, he hears her click down all the locks and smiles to himself. The keys are in his pocket.

The sky is turning deeper blue and it's cooler out of the car. The scent of warm pine is all around and there's a little breeze coming off the water. He closes his eyes, feeling the car rock beneath him. Dixie will be squirming out of that dress as quickly as she can. She's never let him touch anything past her knee. Sometimes he strokes the inside of her arm, which is soft as butter. When he runs his fingers all the way to the top, it makes her shiver and tell him to quit. He doesn't mind; he wants her to keep herself nice for if they do get married. His mama says he shouldn't tie himself down too quick but she also says not to let Dixie get away. It's not easy to do both things.

A duck swoops low, almost touching his head as it lands awkwardly on the water, squawking and flapping, making him open his eyes and curse, and miss her unlocking the doors.

'Elvis.'

His first thought, on turning to see her standing next to the car, is that he ought to have bought her some shoes, too. The playsuit doesn't look as good as it would if she were wearing high heels.

But those thighs. Just as white and smooth as he'd hoped, if a little wider than he'd expected, considering the size of her waist, which he can get both his hands right round, easy.

'Come on over here.'

'Does it look OK?'

'It's beautiful, honey. Come closer.'

She takes little steps towards him, combing out her hair with her fingers as she walks, keeping her eyes on his.

Before she reaches him, he sticks out a hand. 'Hold it right there,' he says. 'Now, sit on the hood, and cross your legs.'

She hesitates, seeming to wonder if he is serious.

'I just wanna see you good.'

She slides herself onto the metal.

'It's kinda hot on here!' she says, springing off.

'Just relax into it. You'll get used to it.'

Biting her lip, she sits on the hood, resting her feet on the fender and raising her thighs off the body of the car.

'Now tip your head to the right, and give Elvis a big, big smile.'

'I feel silly!' she says, but she giggles and pushes her breasts out.

'You look like a goddamn movie star up there on the Caddy, Dixie.'

'Honestly?' she says, tossing back her hair and showing her teeth.

'That's it,' he says. 'Perfect.'

After he has admired her from all angles, they spend a long time necking in the car. Dixie lets Elvis slide his hand up one of the legs of her playsuit. Then she takes hold of his fingers and pushes them further in. Feeling the wetness there, he snatches his hand away.

'Elvis,' she says into his shoulder, breathing quick, 'let me show you how much I love you,' and she tries to put his hand back where it was.

He shakes free of her grip and springs away from her.

She looks at him, and her face is flushed, her lips red. He finds it hard to meet her eye.

'Dixie,' he says, 'you don't have to show me nothing.'

'But you been gone so long!' she says, kneading her fingers on her naked thigh. 'I worry about losing you to somebody else.'

'Why would you even think that?'

She yanks the legs of the playsuit down as far as they will go and sits on her hands, her knees clamped together. Her mouth twists. 'Why wouldn't I, when you got so many girls throwing themselves at you?'

At this, he cannot contain his rage.

'Seems to me like you got plenty of your own opportunities, right here!'

She shrinks back, shocked. 'What does that mean?'

'I heard you was at the Rainbow while I was away!'

She stares at him for a moment. Then she says, in a small voice, 'Well, it gets kinda boring, sitting home and waiting with your mother.'

'You don't have to go around with other guys though, do you? Maybe one of *them* taught you this stuff, huh?'

'What stuff?'

'What you was doing just there. Nasty stuff.'

There's a pause. Then Dixie says, very slowly, her eyes on her knees, 'Elvis, please get out of the car so I can dress.'

He does as she asks, slamming the door good and hard, but as soon as he's outside, listening to the gabble of those goddamn ducks, he pounds his forehead with the flat of his hand and yells, 'Presley! You dumb ass! You heel!'

The ducks take fright and fly across the lake, into the dying sun.

Elvis paces the length of the car, yelling at himself and banging on his own head, until Dixie finally opens the door.

'Get in here,' she says. 'You'll frighten the fish, you keep going like that.'

'I'm sorry, baby,' he says.

She nods, quickly.

He climbs in beside her and says, 'You know that we'll be married some day, don't you?'

'I know.'

The Colonel has already advised him that he must hide any steady girlfriend from the press and never speak publicly of marriage, in case it puts the fans off. But Elvis hasn't yet found the right moment to mention this to Dixie.

As he starts the engine, he can tell from the way she moves closer that she will forgive him, at least for the time being.

* * *

At Sun, Gladys is the only woman in the studio. Miss Keisker had greeted her and offered to take her coat, but Gladys declined, not meaning to stay longer than was necessary. Now Miss Keisker has dissolved back into the office, leaving Gladys surrounded by men in suits, one of whom is carrying the biggest camera she's ever seen. Mr Phillips has sold Elvis's record contract to RCA Victor for $35,000. The papers have been signed, and the man from the *Scimitar* wants Elvis's picture.

This is the first time Gladys has been in the studio that her son has told her so much about, and she's a little shocked at how empty and plain the white-tiled room is. It's a late November day, and it's kind of chilly in here. There's a piano in the corner, and a few microphones lined up along the wall. And then there are these men, who are laughing together, and keep shaking one another's hands and clapping her son on the shoulder. Everyone in the room is smiling at Elvis. Vernon hangs back, his jacket open, giving the occasional nod, saying nothing.

To Gladys's surprise, Mr Parker isn't in the centre of the action. He leans against a wall, smoking a cigar, observing the others, much as she is doing. All summer, he has been making her telephone ring, trying to convince her to sign the contract that would grant him the right to act as Elvis's sole manager. When they'd first met, he'd smoked his cigar right at her kitchen table and assumed Vernon to be in charge. All his talk of million-dollar record contracts and Hollywood deals was directed to Elvis's father. He'd also referred to Elvis as 'our boy', as if he already had ownership of him. And so Gladys refused to sign, even though Elvis begged her to do so. He kept telling her that she just didn't understand: Tom Parker might be an old carny, but he knew everyone who counted for anything in the music business and the movies, too. Without Parker, he'd never really make it. When he'd said that, Gladys had realised the full extent of her son's ambition: being an entertainer wasn't enough; he wanted to be a movie star. How could she stand in his way? By October, she had relented, and Tom Parker promised her that Elvis would make so much money he would no longer have to do live shows. Instead of facing a crowd of frenzied fans, he would be in front of a movie camera. He would be safe. Whenever she doubts her decision to sign, she brings this promise to mind.

Mr Neal clasps her hands. 'You sure look elegant today, Mrs Presley!'

Mr Gill at Goldsmith's fixed her hair this morning, putting on more colour and lifting up the sides with cute little slides. She'd gone on to the department-store restaurant, too, and, encouraged by Vernon, had taken a couple of steadying beers with her lunchtime sandwich.

'Why, thank you, Mr Neal!' Gladys sings. Keeping hold of his hands, she draws him closer and lowers her voice. 'Tell me, are you sure my boy will be all right with these new recording folks?'

Mr Neal is a true gentleman; he never laughs off a mother's concerns. 'Mrs Presley,' he says, seriously, 'Elvis is gonna be more than all right. He's gonna be swell. These folks are the very best in the business.'

She nods. 'Kind of a shame for Mr Phillips, though,' she says. 'Elvis is gonna miss him.'

They both look over at Sam, whose face is split by the width of his grin as he listens to something one of the other men – Gladys thinks it's the man from RCA – is telling him.

'I think Sam did pretty good out of this,' says Mr Neal.

'Elvis said that,' says Gladys. 'And so did Mr Parker. But I can't help but feel sorry. And what about Scotty and Bill? They've been so good to my boy, Mr Neal. Taken care of him real well on the road. But Elvis tells me they ain't a part of this thing with Mr Parker.'

Elvis has also told her that though he feels bad about Scotty and Bill going on the payroll rather than getting a slice of everything he makes, he has to look out for his own career now.

Mr Neal places a firm hand on her arm. 'It's a good deal for everybody, Mrs Presley.' He beams, and she sees his gums. 'Scotty and Bill will be just fine. They're still the band, and any band of your son's is onto a real good thing.'

'I hope so, Mr Neal.'

'Did Elvis tell you the Colonel already has his first television appearances booked?'

'He sure did!'

'You must be real proud. And the great credit to you is that he's such a fine boy. Everybody comments on his good manners and attitude. And that's all down to you.'

He's told her this before, but hearing it in this room makes Gladys glow with pleasure. Looking at her son, radiantly handsome in his dark suit, ringed by businessmen congratulating him, she finds herself giggling.

'I guess I did all right, Mr Neal!'

'You certainly did.'

Thirty-five thousand dollars. He'll see only some of that money, of course, but Elvis has told her it's the most ever paid for a single artist's recording contract.

'Folks! Would y'all be so kind as to line up over there?' asks the man from the *Scimitar*. 'I need to get me a picture!'

The men look up. Elvis grabs his own leg, as if to control it, and says, 'I'm shaking with excitement here!' and everyone laughs, including Gladys.

Elvis takes her by the arm and steers her across the room. 'You look happy, Mama,' he says.

'So do you,' she replies.

As they line up, Elvis keeps her close, so Colonel Parker must stand behind her. Vernon manages to slip in on Elvis's other side.

'All this is for you, son,' she whispers, and, turning her back on the Colonel, she kisses his cheek. The camera flashes.

He kisses her back, and as the camera pops again he says, quietly, 'No, Mama, it's for you.'

And, at this moment, Gladys is happy to believe this might be true.

Graceland, July 1958

A week before they are due to join their son in Texas, where he is completing his army training, Gladys receives a telephone call. Since Elvis left, he's called home every night to fill her in on his activities. As she picks up, she is expecting to hear about the weight of the pack he had to carry, what the other men said about the sergeant, and what horrors the army canteen dished out today.

'Mama.'

There's a waver to his voice which Gladys recognises immediately. Knowing what's coming, she closes the kitchen door, then pulls up a stool and parks herself by the wall, cradling the receiver between her chin and her shoulder.

'What's wrong, son?'

'Mama, I ...' He trails off, and lets out a dry sob.

'I'm right here, Elvie. Whatever it is, you can let it out.'

Often he calls her from his friend Mr Fadal's house. Mr Fadal is a disc jockey who has made Elvis feel right at home; his wife cooks the food he likes, and Mr Fadal has even bought special hi-fi equipment for Elvis to listen to his favourite music. She guesses he must be there now, away from the base and the other recruits.

'Mama ...'

'What's going on, baby? Those army folks treating you right?'

'It ain't that.'

'Then what?'

There's a pause, then he asks, very quietly, 'Am I a good son?'

'Elvie! Of course you are!'

His breath shudders over the line. 'Mama, I want you here.'

'Me and Daddy are coming in a week.'

'You oughta be here. You're sick, ain't you, Mama? Real sick. I know it. I see it with my own eyes. You're in pain.'

She twists the cord around her fist and clears her throat. 'The doctors ain't found but one thing wrong with me.'

'My own mother is sick, and I'm four hundred miles away, doing nothing about it! I'm useless, Mama!'

Gladys steadies herself against the wall. 'Son. I'm fine. Mama just misses her baby, is all.'

He's weeping now. She can picture him precisely: one hand on his forehead, shielding his face. His open mouth straining downwards.

'You at Mr Fadal's?' she asks.

'Uh-huh.' He lets out a moan, and sobs again. 'Mama ...'

'I'm here, baby.'

'Mama, I miss you so much.'

'I know, son.'

'Mama ...'

'Elvis ...'

'Mama ...'

'Elvis ...'

On and on it goes. Every time he says it he cries a little louder, and Gladys takes the receiver from her chin, clutches it tight, and lets a tear slide down her own face. It's such a relief to hear him weep for her, and to weep in return, that she almost takes pleasure in it. But the pain of not being able to hold him is physical. She hugs herself with one arm, feeling the hardness in her belly, and rocks back and forth on her stool. Her throat aches from withholding more tears, but she manages to control herself enough to say, 'Listen to me, Elvie. Mama's gonna be with you soon, you hear?'

A long sniff from the other end of the line.

'We'll be together, and everything will be fine.'

'Yes, Mama.'

'There, there, baby.'

'There, there.'

She doesn't hang up until his tears have stopped.

That night, Gladys sleeps well, and the following morning she feels lighter. Elvis may be in the army. He may be the nation's number-one entertainer. But he still needs her. She sits in her garden chair beneath the shade of the large oak at the back of the house, flipping through *Good Housekeeping* and sipping her coffee, and her legs don't give her a moment's bother until lunch-time.

A week later, she can already feel the morning's heat as she steps outside to check on her chickens. It's a shock after the cool of her air-conditioned house, and she reaches back inside the kitchen to reduce the dial. At least when it's warm all the time, you know what you're in for. And if it's hot in the house nobody can expect her to get dressed quick or go to the gate to greet the fans, many of whom have been weeping on the sidewalk since Elvis left. Gladys hasn't had the strength to go down there, fearing she will say something she shouldn't about Tom Parker, or the army, or Elvis himself.

Today Vernon will drive her and his mother through Texas to join Elvis in Killeen, near his base at Fort Hood. Alberta will follow them by train a few days later. Taking a flight is not something Gladys will consider. She'd rather be on the road, even in the heat of July, than up in a plane with nothing between her and death but the air.

She crosses the grass to the coop which Elvis had built as far away from the highway as possible. The dew clings to her slippers and the tall trees stand perfectly still in the humid air. She looks back at the mansion, softly white in the early-morning sun. She won't miss this place. Elvis called last night saying he'd found them the perfect luxury trailer, and Gladys thought that sounded just fine. Small enough for her to walk from end to end without pain, anyhow.

She sidesteps chicken shit with the practised moves of an expert, still light on her feet despite her weight, unlatches the wire door, and reaches for her favourite bird, Marmalade. She's a fat, ginger, speckled hen with the softest feathers and the neatest turn to her beak. Cradling her to her chest, Gladys coos, 'Don't you die while I'm gone, you hear? Don't let them old maids kill you.'

She lets the hen go and scatters corn on the dry grass. 'Mama will be back,' she says, 'won't she?'

The chickens gurgle and squawk in reply, and Gladys lets each one out of the coop to roam the lawn. With Elvis gone, nobody can tell her not to.

Wiping her hands on her dress, she walks quickly back to the house.

Vernon enjoys driving fast, and he settles himself into the seat of the Lincoln, making small contended noises as they race towards Texas. All the windows are down and warm air batters their heads. Minnie Mae snores softly in the back, one hand on her pocketbook. Gladys removes her shoes, not caring about the smell. She closes her eyes and, for a moment, with Vernon singing along to the radio, she feels like a girl again, being driven someplace in the woods in that truck he used to borrow. He always had a rug in the back, ready for her to lie beneath the pines. She wonders if he still has one in the trunk, just in case one of his women would rather do it under the boughs of an old oak than in some motel room.

'Teddy Bear' comes on, and Vernon sings along, tapping the steering wheel in time to the beat. She's never liked this one too much. When she first heard it she didn't understand why Elvis had made a record for children.

'That's a good 'un, ain't it?' says Vernon. 'Ain't heard it in a while.'

'You know who that was!' says the disc jockey. 'U.S. Army Private Presley! And we want to know what *you* think of Elvis joining up!

Does this mean the end of Elvis the Pelvis? We've got Marie on the line ...'

Gladys reaches for the off switch, but Vernon clasps her wrist. 'I wanna hear this,' he protests.

'I reckon Elvis is serving his country like a good American citizen and we all oughta be right proud of him and he'll be just as popular when he gets out,' says Marie.

'That's two years from now, Marie. Which is a heck of a long time in show business,' warns the disc jockey.

'Well, I'll still love him!' says Marie.

'Course you will, girl!' adds Vernon, grinning.

Steve is on the line now. 'Presley is finished!' he says. 'He can't keep his career going and be in the army! He was getting kinda long in the tooth anyhow.'

'Aw, eat dirt, Steve!' says Vernon, clearly enjoying himself.

'Man could be right,' says Gladys, quietly.

'When he comes back,' Steve continues, 'nobody will remember what all the fuss was about.'

'Who'll they be listening to instead, Steve?' asks the disc jockey.

'Jerry Lee Lewis, maybe,' Steve replies. 'Or Pat Boone.'

'Pat Boone!' spits Vernon.

'He's a good singer,' says Gladys.

'Jerry Lee's all right,' says Vernon. 'But not a patch on our boy. And he's too rough round the edges to get real popular.'

'I don't like him one whit,' says Gladys.

'Presley'll be all washed up, two years from now!' Steve declares.

Vernon clicks off the radio. 'What's wrong with these folks?' he asks.

'Well,' says Gladys, 'maybe when he comes home again Elvis will think about doing something else.'

'Damn well hope not!'

'It ain't like being an entertainer is a stable kind of career.'

'Are you out of your mind? Think of the money!'

'Boy's made enough to last a lifetime,' says Gladys.

Vernon tuts. 'You don't know shit,' he says, not quite low enough for her to miss.

'I know he'll be dead before thirty if he don't slow down.'

'You gotta quit saying that.'

'I'll quit saying it when I know it ain't true.'

Vernon puts his foot to the floor, and Gladys closes her eyes, trying to imagine what a luxury trailer might look like.

RIOT: 1956

1956

Even the air is different in Hollywood. Drier, thicker, dirtier, despite the bright spring sky. It is also rich with the scent of Colonel Parker's cigars. Elvis breathes in a lungful, and starts to cough as his manager steers him towards his screen test at Paramount Pictures. He often smells the Colonel before he sees him. The sweet, woody scent precedes him, and when Elvis gets a whiff of it, he knows he's got to look sharp.

'You're gonna be terrific,' the Colonel says. 'All Mr Wallis will want to know is that you can take direction without any bullshit. What he won't want is some hotshot who thinks he knows it all already. So you gotta show him you're real good at listening. You can do that, can't you?'

'I reckon so, sir.'

'I know you can, son. Like I always say: you do your thing, I do mine.'

Every building is squared off, and the same light cream colour. The dry atmosphere means his hair stays in its sculpted shape. There is a new tightness around his mouth and eyes, but he cannot tell if this is down to the Los Angeles air, or all the smiling he's doing.

Maybe it's just nerves at the thought of acting for real Hollywood folks, or exhaustion from being on the road. When he collapsed a few weeks ago after a show in Florida, the doctor told him he had to rest up or risk serious illness, because what he was doing onstage amounted to a full day's labour crammed into twenty minutes. Ever since, Elvis has been proudly telling everyone that story, and every time he tells it, the Colonel's eyes grow rounder and brighter, like prized marbles.

A young man wearing pale pants strides past with a clipboard beneath his arm and the Colonel raises his hand in crisp salute. 'Fine morning!' he says.

The man shoots an interested look at Elvis, nods, and walks on.

Colonel Parker leans close to Elvis and hisses, 'Don't mix with these Hollywood guys any more than you got to. They're all Jews and faggots. Which is their business, of course. But you need to keep your wits sharp.'

Elvis nods.

'I'm watching your back, but you gotta do your bit, too.'

'Understood, sir.'

'So why you wearing blue jeans, son?' asks the Colonel, looking straight ahead, his short body waddling confidently.

'I figured it'd be more ... actorly.'

'Like James Dean?'

'I guess. Colonel, do you reckon they'd let me do that speech from *Rebel Without a Cause*?' Elvis knows all the words to his favourite film and often performs bits of it for his manager.

'You know the one, don't you?' he continues. 'The one about him feeling so ashamed? Like he don't belong no place?'

They've reached the studio now, and the Colonel pauses to look directly at Elvis. Those round eyes make Elvis fear that his manager can read his mind. Elvis has seen the Colonel hypnotise men; once he had his assistant rolling on the floor and barking like a dog. He's never sure if this is a trick or a real power.

Certainly, there seems to be nothing his manager cannot do. When they'd first met, he'd told Elvis that he would never be more than a regional star without a bigger record label, and he'd made that happen. Then he'd got him on TV. And now here they are, in Hollywood.

'You're a smart boy,' the Colonel says, cocking his head. 'Mr Wallis will want somebody to replace Dean. And you're his ticket to the youth market. But don't forget he'll want something new, too. He doesn't want a number-two James Dean. He wants a number-one Elvis Presley. Wallis called *me*. He's been calling me ever since he saw you on the *Dorsey Show*. He's desperate for your talent, son.'

'Yessir, but—'

'You're my boy, and you're already a star. Got it?'

'Thank you, Colonel.'

'So do the script they sent you, OK?'

'Yessir.'

'And when I've got you a million-dollar contract – which I will – then you can do whatever the hell script you like.'

'Yessir.'

The Colonel chews on his cigar and pats Elvis's shoulder. 'You could make money in your sleep, son. In fact, you are!'

Elvis laughs.

Holding the door open for him, the Colonel adds, round eyes popping, 'And if you ever do anything to shame me, you're finished.'

The following day, Elvis and his manager have an appointment to meet producer Hal Wallis. Mr Wallis's office is as big as the whole studio at Sun Records, and his desk is an enormous marble table set on a raised platform, like an altar. There's nothing on it except a black telephone, a pad and a gold pencil. Behind the desk is a shelf reserved for Academy Awards, and Elvis can't help but imagine what it might be like to hold one of those glinting statuettes in his hands.

Catching him gawping, Mr Wallis says, 'I see you've noticed the spoils of my art! So difficult to know *where* to put these things ...'

He's wearing powder-blue suit pants and a silk tie, and is deeply tanned. Leaning back in his padded chair, he smiles.

'So, young man, what do you make of our little set-up here?'

'I can hardly take it in, Mr Wallis,' says Elvis, shifting in his seat. 'I mean, it's happened so fast and all.'

Mr Wallis nods thoughtfully. 'I can imagine,' he says in a soft voice, 'that it's quite overwhelming. Of course, the real strength of our system here at Paramount is that we look after our stars. It can be a pretty tough business, being famous. And we have plenty of experience in *managing* that process.'

'Boy's already a star in his own right, of course,' says Colonel Parker, dabbing his brow with a brightly patterned handkerchief. 'Do you know how many records he's sold, Hal? Did I give you the update on that?'

'I don't believe you did, Tom.'

'"Heartbreak Hotel" – that's his latest, out just a few weeks – is already over a million, and still climbing.'

'That is truly impressive.'

'I'm fielding calls from the TV networks, night and day. Everyone wants my boy, Hal.'

Mr Wallis forms a steeple with his fingers and breathes across it.

'I've watched your screen test, Elvis, and I'll be honest with you: I haven't seen any male actor whose test impressed me quite as much since Errol Flynn.'

Elvis beams. 'Why, thank you, sir.'

'It's not so much your acting ability – although you do have that – it's more your magnetism. The camera sees it, and magnifies it, and that's the thing that makes stars. And, frustratingly for us, it's the thing that's absolutely impossible to manufacture.'

'Millions of girls across the nation agree!' says the Colonel, slapping Elvis's shoulder. 'And their mamas and grandmas, too!'

'What did you make of the role you played in the test, Elvis?' asks Mr Wallis.

Putting his hands to his knees to stop them jumping up and down, Elvis says, 'Well, it was all real interesting, sir, and everyone was so helpful and all, and I had fun. But – can I speak honestly?'

'Please.'

The Colonel sits forward, gripping his cigar in his teeth. He's warned his client never to speak his mind without first checking that his mind is in full agreement with his manager's. But Elvis can't keep quiet on this, and he feels he can trust Mr Wallis to understand. Although he rates the Colonel as just about the smartest man he has ever met, Elvis suspects that his manager knows little about acting in real movies.

'Well, that character just wasn't anything like me, you know?' he says. 'I mean, he was kinda heartbroken, and real happy at the same time. When I get my heart broke, I'm just sad.'

He'd played a halfwit clown. The director hadn't said as much, but from the moment Elvis first read the script he'd known he was playing somebody not unlike his cousin, Gene. Maybe listening to Gene babble on for so many years had helped him get into the role.

Mr Wallis raises his eyebrows. 'What kind of role do you think *would* suit you, Elvis?'

'I guess just something a bit more like me, more suited to my experience and all ... something that didn't need so much—'

'Acting?' asks Mr Wallis.

There's a pause before he bursts out laughing, his plump cheeks shaking with mirth. After a beat, the Colonel joins in.

Elvis looks into his lap. Before the screen test, his manager told him a story about Hank Williams. Hank made it to Hollywood, the Colonel said, only to blow the whole damn thing by getting uppity when he thought the producer was treating him like a rube. Hank had pushed back his chair and rested his cowboy-booted feet on the producer's desk. The sound of Hank's spurs digging into that fine maple had marked the end of his career in pictures.

Elvis shakes his head and manages to smile up at the two men. 'You got my number!' he says, as lightly as he can.

Mr Wallis dabs his eyes. 'I'll let you into a secret,' he says. 'The project I'm thinking of for you, Elvis, is what I'd call a classic Civil War picture, with plenty of love interest, and a real dramatic role for you. Do you think you could handle that?'

'How many songs?' asks the Colonel.

'We can discuss that, but we'll obviously be including some musical numbers ... the character you'd play, Elvis, is a good farm boy, so that would in fact be closer to your own experience, am I right?'

'Well, not exactly, sir—'

'His daddy was a sharecropper,' states the Colonel, without looking at Elvis. 'Worked night and day. Real salt of the earth.'

'So you'll know what it's like to toil the land,' says Mr Wallis. 'I bet you could chase a hog *and* catch it!'

Elvis looks at his shoes. They are made of crocodile skin, and too soft to make a dent in any item of furniture in this room.

'Yessir,' he says, 'reckon I could, if it was a slow 'un.'

Mr Wallis chuckles. 'Elvis,' he says, 'I think we're going to get along just fine.'

A couple of nights later, he is mobbed by girls after a show at the San Diego Arena, and an entire arm of his jacket is taken from him. He runs to the Cadillac, trailing threads of cloth. Slamming the door shut, he sees naked legs coming from his dressing-room window, and a couple of state troopers, together with his friend Red, who has started coming to shows with him to help out, trying to stuff them back in, as though dealing with a bucket of snakes.

Collapsing in the back seat, Elvis realises the police have become part of his family. His first sight now, on arriving anyplace new, or stepping from a hotel or limousine, is a uniform, a cap and a pistol. Wherever he goes, Colonel Parker sees to it that a band of state troopers are put to work, holding back the crowds. Elvis has thanked his manager many times for saving his life. He tells the Colonel that he is like a father to him, and that he hopes he can prove a worthy son.

Back at the El Cortez Hotel, his mama and his new steady, Barbara, are waiting. Barbara is a friend of Dixie's, although slightly older; from some angles, she looks like Elizabeth Taylor. She and Gladys sit at opposite ends of the vinyl couch in his suite, both clutching their purses in their laps. What Elvis finds both appealing and unsettling about Barbara is her cool watchfulness. She reads books and talks about them, too. Sometimes she even reads him poetry, which he likes. Elvis judges her sophisticated enough to be seen with him, yet homey enough to please his mama.

He and Dixie split a few months ago. Sitting on her porch, Dixie had wept as she told him they'd grown too far apart, and she had to end it. His life was elsewhere, now, and his success was more than she could handle. They'd cried together for hours. By midnight, though, he knew her tears were a way of keeping him there in the hope that he'd promise to turn down the dial on his career. The look of desperate pleading in her reddened eyes had made him relieved to walk away.

Outside, a crowd of a hundred or so girls are chanting his name and occasionally breaking out into squeals.

He leans in to kiss his visitors' cheeks – Mama's first.

Barbara says, 'Sounds like that one was a success.'

'It was crazy!' Elvis says, pacing up and down before them. 'The best yet, probably. They're still real excited.'

She nods thoughtfully. Unlike Dixie, Barbara never bubbles over. He wonders what it would take to make her raise her voice. She still has her hat on, a tiny red velvet thing which puts him in mind of a jewellery box. He can't fathom how it stays on her head; perhaps it's held in place by Barbara's will, alone.

'Red said it was more than crazy, son,' says Gladys. 'He said things got a little scary.'

'There was some girls, after, came into the dressing room unin-vited, that's all.'

Gladys shifts in her seat, dabbing at her hairline with a handkerchief. 'Did you ask Mr Parker about getting more police protection? He promised me he'd take good care of you. Me and daddy would never have signed that contract if we'd known—'

'He's doing a good job, Mama. And it's a miracle, ain't it? *Everyone* wants me! Listen to them!' Elvis gestures towards the window. In fact, the shouting has died down some.

'Just so long as they don't hurt you, son. Barbara here's been worried, too.'

Barbara screws up her nose, but she's smiling. 'Those girls are kinda wild, Elvis. *You're* driving them wild.'

'I'm just entertaining them. I owe it to them to put on a good show.'

'Do you have to do all that ... that *stuff*, on the floor?' Barbara asks.

'What stuff?'

'Elvis wouldn't do anything unchristian,' says Gladys.

'Seems to me those girls need a little more self-control!' says Barbara, glancing at Gladys.

Elvis snorts. 'Control's something you're real good at, ain't it?'

Barbara draws back. 'What do you mean?'

'I mean, you might try getting off your behind to kiss me when I come in!' He hoists her to her feet and plants a kiss on her neck.

Barbara touches her hat, apparently worried that it has moved.

'Now, son, she's just concerned for your safety,' says Gladys, patting Barbara's hand. 'Why don't you fetch us all a cool drink and maybe a sandwich from the lobby, Barbara, dear? Whoever's down there won't bother you ... Elvis, give Barbara some money.'

'I got it,' says Barbara.

Elvis tries to stuff some bills in the pocket of Barbara's dress as she walks to the door. His hands fumble at her waist, and she pushes them away.

'I said, I got it.'

When she's gone, Elvis collapses on the couch next to his mama.

'That girl sure is sensitive,' says Gladys. 'You gotta be real careful with her.'

'I can handle it, Mama,' says Elvis.

'Well, I'm glad she's gone, because I got news.' She takes his hand in hers, and lowers her voice. 'There's no way to tell you this but straight, son. Dixie's fixing to marry.'

Elvis springs from the couch and in two steps he's at the window, checking on the crowd outside. The noise increases.

'Still around a hundred girls out there,' he says.

'You hear what I told you, son?'

He puts his hands to the window, then presses his cheek to the glass. In response, the girls wave their arms, straining upwards as though they could reach him, even from four floors below. It's useless, of course; there is no ladder to where he is, but still they stretch as far as they can.

'I'll never understand why the two of you parted, but now she's found a nice boy with a good steady job—'

'Hi, girls!' Elvis flings open the window and waves, and the crowd erupt into yelling. Several drivers blast their horns at the commotion. The cool air coming from the bay feels good on his face. He wonders what would happen if he were to fall. Would the crowd catch him, or would they devour him?

'Elvis! Come away from there! You gonna get those girls in trouble.'

'Sure mean to,' he mumbles.

'What did you say?'

'I sure am happy for Dixie,' he says, closing the window.

Gladys sighs. 'You know, you didn't oughta let Barbara go the same way. She's a good girl.'

He crosses the room and kneels before his mother, resting his head on the couch. 'Mama,' he says, looking up at her, 'I don't need no wife. I got you.'

She smiles and pats his hair. 'Quit messing around.'

'Nobody's gonna look after Elvie like you do.'

'You gotta do right by that gal, or she'll be gone. Be smart. If you keep Barbara happy, she'll wait for you.'

He gets to his feet once more but doesn't go to the window this time. At his back the sound of the girls chanting his name reverberates up into the air.

'Mama,' he says, 'I got so many girls to keep happy, it makes my head spin.'

'Son,' says Gladys, 'if anybody can do it, you can.'

Elvis stands at the window and throws it open to let the cold air and the sound of his fans surround him. He can smell the ocean. It's close to midnight; his mama and Barbara have gone to their own beds and Red is in the suite's bathroom. Leaning on the sill, he waves down to the girls still on the sidewalk – about fifty, he reckons. Their upturned faces are lit by the hotel sign, which flashes blue and green, giving them an unearthly glow. One of them shouts, 'Take off your shirt, Elvis!'

Pretending not to have heard, he cups a hand to his ear. 'Say what?'

'Shirt off!'

He shakes his head. 'Can't hear you!'

'Shirt off!'

Drawing back, he unbuttons his shirt – pale blue, embroidered with white diamonds – to the rising crescendo of squeals, then dangles it above the crowd with one hand.

'Those crazy females will wake the whole city.'

Red has returned from the bathroom and is standing close to him, looking out. Earlier, it was obvious to Elvis that Red wanted to go out on the town with Scotty, Bill and DJ, the new drummer. But, knowing Elvis couldn't join them, Red chose to stay and keep his friend company.

He lights up a cigarette and blows smoke out of the window.

'Why you half-naked, E?'

'Just having me a little fun,' says Elvis, tossing the shirt into the air. It balloons out, then flutters down with its arms catching on the breeze. The girls rise as one to grab it. It gets hooked by at least four of them, who shriek as they try to tug it from each other.

Red looks down. 'Those gals gonna kill each other,' he murmurs.

Elvis turns to him and says, 'Feel like doing something for me?'

'Sure, E.'

'Go down there and pick me one out. You know the type I like.'

Red looks as though he's about to laugh, but Elvis holds his gaze.

'There's one I seen. Around sixteen. Dark hair. Blue eyes. Kinda small, with a round behind. Bring her up.'

'How will I know which—'

'You'll know,' says Elvis. He's seen no such girl in the crowd, but he can imagine her well enough, and he knows Red can, too.

Red drags on his cigarette. 'All right,' he says, 'but what if there's more than one like that?'

'Hell, bring 'em both up,' says Elvis.

'And what if there's three, E?'

Elvis laughs. 'Then there's one for you, too, man.'

As Red leaves the room, Elvis adds, 'Don't tell Colonel nothing about this.'

The girl's name is Diane. In her pink dress and matching lipstick, she is almost exactly what he'd asked for, and she hasn't said a word since Red brought her up with her friend, Alicia. They both sit on the couch drinking Pepsis while Red and Elvis swap wisecracks. Both girls laugh at everything Elvis says, but Alicia laughs the loudest. When Red takes Alicia off to his room, Elvis suggests that Diane might like to see where he sleeps.

She removes her shoes and sits on the edge of the mattress, studying her bare feet. Her toenails are painted light green, and each one is perfectly shaped and glossy.

'I like your toes, honey,' he says. 'I can tell you've gone to a heap of trouble, there.'

She wiggles them for him.

'Why don't you go wash them?' he suggests.

She frowns, but takes herself off to the bathroom. While she's gone, Elvis fetches a pair of ladies' cream silk shortie pyjamas from his suitcase and places them on the bed. He swallows down a couple of sleeping pills from the bottle he stashed in the drawer earlier. Then he strips to his undershorts and climbs between the sheets. He arranges the covers over his lower half and sits upright, watching the door.

When it opens, Diane catches her breath and stands completely still, unable to look at his face.

'It's OK, honey,' he says, 'I just want to snuggle. Slip on those pyjamas for me, and come over here.'

She puts a hand to her cheek and sways a little.

'I know you're a virgin,' he says, 'and I reckon you oughta stay one. I just want to hold you real close, so I can sleep.'

He can't tell if she's on the verge of laughter or tears, so he smiles. 'Put on the pyjamas, sweetheart.'

In a small voice, she asks, 'Do you want to watch?'

'Well, sure,' he says, stretching his arms along the headboard and resting his head on the wall. 'If you don't mind.'

Diane turns her back to him to unzip her dress, fumbling a little when it gets caught on her bra. She's wearing white under-clothes, and the skin on her back is lighter than that on her arms. From the small indentations above her panties, he can see where the dress was tight on her waist. His cock jumps, but he ignores it and takes a swig of water. He can pick up some other girl tomorrow afternoon, between shows, an older one who has already been spoiled and knows what she's doing. For now, he must focus on rest. It is so hard, these days, to allow himself to slip into the warm darkness of sleep. Even when his body is exhausted, his mind still skips in loops. If he can hold this girl, maybe it will be easier to relax into the oblivion he craves. The pills usually work, but the whole process will be sweetened by the presence of a girl.

He doesn't tell her to turn around. As she steps into the pyjamas, her thighs shiver.

'You look real nice,' he says, and she almost vaults to the bed, diving beneath the covers and lying next to him with the sheet pulled up to her neck.

Elvis clicks off the light, then reaches for her.

'Oh, my God,' she whispers, as he aims his lips at her face. He can already feel the pills' heaviness settling in his limbs. Diane stays absolutely still, apparently frozen to the mattress, until he finds her ear and nibbles it, and then she turns and holds him fiercely. He kisses her lips and feels her body loosen beneath his hands until she is a warm mass up against him. He guides her hand to his cock and together they bring him off with a few swift strokes. Then he buries his face in her chest and allows the drug to take hold.

'You'll be here when I wake up, won't you, baby?' he whispers.

'Yes,' she breathes. 'Yes.'

* * *

Another minute seems too long to wait: he has been on the train from New York for twenty-seven hours. He tells anybody who asks that he won't fly because it makes his mama too jittery, but the truth is he fears being up in the air and would rather endure twenty-seven hours on a train than board any plane. Twenty-seven hours of looking out of the window and seeing nothing much, save his own reflection and that of the Colonel's cigar bobbing as he talks of what's next and when (always *now*) and how much money it will make them. Twenty-seven hours of combing his hair, rearranging the pens in his shirt pocket, swapping jokes with Scotty and Bill and his cousins Junior and Bobby, his travelling companions, there for the ride and, as Gladys has said, to give him that family feeling, even when he's away from home. Twenty-seven hours of intense July heat that has the sweat trickling into his eyes. Twenty-seven hours of checking on Junior, who sits next to Elvis like a dog guarding his master. But the master must also control the dog, for Junior is a Section 8, an ex-serviceman who went crazy in Korea and shot a group of civilians. Throughout the trip, he's sipped bourbon from a flask, twitched at unseen threats, grinned whenever he's managed to tune in to one of Elvis's jokes.

Twenty-seven hours of girls peeping at him and whispering, *Is it him? Didn't we see him on TV? It is, it's him!* Giggles, smiles, longing looks. The occasional kiss.

That, at least, has been fun.

The Colonel has spoken to the railroad guard, and the train makes an unscheduled stop at White Station so Elvis can save time getting back to his new house on Audubon Drive. He tells Junior and Bobby there's no need to come with him; they must be tired and it'll be easier for them to get home from downtown Memphis.

He steps from the train, relieved to be alone for the first time in days, and waves to the guard. Once the carriages have rumbled away, there's no noise save the tapping of his white buck shoes along the sidewalk. He is carrying nothing but the rough cuts from his recent recording session. Junior will bring his suitcase to the house, later. But the acetates are too precious to leave with anybody, even the Colonel. And he can't wait to play them to his mother and to Barbara, who has been keeping Gladys company. She is good at that. The two of them often go out shopping, or for a bite to eat, together. He's spoken to them every night, reassuring them that he's just fine, it's going wonderful well, and he'll be back. Although sometimes he wondered if he'd ever make it.

Squinting at the sun-bleached road, he remembers it's morning, before nine-thirty. Most days he has no idea what time it is. If he's not on the road, driving to the next show, then he's in a hotel, waiting to go on. Every hour of every day is spent antici-pating the moment he will step onstage and become his best self. Each day brings so much pleasure and excitement and terror that he feels as though he is balanced always on the edge of the rooftop of the Peabody Hotel, peering down at the fast flow of the Mississippi and the blinding lights of the city. Sometimes those lights hurt his eyes and that river seems mighty close to his nose.

The Colonel tells him not to worry. 'The thing about it,' he says, 'is not to get too bothered. Nobody ever *died* from nerves, or lack of sleep.' Thank God the Colonel is here to steer him through all this. It seems to Elvis that his manager has seen it all and can deal with just about anything. When the press exploded in righteous fury over Elvis shaking his ass on *The Milton Berle Show*, calling him vulgar and accusing him of *the kind of animalism that should be confined to dives and bordellos* (that phrase had stuck in his mind), the Colonel's only reaction was to announce that he was going to get a wiggle-meter. If Elvis stopped singing, he said, he could still put him onstage and count the wiggles.

Elvis means to walk all the way to his house, even though he's not exactly sure of the route. It's hot already, and his toes are rubbing together in his shoes. When he gets home, his pool should be finished. He imagines diving in, Barbara watching as he parts the cool water like one of those Acapulco guys. Then a taxicab rolls by, and he hails it, just because he can. He has a bundle of money in his pocket bigger than anything his daddy ever brought home. As soon as he gets through the door, he'll hand half of it to his mother.

The driver winds down the window and looks him over. Elvis senses the man's hesitation. The words the Employment Officer used when he left Humes High run through his mind: *Elvis Presley is something of a flashily dressed playboy type.* The driver will have noticed his black sport coat and matching pegged pants, white shirt and white knitted tie, and his long, greasy forelock. After twenty-seven hours on a train, he doesn't smell so good. Possibly the driver assumes he's spent the night in a bordello. Elvis almost apologises for his appearance, wanting the older man to know that he has just been to New York to appear on two television shows and cut a record. But instead he removes the money roll from his pocket and pretends to check it. Immediately, the driver opens the door and asks him where he's going.

'Ten thirty-four Audubon Drive, please, sir.'

The driver sits up straight. Audubon is one of the best streets in Memphis, home to the golf-club set, filled with brand new, ranch-type houses. Frank and Betty Pidgeon have already invited the Presleys over for cocktails.

In the back of the cab, Elvis places his acetates carefully on the seat beside him, resting one hand on the paper sleeve. As they sail through the quiet streets, the driver keeps glancing at him in the rear-view mirror. The sunlight falls through the trees like a blessing. A surge of delight goes through Elvis, thinking of his mother's face as he walks up their wide driveway, earlier than expected.

'Sure is good to be back in Memphis,' he says.

The driver grunts.

Elvis tries again. 'Beautiful morning, ain't it?'

'What number Audubon, again?'

'Ten thirty-four.'

The winding tree-lined avenue opens up before them. Each place – wooden-shuttered, car-porched, hemmed by lawns so green and neat they look like carpets – is immaculate, at least on the outside. He tries to remember what his house looks like, exactly – has it got green or blue board-and-batten sidings? The shutters are black, for sure, as is the door. There's no porch, which was one of the things Gladys first noticed about the house. It didn't matter that they had a large patio out back; where, she'd wanted to know, was she going to sit to greet her neighbours and drink lemonade? And what about that lawn? So much grass. They'd never be able to keep it neat. He'd reminded her that they could get a boy to do that, now. She and Vernon needn't lift a finger. Behind a smile, she'd hidden some reaction he couldn't read.

He unrolls his window to let the warm air in and get a better view of his house. And there they are, waiting for him. Every time he comes home he worries they'll be gone and he'll have to walk through his new gates alone, unwatched. As fast as this thing began, it might disappear. The girls will scream at somebody else. They won't be merely indifferent to him, they'll hate him. He's heard them booing the warm-up acts to his show, just because those entertainers are not Elvis Presley. Pretty soon, he might not be the Elvis Presley that they want.

But, for now, here they are, and he can't help grinning. There are more girls than usual: maybe forty, aged from around thirteen to sixteen, some clutching gifts, all in their best clothes. They'll have heard that Elvis will be back in town; he's playing Russwood Park tonight. A few of them touch the new fence lovingly; some do not take their eyes from the house, drinking in the place where he lives. Mostly, though, they are chatting among themselves, clearly not expecting to see him at this hour.

'What's going on here?' asks the driver, laughing in disbelief at the sight of so many young ladies crowding the pavement.

'That's my house, sir.'

The driver swivels his head around. 'It is?'

'Maybe drop me a little way along the road.'

As the car comes close to the house, a few of the girls recognise Elvis, and there are squeals. Some rush to the kerbside, waving and calling his name. Others stay back, clutching the gates for support, jaws open.

The cab pulls in just beyond ten thirty-four.

'Who they waiting for?' the driver asks.

Elvis pushes a few bills into the driver's hand. 'Sir, I have absolutely no idea,' he says, climbing out.

On the sidewalk, the girls come to a halt a few yards before him, suddenly shy. One bites her own hand. One lets out little yelps like a pup. But mostly they just stare. Forty pairs of young female eyes are on him, and they are hungry for detail.

'Well, good morning, ladies,' Elvis says, holding the acetates loosely by his side. 'It sure is good to see y'all.'

This is not like after a show. Here the girls stand and gawp and giggle, but they keep a respectful distance. And it is a wonderful thing, to be so observed, so loved, by these young women. All thoughts of his aching feet are gone. He keeps walking towards his house, and they part to let him through. He's learned that it's important to keep moving, so you don't have to push anybody out of the way. That would be bad manners. After all, they have done this for him. It is thanks to them that he can ride home in a taxi to his new house on Audubon. It's what he says in any interview the Colonel allows him to give (and they are getting fewer): *Without them, I'd still be driving a truck.*

'Elvis!' A plump girl, younger than the rest, gasps and touches his arm with damp fingers.

'Hello, honey.' He smiles, letting his eyes rest on hers for a moment. And keeps moving.

Record sleeves are thrust towards him. He signs each one with his now-practised flourish, and thanks the girls for buying his music. And keeps moving.

'Whatcha got there, Elvis?'

'My new records, honey. Y'all be able to buy them soon enough.'

Another squeal. He laughs at the strangeness of it, that high-pitched wail of female hysteria splitting the polished air of Audubon Drive before ten in the morning.

One of them, he notices, is petite, dark-haired, bright-eyed in the way he especially likes. Around fourteen, he guesses. Dressed in a pretty little cap-sleeved blouse and blue skirt. Reaching the gate, he stops and holds his hand out to her, and she clasps it.

'Thank you,' she mouths.

'My pleasure, sweetheart.' He kisses her surprised cheek, letting his lips linger there. She exhales a shuddering breath, which smells powerfully of bubblegum.

'What's your name?' he whispers.

'Frances,' she gasps.

Then he straightens up and waves. 'I gotta go see my folks, girls.'

They stay respectfully behind the iron gates. Halfway to the house, he turns and waves again, and the girls, glassy-eyed, give a collective squeal.

By now Vernon is opening the front door. They shake hands and clap one another on the back. Vernon wastes no time in stepping beyond his son, gawping at the girls and waving. Elvis lets it go, because Gladys is waiting in the hallway.

She's wearing the new summer dress that he bought her, and her smile is bright, but, seeing the shadows beneath her eyes, he has to look away. He puts his acetates on the hall table, then falls gratefully into her embrace.

'Son,' she says. 'It's been so long.'

'Baby.'

It's been ten days. But now he's home he feels he's been away for years. He closes his eyes and inhales her scent. It is the only thing that is familiar about this house, and he tries not to notice that other smell on her, the one that's been there ever since he started making records. She's drinking more and more, he knows it. He's seen the empty bottles of Schlitz beer, stashed in paper sacks beneath the drainer. As if paper could hide them. It's like she wants him to know.

'We saw you on the TV show last night. You were wonderful. We're so proud of you.'

She's said it so many times now, but every time it makes him smile.

'Funny thing, singing to that dog,' says Vernon.

Lifting his head, Elvis says, 'About as funny as a crutch.'

'You must be hungry,' says Gladys.

'I ain't had nothing but sandwiches since I left. I didn't want to touch a thing you ain't made for me.'

'I'll fix you some breakfast.'

'I wanna get in the pool first, Mama.'

'There's a problem with the pool, son.' Vernon has shut the door and is beckoning Elvis to look out of the kitchen window.

'Thing won't fill. I tried everything.'

Elvis stays exactly where he is, close to his mother. 'There's no water in the pool?'

'It just won't fill.'

A pause. 'Where's Barbara?'

'She's on her way,' says Vernon. 'We didn't think you'd get here till later. Colonel said—'

'What use is a pool without water?'

Gladys steps in. 'Maybe Elvis can fix it. Why don't you two go take a look together?'

'Not now. Let me use the bathroom first.'

His voice is sharper than he'd intended, and the look descends onto Gladys's face. Since that time she'd carried him from the stage, something has shrunk within her, and now she wears this look more often. It's the look of a woman lost in something she cannot understand. Sometimes she stares into space for the longest time with this look on her face. Even in the beautiful house he's bought her, standing on this thick carpet, she wears this look! It makes him mad to see her pull it now, after he's been gone so long.

Vernon steps aside to let his son pass. But Elvis can't remember how the house is laid out, and he pauses, unsure.

'It's at the end of the hall, son,' says Gladys, quietly. 'First on the right.'

There are seven rooms in this house, and Elvis has yet to work out what they're all for. The one next to his is full of the hundreds of teddy bears he's received from his fans. Gladys has told him she goes in there when he's away and shakes the dust off each one, patting down their synthetic fur and rearranging them so they don't get misshapen. Sometimes she plays the tunes they have hidden in their bellies. He knows some of them arrive wrapped in girls' underthings, and that Gladys keeps those, too, in a trunk out beneath the car porch. He's not sure if she can't bear to put them in the trash, or if she just doesn't want him looking at them.

He closes the door to his bedroom, which is at the back of the house. The room still smells of the earthiness of new plaster. Gladys had it decorated, as he'd asked her to, with pale yellow paper, flecked bright blue and orange. He wishes he could peek at the girls – he can hear the buzz of their voices from here – but instead he has a view of his father, son-of-a-bitching at the pool as he wrestles with the hose. When Vernon stumbles on a cinderblock the construction people have left in the yard, he curses louder.

Elvis sits on his bed and removes his sport coat and shirt, then flings them in a corner. His mother will pick them up later. She'll be glad to do it, after he's been away for so long.

On the flouncy white coverlet is a stuffed blue dog. Gazing into its sad, slightly uneven eyes, he thinks again of singing to that basset hound on *The Steve Allen Show*. At first, he hadn't minded wearing the tux the producers had insisted upon: in it, he'd felt sharp and powerful. He could be Dean Martin in that tux! He could be *better* than Sinatra! Everyone in the New York studio would respect him in such clothes. They'd know that he meant business. But then the director had greeted him with a firm handshake and the words, 'What are you doing to my daughter?' His gaze snagged on Elvis's hair. 'You're driving my little girl to distraction.'

'I'm sure sorry to hear that, sir—'

'Are you aware of what you do, onstage? All that grinding. You can't be, can you?'

'Well, I—'

'Don't get me wrong. I wish you all the luck in the world, son, and I'm glad to have you on the show but … personally? I'm not sure what you do is suitable for young Americans. Think about it. Would you let your own daughter watch something like that on television?'

There was a pause. Then Elvis said, very quietly, 'Sir, I think you oughta give your little girl what she wants.'

The director's gaze fell squarely on Elvis's face. 'My little girl already has exactly what she wants. Enjoy yourself, now.'

And then they'd brought the dog on. The thing was sweating and terrified and kept letting off the most gut-turning farts. But even that had amused Elvis, at first. He'd goofed around in rehearsal, still enjoying the tux, putting the dog's top hat on his own head. Everybody had laughed, the director perhaps the most. When the cameras rolled, Elvis grabbed the dog by the mouth and got a handful of warm slobber. He felt the stuff slide beneath his new ring. Wiping his fingers on his black pants, he suddenly saw himself as Gladys would see him that night on her television set: wailing to a stupid animal, trussed up like a turkey. Nobody would remember the song. They'd just remember the dog in the top hat.

He punches the stuffed dog on the nose, once, twice, driving it into the coverlet. Then he holds it close to his face and whispers, *Sorry, doggie, I'm sorry.* The thing is a present from a fan, after all, and has hearts and kisses drawn on its label.

The doorbell chimes, and, hearing Barbara's voice, he throws the dog to the floor and dashes from the room.

She is waiting for him in the living room. Next to her sits Dodger, who has taken to the new house better than any of them, and appears relaxed on the cream couch, even though her ramrod face hardly ever cracks.

He kisses his grandmother's loose cheek first. 'Where's Mama?'

'Where do you reckon? In the kitchen, fixing you something good to eat.'

'Hi, sweetheart.' He kisses Barbara, right in the dip between her earlobe and neck, just below her pearl-cluster earring, which makes her draw back. She's looking, he knows, at his bare chest, and is clearly embarrassed to see him in such a state of undress with two ladies in this pristine room. But he won't apologise. She ought to have been here when he arrived, as she'd promised.

The wood panelling in here makes it shadowy, even on a bright morning, and Elvis moves impatiently around the room, flicking on all the lamps. When he's on the road, he sends one home from every town, selecting the most elaborate models he can find. He wants his mama to have every corner of every room lit up; there should be no gloomy spots in this house.

Then he produces his acetates from behind his back and puts one on the turntable. 'You wanna hear my new recordings?'

'Sure I do,' says Barbara, smoothing her white dress over her knees.

'This one's called "Don't Be Cruel".'

As the bass line hits, he hovers next to the player, then, seeing nobody else is moving, sits on the couch. Barbara and Dodger stare at the black-and-gold standing ashtrays as if the furniture is singing the song, not him. He leans back on the nubbly fabric, pretending not to care. He can't help glancing at Barbara's face, though, watching for signs of indifference. When he hears himself make the low, slightly comic, *Hmmm!* he's disappointed that she doesn't smile. She just stares at the ashtray, fiddling with her earring.

He knows that whatever she says won't be enough to convince him that she loves it as much as she should. Barbara likes it best when he sings ballads. Sometimes they sit at the organ together and try her favourite duet, 'Make Believe' from *Show Boat*.

He's up before the song finishes, changing the acetate to 'Hound Dog'. This time he stands over her, willing her to move or react. He winces slightly when he hears a note he wishes he'd sung better, but he knows it's a good record. At his urging, they'd done thirty-one takes, and, for once, everyone in the studio had listened when he told them what he wanted, what he thought the song could be, if only they could get it right.

By the second chorus he can stand it no more. He grabs Barbara by the wrists and yanks her to her feet. 'Dance with me,' he says.

She rocks back and forth on her heels, ducks beneath his arm when he holds it out, and smiles. He takes the opportunity to plant a wet kiss on her mouth but she pushes him gently away, glancing at Dodger.

Dodger tuts, then hauls herself from the couch. 'An old woman can tell when she ain't wanted,' she says, leaving the room.

The two of them look at each other and laugh.

'That wasn't nice, Elvis. Poor Mrs Presley.'

'Forget her. What do you think of my records?'

'They're wonderful. The best yet.' Her black eyes shine.

'Do you really think so?'

'I do.'

'They're for you, baby.'

Then she lets him hold her tightly, and doesn't resist when he runs a hand up her skirt.

Elvis takes Red to the Mid-South Fairgounds to spend some time throwing balls at bottles; knocking coconuts off plinths; shooting targets; riding the Pippin, the Whip and the Tumblebug; and winning teddy bears. Aware of how difficult it will be to do this unnoticed, he wears a trilby pulled down low and a pair of sunglasses. Seeing him, Red smirks. 'You look just like Elvis Presley in that,' he says.

It's the night after the Russwood Park show. It isn't long before a crowd gathers, alerted to Elvis's presence by the roar of his Harley-Davidson, and it takes Red and him an hour to reach the shooting gallery. All the way, Elvis knows that Red is keeping one eye peeled for trouble, but he also knows that his friend is watching him as he thanks his well-wishers, signs anything they hand over, and kisses almost every cheek offered, while Red himself is ignored or pushed aside. So it comes as little surprise to Elvis when, after they've managed to get to the Walking Charlies and he's aiming to smack another moving dummy with a baseball, a fight breaks out.

'He ain't no fucking faggot!' he hears Red yell.

By the corner of the stall, Red has a blonde boy, no older than fifteen, by the collar, and he's raising his fist.

Elvis makes a lunge for his friend, grabbing him round the waist, trying to drag him back.

But Red digs his heels into the grass, twists free, and lands a right hook on the boy's jaw. Elvis hears the crunch of bone on bone. The boy collapses into the canvas side of the stall. Just moments ago, the crowd had been cheering for Elvis as he tried to sock those Charlies right in the mouth and win a teddy bear for anybody who asked him. Now everybody goes quiet.

Elvis backs away from his friend.

Red glares at him. 'What do you expect?' he yells. 'Your mama asked me to protect you!'

On the grass, the boy holds his bleeding face and whimpers. Several older women have clustered about him, making dismayed noises. Behind, the dummies keep rolling along, grinning.

Before Elvis can decide whether to check on the boy, yell at Red, or turn and run, the stall's owner appears, flanked by a couple of heavy-looking guys. 'Mr Presley,' he says, an excited expression on his leathery face, 'your friend here better come with me to see a police officer, don't you reckon?'

As he's led away, Red doesn't look back, and Elvis doesn't call after him.

* * *

When they'd worked together at Britling's Cafeteria downtown, Gladys had been impressed by Alberta Holman, even though the two women barely spoke. Gladys had poured the coffee and taken the orders while Alberta assisted the chef in the kitchen. Alberta always wore her hair in a red net and kept her apron cleaner than the other cooks did. She was careful to arrange food neatly on a plate, and not to let tomato juice slop over the lip, or leave grease smudged on the underside. Gladys noticed, too, that Alberta kept the dishes warm but not overheated; she never burned her hand on one of Alberta's plates. Like the other coloured workers at Britling's, Alberta addressed Gladys as 'Miss Gladys', and never initiated a conversation with a white member of staff. But when Gladys had asked her during one brief lull in the lunchtime shift about her family, Alberta had told her that they'd moved from the country, too, in search of more regular work, and a better life.

So when Vernon suggests that now is the time for the Presleys to hire a housekeeper, Gladys thinks of Alberta.

'I'll call Britling's,' she says, 'and offer her the job.'

It is early evening, and they are hiding from the August sun beneath the umbrellas on their patio. Elvis is away again, having recently left for California to make his movie – the first of seven he's signed up for – but there are still a handful of girls peeking through the fence which runs around their backyard. Vernon has dragged an electric fan out and occasionally it blows the front of his unbuttoned shirt open, revealing the sweaty folds of his stomach. Gladys eyes them distastefully, but decides against chiding her husband in the presence of the fans.

He laughs. 'You can't just offer her the job. You gotta get references. We don't want any old darkie coming in here, stealing Elvis's stuff.'

Although she barely knows her, Gladys says, 'Alberta ain't like that. And ain't no call for references. We worked together.'

Flies dip and buzz around their heads. Vernon says, 'Then I guess I got to interview the woman.'

'Don't trouble yourself,' says Gladys, breezily. 'I can do it.'

At three o'clock the following afternoon, Gladys opens the door to Alberta, who is wearing a long-sleeved blue dress, despite the heat, and a pair of black sliders. She is around Gladys's age, but small, with thin wrists and a long neck, and she moves more slowly than she did before. She smiles briefly, but then her delicate features settle back into the carefully blank mask that Gladys now remembers.

Showing Alberta into the living room, Gladys can smell the grease and coffee on her. She tells her to take a seat on the easy chair, next to the coffee table where she's set a pitcher of iced tea in readiness.

Pouring the drinks, Gladys spills a little on the pile of magazines Elvis has placed there. Many of them have his picture on the cover. But she ignores this and tries to remember what she should ask first. She must pretend, now, to be one of those folks who have questions to get through and papers to fill in. As the mother of a new movie star, she must pretend to be more than that, even – but how to begin?

'Well,' she says, wiping her damp palms on her dress.

Alberta waits, her dark eyes focused on Gladys's shoulder.

'I don't know what your wages are over Britling's, Alberta, but we sure would like to offer you more, because I know you're a mighty good cook.'

'Thank you, ma'am.'

'You'd be cooking for visitors, sometimes, because Elvis entertains a good deal, when he's home.'

'I ain't no stranger to hard work, Miss Gladys.'

'Oh, I know. But I'd cook Elvis's meals for him. Ordinarily, I mean.'

Alberta sips her tea and nods. Then she speaks slowly and deliberately. 'So what I gotta do when Mr Elvis is home?'

'Oh, I'm sure they'll be heaps! Shopping and ... cleaning and everything,' says Gladys, with a wave of her hand.

Alberta raises her eyebrows. On her face is a small smile, as if she's amused by something. But it vanishes as quickly as it appeared. 'Sounds just fine to me, ma'am.'

'That's settled, then!' In her relief, Gladys gulps back the rest of her tea. Then she asks, 'Are your folks doing good, Alberta?'

'Oh yes, Miss Gladys. Real good, thank you. But not as good as yours!'

Gladys nods. 'We've been blessed.'

'Amen,' says Alberta, looking around. Gladys watches her take in the contents of the room: the walnut TV console, the brand new three-piece suite, the framed oil portrait of Elvis on the wall, the lamps on every available surface.

'And how are you yourself, Miss Gladys?' Alberta asks.

Gladys glances down at her hands, taken aback by the question. Because they are so keen to know about Elvis, few people ask her how she is. Flesh bulges from beneath the edges of her diamond cocktail ring, and, sensing Alberta's eyes following her own, she wishes she'd taken the thing off before inviting her into the house.

'Oh,' she says, sliding her hands beneath her thighs, 'I'm just fine, thank you. Just fine.'

She is about to show Alberta out, having taken her on a brief tour of the house, when Vernon arrives home.

From the flush on his cheeks, Gladys guesses he's spent the afternoon in a bar, telling strangers that yes, he really is the daddy of Elvis Presley, and yes, it's true that right now he's shooting his first-ever movie out in Hollywood. Seeing Alberta, he pauses in the hallway. Clutched to his chest is a copy of *Life* magazine.

'Well, looky here,' he says. 'This our new maid?'

'This here's Alberta,' says Gladys. 'She's starting as our house-keeper next week.'

'Uh-huh.' Without smiling, Vernon looks Alberta over, taking his time. 'Ain't that just fine?' he says.

Alberta keeps her eyes on Gladys's shoes.

'We're real happy about it, ain't we, Alberta?' says Gladys.

'Yes, Miss Gladys.'

Vernon grins and winks at his wife.

'We'll be seeing you Monday, then, Alberta,' says Gladys, moving towards the door.

Vernon blocks the women's path. 'You know,' he says, addressing Alberta, 'some folks back in my home town used to call me a no-good jellybean. But here I am, in my ranch-style house, with a swimming pool and a housekeeper! How do you like that?'

Alberta is still staring at Gladys's feet.

'I said, how do you like that?'

'It's just swell, Mr Vernon,' says Alberta, raising her eyes to his chest.

'You bet! But have you seen this here magazine?'

He thrusts his copy of *Life* into her face. His eyes are wide, and even Gladys can smell the liquor on him.

'Vernon,' Gladys warns. 'Alberta's gotta be getting along now.'

'It's got a story about my son's rise to fame and fortune, but do you know what they say about him in here?' He taps the cover.

Now Gladys looks at the magazine. Elvis's face is not on the front, but she can see his name. After all the fuss following her son's appearance on *Milton Berle*, she knows better than to expect everything written about him to be praising. He's been accused of causing the young women of America to lose their morals, teenagers to riot and the races to mix. He's been called obscene, and compared to an animal. Some of it has had her and Elvis weeping together.

'Some low-down preacher from Jacksonville has denounced Elvis in church!' says Vernon, clutching wildly at the pages, trying to find the story. 'Now, do you call that fair, Alberta? Elvis is a God-fearing boy who likes to sing a few songs, and this damned preacher has the gall to pray for his soul!'

Gladys tries to snatch the magazine from her husband. 'Who did such a thing?' she demands.

Vernon holds the magazine out of her reach. 'I don't want you to see it, Glad. I'm gonna destroy this thing,' he says, 'and then I'm gonna dance on it!' And with one swipe, he wrenches off the cover.

Alberta stands back, seemingly ready to witness the show. Gladys pushes past her husband and opens the front door.

'Well, so long, Alberta,' she sings. 'Thanks for coming over!'

Reluctantly, Alberta picks her way past Vernon, who has started pulling the magazine to bits. She inches out of the house, murmuring goodbye. Gladys catches her eye and, to her relief, no longer sees any amusement there.

Having firmly shut the door, Gladys turns to watch her husband, who is tearing through the magazine, sending staples pinging off every which way. He rips a page of photographs to shreds. She sees the words 'fads', 'fears' and 'antics' before they are destroyed. With his heel, Vernon grinds the paper into the carpet. Then he stomps on it.

'You finished?' she asks.

'Nope.'

Lifting his arms, he begins to sing. *'I got a new place to dwell, right at the top of dollar street, in cheque-book motel!'* He grabs at an imaginary microphone and runs one hand through his hair, mimicking his son with expert precision.

'I been so loaded, baby, I'm-a so loaded, I could die!' His voice is good, as it always was. Vernon drops to his knees and looks at her with beseeching eyes. All around him, the shreds of the story flutter in his wake.

Gladys shakes her head, but can't help a smile.

'Get up offa your knees,' she says, gently. 'We got us a maid, now. We can't act like fools no more.'

* * *

Even at nine o'clock in the evening, with the September sun almost setting, it's hot. Elvis bobs in his swimming pool, waiting for the girls. Gloria, Heidi and Frances, all fourteen years old, all sweet, all crazy, have been coming over since he returned from Hollywood. His new buddy Cliff, a disc jockey from Jackson who has stepped in for Red, is picking them up for their first pool-and-pyjama party. Vernon and the Colonel told Red after he hit the guy at the Fairgrounds that he was no longer welcome, and Red announced his intention to join the marines. Maybe it's for the best. Cliff is less likely than Red to throw punches around, and he's also better with girls. He knows how to talk to the parents. He sings a little, but with a mouth like a train running at full speed, he's unlikely to steal their hearts.

The pool shimmers orange and yellow. Elvis pushes his fingers back and forth, making the colours bleed, feeling the resistance of the water, telling himself that it's good to have these moments of ease, when he can watch the sunset and feel the water on his skin. He can hardly believe he's spent the last month shooting a movie. During that time, he barely saw the sky. Was any of that real? He's learning, he thinks, how to get through the days even though the days seem like a dream. He's worked out that it's best to think only of what is happening right now. Otherwise there's too much information in your brain. On set, he tried not to think about being a movie star, or how the picture would turn out, or the fact that he was sitting next to the celebrated and virtuous beauty Debra Paget (*Debra fucking Paget!*) but of what his next line was. Kissing Debra had been delicious, and she had responded to him, he just knew it, not a movie response but a real, female response – she even complimented him on his technique. He knows he's good at this stuff; he's tender, starts softly and works his way in. He learned a lot with Dixie and has been practising ever since.

He closes his eyes and submerges himself completely. Mr Webb always said the same thing. 'That was very good, Elvis. Now, let's try it again ...' So he never knew what the director really thought, and, in the end, was glad he didn't. But Mr Webb had seemed impressed with Elvis's theory about the great screen actors – Brando, Dean, Clift. Had Mr Webb noticed that they never smiled? He'd made a study of them all, and they hardly ever looked happy. He didn't mention that he'd spent many hours perfecting his own scowl in the mirror, or that he'd learned it, initially, from his granddaddy, JD. But even the long-perfected scowl hadn't looked right when he'd watched the rough cut. Seeing himself up there, his face as big as a truck, made him want to hide in his mama's lap. He looked like a big goofy hick. And why did they have him singing? If it was a serious project, as the Colonel tried to assure Elvis it was, it was unnatural to burst into song in the middle of the picture. It had felt strange, anyhow, without Scotty and Bill behind him. Mr Webb had decided they weren't hillbilly enough for the movie, which they found funny – at least for a moment.

He'll be laughed out of Hollywood. He knows it.

'Elvis?'

He comes up for air and there's his mother, standing at the side of the pool, frowning.

'You all right, son?'

'I'm fine, Mama.'

'You were under an awful long time.'

'Everything's fine. Why wouldn't it be?'

And he goes under again, so she has to wait, her body casting a shadow across the water. That shadow has grown larger over the summer, despite her diet pills. They'd worked, at first. He'd seen her pleasure at being able to buy new dresses with the money he gave her. One day she'd come home in a loud polka-dot blouse and skirt, declaring, 'If Mrs King could see me now!' Vernon had even obliged her with a soft wolf whistle, and she'd slapped him across the head, overjoyed.

There's a muffled sound above, but he won't come up. Not yet.

The best thing about her diet pills, though, is that it's easy for him to steal them. The first time he'd tried one, it was like he'd been plugged into the grid, despite the few hours' sleep he'd had. He could sail right through the day without getting bothered about one little thing. His brain seemed one step ahead of his body and of everybody else, too, which was useful on the movie set.

'Son!'

Hearing the warning in her voice, even through the water, he emerges.

'The girls are here. You want me to tell them to come on out?'

'Have they brought their bathing suits along?'

'I guess.'

'Then tell them to get changed quick and get in this pool. It'll be dark soon.'

'All right.' But she doesn't move. 'Elvie?'

'Yes, Mama?'

'I like Frances best, don't you?'

She keeps her gaze on the walnut trees at the back of their property.

Gloria came to Audubon first, because her daddy has fixed the Presley automobiles for as long as they've been in Memphis, and Vernon owed him a favour. But Frances is the reason Gloria has been invited back. Gloria had brought her two friends along at Elvis's suggestion, and he'd recognised Frances straight away. She was the pretty one he'd noticed at the gate on his way back from New York earlier in the summer.

'I like her, Mama.'

'She told me she can sew and cook, both.'

'She's only fourteen.'

'By the time you're ready for marriage, Frances will be a good age.'

Elvis laughs, but the thought has crossed his mind, too.

'Are you about done now?' he asks.

'I'll be done when I see you happy,' she says.

'I am happy, Mama. I'm a movie star with a million-dollar future. I'm Elvis Presley. You must be the only person for miles around who don't know that.'

She crouches down and reaches out to stroke his hair. 'You know what I mean, Elvie,' she says, softly. 'Mama's worried about her baby.'

He kisses her fingers and says, 'Go tell them little girls to hurry along.'

As she walks away, he notices that she is too upright and deliberate in her steps to be entirely sober.

The red ruffles on Gloria's bathing suit make her look like a lapdog gussied up for a show. She's already laughing. Gloria is always letting out a high-pitched, uneven laugh, often at nothing. When Elvis imitates it, she does it even more. She has the hair of a poodle – black and fiercely curly. The others are dressed in strictly practical bathing suits – navy blue for Frances, black for Heidi. Frances's calves are exquisitely curved, like expensive pieces of furniture. Heidi is the tallest, and has the most developed breasts, but also the most serious-looking mouth. She is in charge.

They stand in a tight clump on the flagstones at the other end of the pool, gawping at him.

Elvis keeps his body beneath the water. 'Hi, girls!' He waves. 'Come on in! The water's real fine.'

Without taking their eyes from him, they whisper to one another behind their hands.

'Y'all ain't afraid of Elvis, are you?'

'Frances says she ain't coming in,' says Heidi.

'Then why in the world is she wearing that bathing suit?'

'She can't swim.'

Frances stares at her feet.

Gloria runs along the flags, yelling, 'Here I come!' then she jumps into the water, making a splash large enough to soak his head. She comes up laughing, almost nose to nose with him. His hair drips in his eyes but he does not wipe the water away. There's a pause. 'Hi, Gloria,' he says, keeping his voice soft and low.

'Hi, Elvis.'

'Hi, Gloria.'

'Hi, Elvis.'

'Hi, Gloria.'

'Hi, Elvis,' she giggles, a little uncertain.

'Wanna have some fun?'

'Well, sure.'

He puts a hand on her wet curls and pushes her down. Holding her beneath the water, he turns to Frances and says, 'Don't sweat it, honey. I can't swim, either.'

Gloria kicks and wriggles. For a young girl, she is strong. He lets her come back up, wet curls streaked across her face like a mess of turnip greens. She gasps for breath. 'Oh!' she shouts. 'Oh! *You!*'

'Me?'

'*You!*'

She's splashing him with all her might, but he ignores her. 'Frances, Heidi, get yourselves in this pool, or Gloria here's going under again!' He reaches for Gloria's head, but she dodges away, shrieking.

He smiles to himself at the thought of his daddy's irritation at the noise. Vernon is in the den, watching TV with Cliff. He's probably turning up the volume right now. He's warned Elvis about the neighbours' complaints, too. The residents of Audubon Drive have written a letter, which Vernon read aloud to his son when Gladys was out shopping.

We hope you'll understand our alarm at the disruption caused not only by the volume of the music coming from 1034, but also by the multiple vehicles arriving and departing from your property at all times of day, not to mention the frankly riotous presence of hundreds of teenage girls on the street, many of whom seem to think nothing of stealing blades of grass and other 'souvenirs' not only from your garden but also from ours! Mr Presley Junior appears to keep irregular hours, which is obviously his business, but it becomes our business when it keeps us awake nights. We may be forced to make this a police matter if something cannot be worked out—

What they don't yet know, and what he means to tell them, is that he's discovered he's the only one in the street who owns his property outright. If they want him out, let them buy him out.

Frances and Heidi are climbing in gingerly. While they pick their way across the pool, at pains not to get their hair wet, Elvis says to the bedraggled Gloria, 'I'm sorry, honey, but you looked like you needed a good ducking.'

All three squeal as he chases them, lunging for their arms and legs, not knowing which limb belongs to which girl. As he ploughs through the pool, he glances up at the house and sees his mother, watching from the kitchen window. What's strange is that she is looking not at him but at the darkening sky.

After the girls have dressed in the guest room, Elvis invites them into his bedroom. On the dresser, Gladys has left a tray loaded with milk and banana cake.

The girls sit on his flowered coverlet, chewing their cake and looking around. Frances, the shortest, swings her legs to and fro. Heidi cuddles the stuffed dog. Elvis is tired, now, and beginning to wish he hadn't invited these teenagers over. He's had enough of their giggling and their staring. Leaning back, he closes his eyes and suddenly gets lost someplace. This happens more and more, if he lets it. He feels his mind slipping away from the chaos of his life, and it's not unpleasant. Half-heartedly, he tells himself to come back, repeating the words silently, unsure if they are his own or Jesse's. *Where have you gone, Elvis? Where are you?* But still his eyes are closed and here's celebrated-and-virtuous Debra's face, right up close to his, her breath warm on his nose. Then Jesse says, *Look at you, you're surrounded by them! Where's my girl, Elvis?*

A crash from along the hall brings him back. Probably Cliff knocking over another ashtray. Clumsy son of a bitch.

Elvis opens his eyes. The girls are still there, staring. Heidi says, 'Where's your mother, Elvis?'

'I don't know.'

She'll be in bed by now, sleeping it off. But from this end of the house, they won't hear her wet snores.

Gloria widens her eyes. 'So we're all alone with Elvis Presley in his *bedroom*?'

'Well, Cliff's just along the hall with my daddy.'

'Like I said,' says Gloria. 'All alone with Elvis Presley.'

'You wanna go home, Gloria?' he asks, unable to resist a flicker of annoyance. 'I can ask Cliff to drive you.'

'No!'

'Then hush up,' says Heidi, throwing the stuffed dog into Gloria's lap. 'You know nothing's gonna happen with Elvis here. Don't spoil it for the rest of us.'

'That's right, Heidi,' says Elvis. 'You are a very sensible young lady. Gloria, you could take a lesson or two from your friend here.'

Gloria lets out a long huff and flops back on the bed, the dog pressed to her face.

Frances says, 'We're real grateful, Elvis. We know how lucky we are to visit with you.'

Her quiet confidence reminds him of Dixie in the early days. The way she skated neatly round the Rainbow without a shred of arrogance or self-consciousness. Frances's little dimpled smile is so sweet and sincere that he has a sudden longing to keep them all right here, on his bed, throughout the night. It would be better than sleeping alone.

'Let me dry your hair before you go,' he says. 'I got this really neat new hairdryer.' He finds it in the top drawer and plugs it in. It is pink, with a silver handle. 'You don't wanna catch a chill out there. Come on, girls, let's sit pow-wow style.'

He rearranges himself on the bed, sitting cross-legged in the centre, the dryer poised and ready. The three girls follow suit, skirts resting on their rounded knees.

Beneath his fingers, Frances's hair springs like something newborn. Her cheeks flare pink as he runs his comb through to the ends, scattering her blouse with droplets of moisture. She seems to be holding her breath.

'You girls ought never, ever cut your hair,' he instructs, and they all nod.

He switches the dryer off and combs through Frances's damp waves. 'Now. We'd better move on to kissing practice.' Because they'd be disappointed to leave without a kiss, wouldn't they? And he can't disappoint his girls. 'Whose turn is it?'

'It's Heidi's turn,' says Frances. 'Gloria went last time.'

It is typical of Frances to remember the schedule. The others would have cheated. 'Frances, I knew you would tell the truth, honey.'

'Then it's really my turn?' says Heidi, leaning in slightly. Her hair is wild from the pool and her eyes are shining.

'No,' he says. 'It's Frances's, because she was honest.'

'Lordy,' says Gloria. 'Frances? She ain't never been kissed. She's gonna pee in her pants.'

'I am not!' Frances thrusts her fists into the coverlet and looks as though she might cry.

'I'm mighty glad to hear you ain't been kissed, Frances. That's the way it oughta be. You girls are lucky I'm here to teach you.'

'We sure are!' says Gloria.

Elvis laughs, but says, 'Now, girls, this here's a serious moment. Frances's first kiss.'

They all nod and try to compose themselves.

Frances is staring at him, flushed to the neck. Her lips are tight and unsmiling. When he touches her shoulder, he realises she is trembling. 'You don't have to worry none, honey. I'm gonna be real gentle.'

Gloria and Heidi lean in as he moves his face closer to Frances's, until the four of them are in danger of toppling together on the bed.

'Scoot back, you two. Frances, close your eyes.'

'But she wants to look at you, Elvis,' says Gloria.

'Hush up,' says Heidi.

Frances shuts her eyes. Elvis glances at the others, who gape back. He winks, then focuses on his task. As he touches her lips with his, he puts his whole being into the kiss; it is deliberate and studied. Starting gentle, he slowly increases the pressure, and her shoulders go limp beneath his fingers. He thinks of Dixie, that first time in the car, the way she'd opened for him. The way she'd been so grateful. Not like those girls in Hollywood.

Feeling Frances's lips begin to loosen, he draws back and says, 'Frances, that was your first kiss. How did it feel?'

She cannot look at him. She shakes her head and covers her mouth with a hand.

'Frances? You OK, honey?'

But she can't seem to speak. A small stab of panic goes through him. Perhaps she's going to run home to her daddy and say, 'Elvis forced himself on me!' The Colonel will be hopping mad if he finds out the girls are here without chaperones. If the papers get hold of it, he might as well forget his career. This will put the hullaballoo over him grinding his hips on *Milton Berle* in the shade.

Heidi puts an arm around Frances, who buries her face in her friend's shoulder.

'Frances?' says Heidi.

Suddenly Frances lets out a sob and grabs Elvis's arm, tightly. He shakes her off and leaps from the bed as if she were a rattlesnake. 'What's wrong with her?' he demands of Gloria. 'I ain't done nothing wrong! I'd never hurt none of you girls!'

'She's always been a little sensitive,' says Gloria.

'Frances?' says Heidi. 'Are you all right?'

Frances raises her head and looks at him, her eyes wet with tears. 'That was ... the most wonderful thing that ever happened to me,' she says.

Elvis is so jumpy about Frances that instead of going to bed, he paces the patio, waiting for Cliff to return from delivering the girls home. From here, he can hear his mama's snores, and every one grates on his nerves. He thinks about going in the house and shaking her awake, partly to ask for her advice on this, but partly to stop that sound she's making. It's like a spade dragged through wet gravel.

Cliff appears.

'Everything all right?' Elvis asks, aware that he's standing too close to his friend.

Cliff studies Elvis's face for a moment, then says, 'Just fine.'

Elvis looks back towards the house. 'You want something to drink?'

'Naw.' Cliff pulls up a lawn chair and sits, and Elvis does the same. They both look over the pool.

'I was a little concerned,' says Elvis, 'that those girls got the wrong idea ...'

For a while, Cliff is silent. They watch the bats flicker among the trees. Then, very slowly, Cliff says, 'You know, I don't wanna speak out of line here, but you might be careful not to ruin those girls.'

'What did those little bitches say?'

'I only meant – well, think about it, boss. Will they ever get over it? That girl, Frances – she looked like a goddamned zombie in the car. And they was all talking about how you kissed her.' Cliff shakes his head and laughs.

'We was practising, was all,' says Elvis. 'It was a game.'

'It's just – well. Seems to me that girl ain't never gonna have a thrill like that again. I mean, she just kissed a goddamn movie star! How's her husband gonna beat that?'

Elvis looks at Cliff and grins. 'Seems to me like I ain't ruined nothing for her, then.'

'How you figure that, boss?'

'I've ruined things for her husband, is all.'

* * *

It's as cold as a meat locker on the sidewalk, even in her long fur coat, but the golden light coming from Goldsmith's Christmas windows sets the street ablaze. Gladys apologises as she bundles her unwieldy frame past Dottie Harmony's neat little body and into the heat of the store. Once inside, both women stand and gaze around in awe. Every square inch of the high ceiling is festooned with ribbon, taffeta and crêpe-paper frills, and all the counters are edged with tiny multicoloured flashing lights. A giant white teddy bear dressed as Santa waves a greeting and barks out a 'Ho, ho, ho'. Bing Crosby singing 'O Little Town of Bethlehem' seeps over them, and Gladys smiles, despite herself. After all, this will be their first Christmas at Audubon Drive, and the first time she's been able to do all her shopping at Goldsmith's. She even has a charge account. Perhaps this will make amends for having to share the holidays with a Vegas showgirl.

Dottie seems at home in the store. She looks, Gladys reflects, like part of the display. To Gladys's surprise, despite lighting up a cigarette at supper last night, Dottie Harmony – not her real name – has so far proved herself well mannered and cheerful in an almost homey way. She has even agreed to assist Gladys with the Christmas shopping.

Gladys has spent the last week compiling the list now clutched in her hand. She glances at the paper. *Presents – Male* is written on one side, and *Presents – Female* on the other. Beneath each heading is a list of items which have caught her attention in magazines or on TV. She does not know who these items will be for. Her son has told her to buy thirty gifts suitable for women, twenty-five for men. She should spend around $50 each on the first ten, $25 on the rest. He's assured her that the important thing is not what goes to who, but that they buy enough, and that those gifts suit the kind of family they are now – they should be modern, luxurious, top of the range. Dottie can help, he said. She'll know the quality stuff. He gave her a wink, and a glimpse of that knowing smile that's never far from his lips these days. What a showgirl would know about quality Gladys wasn't sure, but she'd resisted the temptation to ask.

If only she could get one of these girls to stay long enough for marriage! Then they could all live together and she'd be sure Elvis would always come home – if not for her, then for his wife and children. But the girls come and go like leaves blown along Audubon Drive. They have little substance or staying power. And her son, she has to admit, doesn't do enough to hold on to them. He enjoys one for a few weeks, then it's on to the next, and she must learn a new name and try her best to make the girl stay, to make her hers, as well as his.

Dottie picks her way through soft furnishings like a flamingo. Everything about her is flushed pink: her cheeks, her lips, her cleavage – exposed beneath her little wool jacket; even her white-blonde hair is dancing and pert, gleaming in the bright lights of the store. When she arrived at the house, Vernon looked at her as if she were the well he'd been walking for days to drink from.

Spotting a sign to Santa's grotto, Dottie claps her hands together. 'Ooh! I loved to visit Santa, when I was a little girl.'

'You don't need Santa now, honey. You have Elvis.'

Dottie examines Gladys's face for a moment before letting out a high laugh. 'You're too much, Mrs Presley!'

Gladys touches Dottie's shoulder. 'This here jacket is just ador-able. Did Elvis buy it for you?'

But Dottie is reaching for a cushion, and doesn't seem to have heard. 'Look at these, Mrs Presley. Wouldn't they be perfect for the ladies' list?'

The list does not say 'ladies'. It says 'female', which is an entirely different thing.

'How about perfume?' says Gladys. 'Come on, dear. Let's go try some ...'

She grabs Dottie's arm and steers her through the aisles towards the cosmetics department. At each polished counter, another young girl looks up and registers the presence of the mother of Elvis Presley. Gladys smiles and nods at every one of them. To her satis-faction, they do not seem to recognise Dottie Harmony at all; in fact, most of the girls scowl at her.

Before they reach the perfume counter, Gladys is distracted by a display dedicated to the Crown Jewel electric shavers she's seen advertised on TV. Beneath a sign saying *Dare to bare more of you!*, dozens of them rest on cerise silk purses. Gladys had been a little shocked at the idea of electric shavers for women, but the woman in the advertisement had seemed so calm and reassuring – and she'd worn the most sophisticated evening gown.

'Dorothy, do you reckon one of these would be, you know, suitable?'

Dottie picks up a shaver and weighs it in her hand. It is pale pink and decorated with tiny crystals. Frowning slightly, she says, 'Sure, Mrs Presley. It's real pretty. Although I wouldn't use one, personally.'

'You wouldn't?'

Dottie whispers in Gladys's ear. 'The electric ones don't get close enough, if you know what I mean.' Then she flips the thing back onto its silk nest and saunters towards the perfume.

Gladys instructs the salesgirl to wrap two shavers and have them sent to the Presley house. Then she takes a pen from her pocket and strikes through *Crown Jewel*.

When she catches up with Dottie, who is trying a lipstick, Gladys tries not to look at her own reflection, but the mirrors glare down from every counter. She knows the fans and the press are disappointed that Elvis Presley's mother is not beautiful – there's a trace of prettiness still there, maybe, but the overall impression, as she glances at her reflection in the mirror of the Elizabeth Arden counter, is of bulk and tiredness. Remembering her mother's comments about the breadth of her shoulders, Gladys tries to ignore the sweat on her top lip and focus on the make-up girl, who is spraying perfume, and saying something about her son's movie being just so exciting. Gladys grips the counter, and the girl chatters, and everything wobbles slightly beneath the lights.

'Mrs Presley, are you all right?' asks Dottie. 'You don't look so good.'

What she really needs is to take this dead animal from her back, sit down, and consume some alcohol. Once she makes this decision, Gladys snaps back into focus.

'How about we take a load off, in the restaurant upstairs?' she says.

'We haven't done much shopping.'

'This nice girl here will wrap us up five bottles of scent, won't you, dear? It's for delivery to the Presley house.'

The girl is blushing. 'I know, ma'am. Right away.'

'Come on, Dorothy. Let's take a little refreshment.'

In the elevator, it's like she's already had that drink. She watches the buttons illuminate and fade as they fly to the top floor, and feels so much lighter that she almost giggles.

It's cooler and quieter in the restaurant. The potted palms are festooned with baubles, but the room is uncluttered compared with the rest of the store. A few ladies turn their heads as Gladys and Dottie cross the patterned carpet, and she is glad that the waiter offers them a table in the corner, away from the others.

It is so good to remove her heavy coat, sit on the padded chair and smooth her hot hands across the thick white tablecloth.

Dottie perches on her seat and looks around. 'Everyone in this room knows who you are, Mrs Presley.'

Gladys shrugs. 'They may know my name, but they know nothing at all about me.'

'But isn't it exciting to be recognised?'

'Oh, sure.' Back in East Tupelo, everybody knew Gladys's name and most things about her and her family. And she knew them in return. It is a strange thing, to be recognised, and to have folks expect things of you, without knowing anything of them. Gladys suspects that if she starts to think about the strangeness of such things, she will need not four or five but six, or even seven, drinks a day. If she thinks about such things, she may have to stop coming to Goldsmith's altogether.

'Let me buy you a snack, Dorothy—'

'Just coffee for me, Mrs Presley.'

'Call me Gladys, honey.'

Dottie moves closer. 'Don't look now,' she hisses, 'but that woman over there is gawping at us!'

Gladys glances over her shoulder and gives the woman a small wave. 'Without these folks, I would not be shopping here at all,' she says. 'Now. Let me buy you something to eat.'

Dottie lets out a sigh. 'I guess I could use a doughnut.'

When Gladys asks the waiter for a club sandwich and a small beer, Dottie's eyes dart up from her purse, but Gladys doesn't care. She's had only one this morning, sitting at the breakfast table with Vernon, who was looking out at the girls beyond the gate. With her son home and sleeping, at last, she'd told herself there was no need for the beer, but then Vernon rose from his seat and tapped on the window, and she'd pictured his face as he gave those girls a wave – increasingly, she sees something wolf-like in those pointed front teeth of his – and she'd gone to the refrigerator. Her husband squinted at her, coughed, but said nothing. If he'd made an effort and said something like, *Gladys, do you really need that?* then she might have put it back. But instead he'd turned to the window again. So she'd gulped the beer, and, later on, just before leaving for downtown, she'd taken a nip of vodka in her grapefruit juice, too.

'Do you believe in Jesus, Dottie?'

The showgirl snaps her purse shut. 'Pardon me, Mrs Presley?'

'Because whatever the newspapers say about him, that's real important to Elvis. He believes in the Bible.'

'Oh, I know. He read to me from it last night ... It was – real sweet.'

Gladys's eyes follow the waiter as he sets down their food and Dottie's coffee. There's no beer, but there's no cause to fret; she must focus on the girl.

'My son always says, when the newspapermen ask him, that his mother and daddy brought him up to be a good Christian, and it's a hundred per cent true.'

Dottie sips her coffee. Gladys takes a bite of her sandwich. Without the beer, it's dry and tasteless.

'Which church do you go to, Mrs Presley?'

'We're all First Assembly of God. But we don't have time to get to church as often as we'd like. And if Elvis went, well! You can

341

picture the scene. But I reckon it's the praying that's important, don't you, Dorothy? I tell Elvis: son, it don't matter if you're at a record studio or on some stage or in Hollywood itself! You can still pray.'

'That's nice,' says Dottie.

Gladys cannot get through her sandwich without a beer. She scans the room for the waiter. The other women are eating salads and drinking coffee from small glass cups. None of them have arms which press at the seams of their dresses. Suddenly she imagines all the food sliding off – coffees, Pepsis, floats, tuna-fish sandwiches – into the laps of these neat females.

When at last the beer arrives, Gladys clutches it hard, drinks, and refocuses.

'What grades did you get in school, Dorothy?'

'Oh, I didn't do so well at school ...' Dottie rubs at the back of her neck, making her curls bounce.

Gladys must be careful now. This one isn't as young as the others, and a Yankee. She may not take the questioning so well.

'You was probably too busy helping your mother, like me. What does she think, Dorothy, about your career and all?'

Dottie flashes a big smile. 'She's mighty proud.'

'Well, I guess she must be!' says Gladys, taking another drink. 'You want to settle down, though, don't you, and have a family?'

Dottie fiddles with the clasp on her purse. 'Eventually, I guess.'

'Because her family is a woman's greatest glory, ain't it? Elvis needs somebody to take good care of him. And I understand some girls don't wanna stay home—'

'Right now I'm enjoying my career.'

'Especially when their heads get turned by a lot of fancy stuff.'

The beer has settled her nerves, and she touches the showgirl on the arm. Her skin is as cool and smooth as the tablecloth, and feels almost too delicate to bear. 'But I'm sure you ain't like that, dear.'

Dottie withdraws her arm and settles back in her chair. 'Actually, Mrs Presley, can I speak frankly?'

There's a new directness in her voice which surprises Gladys.

Gladys motions to the waiter, pointing at her glass. She'll have just one more.

'I don't want to disappoint you,' Dottie continues, 'but me and Elvis – I mean, we're just having fun, you know?'

'But Elvis really likes you.'

Dottie licks a finger, runs it around her plate, and pops it, sugar-coated, into her mouth. 'Oh, I know he *admires* me, but it's mainly a publicity thing! I mean, it looks good for him to be seen with a Vegas showgirl.'

'It's more than that, Dorothy. A mother can tell these things.'

Dottie raises her voice. 'I really don't think so, Mrs Presley!'

Several people nearby glance over. Dottie plants her elbows on the table and lowers her voice. 'What I mean is, a girl has to keep her eyes open in this world, don't you think? It's awful nice to spend time with him, but I know the truth: he just isn't ready to settle down.'

Gladys's beer comes, and she takes a gulp before continuing. 'I'm sorry, Dorothy, but you got it all wrong. Elvis tells me everything. We've always been real close. He mentioned his brother, Jesse, to you, I guess?'

'He said something …'

'Jesse was Elvis's stillborn twin. Lord forgive me, but I often think that had his brother survived, I might have lost something precious, because the bond between me and Elvis would never have been so strong.'

Dottie blinks.

'Anyhow!' Gladys remembers to laugh. 'He told me, he said, "Mama, Dottie's a real special girl."'

Dottie runs a finger around her plate again, but there's no sugar left. 'Well,' she says softly. 'That's real nice, Mrs Presley, but …'

Gladys clutches at Dottie's wrist, and the girl, surprised, draws back, but Gladys holds on. She leans closer, so Dottie can't look away. 'Can't you at least try to make him happy for me?'

Dottie extricates her fingers from Gladys's. 'I don't really see,' she says, 'how I can make him any happier than he already is.'

Gladys gives a bitter laugh. 'You think he's happy without a family?'

Dottie says, 'I sure do, Mrs Presley. Anyway, Elvis has a family. He has you.'

With a weak hand, Gladys motions for the cheque.

Oak Hill Drive, Killeen, Texas, July 1958

The luxury trailer did not live up to Gladys's expectations. The flimsy metal walls didn't offer nearly enough protection from the fans, who found the Presleys out in the woods beyond Killeen, and the whole place was just too hot to bear, even with the air conditioning cranked up to maximum.

So the family have moved to a ranch-style house, a little like the one they had on Audubon. Elvis has invited Anita, Cliff and Gene to spend the weekend in this new rental, and Gladys and Minnie Mae have spent Friday afternoon preparing meat loaf, mashed potatoes, fried okra, fried chicken and two pies: one cherry, one peach. Now they sit together in the early-evening shade of the backyard, iced teas in hand, both exhausted by their labours, waiting for the party to arrive. The truth is that Minnie Mae has done most of the work, quietly lifting dishes from Gladys's hands whenever she had a dizzy spell. Each time this happened, Gladys sat on a stool and laughed it off, blaming the heat. But as she watches the end of the sloping lawn for signs of Elvis's arrival (in order to avoid the fans permanently lodged at the front drive, he sometimes sneaks along the creek running by the back of the house), she knows she hasn't fooled her mother-in-law for one minute.

'You don't look so good,' says Minnie Mae.

'Maybe it's the change,' says Gladys.

'I was fifty, fore that kind of trouble started. You're barely past forty.'

Gladys sips her tea. Only Vernon knows that she's taken a few years off her age ever since she lied on her marriage licence.

'This heat, then.'

Minnie Mae pulls her lawn chair closer to Gladys.

'I'm serious, gal. I been watching you. I seen you grabbing at stuff, just to stay on your feet. Your face is yellow, did you know that? And I ain't seen you smile in I don't know how long.'

Hearing these truths, Gladys's hands begin to shake, and a slosh of cool tea wets the front of her dress, making her curse.

Calmly, Minnie Mae takes the glass from her and sets it down on the grass. 'Now, now,' she says. 'Let's not get excited.'

Gladys clamps her hands together in her lap. She stares down, willing them to be still. Since they moved to Texas, she has known that she is seriously ill. She keeps thinking of her own mama, who took to her bed for years before she died, saying she was weak, and so very tired. Nobody knew what was wrong. It had been Lillian's job to keep the sheets and Doll's nightgowns fresh, and to feed and bathe her mama. Perhaps, Gladys thinks, if she had a daughter of her own to take care of her, she could slip between the covers of her bed and rest until the Lord saw fit to take her.

Minnie Mae pats her forearm. 'I'm gonna have a talk with Vernon. I'm surprised Elvis ain't done something already.'

'He's so busy,' says Gladys, her voice a whisper.

'I'm gonna see Vernon gets you to a doctor. Tomorrow.'

'I already seen Dr Evans. He can't find nothing wrong.'

'You got to go again. We can find a doctor right here.'

'I don't like seeing other doctors.'

'We'll get you to Dr Evans, then.'

'Elvis has his friends for a visit—'

'Well, we just got to go without him.'

Gladys sighs, defeated. 'Maybe Elvis don't need to know.'

Minnie Mae raises her eyebrows. 'Don't you think he'll wanna know, Glad?'

'I don't want to worry him.'

'Bit late for that, ain't it?'

Gladys tries to grasp her mother-in-law's bony fingers, but gets a handful of her frilled cuff, which is edged with lace and comes almost to Minnie Mae's knuckles.

'You gonna be just fine,' says Minnie Mae. 'The doc will soon get you back to your old self.'

Gladys spends a few moments running her fingers along the cuff, then she says, 'The work here is real fine. Did Elvis buy you this one?'

'Gladys!' tuts Minnie. 'Don't you remember? You made it for me.'

Minnie Mae must have talked to Elvis as well as Vernon, because after supper he comes to her bedroom. She's turned in early and is lying on the bed with the lights off and her clothes still on, trying to breathe through her headache and summon up the energy to take her medication.

'Mama?' He hovers in the doorway, and she knows she could pretend to be sleeping and he would turn around and rejoin the others, who are still talking and playing records downstairs.

He opens the door wider. 'You awake?'

Everything in this rented house is unfamiliar, and she has to fumble for the light and try to remember which way to turn the switch.

He sits on the bed and looks at her with such concern that she has to avert her eyes, terrified by what ills he might spot in her face.

'We gonna get you to Dr Evans tomorrow. It's all set. I want you to take a flight. It'll be quicker.'

She props herself up on her pillows, pushing him away as he tries to help. Then she grasps his hand. He's wearing his uniform, and has a good tan on him from all those days spent training outside. He looks so capable, so healthy. Perhaps, she thinks, there is hope.

If she can hold on to him, and if he can keep talking as if he's in control of everything, some of his youthful energy could be passed to her. Maybe she doesn't need to see a doctor at all.

'I'm sorry, son,' she says.

'What for?'

'Being such a bother. I'm sure I'll be well again, if I can just rest.' Her head pounds, and, trying not to let the pain show in her face, she squeezes his hand harder. 'Seems an awful fuss to go all the way to Memphis ...'

'Mama,' he says, 'it's all set up. I can't stand to see you sick. So I gotta get you well.'

She takes a deep breath, relieved that he didn't buckle. 'I can't fly, though,' she says. 'I won't do that.'

He sighs. 'Then you'll take the train. I'll drive you and Daddy to the station myself.'

'Thank you, son.'

He kisses her hand and says, 'You're gonna be all better, ain't you?'

Only now does she hear the fear in his voice.

'I am.'

'Elvis is gonna get you well.'

'I know it.'

He touches her head. 'There, there, baby,' he says.

The next morning, she wakes before six and, unable to sleep again because of the ache thrumming through her legs, decides to go to the kitchen for a drink. She's had a broken night. Every time she managed to slip away from pain into sleep, she dreamed she was on a train journey and the windows in her carriage were blacked out, so she couldn't see the names of the stations.

Opening the kitchen door, she's surprised by the sight of Cliff ironing one of Elvis's army shirts, wearing only a pair of undershorts and socks. He's frowning in concentration as he nudges the iron gently along a sleeve.

'Cliff! Why in the world are you doing that?'

Stepping behind the board in an attempt to hide his shorts, which are bright orange and rather baggy, Cliff keeps a tight grip on the iron.

'Give it to me,' Gladys instructs.

''Fraid I can't do that, Miss Gladys. Elvis has given me his orders. You ain't to touch this.'

'Why ain't Alberta doing it?'

'Has to be a man who irons an army uniform, Miss Gladys.'

'Oh, Cliff! What a notion!'

'It's true, ma'am.'

Gladys moves slowly across to the counter to sit herself on a stool. The ache in her legs eases a little. From here, she can see the trees and the bright lawn outside, still wet from the night. It's already hot, and a veil of steam rises from the grass.

'What's he need that for today, anyhow?'

'He wants to wear it, Miss Gladys. You know how he is about his uniform.'

She does. Elvis has had Vernon arrange for twenty pairs of army pants, ten jackets and ten army ties to be tailored specially for him, and he often wears them, even on his days off.

Cliff pushes the iron's nose into the shoulder of the shirt.

'You're good at that.'

'I got my uses, ma'am.'

'How about sharing a beer with me, Cliff?'

They have done this before in the afternoon, alone in the kitchen at Graceland, both hiding their bottles when they heard Elvis approaching.

To her relief, Cliff doesn't even check the clock. 'Sure, Miss Gladys. In my book, it's always time for a drink with a lady.' He places Elvis's shirt on a hanger and hooks it on the back of the door. Opening the refrigerator, he says, 'I oughta apologise, for my attire and all.'

'I seen worse.'

He laughs. Then he settles himself on a stool next to her, and pops the caps on their beers.

After they've taken a drink, Gladys muses, 'I just can't fathom why Elvis needs so much uniform.'

'He'll be glad of it in Germany,' says Cliff. 'I hear it gets real cold out there.'

Gladys puts down her bottle. 'Germany?'

Cliff looks at her for a long moment before saying, very quietly, 'Oh, shit.'

'Elvis is going to Germany?'

He wipes his face with one hand, pulling down the corners of his eyes. 'Guess he didn't tell you, huh?'

Her head goes light, and she has to lean on the counter to catch her breath.

'I'm real sorry, Miss Gladys,' Cliff says. 'He's getting posted. In September.'

She closes her eyes. Germany. She's not sure, even, where it is on the map. She only knows it as a place of war. She pictures barbed wire, tanks ploughing through mud, and pits filled with dead bodies.

'Can I fetch somebody for you?' asks Cliff. 'Mr Presley, maybe?'

'No,' says Gladys, hanging on to his arm. 'Stay with me, please.'

He pats her hand. She can feel his muscle moving as he does so, and she tries to concentrate on that, on the strong smoothness of his arm.

'Cliff,' she says, looking up at him, 'you'll take care of my son when I'm gone, won't you?'

Cliff frowns.

'You're one of his best friends,' she says, 'so I'm expecting you to do that. And he oughta marry before he leaves the country. He'll need somebody out there, and I can't go.'

Cliff laughs; then, seeing she's serious, clears his throat. 'Well, that's really up to him, ain't it?'

She removes her hand from his arm and takes another drink. 'I don't reckon Anita to be perfect. She's too interested in her own career. But it's better he marries her than keeps on as he is.'

Cliff picks up his beer. 'Why you talking this way, Miss Gladys? You're still young yourself. You could go to Germany. Elvis would fix it.'

She waves the comment away. 'It'll ease my mind to know you're gonna be there for him.'

'All right,' he says. 'I promise.'

They chink the necks of their bottles, then watch the sun blaze up over the trees.

GRACELAND: 1957

1957

'Pretty soon I'm gonna buy you a place even better than this, Mama.'

Elvis is taking his parents on a tour of the homes of the Hollywood stars. They've already got a look at the houses of John Wayne and Carole Lombard. Now he's parked up at the gates of his favourite mansion: Red Skelton's, on Sorbonne Road, Bel Air.

'He has a mile-long driveway and a thirty-five-thousand-gallon swimming pool!'

They can just see the house, beyond the trees on the crest of the hill. With its vine-covered red bricks and tall windows, it looks to Elvis like a lot of things in Los Angeles: as if it's come straight from a movie set.

'Son, it's something else,' says Gladys, touching her pinned-back hat. 'Real high class.'

'At night that driveway is lit up all the way to the house.'

'He don't have no trouble finding his front door, then,' says Vernon.

It's February, and his parents have come to California to visit while he's filming his new movie, *Loving You*. Arriving at Paramount, they seemed unsure at first. Gladys's hand had quivered when Mr

Kanter, the director, shook it, and Vernon talked too loud about how long the journey had taken and how fancy their hotel room was and how he couldn't take his eyes off all these beautiful ladies. But now they've been here a couple of days they seem to have realised that their son truly is the star of this picture, and they've relaxed some. Elvis has pointed out to them that there's a man to do his hair and make-up, another whose job it is to take care of his wardrobe, and a boy whose only role seems to be to tell him when it's time to work. Mr Kanter is in charge, of course, but as the Colonel says, without Elvis, there is no movie.

'How many rooms does it have, son?' asks Gladys.

'I ain't sure, Mama. But we'll have more.'

'So long as you buy me that lilac crêpe dress you promised.'

'It's yours.'

They smile at one another, and, from the back seat, Vernon asks if their next stop can be for a beer.

The following day, Mr Kanter suggests to Elvis that his parents could feature in the scene they're shooting that afternoon. His character, Deke Rivers, whose story is loosely based on Elvis's own, will be singing his triumphant final number, 'Got a Lot o' Livin, to Do', in a coast-to-coast broadcast which will win over the entire nation. Even the middle-aged ladies who'd previously disapproved of the explosive young singer will be cheering him and clapping along.

When his mama mentions her concern about looking fat on film, Elvis tells her not to be silly. Nobody will be thinking of that. She'll look pretty, like she always does: Hollywood will work its magic. Mr Kanter agrees. 'It'll be cute,' he says. 'And I think the fans would love to see your mother enjoying your performance, Elvis.'

So Gladys agrees.

On set, it's up to Elvis to generate all the energy in the enormous studio. Even though there's an audience for this scene, it's nothing like a real show. The metal monster of the camera is always there, for one thing, and for another he's not even singing. The pre-recorded song booms through the speakers, and the men behind him mime playing their instruments as he lip-synchs. At least he's managed to get Scotty, Bill and DJ small parts in the picture, which has smoothed things over with them, for now.

As he dances to the edge of the stage, the lights go up on the audience and he sees his mama sitting on the end of a row about halfway down the aisle. She's grinning like a girl, and doesn't take her eyes off him even for a moment. When he returns her gaze, she clasps her hands together and raises them to her chin, as if in prayer, and he senses he can make this one come alive. Jumping from the stage, he leads the audience in clapping along, then dances down the aisle, swinging an arm and bending his knees, all the time heading for his mother. Her tapping foot never misses a beat, and he remembers how he watched her dance on the porch that day his daddy came home from the pen, and how the man in the truck had applauded, and he dances harder, until he's right up close to her. In that moment Gladys almost rises from her seat to greet him, a little perspiration on her lip and a sheen in her eyes he hasn't seen there for a while, and he worries, briefly, that she'll forget this is a movie and throw her arms around his neck. But she just keeps clapping and beaming. Elvis dances back down the aisle, and before the song ends he glances at his mama again, and she looks right at him, and he knows he is loved.

* * *

'Elvis wants a farm,' says Gladys, 'like the one in *Love Me Tender*.'

Not long after arriving home from California, she and Vernon are in their brand new white Lincoln Continental, driving towards Whitehaven shopping mall to meet the realtor, Mrs Virginia Grant.

'It'd have to be a farm with a big ol' house on it!' says Vernon.

'Not a farm, then,' says Gladys. 'Maybe a ranch.'

'More like a mansion,' Vernon corrects her, 'like Red Skelton's house.'

He takes his time driving. Gladys senses his enjoyment when other motorists come up close behind, or linger in the lane beside them, to get a good look at the car. It *is* wonderful. The leather seats are like lovers' laps, wide and welcoming. They hardly seem to move as they glide down Highway 51, past the empty lots, gas stations, restaurants and signs pointing towards the new airport.

They park up easy in the empty lot. The new shopping plaza is the most upscale mall in Memphis, and the buildings shine in the cold February light.

Vernon cuts the engine. 'Darn,' he says. 'We shoulda been late. Kept her waiting.'

He leans back in his seat and fishes a cigarette from the pack in his pocket. Elvis says his daddy should smoke cigars now that he's made it, but Vernon can't stand the smell.

Another car – much older than theirs – parks on the other side of the lot.

'Reckon that's her?' asks Gladys, twisting her neck.

'Bound to be.' Vernon taps his ash into the tray.

'Don't you think we oughta go meet her?' Gladys's feet, in their pristine pumps, are becoming numb with cold.

'Let her come to us. Then we got the upper hand.'

'You sound like Tom Parker.'

'Colonel's a smart cookie. Ain't he done got you this new car?'

Another vehicle pulls up beside them. A woman in a pea-green swing coat gets out, then opens the door for a small girl in a knitted cap. They do not give the Presley Lincoln a second glance as they walk towards the mall, hand in hand.

'Ain't that girl adorable?' says Gladys. 'When Elvis and Barbara are married, we can bring our grandbabies here.'

'Elvis ain't gonna marry that gal. He don't even see her that often no more.'

'I can't see why not. That showgirl was just a flash in the pan. Barbara's waited for him. She'd make a good wife.'

Vernon chuckles. 'Why keep a cow, Glad, when you can milk one through the fence?'

'That's a dirty thing to say!'

'You never used to be so prissy,' says Vernon, grinding out his cigarette. 'Now, listen. Don't get too excited by what this realtor gal shows us. 'Cause we don't wanna pay what she's asking.'

Gladys stares out of the window. The woman is holding the glass door of the grocery store open for her child.

'It's like a game, see?' Vernon continues. 'We gotta act like we don't care. If they know we care, it's in the bag for them.'

'What does it matter, if Elvis can afford it?'

'We don't want her thinking we're green. Don't forget we're the Presleys. Boy! I bet that old maid over there is getting herself pretty worked up, thinking she's gonna meet Elvis's daddy!' He grins at Gladys.

'She might not care for Elvis's music.'

'It ain't just about the music, Glad! Our boy's a superstar! And that means money. And just about the only thing real-estate folks care for is money.'

'Here she comes,' hisses Gladys, spotting a woman climbing from the car behind them.

They get out to watch Virginia Grant approach. She is tall with a wide nose and hair the colour of Gladys's when she was a girl. She is not, Gladys notices, young or particularly attractive, which comes as something of a relief. Mrs Grant walks swiftly, swinging a folder in her hand, giving Vernon a businesslike smile. Vernon leans back on the car, openly assessing the realtor's appearance in a way that makes Gladys so embarrassed that she steps forward to speak first.

'You must be Mrs Grant,' she says, offering her hand. 'I'm Gladys Presley, and this is my husband, Vernon.'

'Such a pleasure!' says Mrs Grant.

Vernon does not move. 'Whatcha got for us, ma'am?'

'We're so excited!' says Gladys. 'We can't wait to see it, whatever it is!'

Vernon hangs his head. 'You gotta forgive my wife, Mrs Grant. She gets herself awful worked up over nothing sometimes.'

'You said on the phone you wanted privacy, and somewhere more rural, perhaps?' says Mrs Grant, being careful to address them both equally. 'I think I have just the place for your family. It's not far from here, and it's an absolute dream of a property, perfect for your needs—'

'Our son has said he wants a plantation-type mansion,' states Vernon.

'Or a farm,' adds Gladys.

'Well, this is both,' says Mrs Grant, firmly. 'But instead of talking about it out here in the cold, why don't we go on over? Do you want to follow me in your car?'

'No need,' says Vernon. 'We can give you a ride.'

'That's kind,' says Mrs Grant, holding her folder to her chest, 'but it's really not necessary—'

'Don't you wanna ride in Elvis Presley's car?' asks Vernon, caressing the Lincoln's roof.

'Well,' says Mrs Grant, glancing at Gladys, 'since you put it like that ...'

Vernon holds open the passenger door.

Gladys arranges herself in the back. She knew her husband would not tolerate following Mrs Grant around town. He's already stated his opinion that real estate is no job for a woman, a sentiment with which Gladys cannot help but agree.

When they're on the road, Vernon asks, 'How much is this house you have in mind, Mrs Grant?'

'Sixty thousand dollars.'

Vernon smiles. 'Sixty thousand? Is that all? I reckon we can do a whole lot better than that. That won't get us much more than we already got.'

'I didn't want to presume—'

'Presume nothing,' says Vernon. 'The Presleys are looking to double their property investment. My son has instructed me, as his

360

financial manager, to look for properties in the region of ninety thousand dollars.'

'I beg your pardon, Mr Presley. I hadn't realised your son was doing quite so well.'

'Elvis is in the movies, ma'am. Hollywood. California.'

'Can we turn around here?' Mrs Grant asks. 'I have someplace else I'd like you to see.'

Vernon makes a slow and careful U-turn on the empty highway.

After ten minutes, the new buildings of Whitehaven run out, and everywhere Gladys looks is open country.

'Where you taking us, Mrs Grant?' asks Vernon. 'Back to Tupelo? We're almost at the state line!'

'It's right here,' says Mrs Grant, pointing to a low gate by the road. 'Thirty-seven sixty-four Highway fifty-one South. But this house also has a name. It's called Graceland. If you pull over here, Mr Presley, I'll walk you up the driveway.'

Although bare now, the trees which surround them are taller than the house, and look as though they have been in this ground for ever. As Mrs Grant has pointed out, this is not just a mansion, it is an estate of thirteen acres. The house was built about ten years ago on what was left of a cattle ranch owned by the Moore family. Mrs Moore, the proprietor, is too old to take care of it all, and has been loaning out the downstairs rooms to the nearby church, who use them for choir practice and Sunday-school sessions.

The choir is practising today, in fact. As they walk up the sweep of the long driveway, the sound of 'Bosom of Abraham' comes from the house, and Vernon hums along.

It reminds Gladys of the first time she visited Memphis Zoological Gardens and saw those landscaped lawns and pathways that seemed to have been created not for walking on but for looking at. There is something ordered and regular about the place that relaxes her mind.

Nearing the steps of the house, all three of them stop and stare. The walls are built from stone the colour of bread. The columned portico, as tall as the house itself, is so white that it looks iced. To each side of the porch are four green-shuttered windows, and hanging above the front door is a large glass lantern. It's the kind of house a city governor or county judge would live in. It's the kind of house, Gladys thinks, in which you might find Sleeping Beauty. She imagines, briefly, her son lying on a bed within, a rose at his chest, waiting for the awakening kiss of his true love. With the welcoming swish of the trees all around him, and the highway far enough away to be quiet, but close enough to take him where he needs to go, she's sure he'll be able to sleep here.

Glancing at her notes, Mrs Grant says, 'Downstairs there's a living room, dining room and parlour, plus a big kitchen, a pantry, a butler's pantry, a utility room, one bedroom and a bath and a half. Upstairs are four bedrooms and three baths. And in the basement there's a wood-panelled den and a playroom. And the car porch has space for four cars.'

Vernon threads his arm through Gladys's. 'This looks like the right kinda place for us,' he says.

Gladys whispers in his ear, 'You said not to show her we wanted it.'

Vernon laughs. 'Aw, hell,' he says, 'we want it.'

* * *

Driving down South Main early one evening in March, Elvis tells his friends about his new house.

'It's kinda a mansion, real classy, nicer than any of those Hollywood homes you see on the TV, nicer than any I been in, anyhow. And I'm gonna make it bang up to date inside. Mr Golden, who did Sam Phillips's house, is fixing up the whole place. It'll be all done by the summer.'

Cliff, riding next to him, says, 'Sam's house looks like something offa Commando Cody.'

'Sam's house makes Commando Cody look old-fashioned,' says Elvis.

He's spent the afternoon showing his friends how to use the prop gun he brought back from the film set of his latest movie, and they've all got pretty good at it. Now they're on their way to the Hotel Chisca to drop in on local disc jockey Dewey Phillips, so Elvis can update him on the movie. He wants to tell him what it was like to kiss Dolores Hart, and how Lizabeth Scott is a lot of fun, despite being one hundred per cent lesbian.

It's noisy inside the car and the windows are starting to steam up. He and Cliff picked up Heidi, Gloria and Frances on the way, and the warm buzz of the pill he took to keep him on top for the night, plus the sugary smell of the girls' perfume, has him winding down his window for air. The plan is to stop by Dewey's, then head to the Fairgrounds, which Elvis has rented privately for the night, so he and his friends won't be bothered by strangers. Gene and Lamar will meet them there later with two more carloads of friends.

At the sight of his Cadillac, other drivers sound their horns. One girl leans out of her passenger-seat window and yells his name as he speeds past. The long syllables stretch after him down the street.

Elvis pulls up outside the towering red bricks of the Hotel Chisca and slams the car into park. He takes a moment to check his hair in the mirror.

Cliff, who knows the drill, hops out first to look up and down the sidewalk for any obvious trouble, then opens the door for Elvis.

'I'll be back!' Elvis tells the girls, leaping into the cool evening.

Cliff nods and stretches an arm towards the hotel, but there are already five or six girls approaching them, and although Elvis knows he should head straight to the double doors, he pauses. One of them has a little of Dolores Hart about her. More girls appear, as if from nowhere, and soon he's in a crowd of fifteen or so, all waving odd pieces of paper snatched from purses and pockets. It's remarkable how many till receipts, grocery sacks and shopping lists he's signed. Paperback novels and sides of milk cartons. Dollar bills. Even, one time, a baby's bonnet.

'Great to have you back in Memphis, Elvis!' shouts an older man from behind the girls, and Elvis calls back, 'Thank you, sir! Sure is good to be home!'

Then there's a shout, and it's unmistakably male and full of rage.

'I got something to settle with you, Presley!'

Elvis looks up and the crowd stills. A young man in a marine uniform is ploughing towards him.

Catching Cliff's eye, Elvis tries to walk on, thinking he can just ignore the boy. This sort of thing happens more now he's in the movies, especially with young men who are jealous of his effect on their wives and girlfriends, and he knows it's best if he can just sidestep his way out of it.

The girls have parted for the marine, who now plants himself in front of Elvis, blocking his path.

'You pushed my wife a month back,' he says. 'That ain't no way to treat a lady.'

Elvis studies the marine, who appears younger than him, with a puffy face and a dark brow. He's breathing hard.

'I got no idea what you're talking about,' he says. 'Now, if you'll excuse me—'

The marine shakes his head. 'You need to apologise.'

Elvis tries a smile. 'I was out in Hollywood a month ago, so I think you've got this wrong, friend.' He takes a step forward, but the marine grabs his arm.

'I ain't your friend,' he says.

Elvis can feel the crowd holding its breath. Somebody calls, 'Don't let him get away with that, Elvis!'

'Turn me loose,' he says, quietly.

The marine's face is real close now; there's coffee on his breath and Elvis can feel the heat and power in his fingers. He thinks of his mama asking for more protection. Vernon has said they should build a bigger wall around Graceland. Elvis had expected Gladys to baulk at this, but she'd nodded solemnly and that stricken look had descended.

'Maybe we should settle this like real men,' the marine says.

Elvis's blood rises. He feels its pressure in his lips, behind his eyes, in his fingertips. It's not unlike being onstage. Then, in one swift movement, he pulls the prop gun from inside his jacket and jabs it into the marine's chest.

'Come any closer,' he hisses, aware that he sounds like a character from one of his own movies, and not quite sure, yet, whether he's kidding around or not, 'and I'll blow your damn brains out, you punk.'

Immediately, the crowd moves back, all eyes on the gun in Elvis's hand, which he knows looks real enough.

'Jesus!' says the marine, holding out his hands as he backs away.

Cliff puts a hand to Elvis's shoulder. 'Get in the car, man,' he says, softly.

But Elvis stands his ground, sure, now, that he's absolutely serious. 'Go on!' he yells at the marine, waving the gun. 'Get!'

The marine turns and sprints down the sidewalk.

Slowly, Elvis slides the gun inside his jacket and scans the crowd, pleased with his performance. The faces look back at him, changed. Each one is pale. Several girls hold their hands over their mouths, not to stop the squeals coming out, but to keep back some objection. Nobody offers up any more pieces of paper, or baby's bonnets.

'I'm real sorry,' Elvis says, 'if that man there scared anybody.'

Then he ducks into the car, and Cliff speeds away.

Nobody says a word, all the way to the Fairgrounds.

Riding the Pippin in the front carriage, his knuckles straining at the bar, the coloured lights, the chill breeze and the smell of the hot-dog stand hurtling towards him, he can still feel the prop gun inside his jacket, poking into his ribs. Seated next to him is Gloria, and in the car behind are Heidi and Frances. Barbara hasn't joined the group at the Fairgrounds tonight. He senses she's had enough of it all, and he's not particularly sorry. He knows how she would feel about that prop gun. Barbara has made her dislike of firearms more than clear.

He's picked Gloria because he suspects she'll scream the loudest when their wooden truck ratchets up to the ride's highest point and tips over the edge of the seventy-foot drop, and he wants to scream right along with her. The air pushes him back in his seat, lifting his hair and pummelling his cheeks. When he opens his mouth to yell, the wind rushes down his throat, almost preventing the sound coming from him. But when he forces it out, closing his eyes and screaming for all he's worth, it's ecstasy, this flying through the night in a roller-coaster car with nothing to do but scream and hold on. Elvis yells and yells and yells.

That night he rides the car ten times in a row, screeching into the dark like one of his own fans. And every time he rides it, he pictures the fear on that marine's face, and tells himself that he had every right to put it there. Any other man would have defended himself. Why should he be different? But he knows he cannot let something like that happen again. If the Colonel finds out, he'll never let Elvis forget it. *Be smart, son, and let those other fools take the rap*, he'd say. He must have more guys around at all times. Armed, if necessary.

Much later, in bed, he takes two sleeping pills but he doesn't tumble directly into oblivion. Instead he travels through several dreams in which he's back sleepwalking in East Tupelo, the gravel road rough and warm beneath his feet. A truck's headlamps sweep over him, and he tugs his too-small nightshirt down, aware, suddenly, that anybody could see his peter, that those lights could display everything he thought he'd hidden, and that his mama isn't coming to save him.

* * *

It is as if, for the first time in his life, he is really going home.

At least, this is what Elvis tells himself as he races through the June night with Cliff snoring in the seat beside him. He's impatient to see his new house, which he visited over Easter but has yet to spend a night in. Hollywood and his latest movie shoot – they had him dance in a jailhouse, which struck him as both ridiculous and wonderful – are finally behind him. Joining Highway 51 into Memphis, he imagines he can already see the glow of the new lights lining his driveway. On the phone, Vernon had complained about that many blue and gold lights making Graceland look like an airport, but he has promised they'll be working by the time his son gets home.

Elvis guns the engine and sounds the horn, just for the hell of being back in town. He feels as though he owns the whole state. He doesn't know exactly how much money he has now – he leaves the details to the Colonel, and the counting to Vernon – but he knows it's more than a million dollars and it keeps on coming. Still, he wishes some special girl were here to witness him whizzing past the motels, the car dealerships and Chenault's Drive-In. He considers picking up Heidi, Gloria and Frances, or even some girl off the street, just to give them a thrill.

Every night he's been away, he's called home and received a report on the latest developments in the decor. Gladys knew exactly what he wanted: purple corduroy drapes and a white couch the length of the entire front wall in the living room; his bedroom to be painted the darkest blue there is, with navy drapes, a white carpet, a mirrored wall and a ten-foot-square bed; and in the front hallway, the ceiling to be painted like a night sky, with stars picked out in tiny bulbs. When they'd moved from house to house and room to room in Tupelo and Memphis (how many times? he's lost count, but it's at least fifteen), nowhere had truly belonged to them. Even at Lauderdale Courts, which had felt the most permanent of his homes, the family were not free to choose the colour of the walls. And Audubon Drive, now he looks back on it, could never have been home, with the golf-set surrounding the place. Graceland will be different. He means to write his name on every inch of his new home.

Elvis unwinds his window to take a gulp of the warm, damp Memphis air. The streetlamps stain the dark sky fuzzily orange until he comes close to his house, where trees begin to outnumber lights, and the new developments run out. He slows down to take in the first sight of his mansion. Drawing close to his gates, he nudges Cliff.

'Wake up, man! We're home!'

He pushes the thought of the special girl from his mind, because it's all perfect: the wrought-iron guitar man on each gate is obviously him, but could be seen as a more general symbol of rock 'n' roll. The blue lights along the driveway lead right up to the house, which is so illuminated it seems to float, shimmering, among the trees. The columns rise up like golden fountains. And there are around thirty fans clustered at the entrance, all starting to wave and call out his name.

Cliff yawns and stretches. 'Sorry 'bout that,' he says.

'Get out there and tell Uncle Vester to open up,' says Elvis.

Cliff fumbles with the handle and almost trips from the car onto the sidewalk. He inches his way through the crowd. Elvis keeps the engine running, drumming his fingers on the wheel. He smiles and waves to the fans but keeps his window up now, despite their demands. He hasn't time for them. All he wants is to get inside his house.

Finally the gates swing open and Elvis drives in fast, leaving Cliff to walk up the driveway. He slows a little on the first bend, sounding his horn three times to let them know he's home. Seeing his parents silhouetted in the doorway, his whole body goes weak, as if washed through, and he has to concentrate on his breathing. It's like that time at Brother Mansell's when he was saved. He stops the car and lets the feeling overcome him, half-wondering if he will float up into the trees. Then he lowers his head in prayer, thanking God and Jesse for his success.

Leaving the engine running, he leaps out and jogs the rest of the way, laughing and calling to them.

On the porch, Gladys opens her arms and says, 'Welcome home, son,' just as he'd hoped she would. He nestles himself against her and breathes in her good Mama smell.

Inside, there is no canopy of stars, and the drapes are not purple corduroy but ivory brocade, because his mother decided they would hang better. She explains how the electricians couldn't wire in all the tiny bulbs without weakening the ceiling, but he's not listening. He'd wanted to bring the sky inside his home, so every time he returned he could look up and see the perfection he'd created right above his head. At night, those glittering stars would have welcomed his guests, letting them know that this was no ordinary house, but a mysterious mansion on the hill, a place where magic happened. Ever since he first set foot in the place, when there was just a dusty schoolroom piano in the corner of the living room, he's dreamed of that night sky.

His mother is kneading her hands together as she apologises, and his father is coughing nervously.

'Couldn't be helped, son,' Vernon says, patting him on the arm.

Seeing his parents' discomfort, Elvis manages to swallow his disappointment, for now.

'What about my bedroom?' he asks.

'That's just exactly as you wanted it, baby,' says Gladys.

Before his daddy can agree, Elvis has mounted the stairs. In his rush to get there, he barely takes in his reflection on the mirrored wall.

The following afternoon, Elvis sits on his bed, watching TV and eating potato chips from a china dish. He's just ended a call to Scotty to ask what it would take to get him and Bill to change their minds about going it alone. The Colonel and the guys at RCA aren't sorry; they've long wanted Scotty and Bill gone, saying the two musicians just aren't up to the job. Elvis is a number-one entertainer, now. He needs professional backup, not a couple of hicks who've barely set foot in a real recording studio. Scotty said he reckoned Elvis owed him at least ten thousand dollars by now, which made Elvis laugh. The Colonel will never agree to such a sum. Scotty, though, hadn't laughed one bit. He'd told Elvis that he and Bill were mighty disappointed. He'd told him that without them Elvis would never have made a record. He'd said that Elvis owed them both a decent living, not the peanuts they were getting on the payroll. As Scotty spoke, Elvis looked out of the window, watching his daddy driving his new tractor round in circles on the lawn. He could think of nothing to say. He hated to think of Scotty being upset. But he hated the thought of the Colonel's wrath even more. So he made no promises. But he knows it won't be long before he has to leave Scotty and Bill behind.

He pops another potato chip in his mouth. His bedroom is the blue he wanted, the blue of the East Tupelo sky on a summer's night, or a police officer's uniform. But Elvis feels the need for a girl more keenly now. The right girl would help him forget the pain in Scotty's voice. The right girl would make this room perfect. Without one, it's just too cold in here.

On the screen is *Top Ten Dance Party*, a new local show featuring kids dancing to the latest hit records. A girl who looks like Grace Kelly but sounds like Magdalene Morgan, cloud of bobbed blonde hair displaying her long pale neck, is introducing the next record. She has bright eyes, something shy in her smile, and a waist he could get both hands round. When he worked as an usher at Loew's State, he sometimes used to imagine the starlet on the screen pausing the movie's action to look right at him. All he'd have to do was beckon her, and she'd step into the auditorium. Then they'd run off together, up the aisle, through the curtain, down the sweeping stairs into the lobby, and out into the sunshine on South Main.

It dawns on him now that he can realise this fantasy. He can reach into the TV screen and pull that girl right out.

He calls a new friend, Lamar Fike, who Cliff has brought to the Fairgrounds a couple of times. Lamar is smart, full of jokes, and must weigh around three hundred pounds. Elvis has decided to call him Buddha, because he is fat and thinks himself wise. He's also decided to count on him for a few things, and see how it turns out.

When he dials the number, Lamar's mother answers.

'Hello, Mrs Fike. This is Elvis Presley, calling for Lamar.'

There's a pause, and then he hears her yell, 'Lamar! It's Elvis Presley for you again!'

There's some murmuring before Lamar comes on. From the crashing and banging, Elvis figures that the phone in the Fike household is next to the stove.

'Hi, Elvis! How's it going, man? I heard you were back in Memphis.'

'Buddha, you need to get your own line.'

'What I need is to get my ass out of here,' Lamar says in a low voice. 'Sorry about my mother. She's a little tired this afternoon.'

'I'm gonna get another line installed for you. You want one in your bedroom?'

'Naw! I mean, that's kind, but—'

'I'll have my daddy take care of it. He'll have it all installed for you in a couple of days. Your mother would appreciate that, wouldn't she?'

There's another loud crash.

'I guess she would.'

'Well, OK, then.'

'Thanks, man.'

Elvis smiles to himself and shifts closer to the TV. 'You watching WHBQ?'

'Sure am.'

On the screen, the girl is pulling a sweetly puzzled face at something her co-host is saying. Elvis decides that she's a virgin. He can tell by the way she holds herself; there's something pure about her posture.

'You see that blonde on there? The hostess?'

'Anita Wood. She's a Memphis girl. Real beauty queen.'

'I want you to set up a date with her for me. Call her up, will you?'

There's a pause, then Lamar says, 'Sure, Elvis. I can do that.'

The show's end credits start to roll. Elvis says, 'Give her an hour or so to get home. Then call. And, Lamar?'

'Yeah?'

'Tell her she's special. Tell her I'm real serious about this.'

Because Anita already had plans to see somebody else, it took Lamar a couple of weeks to set up the date, but now that Elvis has got her in the Cadillac, he sees this as a good thing. It proves that Anita is loyal, and she doesn't take other people's feelings lightly. On the front seat, she looks contained and pale, holding her white hands in her lap and keeping her knees pointing away from his. Her perfume smells expensive and her pink dress seems to be made of satin. When he picked her up, her landlady, Miss Patty, insisted on Elvis coming to the door himself before she'd let Anita out. Bounding up the steps to meet her, he'd wondered if a velvet shirt was such a good idea for a hot night in July. When he took off his motorcycle cap and ducked his head at Miss Patty, he'd felt Anita's eyes taking all of him in, and he sensed it would work out just fine.

On the back seat are Lamar and Cliff. They are heading to Chenault's for burgers in the private dining room, but on the way Elvis takes a detour to the Strand to show Anita the enormous cardboard cut-out of himself outside the theatre. It's part of the advertising display for *Loving You*.

He draws up to the kerb on the opposite side so they can get a good view.

'Nobody's torn it down, Elvis!' says Cliff, laughing.

'Not yet,' Elvis says. He turns to Anita to explain. 'The theatre manager had to replace it five times this week already, because the fans keep stealing me.'

'That's what *he* thinks,' says Lamar. 'Truth is, Colonel Parker comes up here every night and rips him down.'

'Hush your mouth, Buddha,' says Elvis, without looking at him.

'What's it like,' Anita asks, 'in Hollywood?'

Elvis hangs his head for a moment, as if considering her question deeply. The truth is that most of the time he's in Hollywood, he longs to be back in Memphis; he's just never been able to shake the feeling that people there are laughing at him.

'Well,' he says, 'it's just wonderful, honey. It's my dream come true. But folks out there are kinda strange. Some of them are downright insane! So I figure it's better just to get my work done, then come on home.'

'It must be a lot of fun, meeting all those movie stars,' says Anita, her eyes shining.

'Know what was most fun?' he says. 'Seeing my mama and daddy on the set. They were real proud.'

'I'd love to go there some time.'

Elvis leans closer to her. 'Anita,' he says, 'what goes on in California is what goes on in hell. Ain't no place for a good little girl like you.'

She giggles, but when he fixes her with what he hopes is a serious stare, she composes herself.

'I mean it,' he says. 'I'd hate to think of a pure girl like you getting led astray.'

By this time, a group of girls on the sidewalk have noticed him. One of them puts her face close to his window, where she gapes like a fish on a hook. Then she slaps the glass and yells, 'It's him! It's really him!'

Elvis puts the car into drive, revs the engine, then winds down the window. 'Bye, girls,' he says, blowing them a kiss before pulling away.

The car squeals off down South Main, and Anita squeals with it.

At Chenault's, the sun glaring through the pitched glass roof lights up Anita's hair. Her dress complements the pink leatherette seats and white vinyl tables. She nibbles on an order of fries and tells him quite freely about her job at WHBQ and her lack of steady boyfriends. She's not ready, she says, to get serious with anybody.

Back at the mansion, it isn't long before he invites her upstairs, to see his office. She murmurs her approval of his leather swivel chair and huge walnut desk, and listens politely as he takes her through his collection of gold records.

Grabbing her hand, he pulls her down the corridor, past his closets, and into the adjoining room.

'And, well, you can guess what this room is,' he says, sitting on the bed. He tugs at her fingers. 'Take the weight off, honey. You can trust me.'

She sits next to him, but when he moves his face close to hers, she puts a hand to his lips to stop him.

'Elvis,' she says, 'it's like you said. I ain't one of those girls.'

He tries to nibble one of her fingers, but she inches away and curls her hands in her lap. Back at Chenault's, she'd seemed confident and full of talk. In fact, he'd wondered if she had too much to say for herself. Now she seems younger, and a little lost.

Since he's been in the movies, he's found these moments with girls have taken on an unreal quality. He wants to act like a star, and he senses that the girls want that too. But the whole thing can make him nervous, and he sometimes gets the feeling that what he's doing is being recorded somehow. He wishes he could slip away from her and take another pill.

The air conditioning whirrs, and she gives a shiver. She'd removed her shoes before coming upstairs, and he looks at her naked feet, pale as moons.

'I like your sooties,' he says. 'You got a chip on the polish there, though.'

Anita bends to examine her toes.

'Seems a shame to spoil perfection, don't it?' he says, laughing.

She straightens up. 'Do you always notice girls' feet?' she asks.

'Only pretty ones, like yours. Ones like tiny flowers.' He takes her by the shoulders and notices her glance at his diamond pinkie ring.

'Will you keep them perfect for me?' he says. 'Just like you, little one?' He kisses her forehead, and tastes salt. 'That's what I'm gonna call you. *Little*,' he murmurs into her hair.

She draws back. 'Like a doll?'

'Exactly.'

Anita laughs.

'What's funny?' Perhaps he's made a fool of himself. Perhaps he'll have to try another girl, if Anita is going to laugh at him. 'Don't you like me?'

Instead of replying, she plants a long, wet kiss right on his lips.

Before Elvis can speak again, she says, 'You can take me home now.'

* * *

It's six o'clock in the evening, and Gladys is in front of the mansion, feeding her chickens. Her flock chuckle and flutter around her slippered feet as she pushes her hand into the bin and savours the cool, pearly feeling of corn slipping over her fingers. Tossing a handful onto the grass, she reflects that there's more pleasure in this act than there is in touching the real pearls her son has bought her. She has so much jewellery now that she's embarrassed to look at it. On her dresser, it hangs on a silver contraption which is moulded to look like a tree. It is also crammed into mahogany boxes, inlaid with more jewels. It is stashed in velvet purses among the handkerchiefs and lavender sachets in her top drawer. And still it spills over. She has told him, many times now, to stop. Just stop. She has enough. But he won't listen.

'Mama!'

She'd known Elvis would be coming out soon; it was after four a.m. when she heard him arriving home, and he's been in bed until about an hour ago. But she pretends not to have noticed his call. After all, it is a breezy evening, bringing a little respite from the heavy August heat. It's been over ninety degrees for days, but it's cooler out here, now. The wind blows the tall trees around as if they were no more than cotton plants. She could very well have missed him.

She feels her son watching her from the steps as she scoops another handful of corn, so round and full. But she won't make it easy for him. Not today. Not with her legs in the state they are – when asked, she blames the swelling on the long hours she spent standing at St Joseph's Hospital. Privately, she knows this to be a fiction. Her legs never gave her a moment's worry until the family moved to Audubon Drive.

'Mama!'

She focuses on her task, clucking to her birds as she feeds them. Let him come closer, if he really wants to. Let him smell the chicken shit.

'Mama!'

Let him get it on his buckskin shoes.

'Mama,' he says, striding across the grass, 'didn't you hear me calling?'

'No, son, I guess not.'

His pale face looks a little creased after another night at the Fairgrounds. He needs to blow off some steam, she knows that. And after being surrounded by those Hollywood folks, it's good for him to spend time with his friends, just fooling around. Gladys herself used to love riding everything from carousels to Ferris wheels, and recalls fondly that feeling she would get of being on the brink of something wonderful whenever she bought a ticket.

'Mama, can I talk to you?'

He looks paler because his hair is permanently dyed black now, like hers. He got it done for the picture he made earlier in the year, *Loving You*, and he's kept it ever since. That unrelenting, thick blackness which reflects nothing. Although it suits him well enough, especially with his eyebrows and lashes dyed to match, she preferred his hair when it was the colour of wet sand. It seemed less fixed, somehow.

She knows what this is going to be about. Without meeting his eye, she scatters more corn and says, 'Sure, son.'

'Let's go on inside.'

'We can talk right here.'

He hesitates. 'But anybody can see us.'

'Not through them trees.'

He bends his knees a little to peer towards the gate. The fans are there. They are there twenty-four hours a day. But there aren't that many this evening. And, anyway, this part of the grounds is mostly hidden.

'What is it you wanted to say, son?'

He steps closer to her. 'You gotta quit feeding them chickens.'

Her hand goes in for another scoop of corn.

'Mama, you gotta quit—'

'I heard you, Elvis.'

'Colonel says it ain't good for business.'

She turns to him, weighing the corn in her hand. 'I just can't see what feeding my chickens has to do with his business.'

'It's my business, Mama. His business is *my* business. It's all of ours—'

'Last I heard, you was an entertainer.'

His eyes look tired. 'I am an entertainer,' he says, slowly. 'I'm the best entertainer in the business.'

'What does feeding my chickens have to do with the entertainment business? I ain't entertaining nobody.'

He looks to the ground and his shoulders sink forward. Perhaps she has been too harsh. She's yet to have her evening beer, and hardly slept a wink last night. And this pain keeps stabbing at her calves.

'Mama. You know what Colonel Parker said. It just don't look good to feed chickens outside a mansion. What if the newspapermen see you?'

'What if they do?'

'Well, what do you figure they'd say?'

'Don't you like my chickens, son?'

He laughs, a little. Then he crouches down and scoops up Ruby, the one with the bad foot. Her eyes pop and she stretches her neck but he holds her tightly as he draws her close to his face. 'I like you, don't I?' he says, shaking her more roughly than Gladys would like.

'Turn her loose.'

'Sure Elvis likes you, you stupid old hen.' He bunches up his lips and pretends to kiss the animal on the beak.

'Elvis. Turn that bird loose.'

He does as he's told, and Ruby scuttles away.

'You done scared her, now.'

He dusts off his pants. 'Look, Mama. You know what they'd say, don't you? They'd say, Elvis Presley's mother is so down-home Southern, she keeps chickens outside their big old mansion. And that makes Elvis no better than a hick. Do you want them to say that?'

She looks towards the house. The sun is getting lower, and the columns are golden. Above their heads, the leaves swirl in the warm breeze. It is a beautiful thing, to have this kind of luxury. Each day she tries to remember to thank God and her son for her luck. But she doesn't feel lucky this evening. Lately, she keeps asking herself what is the point of such beauty, of such luxury, if she feels only boredom? One by one, her daily tasks have been taken from her. At Audubon, she'd tried to continue hanging out her laundry, but the neighbours had complained. Then Alberta had arrived, and there was no longer any need to shop or fix meals. Now there are three maids to clean, to wash her sheets, run her baths, iron her clothes and fold them into the closet. It is as if she has been removed from her own life. Her place now is to watch others work, and do nothing herself. Feeding her chickens was the last thing she had. And she loves her chickens, every one of them, even Clarence the cockerel, whose proud head hardly ever reaches for her hand, no matter how she loads it with corn.

'It's like the Colonel says, Mama. It's bad for my image.'

At this, something in her snaps, and she slings a handful of corn at her son's chest. 'I am not part of your *image*!' She is close to tears, but she won't let them break. 'I'm your mother! I'm a person!'

Elvis brushes down his shirt and shakes his head. If he laughs at her now she will wallop him, hard.

'Now, don't get excited—'

'The fans like me! I've always gone out of my way to be good to them!' She points towards the gate. 'Why don't we go down there and ask them if they care about me feeding chickens?'

They stare at one another.

'I'm sorry, Mama. Really I am.' His voice is soft. 'But you got to quit. I'm gonna get the coop moved to the back of the house, and Daisy can feed them from now on. Daddy's told her to do it.'

'*Daddy's* told her?'

Since when has Vernon been in charge of anything in the house?

'And I don't wanna hear nothing about you trying to stop her.'

Daisy. The maid. Memphis born and bred. Wears a little too much eye make-up.

'What does a city girl like her know about chickens? They need special care and attention. You gotta talk to them, or they won't lay.'

'Mama. I know you love them old birds. But please understand. It's out of my hands.' He pauses, then smiles. 'What would make it up to you? Just tell me what you'd like, and I'll get it for you.'

She touches his hand, because she's too weary to continue. All she wants is her chair by the kitchen window, and the cold beer that's waiting for her in the refrigerator.

'How about a little dog?' he asks, his face brightening.

Putting down her corn scoop, she walks away from him, towards the house.

* * *

Around ten o'clock the same evening, when Elvis's new girl and some of his other friends have arrived, Gladys sits in the kitchen, listening to him playing piano and singing 'Little Cabin Home on the Hill'. Cliff is harmonising, and occasionally Anita joins in. Her high tinkling voice is pretty enough but, to Gladys's mind, has no real power. Anita is a local girl, like Barbara was, but she just doesn't have Barbara's homeyness. Gladys had rushed to embrace her when they'd first met, fearful that the girl would dissolve before her eyes like all the rest, and she'd felt Anita bristle at the contact.

The sound of Elvis singing one of her favourites puts Gladys in a better mood. Her legs are feeling a little lighter now, and she decides she will put some biscuit dough together, ready to bake in the morning. Alberta has gone home and Daisy has yet to appear, so she can work without being overlooked. She slips on her apron and sets about measuring the flour, butter and lard, spreading her ingredients across the counter. She also fetches herself a small glass of beer to enjoy while she works.

She has her hands in the flour when she hears the side door open and her husband's quick footsteps along the carpeted hall. He almost passes the kitchen without stopping. Not wanting him to get away with this, she sings out, 'Evening, Vernon.'

He stands in the doorway wearing a sheepish grin. He's in a pair of overalls, and his cheeks are flushed.

'Why in the world are you wearing those?' she asks. She hasn't seen him in such dirty old clothes since he worked at United Paint.

Glancing down at himself, he chuckles. 'Well,' he says, 'folks notice Elvis Presley's daddy out on the street. And I'm kinda tired of the attention. So I figured I'd try me a little disguise.'

He's never mentioned being tired of any of it, before.

He runs a hand down his front and eyes her mixing bowl. 'You know you don't have to do that stuff no more, Glad.'

She continues rubbing the lard and butter into the flour, stirring in the baking soda.

'Well,' he says, stretching his arms to the ceiling. 'I'm about beat. Reckon I'll turn in for the night.'

She asks, as lightly as she can, 'Where you been?'

Vernon sighs. Then he steps into the kitchen and leans on the counter next to her, breathing all over her flour. The scent of perfume hits her, and she recognises it as the same one she's smelled at the breakfast table. She notices, too, how shiny his eyes are. He is apparently unaware of how he smells.

'Had to see a man about a dog. You know how it is.'

'Oh, I know,' says Gladys, reaching across him for the buttermilk.

'Elvis told me he talked to you about them chickens,' he says. 'I reckon it's for the best.'

'I ain't giving up my chickens.' Gladys pours the liquid into the bowl and keeps her voice even. 'And I know what you're up to, Vernon Presley, and I also know you're a goddamn steercotted bastard.'

She sets the pitcher down and plunges her hands into the mess, letting the buttermilk squirt between her fingers.

Vernon lets out a small noise, something between a cough and a laugh, and says, 'What did you just call me?'

Gladys concentrates on squeezing the fat and flour and liquid together so it will come out light and soft, as Elvis likes it. As she works, she says, 'You oughta know, Vernon, that I turned a blind eye to your other women for the longest time. The *longest* time. But I ain't gonna do that no more. Elvis is grown now, and it don't matter if he finds out what his daddy really is. In fact, I've a mind to tell him a few home truths about you.'

The dust of the flour catches in the lined skin of her hands, clumping around the gaps between the stones of her cocktail ring. She hears Vernon's breathing quicken, but she doesn't look up because she knows that if she does she will weaken, so when she feels the first blow across her head she is confused, and wonders if something has fallen from the high shelf.

But then she sees Vernon's fist coming towards her again, and she ducks. It's too late for him to draw back, and he thumps the metal mixing bowl, sending it skidding across the counter and smashing into the Mixmaster. He holds his hand to his chest for a second, cursing, then swings for her again, his knuckles driving into her cheek this time. The force of the blow has her staggering backwards, and her feet become tangled with the legs of a stool. As she crashes to the ground, taking the stool with her, she cries out.

From her position on the carpet, she notices the gleam on her husband's new shoes, which look odd peeking from beneath the frayed ends of his overalls. She blinks. Her head feels as though it's been stuck in an ice box, and she's not sure where the rest of her body is, but she knows pain isn't far away. Then Elvis is there, kneeling beside her and taking her head in his hands and saying, *Mama*. She tries to tell him it's OK, but she can't get her lips to move. She hears him crying and telling his daddy that if he ever touches her again he'll kill him dead, and she tries again to say it's OK, but Vernon and Elvis are yelling and the pain has burned a path from her jaw right into her spine. She closes her eyes, wondering where the strength of that girl who once threw the blade of a ploughshare has gone, and waits for it to be over.

When he wakes, it takes Elvis a moment to figure out whether he is in California, Memphis, or some hotel between live shows. Then he becomes aware of his own silk sheets and the pillowy quiet of the mansion, and he remembers what happened to his mama two nights ago, and he turns over, determined to lose himself in sleep. Recalling that Anita stayed in his bed for the first time last night, he reaches out for the comfort of her body, but there's nothing beside him.

He lifts his head. 'Little?'

She's sitting at the foot of the bed, fully dressed in a lemon blouse and matching skirt. Even in her bright coral lipstick, she looks serious.

'What you doing out of bed, honey?' he mumbles.

'It's four in the afternoon,' she says. 'I couldn't sleep any longer.'

'Well, get yourself in here.' He pulls back the sheet. 'I hate to wake up alone.'

'You're not alone.'

She's opened the drapes and the light is making his eyes itch. 'It's cold in here without you,' he moans.

She moves closer but doesn't get between the sheets. 'Elvis,' she says. 'How am I going to go downstairs?'

'It's easy, honey. You just take one tiny step at a time.'

'I'm serious. Your mother's going to be down there, and I can't look her in the eye. She'll know I've been up here all night.'

'Then come back to bed,' he says, kissing her wrist.

'I can't. I'm expecting a call from that New York agent.'

A few weeks ago, Anita won the South's Hollywood Star Hunt talent contest. The prize was a small role in some B-movie. Now she's waiting on a call from the agency that signed her up.

'I told you, don't take them two-bit parts,' says Elvis, now fully awake. 'You deserve better. And I also told you about Hollywood, and what goes on there—'

'Can't you go down and distract her so I can slip out without her noticing?'

He groans. 'Anita. We didn't even do anything.'

'That's not the point,' she says. 'She'll think we did.'

'Then I'll tell her we didn't.'

'You won't!' She tears the sheet from his shoulder and leans over him, scowling. 'Don't you tell your mama I stayed all night!'

They'd fooled around some, as they've been doing all summer (she loves it when he kisses her up and down her spine), but when Anita had said she'd felt ready to give all of herself to him, Elvis had refused to take her virginity, saying that she should keep herself whole. Because if they did get married, he wanted it to be perfect.

'You look pretty when you're angry,' he says. He reaches up to touch her face, but she bats his arm away so hard that he knocks over the glass of water on his nightstand, soaking the sheets.

He leaps from the bed. 'Hot damn!'

'I'm sorry—'

'Call the maid.' He brushes past her. 'She'll change them.'

'Elvis, I—'

'Call the maid!' he yells, slamming the bathroom door behind him.

Once he's relieved himself, he opens the cabinet and finds the packet of Dexedrine. He no longer has to pilfer them from his mama. And this is definitely one of those mornings when he needs two. He slathers his face with foam and starts to shave.

There's a soft knock at the door, which he ignores.

'Elvis,' Anita calls, 'I'm leaving now.'

He drags the razor up his neck and along his cheek.

'I'm real sorry about the sheets,' she says.

He washes the blade, then pulls the plug and watches the water disappear, leaving streaks of stubbly foam. Leaning on the sink, he studies his face, wondering if he need worry about the slight puffiness along his jawline. He considers himself from the side, tilting his head so his chin goes tight, and remembers the way his mama's face was mashed by his father's fist.

Then he opens the door.

'Wait. Don't go down there alone, Little,' he says. 'I don't want you adding to Mama's worries.'

He selects a pair of pants and a shirt from the closet.

'We're gonna go together,' he says, buttoning his shirt. 'If we see Mama, I'll tell her it got late and you slept on the couch in my office.'

'But—'

'You wanted me to fix this.' He catches her hand. 'So I'm fixing it.'

She doesn't protest as he leads her to the main stairs, calculating this will give him more time to get her out of the front door before Gladys appears.

As they descend, Anita taking cringing steps just behind him, Elvis feels the pills begin to kick through his blood and he races to the bottom, making her flap her hands around and hiss at him to be quiet.

In the hallway, he laughs and impersonates her, hunching his body and creeping along the carpet like a cartoon burglar. Scowling, she tries to reach the front door, but he grasps her around the waist and pins her against the wall.

'You love me, baby, don't you?'

She looks even prettier here, seeming to glitter for him beneath the reflected light of the chandelier.

Anita nods and holds a finger to his lips to shush him.

'You're my best girl,' he says. 'You know that, don't you?'

Anita looks over his shoulder. Her face falls.

'Elvie?'

He twists his neck to see his mama standing behind him, wearing her pink housecoat. Her face looks much worse this afternoon. Yesterday he'd tried to persuade her to let him fetch the doctor, but she'd refused, saying she didn't want more trouble, and, concerned that the papers would get hold of the story, he didn't press her. He'd sat with her all afternoon in the music room, fooling around on the piano before joining her on the couch to eat Reese's peanut butter cups and watch her favourite shows on TV. Her face hadn't looked too bad, then. But now the bruise has blossomed into a dark purple flower, yellowed at the edges, and her jaw has swollen, making her head look lopsided.

He releases Anita. 'Mama.'

'You two want something to eat?' Gladys says.

She doesn't touch her face or try to hide it in any way. In fact, she steps into the light of the chandelier and looks right at him. The sight of her makes him feel nauseous, but he knows he mustn't show it, for her sake.

Anita's eyes dart uncertainly between Elvis and his mother. She is aware there was a fight, but Elvis had told Lamar to get her out of the house as soon as he heard the commotion in the kitchen, and she hasn't seen Gladys since. Last night Elvis told her his mama was fine; that it was just a scuffle; that his father was real sorry and everything had been straightened out.

'Mama,' Elvis says, slowly, 'Anita here stayed on the couch last night—'

'Well, I figured she did, son.' Gladys touches Anita's arm. 'And don't you look fresh and pretty even so, honey?'

It takes a moment for Anita to mouth the words, *Thank you*.

'Now come on and let me fix you something.'

Because he can't think of how to refuse, Elvis guides Anita into the kitchen and they sit together at the counter. All through the meal, he keeps his eyes on his plate as his mother chatters on about his next movie project, which is to be filmed in New Orleans, and how she loved it when Elvis took her there for a visit and has Anita ever been, and shouldn't Elvis take her some time? Anita nods and swallows and nods and smiles and nods some more. When Dodger comes in to pour herself some coffee, she puts a hand on Gladys's shoulder and says, 'Sure is good to see you up on your feet.'

Elvis can stand no more. Almost toppling his stool in his rush to escape, leaving his food half-eaten, he tells them Anita's got somewhere to be, and, ignoring the women's protests, ushers his girl from the room.

He walks Anita to her car, a year-old Ford that he gave her earlier in the summer, and holds the door open.

'I'll call you,' he says.

It's hot as hell out here, and he wants to get back in his air-conditioned house and ask his mama where his daddy has disappeared to, so he can find him and make him pay.

'Elvis,' she says, clutching her keys, 'your mama didn't look so good. Maybe she should see a doctor.'

'She won't see no doctor.'

'Maybe she would, if you told her she's got to.'

'I already told her!' He slams a hand on the scalding roof of the Ford.

There's a pause. Then Anita asks, in a small voice, fiddling with her keys, 'Where's your daddy now?'

'Gone off someplace.'

She nods. 'I just couldn't stand it if I knew my daddy was hitting my mama.'

At this, Elvis has to ram his fists deep into his pockets to stop them beating on the car again. He grits his teeth. 'Daddy's been under a lot of pressure.'

Anita gives a little snort. 'How can you defend him?'

He looks her in the eye, and sees her recoil as he hisses, 'You don't know one thing about my daddy. He's been through more shit than you've smelled your entire life.'

Then he turns on his heel and stalks towards the mansion in silence.

Gladys had refused to be drawn in to a conversation about Vernon's whereabouts, saying that her husband had to answer to God, and his own conscience, now. Her son should go out with his friends and enjoy himself while he could, because he'd be working again soon enough. She'd be just fine at home with Alberta and Dodger.

Telling himself that he'd think about it later, Elvis took another pill and did as she suggested. Now it's past eleven o'clock, and he's on his way to his private party at the Rainbow.

In order to get around the city without being recognised, he's started using a truck again. It's a beat-up old Ford, not unlike the one he drove at Crown Electric, and he keeps it parked at the back of the mansion. He refuses to wear a disguise – tonight he's in a pair of black pants and an orange-and-black knitted shirt – but the truck itself seems to be disguise enough.

To wrong-foot the fans, Cliff puts a hat and dark glasses on and drives the purple Cadillac out of the gates. Then, while the fans are still gazing and calling after that car, Elvis races out in the truck, and heads in the opposite direction.

All evening, he's been fantasising about smashing his daddy's face to a bloody pulp. Maybe he could get one of the guys to do the job for him. If Red were here, Elvis is sure he'd be more than happy to oblige. Or maybe he could pay somebody to beat Vernon, and make it look like a ransom thing. He overtakes a Chevy, putting his foot to the floor to get past it before a junction. He can see the headline: *Elvis's Father Tortured in Ransom Drama*. No broken bones or anything, just mess him up good, so his face gets all puffy and dark like Mama's. When he'd looked at her before he left the house, he'd wanted to whimper and crawl beneath some porch to hide his own face. And when she'd told him she'd be fine, all he wanted was to hold her so he could comfort her, but also so he could comfort himself. For some reason, the look on her face and the way she held her body – which looked so broken, even though it was big – told him not to try it, and he'd let her usher him out of the door.

Realising he's close to Anita's apartment, Elvis suddenly swerves the truck across the street, almost crashing into the stop lights. It's all too much. He needs his girl by his side.

He has to ring the bell several times before Miss Patty opens the door. She's wearing an embroidered housecoat and has rollers in her hair. Seeing him, she folds her arms.

'Why are you hauling decent folks from their beds at this hour?' she says.

'Hello, Miss Patty. Sorry to call so late. Can I see her?'

She tuts. 'Why should I let you, when you treat her so bad? She's been crying all evening.'

'I don't know what she's told you, ma'am, but—'

'She don't need to tell me nothing. I can see it all in her eyes. And I read about your exploits in the newspapers, just like she does.'

He looks up at the murky sky and takes a breath, knowing what he must do.

'You're right, ma'am. I've come to apologise. I acted plumb crazy, earlier.'

Miss Patty touches her rollers. 'You oughta be telling this to Anita, not me.'

'Well, I will, if you'll let me.'

Anita must have been listening on the stairwell, because as soon as Miss Patty calls for her, she's at the door.

'Forgive me, Little,' he says, and she falls into his arms.

Mrs Pieracinni, who owns the Rainbow, has done a good job of organising the party. Her nephews, all tall and broad but with the same miniature nose as her, stand by the doors to keep out uninvited guests. The Rollerdrome is decorated with multicoloured bunting and streamers, and the lights, which usually brighten every corner, are turned low. The tables beside the rink are groaning with hot dogs, popcorn, potato chips, and paper cups of Pepsi. The music's up so loud that Elvis feels it coming through his shoes. Ricky Nelson, unfortunately.

There are already twenty or so people in the room, including Heidi, Gloria and Frances. The three girls are huddled round the jukebox, sipping their drinks and taking everything in. Spotting them, Elvis raises a hand in greeting and they all break into wide smiles and frantic waving, but only Cliff and Billy, Elvis's younger cousin, approach.

'You made it!' says Cliff, slapping him heartily on the back, as if Elvis has completed the journey from overseas.

Elvis grins at Billy. He's fifteen, and this is his first time out with the group. He's styled his pale hair just like Elvis's for the occasion.

'You sure you're good and ready for this, Billy-boy?' Elvis asks. 'It can get a little rough out there.'

'I'm ready,' says Billy, holding his freckled face still and serious.

'Cliff, I want you to take care of Billy here,' says Elvis. 'Don't let him mess up his hair.'

'Sure, boss.'

Anita grips his hand. He can feel her scanning the room for other, younger, prettier girls. He doesn't recognise any of them, apart from Cliff's date and the three teenagers. Lamar has picked them all from the crowd at the gate. A few of them were skating when Elvis came in, but they've stopped now and are leaning on the barriers, watching him intently.

He thinks of Dixie in her white skirt and pantyhose, as he always does when he comes to the Rainbow. Of how he'd been amazed that she wanted to talk to him. He's heard she's settled into her own home now. He can just picture her, serving up meat loaf to some white-collar guy who has no idea how his wife's cherry ball was fondled by Elvis Presley.

'Let's get the games started,' he says, and Cliff claps his hands to gather everyone to the rink.

'Why don't you take the weight off, baby?' Elvis asks Anita.

'I'd like to skate some,' she says.

He touches her cheek. 'We don't want you to chip your nails,' he says. 'You're too special for this stuff.'

And he's gone before she can protest.

They start with Crack the Whip. Not wanting to be the leader every time, Elvis lets Cliff head up the line. He tells Lamar to be the caboose at the back of the chain, and takes his position in the middle, holding hands with Frances and Gloria. Cliff gets up some good speed, then changes direction suddenly, causing the end of the whip to curl in on itself. Lamar hurtles to the ground, and Elvis doubles over with laughter.

His recording of 'Ready, Teddy' comes on, and the speed of the line increases, with the girls squealing when their hands slip from his. As Frances lets go, he says, 'Too bad, honey,' and watches her fly, arms flailing, into the railing.

Elvis lifts his hand, the signal for everybody to stop, and goes to check on her. A kiss on the forehead and a couple of the painkillers he gets from his dentist seem to make everything all right again. The pills are strong enough to allow him to play these kinds of games without hurting too much.

After a few more rounds of Crack the Whip, he peels off his sodden shirt and plants it in the trash. Anita brings him a clean one from the truck.

'I wish you'd let me play,' she says, grasping him around the waist. 'I'm lonely here.'

He kisses her on the mouth. Then he whispers in her ear, 'Will you wait for me, Little? Till I'm through this crazy part of my career? Then we can be together, really together. I meant what I said, about marriage and all.'

She looks up at him with shining eyes, and he wants to take her back to the mansion right away and tell his mama he's going to marry this girl. It would make Gladys so happy. She'd embrace him, and everything would be good again.

Lamar calls out, 'Knock Down!'

Elvis looks over to the rink. Everyone is clapping and chanting for him.

Anita sighs. 'Go on and play with your friends.'

First, he hands out some painkillers, because this one can get a little rough, and is for the boys only. The aim of the game is to knock everyone else on the rink down. Whoever is left standing is the winner.

The girls line up along the barrier to spectate, Anita included. Elvis skates around the edge, avoiding the blows for a while, letting the others get started. Cliff and Billy are the first to be knocked down, but they get up and skate towards one another again. Billy goes down once more, knocked to the floor by Cliff, and drags himself to the side. Elvis skates over to his cousin. 'Don't feel bad,' he says. 'Bound to happen. You're the youngest.'

While he's talking, a friend of Cliff's – Elvis doesn't know his name – skates past and whacks Elvis with his elbow, making him yell and stumble backwards. Righting himself, Elvis skates as fast as he can at the first body in his path. It's Cliff's, and he falls easy. Elvis hears the smack of Cliff's head on the floor, even over the din of his own music, but he doesn't stop skating. Picturing Vernon in those goddamn overalls, he heads for George, walloping him with his whole body and sending him spinning across the floor. A cheer rises, and Elvis looks up to see all three hundred pounds of

Lamar coming towards him like a bull, head low, shoulders hunched. Elvis stops skating and laughs. He stretches his arms wide and says, 'Come on, man! Come get me!', figuring he can skate out of Lamar's path. But as he twists away, his skate comes loose, and he stumbles. Lamar slams into him, pushing him backwards. They travel together for a few seconds, Lamar holding Elvis by the shoulders and grunting.

'I'm gonna kill you, you son of a bitch!' Elvis yells.

They smash into the railing. Luckily for Elvis, his friend goes down first, breaking his own fall.

With his face squashed against the folds of Lamar's sweating, fleshy neck, Elvis considers biting down on it as hard as he can. But then he remembers the girls at the barricade and he swiftly disentangles himself from Lamar's big body and holds up his hands so that everyone can see he's all right. Using Lamar for ballast, he scrambles to his feet. Then he skates across the rink, turning circles and waving despite his trembling legs.

He feels absolutely no pain.

Lamar manages to sit up. 'You OK, boss?' he calls out.

'No damage at all, Buddha,' Elvis calls back. 'Not one scratch.'

Everybody applauds, lightly. He glances at Anita, who is watching the other girls.

Perhaps there's no need, he thinks, to rush into a marriage proposal.

* * *

After Gladys's bruises have disappeared and Elvis has left for another tour, Lillian visits Graceland.

'Vernon must sure be worried about you, if he's calling on *me*,' she says, patting at her hair, which looks like it's got a stiff new permanent on it.

It's a Sunday afternoon in October, and they are sitting in the dining room, sipping tea from crystal tumblers. Gladys knows her sister would be more comfortable in the kitchen, but it's been months since her last visit, and something made Gladys want to subject Lillian to the fancy room, with its uncomfortable modern chairs and relentlessly glossy tabletop.

Lillian lowers her voice. 'He said you been drinking more than you oughta, Glad. Is that true?'

It is useless to deny it. Her sister always could see right through her.

Lillian sighs. 'I just don't understand it,' she says, leaning back in her chair. Her gaze lingers on the new TV console in the far corner. 'You got it all, Glad. Every little thing.'

Gladys eyes her sister – still thin, still upright, still getting on with her life, and a deep shame seeps through her body, weakening her aching limbs.

'You want something?' Gladys asks, hauling herself upright. 'I got more jewellery than I know what to do with, Lillian. You can have it. I'll go fetch it for you right now.'

'Sit down,' says Lillian, quietly.

'How about a Mixmaster, then?'

'No, thank you.'

'Or a new vacuum cleaner?'

'Glad. I don't want none of your stuff. I came to check up on you, is all.'

Gladys sinks into her chair. 'Well. You can see with your own eyes. Your sister is low-down miserable.'

'But how come?' asks Lillian.

How can Gladys explain anything about her own existence to her sister, who still lives in a small duplex across town, works regular hours at Fashion Curtains, and – unlike many other members of the family – doesn't come knocking on Elvis's door for handouts?

'Is it Vernon?' Lillian asks. 'I know he can be kinda cold sometimes, but that's just how men are.' She gives a little laugh. 'You never could understand that, could you, honey? Seems like you always expected more.'

Gladys shakes her head. 'Elvis ain't cold. Never has been.'

Lillian sighs. 'Elvis ain't here.'

Gladys stares at the window, which is lit golden by the setting sun. There's a long silence.

'Here's what we're gonna do,' says Lillian, pushing her tea aside and grasping Gladys's hand. 'I'm gonna come visit every day, just to see how you're getting along. OK?'

Gladys nods, but keeps her eyes on the window. If she looks at her sister, she fears she may weep. Or draw her hand back and slap Lillian's face.

* * *

Elvis is alone in his dressing room, shrugging on his gold lamé jacket. The full tuxedo – named 'the ten-thousand-dollar gold suit' by the Colonel – is, he thinks, a joke. Made from $2,500 worth of gold leaf by Nudie Cohn, who has designed suits for Hank Williams and any number of exotic dancers, it has diamanté-encrusted lapels and cuffs, and comes complete with a gold belt and gold lace tie. When he'd first worn the full outfit, the Colonel had warned him not to perform any knee slides, in case the gold wore off the lamé pants. Elvis had felt like he'd stepped into a magician's box and was about to get sawn in half.

Tonight's show at Los Angeles's Pan Pacific Auditorium is important enough for him to want to wear the jacket, though, because nothing shines quite like it. Onstage, it's as if the jacket is lit from the inside. He can wear it with black pants and a black shirt.

The Colonel says half of Tinseltown will show up. Hal Wallis. Debra Paget. Nick Adams. Carol Channing. Sammy Davis. Tommy Sands. Vince Edwards. As usual, the critics have panned Elvis's new movie, *Jailhouse Rock*, calling his acting effort 'grotesque'. Tonight he means to show Hollywood what he's really made of.

He's applied his own make-up, having perfected his technique with guidance from the artist at Paramount, and sculpted his hair. Cliff and Lamar ought to be back from the Pepsi machine by now.

Elvis stares at the dimples in the cinderblock wall, trying to control his breathing. It's always like this before a show, no matter how well the last one went. In fact, he thinks that maybe it gets worse, every time. Every time he fears he will have no voice at all out there; that his body will betray him by collapsing; that his mind will go blank and he'll become a limp, empty ghost, like Noreen after Preacher Brown rid her of her demon. He swallows a couple of Dexedrine before pointing at himself in the mirror and clearing his throat. 'My name is FEAR!' he says, with as much menace as he can muster. 'People tremble and shake when I am near!'

Finally, unable to sit any longer, he knocks on the band's door. Although they've officially resigned, Scotty and Bill have agreed to play on this short tour for a flat fee. So far, they've stayed in their hotel room at the Knickerbocker (Elvis is in the plusher Beverly Wilshire) and have done their work without saying a word about their resignation letter.

Scotty opens the door, but doesn't invite Elvis in.

'Everything OK for tonight?' asks Elvis, leaning on the door frame, tapping his foot. The jacket is already scratching at his wrists.

'Yep.'

Elvis can see Bill sitting behind Scotty. When their eyes meet in the dressing-table mirror, Elvis tries a grin, but Bill says nothing.

'Was there anything else?' asks Scotty. His wide face remains smooth, the ironic smile still in place.

'Just, you know, I'm real glad you fellas are gonna be out there with me.'

Elvis offers his hand for a shake. Scotty considers it for a moment, then pumps it up and down, firmly.

'And,' says Elvis, 'as Sam would say, don't make that guitar too damn complicated!'

Scotty smooths his hair. 'It ain't complicated,' he says. 'We just follow your ass.'

* * *

"Love Me!" he commands.

There are over nine thousand people in the auditorium, and it seems that they are all screaming. As he sings, he pulls the gold jacket from one shoulder and shimmies towards the audience, then circles his hips slowly, going up onto the balls of his feet to bump his groin towards the mike. The girls in the front rows are out of their seats, but that's not enough for Elvis. He wants the whole of Hollywood on its feet. He wants Carol Channing and Debra Paget to grip their own flesh and scream the hell out of their lungs. He wants Hal Wallis to split his britches, begging for more. He wants Nick Adams to bark like a dog.

He turns to check on Scotty, who returns his grin. Bill does likewise. Perhaps they don't hate him, after all. He shrugs and winks at the audience, who roar and whistle back.

He clasps the microphone in both hands as if it's a woman, hooking a leg around its body, touching the mesh of the mike with his lips. The New York songwriters, Jerry and Mike, told him they wrote this one as a kind of joke, but tonight Elvis can see nothing funny about it.

Bending at the knees, he pulls the mike stand between his legs, running the metal against his thigh. The crowd rise as one, and their noise billows up to the wooden rafters and down to the concrete floor. Then he sees a flash of red hair, and his already inflated heart rises to his throat. He blinks and stumbles on the lyric about begging and stealing, because this girl's hair springs from her head like flames and for one second he's convinced that it's Noreen. The girl makes her hands into fists and brings them to her face and bellows his name, and it seems that maybe he's undone whatever it was the preacher did all those years ago. He's told Anita that being onstage is like making love, but now he realises it's better than that, because it's not one girl but nine thousand, and he's setting the whole lot of them loose. When he looks again at the crowd, he sees them all: Noreen, Magdalene, Betty, Dixie, Barbara, Dottie, Anita, and he feels he has enough for everybody. If he can give them this song, they'll love him for ever. He's sure of it.

He promises the audience that if they ever go, he'll be oh, so lonely, and then he's on his knees, reaching out to them. They return the gesture.

To finish, he introduces 'The Elvis Presley National Anthem: "Hound Dog"'. On the side of the stage, as always, is his record company's mascot, a three-feet-high plaster dog called Nipper. Halfway through the song, Elvis starts singing to the dog, but not in the way he sang to that basset hound on *The Steve Allen Show*. Instead, he slides to his knees and takes it by the neck, then rolls on his back with the dog in his arms, still singing. From the corner of his eye, he can see Scotty and Bill glancing at one another nervously. On the final slowed-down verse, Elvis rolls over, taking the dog with him. With one leg slung across its back, he grinds himself against the creature. He sings the chorus as slowly and as wildly as he can, scattering sweat and gold leaf across the stage. He sings it again and again and again, slower each time, clasping the dog to his zipper as he howls the words. Each time he sings it, the uncertain, disbelieving, thrilled pause in the crowd's whooping becomes longer. When he's finally through, he lets the song's last words come out of his mouth in a laughing rush, releases the dog, and lies with his arms and legs spread out on the stage.

When he looks up at the lights, he half-expects them to explode, along with the audience.

Memphis, August 1958

Since making the journey back from Killeen to see Dr Evans, Gladys has been in hospital for three days, and each morning she looks forward to sleep.

It's nine-thirty a.m., and the nurse has just given her the medication that will alleviate the pain in her stomach, enabling her to drift off. When Gladys does sleep at night, she is visited by Jesse, who slips into her dreams to ask where she is, and when she's going to come fetch him. Last night, when she woke at three a.m. with that old feeling of terrible lightness in her chest and pain so bad it made her moan, she'd groped around the bed for the child she'd lost, and it wasn't Elvis's name she called out, but Jesse's. Then she'd prayed. *Jesse*, she whispered. *Son. Forgive me. I told your brother he had your strength. What else could I say? I didn't want him to go through life blaming himself for your death. Or blaming God. Or me.*

Jesse never makes his presence felt during the day, so now she can safely allow herself to slide into drowsiness. She places her arms outside the thick white sheet and watches the huge window. It's double-glazed and renders the room absolutely silent, save for the low whirr of the air conditioning. The bright clouds scud past. Closing her eyes, she feels warmth on her lids, and her limbs begin to soften. She thinks of her mother, who'd spent months and months dying. With her body lightened by the drug, Gladys tells herself that this is all too sudden to be her own end. Vernon keeps saying that Elvis will come and she'll soon be up on her feet. Deep down, though, she knows she will never be well again. Because if she ever gets out of this room the first thing she will do is take a drink. Nothing fancy. Just a long, cool beer. It will be the best she's ever tasted.

She longs for Elvis to appear, though, not only for the comfort his voice and body always bring, but also so he can witness her bravery in smiling through the sickness. And she'd like him to appreciate her refusal to die until he's arrived.

Then her husband comes in, bringing with him outdoor smells of exhaust fumes, hair pomade and coffee.

He's fetched her baby-blue bed jacket from home, and is sitting on the mattress, waving it in her direction. Gladys lets her lids droop again. Perhaps she can pretend to be in a deep sleep already. She can't stand the burden of Vernon's face. Ever since she's been in hospital, he's looked like he did when she'd first plopped Elvis into his arms: as if the world had shifted so suddenly it had left him behind.

'Glad,' he says softly, 'Elvis is on his way.'

She opens her eyes.

Vernon is holding his jaw at an odd angle. 'He got a pass out.' He swallows. 'Had to fight his goddamn lieutenant for it. But now he's coming.'

Gladys touches his hand, then succumbs to blackness.

She sleeps most of the day, dreaming about being a girl again, dancing for Vernon on an upturned crate. In the dream, her mama is behind her, keeping an eye on her daughter from her bed, and when she finishes dancing, Doll holds her mirror up to Gladys's face and says, 'Watch yourself, gal.'

When she wakes, she wonders if she is dead already. The room is dazzlingly white from the afternoon sun blasting through the window, and everywhere she looks she sees flowers. Pink lilies, babies' breath, hollyhocks, zinnias, poppies, larkspur and yellow roses. But Vernon is sitting on her bed once again (or perhaps, she thinks, he never left his spot), squeezing her hand as he says her name. And then Elvis's voice comes from the corridor, thanking strangers for their concern, telling them he's sure his mama's going to be well, that he's happy to be here at last, that he knows they're all doing a wonderful job.

'Help me,' she says. Vernon pulls her into a sitting position, and she leans against him as he props up the pillows, her head spinning, pain gripping her stomach.

'I need water,' she says, not because she wants to drink but because she doesn't want Elvis to smell the sickness on her breath. Vernon pours her a cup from the pink pitcher on her bedside table. It's the exact same colour as one she had in Lauderdale Courts. Before she can ask her husband to comb her hair, Elvis is coming through the door, rushing to the bed and throwing his arms around her, forcing his father to step back.

'Mama!' Elvis cries, burying his face in her neck.

'My son,' she says, grasping his shoulders as tightly as she can. He's in his army shirt and the fabric feels rough beneath her fingers. He smells different, too: of boiled food and boot polish.

When he lifts his face, she tries not to look at the terror in his eyes.

It takes all her strength to smile and ask, 'Now, what in the world is wrong with you?'

He looks confused.

'I don't know why y'all keep fussing,' she continues. 'I'm gonna be up on my feet in a couple of days.'

'You're talking,' he says, letting out a breath. 'That's good, Mama.'

'Sure I'm talking.' She knows her voice is faint, but she won't let it waver. 'Why wouldn't I be talking?'

Elvis glances across to his father, who is standing in the corner of the room, chewing on his thumbnail.

'Daddy said . . .'

'What did Daddy say?'

'Nothing.'

She takes his face in her hands. Since he joined the army, he's lost weight, and he is, if anything, even more handsome than before. 'You eating good?'

'I'm fine, Mama.'

She releases him. 'Well, tell me boocups.'

He hangs his head. 'Mama, I thought ...'

She cannot stand for him to cry now. If he does that, she will have to order him to leave. Patting the mattress, she says, 'Elvis. Tell me boocups.'

He clears his throat and begins. 'I went out in the tank. A real big one. It was fun. They let me drive it.'

'That's good, son.'

'And Sergeant Norwood's real pleased. I think I'm convincing them, you know, that I'm just one of the guys.'

She nods.

He pauses, mashing the sheet in his hands. 'You know I prayed, Mama, that you'd be well. I prayed to Jesse.'

'He's always with us.'

Vernon moves to the window and rests his forehead on the glass.

They're all quiet for a while. Gladys closes her eyes, wishing Elvis would leave the room so she could call on the nurse for more medication. All this talking makes her sweat, and the pain is growing stronger. She's struggling to breathe easy, and doesn't want him to notice.

'Couple of hundred people out there, at least,' says Vernon, tapping the window. 'Those gals never give up on you, son.'

'You see?' says Gladys. 'I was right. Being in the army ain't gonna make you one whit less popular.'

Elvis kisses her cheek. 'It's you they're worried about,' he whispers. 'They're here for you. Who do you think sent all these flowers?'

'Why,' she says, 'I figured you did, son.'

Her lids droop. Although she knows Elvis is still there, waiting for her to reassure him again, she does not open her eyes. If she opens her eyes, she will have to moan and cry until she gets the pain relief she craves. If she opens her eyes, she fears the noise she'll make may never end.

MY BEST GIRL: 1958

1958

After Gladys has closed her eyes, Vernon tells Elvis to go on home and get some sleep.

Elvis kisses his mama's cheeks quickly, ashamed by his own repulsion at the bloated feel of her yellow flesh.

'I'll come back, baby,' he says.

She squeezes his hand.

He lingers by the bed, hoping she will look at him once more. 'I'll come back tomorrow,' he repeats. Her eyes remain closed.

Vernon stays by his wife's side, saying he'll see his son in the morning.

Leaving the hospital, Elvis thinks about calling Anita up, but decides he can't deal with her questions about his mama right now. Yesterday, on the phone, Vernon had told him the doctors were talking about acute hepatitis and severe liver damage, saying Gladys's condition was critical. When Elvis first saw her this afternoon, he was shocked by the purple veins popping in her neck, the tremble in her hands when she touched his face, the weariness in her voice. But, he tells himself, she had at least been sitting up and talking some. And she'd seemed steadier before he left.

What he really needs is something to distract him. So he takes a pill – just one, just enough to see him through – and fetches his cousin Billy. Together they pick up Gloria, Heidi and Frances and head over to the Memphian, which will always open after hours for him, to watch *The Vikings*. For a while he enjoys the sight of Kirk Douglas on a longship, but he can't lose himself in the picture as he usually would. He keeps thinking of those bloated cheeks, those purple veins. Driving home, the others discuss the heat, the army, and Tony Curtis with a beard. Nobody talks about Gladys.

It's midnight by the time Elvis drops off the girls. Before climbing from the car, Frances looks back at him with serious eyes. 'I just know your mother will be home soon, Elvis,' she says. 'Will you be OK, all alone tonight?'

He catches her hand and kisses it. It smells of popcorn. She really couldn't be any sweeter, he thinks, and for a moment he considers pulling her back, driving off someplace with her, and never returning.

Instead, he says, 'Billy here will take care of me.'

Elvis hasn't been back to Graceland since he started basic training at Fort Hood, and as he drives along Highway 51 he begins to feel a little excited. Approaching the gates, though, he sees that something is wrong. There are no blue and gold lights. Billy's father, Travis, who Vernon employs as a groundsman, has been checking on the house every day, but he has obviously forgotten to turn them on. The lantern over the front door is just visible, a blur of light amidst the gloom of the trees.

Elvis stops the car at the gates. There's nobody in the gatehouse, either.

'Goddamn!' he says. 'What do I pay people for, Billy?'

'To do their jobs?' Billy ventures.

'So why won't they get off their asses?'

Billy shrugs.

'You gotta climb over them gates, Billy boy.'

'Say what?'

'You heard me. Go on.'

Billy is fifteen and skinny, and he scrambles up the metal music-man in no time. Elvis tries not to wince when Billy hooks his foot inside the iron rendering of his own head.

Once the gates are open, Elvis picks up his cousin and they drive to the steps of the mansion.

'Lights are off, and nobody's home,' Elvis says, more to himself than to Billy. Billy smiles, uncertainly.

Elvis gets out of the car. The night buzzes with the sound of insects. The white lions glow faintly in the darkness.

As they mount the steps, he hangs back, saying, 'You go first.'

Billy peers up at the silent house. 'Me?'

'Go on. Ain't no ghosts in there,' says Elvis, handing his cousin the keys and giving him a little shove towards the door.

In the gloom, it takes Billy a while to figure out the locks and push the big door open. 'Where's the light switch?' he asks.

Elvis has to think before he answers. He's never before arrived at an empty Graceland.

'Try the left.'

He doesn't step into the house until Billy has turned on the chandelier in the hallway. Inside, it's uncomfortably warm, having been shut up for weeks, and still smells of Vernon's cigarettes and Alberta's bean pots. Billy stands beneath the chandelier while Elvis first finds the switch for the outside lighting, then rushes from room to room, turning on the air conditioning and every lamp. The whole place feels unfamiliar without Gladys. In each room, Elvis paces the length of the floor, checking that everything is as it ought to be, and that nobody is lurking in the shadows. He peeks behind the piano. Runs his hand along the back of the couch. Twitches the drapes. He even looks beneath the dining-room table. There's nothing.

'Hang on there a minute,' he tells his cousin, who is still standing awkwardly in the hallway, waiting for instructions.

'You OK, Elvis?' Billy asks.

'Don't move.'

If he finds some stranger in his house, he means to kill them.

In the kitchen, he spots a crack in the window. It's small, and runs across the corner of one pane, but the sight of it sets his heart jumping. He wrenches open the back door and his land stretches before him; he can just see the outline of the fence and the tall hands of the trees. He holds his breath, listening to the night. There's the long wail of the goods train. The rustle and whirr of insects. A dog yelping somewhere. A faint hum from the lights.

'Who's there?' he calls.

Only the dog's bark comes back at him.

'I got a gun here!' he yells, touching his hip. 'I ain't afraid to use it!'

The insects carry on singing, regardless.

Elvis slams the door and calls Billy in.

'You see this?' he says, pointing to the crack. 'Looks like some-body's tried to get in here. We'd better call your daddy. Maybe the police, too.'

Billy stands by his side, examining the glass.

'Naw,' he says. 'Daddy done told me what happened here. Aunt Gladys fell, and cracked the window.'

'She fell?'

'That's what he said. Went clean over. She was getting up to fix herself a drink and she blacked out.'

Elvis says nothing.

'Daddy was fixing to get it done, but nobody figured you'd be home so soon,' Billy adds.

'When was this?'

'Just before Aunt Gladys and Uncle Vernon went out to Fort Hood, I reckon.' There's a pause, then Billy says, 'Didn't nobody tell you?'

'Billy,' says Elvis, 'nobody tells me nothing about what goes on around here no more. Maybe you can be my eyes and ears on the ground, huh?' He slaps his cousin on the back, making him jolt forward. 'Could you do that for me?'

Billy nods, slowly, his young face lighting at the challenge.

They make up a pallet on the bedroom floor for Billy, then Elvis takes his sleeping pills. He hopes that Jesse will come visit him tonight. He hasn't heard from his brother in a long time. But, in fact, as soon as he closes his eyes, he's sucked into an empty, black sleep.

Once Elvis had left, the nurse gave Gladys something to help her through the night.

When she begins the climb back into consciousness, the hospital room has darkened, and she has no clue where she is until she hears Vernon's snores coming from the cot beside her bed. She reaches out for him, but he's too far away; she has only enough energy to move her arm, and it flaps uselessly in the empty air.

The effort has her closing her eyes again, and her mind slips back to East Tupelo. She's running after Elvis, pushing through the thick branches of the pines. The moon is high and yellow and the air is hot on her naked calves as she crashes down the hill. She's going so fast she can barely breathe; her heart hammers, not only in her chest, but in her ears, her throat, her eyes, and still she can't reach her boy, even though she can see him sleepwalking through the dark trees, towards the highway. His steps are quick and deliberate, as if he's fully awake and has chosen this crazy path. All she wants is to bundle him to the ground, drag him into the safety of the ditch, cover his skinny body with her own. Gladys tries to run faster, to call her son's name. But she hasn't enough breath, and Elvis keeps on striding away until she has no choice but to watch him disappear through the branches, towards the highway.

Something presses on her chest. Pain scorches her insides, and she strains to lift her head so she can catch her breath. There must be air up there, somewhere. But her body will not budge one inch, although she can hear the trundle of trolley wheels from the corridor, and Vernon's cough, and another sound, a sharp rasp, like scissors slicing through thick cloth. That sound comes again, and the pressing on her chest is terrible now, as though she is trapped beneath something cold and heavy. A ploughshare, maybe. A light comes on and Vernon is looming above her, grey stubble in the pits of his cheeks, pink threads in the whites of his eyes. The scissors make another decisive cut and she realises this noise is coming from her. Vernon calls for the nurse and grips her hand. He begs Jesus to help her, to help them both.

As Vernon hollers, Gladys tries to focus on the pink pitcher on her bedside table, imagining it full of milk for Elvis. His favourite: butch with a little molasses in it. She can almost taste that creamy liquid in her mouth. She'd like to say the words, *Here's your butch, Elvie,* but the scissoring is the only sound that comes, and the pressure is so intense now that she cannot move her lips, cannot breathe, cannot tell Vernon to quit yelling for the goddamn nurse and holler for her boy instead.

He's woken by the phone. It drills into the quiet house with absolute insistence. Elvis knows it means bad news, even before he's aware of Billy rushing into his office to pick it up. There can be no other reason for calling at three a.m. He turns on the light and leaps from his bed, meaning to snatch the phone from his cousin. But then Billy dashes back into the room.

'That was the hospital,' he says, his voice oddly flat. 'They said you might get over quick as you can. Aunt Gladys is bad.'

From Billy's pale face, and the way he's looking at him as if Elvis is the one who's sick, Elvis understands it's useless to ask questions. So he goes to his closet and grabs his mama's favourite of his shirts: white, with a row of delicate frills running down the centre. He imagines that if he wears this shirt, it might in some way prevent the worst from happening.

Billy has to help him button it, his hands are shaking so badly.

* * *

From the end of the tiled hospital corridor, he hears his father's long, high-pitched wail.

Seeing his son, Vernon bars the door to Gladys's room with his body. 'Don't go in there,' he says. 'She's gone. You can't go in.'

Elvis takes his father by the shoulders and throws him aside.

His mother lies completely still beneath a white sheet. The room is full of grey machinery: metal trolleys holding abandoned pumps and wires and tubes, plastic monitors on wheels, and the large canopy of an oxygen tent, pulled back now from Gladys's head like a theatre curtain. And everything is switched off. The only sound is Elvis's own shuddering breath.

He rushes to his mama's side.

'Mama,' he whispers, 'wake up, baby.'

Her eyes are closed, her lips fixed in a downturn. He licks a finger and rubs away a crust of saliva from the corner of her mouth.

'I came back,' he says, 'I came back for you! Come on, Mama!'

He unpeels the sheet and gazes at the solid lump of her body. Her nightgown is pink, printed with tiny roses, square at the neck and gathered on the shoulders. It is not one he recognises. He takes her by the upper arms and attempts to shake her, but she will not move for him. So he climbs onto the bed and shoves his arm beneath her back so he can haul her towards him. The weight of her is a shock, and he can clasp her only for a few seconds before he has to let her already stiffening limbs fall back on the bed. He puts his face to her bosom, wanting to bury himself there, to sleep in her arms as he used to, but nothing is as it ought to be. His mama smells sour, her flesh is cold, and he feels only the scratchy cotton of her brand new nightgown against his own cheek.

Then he begins to holler, and he keeps hollering until Vernon, Billy and several nurses drag him from the room.

The next day, still in the white frilled shirt, Elvis sits on the steps of Graceland with his daddy, weeping for his dead mother. When they came home from the hospital, he'd tried to walk through his front door, but the journey from car to porch had seemed so long, and the heat was so heavy, that he'd sat on the steps instead.

The cardinals chatter brightly in the trees. The stone lions look on impassively. From the road comes the sound of cars pulling up to his gates, full of people eager to know the news. Vernon and Elvis clasp each other, and sweat, and cry. His daddy's breath smells terrible, like a hog's, but Elvis pulls him closer so their pain can become one sound.

Some men from the press stand in the drive and take photographs. Elvis doesn't know who let them in, but every time he thinks he must tell them to go, his daddy starts to cry again, and so does he, and he cannot think of any words to say, let alone speak them aloud. So the men get their pictures.

Two days later, Anita comes.

'Come on,' Elvis says, taking her by the hand and leading her into the mansion, 'Come say hi to Mama.'

When the men from the funeral parlour had carried in Gladys's copper-and-silver casket, placing it in the opening between the music and living rooms, Elvis had felt almost happy to see her again. Now the air is rich with the headachy stench of lilies, which cover the top of the grand piano. Next to the instrument, the glass lid of the casket is propped open. Gladys is dressed in the lavender-blue crêpe gown he's chosen, and her hair has been touched up and set nice. No greys in there now. Her lips have been painted pink and the diamond drops he bought are in her ears. He's aware of Anita drawing a sharp breath as he leans over the casket to kiss his mother's cold cheek. Gladys's skin is so hard now against his lips, it's as if she's moulded from wax, and instead of her smell there is a chemical aroma.

'Look at her little sooties,' he says to Anita. 'Ain't they pretty? So delicate, just like yours, baby.'

Anita doesn't seem to want to look. Instead, she touches his arm and says, 'I'm so sorry.'

'She's with God now,' says Elvis.

'She is.'

'And Jesse, too.'

'Uh-huh.'

'I can't believe she left me.'

'Elvis,' says Anita in a soft voice, still clasping his arm, 'your mama didn't leave you. She passed on.'

Elvis steps away from her and clutches the edge of the casket. 'She's right here, though, ain't she?'

'Pardon me?'

'She'll always be right here in this house. Graceland is *her* house, Little.'

Anita twists her hands together and gazes at the window. Outside, beyond the trees, hundreds of people are waiting at the gate, murmuring their loss to the policemen guarding the house. In the August heat, the flowers they've laid on the sidewalk are turning brown and soft.

'Everything I ever did, I did for her,' Elvis says.

The worst thing, the thing that makes his whole body shake with fear now, is that he knows this is a lie. But he keeps saying it, trying to convince himself that his fame was nothing but a joy to Gladys, even though he suspects that it may, in some way he can't quite fathom, have made her sick.

Anita rubs his back, and he says it again, through chattering teeth. 'Everything I ever did, Little. Everything.'

'Everybody knows that,' she says.

Later that day, the Colonel comes.

Elvis rises from the couch and is embraced by his manager's clammy arms.

'Son,' says the Colonel, patting him on the back of the head.

'Mama's gone, Colonel,' says Elvis. 'She's gone.'

'I know, son, I know.'

When he's released, Elvis sees that the Colonel is wearing an *I LIKE ELVIS* button on the breast pocket of his seersucker shirt.

Saying that any business was good business, he used to sell those at shows, right along with his *I HATE ELVIS* ones.

'Mama,' says Elvis, clasping the lip of the casket, 'Colonel's come to pay his respects to you.'

The Colonel nods, briefly, towards Gladys's body, then turns to Elvis's father, who has slipped into the room. Vernon has freshened his pale suit with a silk necktie, and the puffy redness in his face has subsided.

'Colonel,' he says, shaking Tom Parker's hand, 'we just can't get a hold on any part of this thing.'

'That's why the Colonel is here,' says Elvis's manager, fishing a cigar from his pocket. 'I'm gonna take care of this for you. You don't have to worry one bit. The Colonel will fix everything.'

'Well,' says Vernon, with a long sigh, 'that would be more than kind.'

The Colonel holds up a hand. 'I ain't doing this out of the goodness of my heart, Mr Presley. The truth is – and it's hard to say it, but we got to face facts here – the truth is that the newspapers are gonna want a piece of this, and my aim is to protect our boy. That's always my number-one priority.'

Elvis sits on the couch and stares at the casket.

'Which is why,' the Colonel continues, rocking back on his heels, 'I really think we should make this a public funeral. The members of the press will want to get their pictures of the procession and all, and nothing we can do can stop them, but if the funeral is in a public place it'll be easier to police the whole event—'

'This ain't no event,' says Elvis, looking up. 'This here's a funeral.'

'And it will be the best funeral ever seen in Memphis,' says the Colonel, lighting up his cigar, 'as befits your mother.'

Elvis glances at his father. 'Mama would want the funeral right here at home.'

Vernon sits next to him and puts his face in his hands. 'I don't know, son,' he mumbles, 'I just don't know ...' He's shaking his head and breathing ragged, but Elvis can tell his daddy is not crying. Not any more.

The Colonel pats Elvis on the shoulder. 'I don't think your father is in any condition to deal with this, Elvis,' he says. 'You want your fans to be able to say goodbye to your mother, don't you? I know they had a special relationship.'

Elvis blinks at him.

The Colonel puffs on his cigar and tilts his head. 'Maybe we can talk about this later.'

'Mr Parker,' says Elvis, keeping his voice low and his fists balled in his lap. 'I want you out of my house.'

'Now, son—' says Vernon.

'Get out!'

The Colonel sighs, opens his mouth to speak again, then seems to think better of it. Before leaving the room, he pats Vernon's arm, and Vernon clasps his hand, hard.

When the Colonel has left, Elvis wanders the house with Gladys's pink housecoat in his arms. His daddy has gone out, Elvis doesn't know where. He wonders who Vernon will become, now Gladys isn't around to remind him who he once was. He sits on the stairs and brings the housecoat to his face, trying to breathe his mama in, terrified he will forget how she smelled, that all he will remember is the chemical whiff of her embalmed body. Sitting there, he buries his nose into the rayon, shuts his eyes, and talks to Jesse.

Jesse, he says, silently, *is she with you now? Are the two of you together?*

The only answer that comes is the hum of the air conditioning.

Cliff, Lamar, George and Billy, and Red, who has come back to Memphis for the funeral, sit in the dining room, waiting for him to appear. Elvis doesn't know what to say to them, so he hides in the kitchen, still holding the housecoat. Alberta pours him coffee, butters him some biscuits and stands over him until he eats. She

415

doesn't say a word but he can see that she's been crying, too. As he is swallowing his coffee, which is sweet and good, he thinks of asking her to hold him. Although she is small, she looks so solid and comfortable, standing there in her maid's apron. She doesn't look like she'd break, if he were to touch her.

He says, 'Who's gonna take care of us now, Alberta?'

Alberta shakes her head. 'I'm sure sorry for your loss, Mr Elvis,' she says, clearing the plates.

'I ain't letting go of this housecoat,' he says.

She piles the dishes in the sink, then looks at him. 'I ain't asking you to,' she replies.

The Colonel gets his way, and Gladys's funeral is held in the Memphis Funeral Home. The chapel is crammed with people, though Elvis barely looks at anybody. He hasn't slept and has hardly eaten for days. It's so hot he finds it hard to breathe. He keeps pulling at the collar of his funeral suit jacket, fighting the urge to fling the thing to the floor. During the service, Red holds him around the shoulders to keep him upright and whispers to him that it will be all right. Red is the only one who says this. Everybody else, even Vernon, looks at Elvis with fear, as if they no longer know who he is. The Colonel, wearing a crumpled suit, doesn't look at him at all. So Elvis keeps on passing notes with requests for more songs to the Blackwood Brothers, who are performing Gladys's favourite hymns for the service. 'Precious Memories'. 'The Last Mile of the Way'. 'Farther Along'. 'Nearer My God to Thee'. 'How Great Thou Art'. He'll keep everybody in here for as long as it takes to get through the music.

At the cemetery, three thousand fans stand outside in the intense heat, wanting to share something, anything, with Elvis. For the first time, he is not happy to see them. Doing his best to stay on his feet at the mouth of his mama's grave, he has no wish to have his picture taken, or for his name to be screamed as though it is a plea for life.

* * *

Afterwards, Dixie comes to the house with her husband, to pay her respects.

In the hallway, the three of them stand together beneath the chandelier. Dixie's husband is taller than Elvis, with sandy hair and a bushy moustache. His expression is fixed somewhere between terror and awe. Dixie tries to introduce him, but Elvis mumbles an apology and says, 'Come on upstairs with me, honey. I want you to have something of Mama's.'

Dixie's black dress is too short for a funeral, he thinks. But he lets it go. Her wavy hair, her lifted chin, her way of standing as if she's about to skate across the rink, are all unchanged. He wants to get her in his room so he can hold her tight and tell her how much he needs her now. With Dixie in his arms, he might even sleep.

Dixie hesitates, glancing at her husband.

'Come on now,' says Elvis, grabbing her hand. 'He don't mind.'

She follows him up halfway. Encouraged, he catches her around the waist and whispers in her ear, 'I know you won't never love nobody like you love me, baby,' which makes her wriggle free. They stand staring at each other, and he realises that she's wearing eye make-up now, which makes her look more like the rest of the girls.

When he reaches for her again, Dixie slaps his hand away, making him yelp with surprise.

'I can't,' she says. 'I'm sorry.'

As she hurries down the stairs, he calls out, 'Congratulations on getting married and all! I'll send you two a gift. Anything you want! Just name it!'

Then Elvis's eye is caught by his reflection in the mirrored wall. He blinks, surprised to see himself. He hasn't looked at his own face since his mother died. The wall trembles before his eyes, making his reflection seem to bend. He points at it and laughs, and the image does the same, which makes him laugh some more. Then everything goes double, and his image repeats itself across the wall.

'Look!' he says, stepping back to get a better view. 'Thousands of little Elvises!'

When he takes his eyes from the mirror, Dixie is slamming the door, and his father and Colonel Parker are coming for him with Dr Evans, who is carrying a pouchy brown medicine bag.

Elvis's legs go liquid, but Vernon catches him by the elbow. 'The doc's gonna give you a shot, son,' he says.

'Let's get you into bed, now,' says Dr Evans, his balding head sweating. 'You need rest.' He takes a firm grip on Elvis's other arm.

Elvis smells the Colonel's cigar, and feels a pressure on his back.

The three men steer him up the stairs. It is nine days before he leaves his bedroom again.

He cannot leave his bedroom, because Mama is talking. Every time Elvis removes his sleep mask, a nurse – he notices Dr Evans has sent his oldest, most matronly staff member – is right there, offering a milkshake and a shot. She asks if he would like her to send down for food, and he tells her to just give him the damn shot. Because every time she does, Mama is waiting, wearing her lilac crêpe and her diamond drops. The two of them curl together in their shared bed, back in East Tupelo. Outside, the wind shakes the house and the Frisco train releases its long whistle. She talks and talks, her voice light and smooth, saying things he's never heard her say before. He doesn't dare look her in the eye in case she vanishes, so he buries himself in her arms and listens.

My son, she says. *When Jesse was lost I thought everything was gone, but then you came. I'd reckoned on two babies but couldn't know for sure till you was born. I thought I'd die that cold January morning. But you made me live.*

You always said you was gonna be home soon. I asked if those Hollywood folks was treating you good and you said yes. But I never believed a word of it. They don't know you like I do. When I saw your face on the movie screen I wanted to turn away, because how could it really be you, if you couldn't see me?

He buries his face deeper into her chest. In this sweet spot, everything drops away, and Mama keeps on talking.

Is Daddy still at the gate, with the girls? They're all yours, those girls, but Daddy reckons he has a claim on them. He's wrong. Don't forget that.

He opens his mouth to speak, but she tells him to hush up and let her say her piece.

Listen, now. I know you won't wanna listen, though you'll put on a good show of it. You're the world's best at putting on a show, ain't you? But listen, now. Listen. Because Mama is telling you her dreams. And you know that Mama's dreams come true. Didn't I dream that your car would burn up beside the highway? That you would sing to a dog? That you would dance in a jail? That you would be torn apart by little girls?

He wakes with a start and peeks out of the mask. It's night-time. The pink housecoat is still in his arms; he can smell his mama there, and he inhales her deeply. He can see nothing in this room – Mr Golden did a good job with the decor, and it's the darkest blue, just as he wanted – but he senses the nurse has gone. He wonders if she was ever there. He takes a couple of pills from his bedside drawer, swallows them, and goes back to sleep before his mind can remember what it is he must face.

* * *

Before returning to Fort Hood, Elvis takes Cliff, Red, Anita, Lamar and Billy to the Rainbow.

At the door, Mrs Pieracinni is waiting for them, together with her strapping sons. She's all in black and is wearing no lipstick, which makes her look even smaller than usual.

'I couldn't make it inside the chapel,' she says. 'The crowds were so crazy.'

'I'm glad you weren't there, Mrs Pieracinni,' says Elvis. 'It was a circus. The whole thing.'

'I wanted to pay my respects to your mother. I heard she was a real fine lady.'

'She was an angel,' says Elvis. 'She was my best girl.'

Inside, the rink looks as though it has been polished in his honour, it gleams so deeply. Instead of the usual popcorn and teenage sweat, there's a whiff of beeswax and Lysol, and the music is turned low. He's instructed Lamar to keep an eye on the jukebox and to select his mother's favourites – Jimmie Rodgers, the Blackwood Brothers, Hank Williams – where possible. There is to be no rock 'n' roll tonight.

As Elvis stands by the door, looking the place over, the others hang back, unsure what to do. The tables to the side of the rink are full of food, but nobody helps themselves. He feels watched, as never before. He's used to all eyes being on him, to his every move being followed, but this is different. Now he is being scrutinised, and he senses that nobody will utter one word without his encouragement. They are waiting for his reaction in order to decide what their own should be. And he has no idea how to act out this new, motherless Elvis.

So he simply crosses the dimpled rubber floor, sits on a chair, and removes his shoes. He slips his feet into his roller skates and laces them good and tight. Roy Acuff's 'Wabash Cannonball' comes on the jukebox. Once he is up on the skates, and the Wabash train whistle is blowing, Elvis feels something lift from his shoulders, and he soon gains momentum.

'Turn it up, Lamar,' he yells, and Roy sings louder.

On the glossy surface, Elvis spins in wide circles, gathering speed, letting the skates take him where they want to go. Roy sings of the rumble and the roar, and the wheels vibrate beneath the soles of Elvis's feet, making his legs thrum. That train is coming. He can hear the mighty rush of the engine. Nothing can stop it. So he gathers all his strength and pushes on, pumping his arms, leaning forward, his lungs expanding, his feet driving the skates, his whole body balanced and ready for whatever is coming to meet him.

When the song is over, he tells Lamar to play it again. Then the others follow Elvis onto the rink, and together they glide round and round to the music.

Acknowledgements

I am very grateful to the Royal Society of Literature for awarding this book a Brookleaze Grant, which enabled me to travel to Tupelo and Memphis, and to the Royal Literary Fund for granting me a Fellowship while I was writing this novel.

Many sources were useful in researching Elvis's story, but particularly valuable to me were Peter Guralnick's *Last Train to Memphis* and *Careless Love*, Elaine Dundy's *Elvis and Gladys*, Karal Ann Marling's *Graceland: Going Home with Elvis*, and *We Remember Elvis* by Azalia S. Moore, Guy Thomas Harris, Sybil Presley and Lee Clark.

I'd like to thank the following people for taking the time to talk Elvis with me: Mike Freeman, Roy Turner, Larry Geller, Tish Henley, Guy Thomas Harris, Wayne Mann and Neil Cameron. Jennie Bradford Curlee looked after me in Tupelo, and Alexandra Mobley let me sleep in the Elvis apartment at Lauderdale Courts.

The following writers were generous enough to read and comment on drafts of the manuscript even though they don't particularly dig Elvis: Hugh Dunkerley, Karen Stevens, Edward Hogan and David Swann. I'm grateful, too, for the advice I received from Claire Keegan.

I'd also like to thank Poppy Hampson and Véronique Baxter for their advice and support. And Mum for starting the whole thing. And Hugh and Ted for their love.

Thank you. Thank you very much.

penguin.co.uk/vintage